"*Shepherd's Fall* is a clever, creepy and inventive tale that puts a disturbing new spin on the classic haunted house story. This one will catch you totally off guard."

— Jonathan Maberry, New York Times bestselling author
of *Assassin's Code* and *Dust & Decay*

"Fans of *The Amityville Horror* will devour this debut novel by George Appelt. If you dream of owning a big, old country house, *Shepherd's Fall* may change your mind. The nonstop action and chilling scenes will keep you reading into the dark of night and frighten you into wishing for the light of day."

— Dennis Royer, author of *Earthburst*

"Appelt's fast-paced, debut novel grabs your spine in a death grip from the first chapter, and doesn't let loose. I simply couldn't stop reading!"

— Ralph W. Bieber II,
Bram Stoker Award nominated bestselling author
of *Ashes* and *The Epicure*

AUTHOR'S NOTE

Although Harrisburg, Pennsylvania, the Susquehanna River, and Chickies Rock are all actual locations, they are used fictitiously in *Shepherd's Fall*. And while the town of Templeton and the house at Shadow's Forge are products of my imagination, sometimes I am almost certain that if I drive north from Harrisburg and turn east I will find them both waiting there for me.

Special thanks go out to my wife, Diane, and to my children, Anthony and Katie, for their love and understanding while I disappear into my own worlds. I also want to thank my parents for encouraging me to dream big. And thanks to all my extended family for their support.

Writing can be a lonely undertaking, so thanks to the Central Pennsylvania Writers Group and to the Pennwriters Fourth Wednesday Writers Group for their moral support and excellent critiques. Thanks also to Jonathan and Ralph for their guidance and encouragement.

I also need to thank my first readers – Erica Grumbine, Pastor Bennett Harris, Dennis Royer, and Wade Fowler.

And although my sister Lisa doesn't like scary stories, I have to thank her for all her help and encouragement.

I have tried to stay accurate in my use of historical details, but have fictionalized the accounts of the Susquehannock Indians to serve the story. Any historical inaccuracies can be attributed to artistic license. I hope you enjoy reading *Shepherd's Fall* as much as I have enjoyed writing it.

To Diane, your love, faith, and support lift me into the light.

CHAPTER ONE

Will Shepherd had never seen anyone die before. Nothing he had witnessed until that point in his life had prepared him, but deep inside some inkling had started to warn him before the actual event. Later he would think back and realize he had been waiting for something to happen, he just hadn't known what to expect.

He woke up that Saturday morning with a sense of dread he couldn't explain. During the drive from Philadelphia, he found no rational justification for his deepening mental funk. It should have been a happy day, and he wanted to ignore the hollow feeling. He blamed his ill humor on his daughter Ellie. She had been kicking the back of his seat for the past two hours. The constant bumping irritated him more each time, and he felt his composure slipping away.

"Your greatest desire, what would you sacrifice to obtain it? Your free time, your family, or perhaps your soul?" The Amazing Charles Cooper's question thundered from the car's CD player like a fire and brimstone preacher's sermon.

Will's forehead twitched, the beginnings of a headache. Motivational speaker Charles Cooper never seemed to struggle for the answer.

Will's wife Sara shifted in the passenger seat. "Honey, two and a half hours of this self-help crap is enough, especially on a Saturday morning. Can we please change it?"

Her green eyes hinted at mischief. He loved those eyes.

He smiled and wondered *how did I get so lucky*?

Sara swept a loose lock of long red curls off her face. Her loving gaze still quickened his pulse, even after twelve years of marriage.

"Yeah. How about some music?" Ellie called from the backseat. Her gaze met his in the rearview mirror. She grinned. Like her mother, the strawberry blond eight-year-old possessed an inner glow. In fewer years than Will liked to admit she would be breaking boys' hearts. He wasn't ready for that.

The twinge in his forehead danced, growing closer to a respectable headache. He sighed. "Okay, if you guys don't want to learn the Amazing secrets of success, I give. Go ahead, put on some music."

"Sorry Charlie," Sara said and punched one of the radio presets. The speakers blasted a song by some band Will didn't recognize, something upbeat with a quirky hook that brought a smile to Ellie's face. It did nothing to sooth Will's headache, and he rubbed the bridge of his nose, trying to ease the tension.

A cloud drifted in front of the sun casting shadows over the valley and darkening the cornfields. Ellie hummed along with the song. As the sky dimmed, Will's mood sank lower. The passing trees grew thicker and their upturned leaves foreshadowed a storm.

A sudden chill bit his exposed flesh.

Sara touched his arm. "Are you okay?"

His head felt like it was being hit by a jackhammer. "Yeah, just a little tired," Will said. No sense ruining the day for her, even though this drive felt like a journey to his execution. He had thought he could live with their decision, now he wasn't so sure.

The clouds parted and the bright sunlight glared on the windshield. Will blinked. His eyes were only closed for a second, but when he opened them, pain exploded in his head. It all happened in seconds that seemed to span into hours. A young boy raced down the hill on the other side of the intersection on a blue Schwinn bike. A brilliant blue, a bright blue — Sara would've known the exact shade, but to Will it was just blue. Coming out of nowhere, the kid blazed along like a lightning bolt, almost a blur. Instead of pausing at the stop sign, the boy accelerated, picked up speed, and shot into the crossroad on a head-on trajectory with the front of Will's Civic.

Will nailed the brakes, sending his car skidding. The front bumper smashed into the boy's bike with a sickening crunch.

The child flailed his arms and legs as he rocketed through the air. His head smashed into the windshield. The impact wove a spider-web pattern in the safety glass around a red splotch.

Sara and Ellie's screams amped up during the wild slide and then faded into silence as the car stopped. Will's body temperature plunged as if someone had drenched him in ice water. He drew a long breath and held it. His heart pounded. His gaze fixed on the contorted child, close in age to Ellie, sprawled there only inches away on the car hood, staring into the blue sky with unseeing eyes.

Shit, what have I done?

CHAPTER TWO

Sara touched his shoulder startling him. "Will, are you all right?"

"What!"

He blinked. It was like waking from a dream. Glancing around the empty intersection, the knot in his stomach relaxed, replaced with a hollow sinking sensation. The child's broken body had vanished. Only the bright patterns formed by sunlight streaming through the trees danced on the Civic's hood on the other side of his unblemished windshield.

Will relaxed his grip on the steering wheel. "You didn't see that?"

Sara eyed him suspiciously. "See what? All I saw was you jamming on the brakes and scaring us half to death."

He scanned the empty intersection once more. The boy couldn't have vanished, yet he had. Will didn't understand what had happened, and he didn't want to try to explain it to Sara in front of Ellie.

"Yeah, Dad, that was really scary."

"Sorry, honey."

The street signs indicated they were at the intersection of Old Creek and Pine roads. It felt as if they were a million miles from civilization. The knot in Will's stomach tightened when he realized they were only a mile-and-a-half from their new home.

He fought the urge to get out of the car and examine the hood for some trace signs of the accident. Will turned onto Old Creek Road, glancing once more in the rearview to double check. Only long black skid marks marred the macadam. A chill crept down his spine.

Relax. There was no body, no bike, and no accident. It was just a day-

dream, nothing else.

It couldn't be, not now. Not when he was so close to everything he wanted.

CHAPTER **THREE**

Will eased the black Civic down the long gravel driveway and parked under the huge oak trees in front of the Gothic Victorian. His hands trembled on the wheel, and he tried to banish the image of the boy's crumpled body from his mind.

It wasn't real.

The ridiculous idea of doubling back to confirm the child wasn't there still tempted him like a scab that begged to be scratched.

Sara would've seen a real accident.

Logical thinking did little to calm his nerves.

Sitting in the driveway of his new home, the hallucinations inspired more fear than an actual accident. What could've caused the vision? Was it stress, insanity, a brain tumor? None of the possibilities offered comfort. The roar in his head melted back into a dull ache as he climbed from the car.

The scent of lilac wafted through the morning air, and the sun's warmth radiated from the clear blue sky, but Will sensed storm clouds on the horizon. They were not visible, but they were there, just like the lilac's fragrance failed to cover the stench of decay that hung just beneath it.

Disconcerted, he stretched, trying to loosen his stiff muscles.

Stress, that has to be the answer. The new job, the move, even good changes cause stress.

Will tried to shake off his growing anxiety. He shielded his eyes, and scanned the road.

"No sign of the moving vans," he said.

He studied the old structure, their new home. The skin prickled on the back of his neck. Something disturbing lingered in the shadows of the gothic Victorian with its steep mansard roofs and its widow's tower pointing accusingly toward the heavens. Sara loved the architectural trimmings that modern structures lacked, but he found all the extra wooden adornments antiquated and creepy. He had felt it on both of their previous visits. Something dark prowled the depths of his consciousness.

It's old.

That presented a huge problem. Will had hated old things, old places, anything to do with the past. Maybe he hated them because the objects reminded him of their previous owners? Will didn't like to think about the people who had used the items, possibly even cherished them during their short time on this earth, but now they were dead and gone. Each antique served as a reminder that all we struggle for is folly in the end.

This place stinks of death.

An odd and illogical thought, not the kind of association one wanted with a new home.

His spirits faltered further as he scrutinized the faded yellow paint and the cracked green trim. Dark cavities loomed where shingles were missing from the veranda's roof, and some of the shutters tilted at odd angles.

Will frowned and ran his right hand through his hair. "It needs a lot of work."

Sara slid her arm around his waist. "Think how great it'll be after renovations."

He tried to envision it, but saw only the deterioration.

Nope, not seeing it.

Sara's eyes searched his face. "You're still okay with this?"

"Just tired from the drive. I'm getting old."

She pulled away from him. "Thirty-five's not old, and you're the one who had to take a job out here in the sticks. It's your idea to move halfway across the state."

Will raised his hands. "I know. I signed the mortgage papers, remember?"

"I just don't want to feel like I forced you into a home you hate."

He wrapped his arms about her, drew her close. "We could've

looked at other listings. Twenty acres is a lot of land. We didn't have to settle on the first one."

Sara grinned and squeezed him. "Look, it's got to be better than living in that hotel room for the last three months. And it's the house of my dreams. Besides, most of it's forest. We can let it grow wild, and look at that view. It's breathtaking."

The Appalachian Mountains to the north and the farm country to the east were spectacular, quite a change from the housing development back in Horsham.

"Okay, then I'll love it too," he said.

Fat chance.

The house was a concession. Sara had always wanted a Gothic Victorian home. When the job offer had materialized to manage a multi-million dollar web project in Harrisburg, he had needed leverage to convince her to move away from Philadelphia, their friends, everything they had ever known. His agreeing to purchase an old house had sealed the deal. Now he wondered if he had made a deal with the devil.

Sara kissed him on the cheek.

Ellie ran across the lawn to examine the stone angel in the center of the large cement birdbath. The statue faced the house, its arms raised in adoration. Ellie circled, paused in front of the statue, turned to face the house, and mimicked the statue's pose. So dramatic, a quality Will adored. He choked on a chuckle as the angel's shadow slithered across the grass and engulfed Ellie like a black wave washing over her.

Will sucked in a breath. The moment passed, and the shadow receded back to normal. He rubbed his eyes. Ellie was fine, and Sara seemed oblivious.

What the hell's wrong with me? It must've been a trick of the light...

Not very likely, but whatever gets you through the night.

Sara started toward the porch. "Let's wait inside."

Ellie dashed after her. Will glanced at the statue once more before he followed. *I need to relax. I'm really losing it.*

CHAPTER **FOUR**

Will unlocked the front double doors and stepped into the dim foyer. As his eyes adjusted to the light, his gaze followed the open staircase to a large, round, stained glass window on the second floor. He studied the intricately carved angels that encircled the newel posts at the bottom and top of the banister, ornamentation that he found dark, antiquated, and somehow foreboding. Whatever the original architect's intention, the angels generated goose bumps on Will's flesh.

Ellie and Sara crowded past him. Sara caressed one of the carved angel's raptured faces that lifted toward heaven. Ellie joined her mother at the foot of the stairs, and traced the angels with her small fingers. "Oh Daddy, how pretty."

Sara possessed the beauty of a true heavenly creature, not some stunted wooden mockery of the celestial beings. He grinned as he watched Ellie. Seeing them happy eased the tension in his head.

Sara stepped closer, hugging him, and whispered in his ear, "I've come home."

Lost in the moment, Will closed his eyes and held her. She felt good. Maybe if he just went with it, everything would work out fine. He wanted Sara to be happy.

Why shouldn't she have the house she wanted?

In the end, one old house would bother him as much as another. The whole idea of old things presented the problem, but it was his problem. Over the years he had sort of gotten used to Sara's antique collection. If this was that important to her, he could work through his discomfort.

Ellie's shout from the doorway startled him. "They're here. They're here."

Two moving vans kicked up dust in the driveway. Will blew out a long breath. Living in the country would take some getting used to. Grit coated everything. This environment felt less sanitized than back in their old upscale suburban neighborhood.

Ironically, he had spent years climbing the corporate ladder to purchase a fine house in a good neighborhood, and now they were trading it all in on this Gothic disaster.

The vans coasted to a stop and the moving company owner and foreman, climbed from the cab of the first truck like an astronaut stepping on the moon. The large man began barking orders at his three helpers. They scrambled from the vans, opened the back doors, and started unloading boxes and furniture.

Will sighed. There was no turning back now, even if he wanted to, and that temptation lingered heavy in his thoughts. No, he was committed to this course of action and would see it through.

He spent the next few hours assisting the movers, and by mid afternoon an exhausted Will entered Sara's new studio carrying a box of chisels.

The sunlight streamed through the glass ceiling, bathing the area in a warm glow. A lingering whiff of plants and earth drifted in the air. Previous owners had grown things here. This room presented the only space in the entire house that didn't feel cold.

On their first visit, Sara had raved about the arboretum's fieldstone floor and glass walls and ceiling. She insisted it would be the perfect place to sculpt. Will had no clue about Sara's career, nor did he often give it much thought. His take on art was limited to the old cliché, 'I know what I like when I see it.' Beyond admiring the beauty of his wife's art, he hadn't the first concept of her actual creative process.

He lowered the chisels on a table and turned slowly in a circle, studying the space. This room had clinched the deal. He despised it.

Will returned to the parlor, where he discovered the pastor from St. Mark's Lutheran Church chatting with Ellie.

"I love it here. I'm making all kinds of friends," Ellie said.

Pastor Wheeler smiled and hoisted his portly frame from the couch to shake Will's extended hand. "Hello Will. It's our tradition to welcome new people into the parish. I hope I'm not interrupting."

"No problem, we're just about finished, and I'm glad for an excuse to take a break."

Both men chuckled, but the Pastor's sounded forced.

"We have enjoyed attending your church services the last few Sundays. Sara and Ellie joined me on the weekends to search for a house and Ellie loved your Sunday school," Will said.

He had always liked the older man, but today the Pastor seemed distracted. Beads of sweat dotted his pasty white forehead.

I hope he's not having a heart attack.

The thought stopped Will for a moment.

"I'm pleased. We would be delighted to have you as members. Sara tells me you have a beautiful voice. I hope you'll consider singing in the choir."

"Yeah, once we get settled, I'd consider that," Will said.

"Mommy and Daddy both sang in our last church's choir," Ellie said, "I like to sing too."

"I already told him I would," Sara said from the doorway.

Ellie asked to be excused and ran back the hall toward the kitchen.

"Stay close to the back porch," Will called after her.

A fleeting thought of the statue's shadow in the front yard crossed his mind, but he dismissed it when movement in the foyer, visible through the archway, distracted him.

Two of the movers worked their way up the staircase with the large rosewood framed antique mirror that would soon hang above the bureau in the master bedroom. Sara was particularly fond of the piece because she had inherited it from her Aunt. The heavy, thick glass weighed a ton.

The pair struggled with the mirror, trying not to lose their grip.

The first mover worked his way up the steps backward. He was thin, and the muscles in his arms bunched in wiry cords. With his long brown ponytail and thin scruffy beard, he resembled a malnourished folk singer.

Helping him was a younger man they called Tony. His dark blue creased jeans and a crisp clean T-shirt marked him as new. Will had learned earlier in the day that Tony was the owner's nephew, who was helping on his summer break from college.

Together the two men inched up the staircase one step at a time. The first mover backed onto the landing, and Pastor Wheeler distracted Will when he said, "I'd like to bless your new home. Let us pray."

Will bowed his head and closed his eyes.

"Dear Lord…"

The crash cut off the Pastor's words. Will's eyes flew open seeking the source of the crash. The first mover sprawled on his back. The mirror had smashed against the top newel post.

Sara gasped, and Will felt weak, like all the air had left his lungs.

Somehow Tony had managed to lay the large frame on its side and fought at one end to balance it on the stair's handrail. He staggered back down the steps, struggling to support the weight by himself. A spider web pattern, like the one in Will's windshield earlier in the day, wove across the large sheet of glass.

Everything slowed down as Tony stumbled on the steps. His feet flailed about in what would've under other circumstances been funny movements. They reminded Will of an old cartoon's slapstick from when he was a kid. Dance, funnyman, dance. The frame slid along the handrail, the vibration jarring loose pieces of glass. Will raised his right hand in desperation, wanting to reach across the space and snatch the young man out of harm's way.

Sara's screams echoed off the foyer walls as Tony crashed to the floor and landed hard on his back. The concussion jarred free the remaining razor sharp pieces of glass. Will's feet felt nailed to the floor, as the large jagged section caught Tony squarely in the stomach. A wet sound cut through the air as the glass sliced through the young man, and a heart-stopping thunk sounded as the largest point dug into the hardwood and pinned him to the floor.

Bile rose in Will's throat, and he swallowed desperately trying not to vomit. Pastor Wheeler stumbled backward into a chair, and Sara stood frozen, a strange faraway look in her eyes.

A scarlet fountain exploded from Tony's mouth. The eruption coated his fresh white T-shirt. He grabbed the large shard of mirror and sliced his palms on the glass.

Will flinched, feeling the pain in his own palms. Tony held on for a second and then his hands fell to the floor. Blood pooled on the floor around the body. The glass had almost severed him. The fountain from his mouth slowed to one final ruby bubble. Will held his breath, waiting for it to burst. When it did the world spun back into real time.

The mover on the landing scrambled to his feet and peered down the staircase for a second before he staggered away from the edge, gagging.

Tony's uncle appeared on the landing. "Tony?"

He raced down the stairs to the young man, slipped on the wet floor, and fell to his hands and knees in his nephew's blood. His sobs filled the foyer as he grasped the large piece of glass and tried to pry it from the floor. Blood from his own sliced palms mixed with his nephew's.

Sara's screams echoed in Will's ears as he hit 911 on his cell phone. *Ellie can't see this.*

Will turned to Sara. "Get Ellie. Keep her out."

A coppery metallic scent assaulted Will's nostrils. His head swam, and he steadied himself on the door jam. The boy on the bike, and now this. He felt his mind slipping over the edge of a dark precipice.

CHAPTER FIVE

Later that night, Will braced himself against the banister and stared down into the dim foyer. Sleep eluded him despite his exhaustion. Maybe sleep would never come again. The paramedics and police had removed the body, but the scene still seared in his memory. His breath formed a crystallized cloud of vapor.

How can it be this cold in June?

Outside, clouds must have passed in front of the moon, because the room darkened. Gusts of wind stirred the old house. It creaked and moaned. Sweat formed on his brow. Will shivered.

Standing in the darkness, listening to the sounds of the night, unable to banish the horrific images from his head, he only took comfort that they were different than his vision of the boy on the bike.

Of course the bike accident hadn't really occurred. It was a hallucination, probably induced by stress. Will swallowed and tried not to
think about it. He hadn't experienced anything like that since he
quit drinking. And even then it had only occurred once. For the first
time in years a drink seemed like just what he needed.

The hand on his shoulder startled him, and he barely suppressed
a shout.

CHAPTER SIX

Sara found Will standing at the banister staring down into the
dim foyer. Silhouetted in the moonlight, he resembled a slimmed
down version of the heroes from the trashy historical romances that
she loved to read. She smiled. The thick short wavy blonde hair
gave him a boyish charm, and his two mile morning runs kept his
body in decent athletic shape despite his desk job.

His muscles tensed when she touched his shoulder. She slipped
her hands around his waist. "What are you doing up?"

He shook his head. "I couldn't sleep. I didn't wake you when I
got out of bed, did I?"

"No. I just noticed you were missing. I'm having a little trouble
myself."

She leaned into him as he drew her close enjoying his comforting
embrace. They stood quietly listening to the night world outside.
She always felt safe in his arms. Safe and protected, because he was
the one person she could always count on to stand with her against
the world.

After a long pause he whispered. "Do you think we made a mistake moving here?"

Sara gazed up into gentle blue eyes she had first stared into fifteen
years ago at an art festival in Fairmount Park. "I know today was
horrible, but we can get past this. We must."

Will closed his eyes and shook his head. "I don't know if I can.

This may be too much."

Sara squeezed him tighter. "I've had to live with tragedy. We can do this. Are you sure this isn't second thoughts about the job? You had three months to decide if you liked it before we bought the house."

She hadn't wanted to move. At first she had resisted. Her whole life was in Philadelphia. She had built a successful career by placing her sculptures in galleries; she had many contacts, and was active in the cultural scene.

It had taken a lot for Will to convince her that her career wouldn't suffer by making this move. His job offer was spectacular and it seemed like a golden career opportunity.

In the end she couldn't stand in his way, and after a lot of thought, she realized with a little extra effort she could stay in touch with her contacts in Philly. After all, Harrisburg was only two and a half hours away, not another planet.

Then of course they had found this wonderful house.

But now he's having second thoughts?

"No the job's fine. It's this place," Will said.

"You made a deal. Now you want to renege?"

Sadness played in his eyes. "No, but today was terrible. You say we can get past this accident, but I'm not so sure."

Sara studied the spot she had scrubbed for hours after the police and coroner had removed the body. A faint stain remained. Most people would never notice it, but she didn't think she would ever not see it. What could she say? It had been a horrible accident. But, people do recover from tragedy. Sara knew that first hand.

And there was something about the house. She couldn't explain it to Will, wasn't even sure how to try. Even though it was now tainted with a tragedy, she still loved the place.

Not that the accident hadn't left her shaken. All that blood, broken glass, and the coppery scent had reawakened the memories she had struggled for thirty years to bury.

Since the horror of the afternoon, small pieces started to surface from that night many years ago. Once again, she heard her mother scream: "Watch out!" She saw the woman standing in the road transfixed like a deer in the headlights. She recalled the screech of tires, and the crunch of metal on flesh, father's slumped body behind the wheel, and the gaping hole in the windshield on the passenger's side.

Sara remembered climbing from the car and cutting herself on broken glass. Soaked by the driving rain that merged with her tears, she had searched for her mother. Stumbling through the dark, she had located a crumpled heap by the road. When she had touched it, she had recoiled. Lifting her blood soaked hands to her face, she had screamed until a policeman had carried her to a squad car.

The screams of that five-year-old still echoed in her mind and threatened to devour her. Over the years she had smothered that scream. She understood that there was no safe place in this world.

She rested her head on Will's shoulder. "Today was horrible, but it was an accident. It could've happened anywhere," she said.

"But it happened here."

"I know and it scares me, but this house still feels like I've come home."

Will's embrace tightened. She didn't expect him to understand, but she wasn't going to change her mind.

"Come to bed. It's late." She led him back the hall by the hand.

She was home. She loved this place and wouldn't let the tragedy, no matter how horrible, diminish her joy. She had survived the accident of her childhood, and they would find a way to survive this, too.

CHAPTER SEVEN

Monday afternoon, Will leaned back in his desk chair and paused to marvel at the view of rolling fields and mountains in the distance beyond the perimeter of the business park. He liked this job perk the best. He had spent most of his career writing code in cubes that Sara referred to as "cloth-covered boxes." As Director of Web Development, the novelty of having a door and windows still hadn't faded, three months after starting at Compu-Gear.

He tried to block Saturday's tragedy from his mind. Although he was normally good at compartmentalizing problems and only focusing on the task at hand, grisly sights and sounds kept intruding. And then there was the moving company owner's grief. Will couldn't imagine how the man felt losing one of his family members right in front of his eyes. He didn't want to even try.

His mind also wandered back to the boy on the bike. Where had that strange hallucination come from, and what did it mean? He was trying not to think about that when a knock on the door interrupted him.

Kerrie Andersen, the lead programmer on the project, entered, handed him a stack of printouts, and slid her petite frame into the chair in front of his desk. She brushed a long strand of dark hair back into place with her crimson polished finger tips. "The printout of the site map you requested. Pages that are coded are marked."

Will examined the stack of papers. "Still problems with the Login?"

"Yeah, Bill and Steve are working on it, but it could put the project at risk."

Kerrie crossed her legs, and her black skirt hiked up a little higher on her thigh. Will tried not to glance at her legs or the top two undone buttons on her silky blouse; he didn't want to be that guy. He thought he detected the hint of amusement in her big brown eyes.

Embarrassed that she caught him, he felt heat rise on his cheeks as he flipped through the layout of the site. At least the site map looked good, the ultimate sports portal was taking shape. Soon it would contain images of real time video of college and professional games, the latest scores and schedules, chat rooms, and a full interactive catalog of new and used sports equipment.

He glanced at the time on his computer screen. "4:30 already. Looks like another late night. I better give Sara a call."

Kerrie shifted in her seat, and the skirt inched up a little more. "That's right, this weekend was moving day. How'd that go?"

Will tried to remain focused on her face and shrugged. "You

wouldn't believe it."

She raised her eyebrows in question. Wanting to avoid the topic, he shook his head and smiled. "Sara and Ellie love the place. Thanks again for the Realtor's name."

Kerrie rose. "No problem, I aim to please. Frank's going to call The Golden Dragon for takeout. I could try to catch him if you would like anything special?"

He thought for a moment. "The usual is fine."

The team had fallen into a routine over the last few months. They arrived at work early, and toiled late into the night. They ate most of their meals together in the break room. Will hadn't minded when Ellie and Sara were living in Horsham, and he had nowhere to go except his lonely hotel room. Now that they were here, he resented spending evenings at the office.

When Sara picked up, she sounded distant.

"Not tonight," she responded when he told her he had to stay late.

"Look, it's only five weeks till implementation," he said.

"Sure." Her voice was flat.

"Then things will ease up, I promise."

Although true, this job would always require more time, more effort, and more attention.

There was a long pause. "All right."

"I love you." This was an apology as much as a statement of affection.

"Me too, be careful coming home."

Disappointment infused her words; she sounded dejected. His anger flared.

Doesn't she understand I'm doing this for her, for Ellie, for the three of us? This is how you get ahead. You work your ass off and hope somebody important notices.

He tried to control his irritation, dropped the receiver back in the cradle, and glanced up to see Frank Morgan enter his office. Frank flopped into the vacant chair. "Chinese again tonight? Man, I'm starved."

"You made the call? Kerrie said you were ordering my usual."

Frank folded his hands behind his head. "Yeah. I saw her leaving your office. You better watch out for that one. She's a man eater."

Young and attractive, Kerrie was seductive, but Will wasn't going to admit that to anyone, not even himself.

"I'm married. You're the one that has to watch out."

Frank guffawed, and his thick glasses slid down his thin nose. He adjusted them and snorted again before he continued. "Yeah, right. I'm not in her league."

Will raised an eyebrow. "And I am?"

Frank's cheeks grew crimson, and he stared at the floor. "I'm not the one she recommended for the position of Director of Web Development."

"That doesn't mean anything. We worked together back in Philadelphia. She thought I would be a good fit."

Kerrie had been a young contractor right out of college when she had worked with him at Allied Tech. Will had always liked her. She was a nice kid and good at her job. Then she moved on, and he hadn't heard from her in over a year. She had surprised him four months ago with a call about this new position.

Frank continued. "I dig her, but she goes more for your type."

Frank combed his long thinning hair over his bald spot, and Will wanted to ask if he meant guys with hair, but resisted. "Not to be rude, but is there a point to this visit?"

"Nah, it's all good. I just couldn't take Steve anymore. He gets pretty hot when things don't go right. You better watch out for him too," Frank said.

Will hit the control-alt-delete keys to lock his system. "I don't go that way."

Frank's face grew beet red. "No, that's not what I mean. He has it out for you."

"Come on, Steve's doing a great job."

Frank slid forward in the chair and seesawed his hand back and forth. "Maybe, but he's still cheesed off because you swooped in out of nowhere and got the job he wanted. Not your greatest fan, pal."

Will sighed and tilted back in his chair. "I've picked up cold vibes from the guy. I thought it was just his personality."

Frank hooted and readjusted his glasses. "His personality is all ego. When your predecessor resigned, Steve thought he was a shoo-in. Then — *wham* — Kerrie torpedoed him with you."

Will's stomach tightened. He didn't like the course of this conversation. "I'm not sorry I got the position."

"No I guess not, but Kerrie..."

Frank's words were lost as blue flames ignited on the edges of his shirt collar like a pilot light igniting a gas stove. In a loud whoosh they engulfed his head in a halo of fire and singed away his hair and eyebrows. The unnatural blaze illuminated his skull beneath the thin membrane of skin. The frames of his glasses melted and the lenses shattered. His eyes swelled until they bulged to three times their normal size and finally exploded, spraying goo across Will's desk.

Will launched back in his chair, smashing into the shelves behind him.

The skin on Frank's face darkened and peeled. His tongue flashed behind teeth as he continued to talk apparently unaware and unconcerned that he was ablaze. "Hey man, you okay?"

Will blinked. Frank stared back at him through his thick glasses with perfect eyes, his long hair still combed over his bald spot. "You look pale."

Will righted his chair. Shaken, he tried to cover his actions with a dismissive wave and smile. "Yeah, fine. I'm just a little tired. I guess I lost my balance."

Balance? I'm losing my mind.

Will remained calm, but it required every ounce of control he could muster. He didn't want it getting around the company that he was cracking under the pressure.

Frank adjusted his glasses. "I'm just telling you watch it with her."

Will rose from his chair and dropped the screenshot pages onto his desk. He tried not to stare at Frank, who now appeared fine. "Our relationship is purely professional."

Frank stood. "Sure, but does your wife believe that?"

Will didn't know. He hadn't told Sara about Kerrie.

CHAPTER **EIGHT**

Around midnight, Will slipped through the front door of their new home, his heart pounding as he dropped the keys into his pocket. Sara left a small table lamp on in the foyer when she had gone to bed, but darkness engulfed the far recesses of the hall, parlor, and most of the upstairs landing. Even through the oppressive silence, he sensed someone watching him from the shadows.

"Hello?"

No answer.

He felt foolish, a grown man afraid of the dark. But after the hallucination at the office he wasn't sure what to expect.

The chiming grandfather clock in the hall shattered the silence sending a tingle of low current through his chest. He froze. His gaze lingered at the foot of the stairs, searching for any sign of Saturday's tragedy, afraid he would see a vision of the dead young man. How could he face each night coming home to this place?

Navigating the parlor, careful not to knock into any of the antique furniture silhouetted by the moonlight, he made his way toward the kitchen.

Will fumbled in the dark to find the switch for the dining room chandelier. It felt like invisible fingers caressed his face and arms. He drew a deep breath trying to slow his racing heart. The old damaged chandelier with a majority of burnt out bulbs failed to ease the sensation.

Only the white curtains that adorned the studio's French doors lifted his spirits. True to her nature, Sara never let anyone, including him, see her sculptures in progress. Her studio remained off limits while she wrestled with her muse.

After twelve years of marriage, her career still remained a mystery to him. He had no talent or desire to comprehend the aesthetic.

He paused halfway across the dining room and glanced back at the darkened parlor. Exhaustion from the long day explained why the shadows seemed alive, like something lurked there waiting to pounce on him.

He snapped on the kitchen light, wishing the pale illumination were more comforting.

Retrieving a glass from the cabinet, he turned the cold water tap. Deep in the bowels of the house, somewhere below the kitchen, pipes groaned and knocked, and then the liquid spilled into his glass.

Great, something else that's worn out.

He glanced around the dingy room. Sara was excited about the daunting task of remodeling. For the one-thousandth time he wondered if they had made a mistake buying this place. Not just because of his unease, but because the restoration would require a monumental effort.

Mr. Whiskers rubbed against his leg. Startled, he jumped, drenching the front of his shirt. The cat stalked off, possibly in search of rodents. The walls were probably full of them, gnawing and scurrying. Will glanced down at the scuffed oilcloth floor, seeking signs of infestation. Expecting to see movement in the shadows, it almost disappointed him when he spotted none.

He refilled his glass. The room temperature plunged and the acrid scent of burning wood and charred meat assaulted his senses. The hair on his arms tingled, and the water glass shattered, exploding in his hand. He dropped it into the sink and sprang back. Breathing hard, he scanned the kitchen convinced he was not alone.

Damn it. This is too much.

Gathering the shards of glass, he tossed them into the trashcan. The smoke alarm above the stove remained silent. The room warmed, and the burnt scent dissipated. He tested the alarm and it sounded. He quickly released the button afraid it would wake the girls. He must have imagined it. Another hallucination. Unsure what just happened, Will fled upstairs.

At the landing he paused, because he heard whispers off to the right in Ellie's room. She should have been sound asleep. He eased open her door.

"That must have been really loud," Ellie whispered.

"Are you still awake?" He entered the room without turning on the light and approached her bed. She was buried among all the stuffed animals. She peeked from under a large stuffed tiger that was almost her size.

"You're home. I waited up for you," she said and sprang into his arms.

Glad to see her, he hugged her and guided her back into bed. "You need your sleep."

"I'm not tired Dad, I was talking to Celeste."

Like Sara, she had a vivid imagination. He covered her, trying not to dislodge too many of the stuffed creatures. He shivered. The room felt frigid, especially for July 1st.

"Who's Celeste?" He asked.

"She's my friend."

He hugged her and a kissed her on the forehead.

"Well, it's time for bed, so tell her you have to get some sleep."

"Would you like to see her picture?" Ellie produced a small, framed photo of a blonde woman wearing a white flapper dress. She stood in front of a Model-T Ford.

"Where did you get this?"

"Celeste gave it to me."

He studied the sepia tone and swore he recognized the woman, but couldn't place her. Ellie must have found one of Sara's old family photos while they were unpacking. It was probably one of Sara's relatives.

Isn't she a little old for imaginary friends?

He shrugged off the thought. Why would he even think that? Unnerved and exhausted, he couldn't begin to confront his child's mental development tonight.

Besides, what did he know about age-appropriate imaginary friends?

He placed the picture on the nightstand. "She's very pretty."

"She's right over there." Ellie pointed toward the window.

He thought he caught movement in the corner, but when he turned there was nothing there. It must've been the white sheer curtains fluttering in the breeze. He gave Ellie a final hug and started for the door. "Get some sleep. I love you."

"Good night, Daddy. I love you too."

As an afterthought, he checked the window, but it was already closed.

Somewhere deep inside doubts raced to the surface, but he fled the room, not willing to entertain his growing fears. He needed a good night's sleep.

CHAPTER **NINE**

Will studied the way the moonlight painted the front of the large house. It cast eerie starkness across the mammoth facade that rose out of the mist. He had no memory of stepping outside. The last thing he remembered was climbing into bed beside to Sara.

His stomach tightened at the possibility of another bizarre hallucination.

Am I sleepwalking?

The damp moss squished between his toes, sending a chill up his legs. The canopy of leaves overhead blocked out most of the moonlight. He tiptoed across the gravel driveway cursing each time he stepped on a sharp stone.

Sweat trickled down his forehead, and the salt stung his eyes. He trembled as a thin trail of moisture slithered down his back. Exposed and vulnerable, outside clad only in his boxers, he wanted to retreat back inside.

The porch steps groaned under his weight. The wood felt rough, and the hair prickled on his arms.

At the doors he paused. Not ready to face the foot of the stairs, he feared what his imagination would create. How could his mind conjure up something more hideous than what had actually occurred? It might be the final push to edge him into full-blown insanity.

Reaching for the antique handle like it was an adder poised to strike, he inched the door open. Mercifully only the empty foyer greeted him. He sighed and stepped inside. The faces of the intricately carved angels on the banister twisted in grotesque agony.

Somehow their expressions had transformed. The impossibility only increased his dread.

Music drifted from the parlor. The hisses, pops, and distorted echoes of the Victrola sounded haunted and far away. Flames caressed the logs in the fireplace illuminating the room.

Will stepped into the parlor.

The mahogany coffee table with the round marble top, the green velvet couch, and other assorted antiques were unfamiliar. When had Sara moved all this creepy old furniture into their parlor? Almost as if he had conjured her, Sara emerged from the shadows just beyond the dining room archway. When she moved into the firelight Will gasped.

Her amber curls flowed over her shoulders like glimmering rivers. The white translucent nightgown revealed every detail of her form, causing Will's heart to race. He ached to touch her breasts and run his hands along the soft curves of her hips.

"I've been waiting," She said.

"How did you do all this?"

She smiled and surveyed the room. "I've been busy."

Glancing at the stairs, Will gestured toward the landing. "What about Ellie?"

Sara stepped closer. "She's sound asleep."

"But what if…"

"Shhh." She raised a finger to her lips and closed the distance between them. Her flesh was inviting in the soft firelight, her lips forming a seductive smile.

She reached out for him and slipped her arms over his shoulders, drawing him to her. She pressed against him, and they swayed to the music. His body responded to hers. Her embrace tightened as his fingers traced the familiar contours of her back. She felt as good as she looked. Their lips lightly caressed, teasing at first, and then locked. He lost himself in her sweet fragrance and the rhythm of the music.

Home at last.

In her arms none of the insanity mattered.

When the kiss ended, he tensed, and all the heat drained from his body. Large turquoise pools had replaced Sara's emerald eyes, and her hair had shifted to golden yellow. Will now held Celeste, the woman from Ellie's picture.

She kissed him again and her sour breath tasted like spoiled milk. He gagged and drew back from the embrace, his gaze fixed on her as the transformation continued. The light faded in her dull, sunken eyes, her long curls shifted into dirty twisted and matted hair, and her soft flesh turned gray, cracked and flaked away to reveal the bones beneath.

"What's wrong?" She asked.

Will broke free from her unnaturally powerful embrace. Bile rose in the back of his throat. He swallowed trying not to gag again. Disoriented, he stumbled backward into an overstuffed wing chair.

She drew closer, her skeletal arms outstretched as the music grew louder, the pops and hisses more pronounced. Her dried, crumbling face distorted in pain. The bones peeked through missing skin and muscle. Her large empty sockets fixed him in a vacant stare.

He attempted to rise as a dozen skeletal hands tore through the chair's fabric, seizing his arms, clutching his chest and pinning him. The more he struggled, the tighter they gripped, like steel shackles binding him in place. His skin burned as dirty fingernails dug into his flesh.

God help me.

Through the searing pain, he saw her bend toward him. He felt her hot smoldering breath and smelled the terrible stench. He went rigid when he saw the maggots crawling in the back of her open mouth. One last time he tried to scream, but only moaned as her mouth closed over his.

CHAPTER TEN

It was five in the morning on Tuesday, and Harry Weaver sat at his faded, lime green kitchen table, absentmindedly trying to cut the brown crunchy part of the fried egg whites with his fork. He had already finished sopping up the runny yoke with a piece of buttered toast and polished off half a syrup-drenched piece of scrapple. He washed down a bite of egg with a long swallow of cream soda. For a man in his eighties, he supposed he should have been thankful his arteries didn't crunch when he moved.

His thoughts were not really on his diet, or lack of one. Harry struggled with his conscience as he had over the past three days, as he often had over the past seventy-five years.

"It's none of your business you old fool," he told himself.

"What if they are in danger?" said another voice in his head – the one that kept coming back, pulling and tearing at his conscience like a rabid pit-bull, trying to destroy his common sense

Three days ago he had watched the ambulance's flashing lights through the fence line between his farm and Martin's property. He corrected himself. It wasn't Martin's property anymore. Later, during a visit to town, he learned that a young college student had died while moving furniture for the new owners.

That house again. How much sorrow could one place contain?

Harry had no answer as he sat in his old kitchen with its heavy wooden cupboards and faded oilcloth floor. The soft glow of the overhead light bathed the room in a yellow hue in the predawn hour. This room had hardly changed in his lifetime. He had eaten breakfast here as a boy. He still cooked his eggs in the same black, cast-iron frying pan his mother had used. Martha, his wife, had made only a few superficial changes in all the years of their marriage, God rest her soul and, after her death, he had changed nothing.

Growing up on the farm, he had learned at a young age that manual labor could be dangerous. His older brother Alvin had fallen through one of the hay holes in the second floor of the barn when they were young. He broke his leg; he was lucky it hadn't been his neck. A slip or miscalculation could get someone injured or killed. This sounded like one of those unfortunate accidents.

But, it happened on the stairs.

"That's just a coincidence," Harry argued, but he wasn't sure.

Six months earlier, Harry had found his best friend Martin crumpled in a heap at the foot of those damn stairs with their smiling cherubs. Martin had lain there for over eight hours.

"Don't go there," Harry warned himself, but he couldn't banish the images of his frail friend as they loaded him into the ambulance.

Later at the hospital, Martin asked Harry about the young woman.

"You didn't see the woman?" Martin asked.

"Woman, what woman?" Harry said.

Martin stared at the uneaten dinner on his tray. "A blonde in a white dress."

Harry chuckled, not really amused. "That shot to your head must have addled your brains; there was no young woman at your place. Believe me, I'd of noticed that."

"Yeah, I must have dreamed it," Martin agreed. He gave Harry a weak grin. Then he grew quiet. "I thought I saw her while I was on the floor."

Harry thought about that for a moment. Martin was a sensible man. He had been a bank president after all. "What would she have been doing at your place?"

"I don't know, but I swear I smelled perfume and felt a hand on my back before I fell."

There was nothing amusing about it, because the first woman that sprang into Harry's mind had to be long dead.

After his visit at the hospital, he checked out Martin's house, but found no one. He re-checked over the three days that Martin stayed in the hospital and never found a sign of anyone.

The doctors ran a battery of tests, but discovered nothing, and released Martin. Harry thought Martin would be thrilled to escape the hospital, but his friend seemed more depressed.

Both men remained quiet on the drive home. He worried about Martin, who had dark circles under his eyes and seemed dazed as they traveled. Martin told him that the doctor had prescribed sleeping pills, and that he slept longer each night. Before his fall, Martin had often complained that he couldn't sleep. Harry figured that was part of growing old, he woke up to piss several times a night himself.

"You know Harry, I've been thinking. Maybe we should head down to

Florida. We could live it up on the beach for the remainder of our days. I have the money. We could bask in the sun, drink beer, and watch the young women."

Harry chuckled and studied his friend. "That's not a bad plan. I could sell my farm. The boy's out in Ohio, I've got no reason to stay."

Adam, Harry's only son had married and moved to Ohio. He had gone into electrical engineering and didn't want the farm. There was no reason to hold onto the old place any longer.

"Yeah, we should do that," Martin's voice trailed off as he stared out the old pickup truck's side window.

Large snowflakes began to splatter against the windshield, and Harry started the wipers. The snow fell fast, and the grass along the side of the road disappeared under a white blanket.

"Storm's coming," Harry said.

"I'm ready for it," Martin said. Something in his voice made Harry think he wasn't referring to the snow. When they pulled into the gravel driveway in front of Martin's house, Harry asked, "Want some company?"

Martin shook his head. "I'm tired. I need to get some sleep. Thanks for everything. You're a good friend."

"Sure, have a good night. I'll see you tomorrow," Harry said.

He watched Martin climb the porch steps, wave once, and disappear through the front doors.

Back at his kitchen table, Harry groaned and slid his plate away. "We should have gone that night, Martin. I should've driven straight to the airport. I'm sorry."

Should've and could've, the language of the recently damned.

Harry slammed the table with his fist. "I don't want to get involved."

Oh, but you are Harry. You always have been.

The voice was relentless.

Harry rose, clearing his plate and silverware from the table. He dropped his glass soda bottle in the bin under the counter and started the tap. As he watched the water fill the sink, he noticed a man come out of Martin's old house.

It was the second day in a row that the new owner had gone for a morning run. The young fella stretched for a few moments then started down the driveway. Harry watched as the jogger reached the end of the lane.

Harry absentmindedly wiped his plate as he followed the young man's progress. By the time he had dried his fork, knife, and plate, and returned them to their rightful places in the cupboard, the young man had jogged out of sight.

Harry sighed and supposed he was going to have to surrender to the voice in his head. Still this new family wasn't his concern, and the last thing they'd want is some crazy, old codger poking his nose into their business.

But his conscience needled him. Martin had died in that house. Harry had failed to save his friend, what if the new family was in danger as well? Harry sighed, Martin and June had lived there for years and nothing bad ever happened.

Are you sure?

"Martin would've told me, and I've always kept an eye on the place."

Yeah, because of that other thing with the senator.

Harry shuddered. He was letting his imagination take him places he didn't want to go. He walked into the parlor, sank into his easy chair, and closed his eyes. Hadn't he paid enough? How much could a person give up to make amends for a past mistake? He had spent most of his life paying.

You should've told.

The voice roared, and tears ran down Harry's cheeks.

You could've saved Martin and maybe June. You might be able to save this new family.

Harry knew his conscience was convicting him, but he'd made his decision a long time ago and he would stick to it now. He shook his head, sighed, and slammed his hand down on the chair arm. He had never mentioned the event to another soul. Some things should remain dead and buried, and that's exactly what that incident was going to do. After seventy-five years it really couldn't make a difference.

His conscience, not willing to surrender, played its last card —
Martin's words.

*I don't know, but I swear I smelled perfume and felt a hand on my back
before I fell.*

Harry didn't know if it was a coincidence that the young man had
died on the stairs or if something more sinister was a work, but he
knew he couldn't ignore the possibility.

"Okay, that's it. Today I'll stop by to say hello."

In the end it always came back to that old house next door. Harry
had spent most of his life watching that place. He guessed he was
too old to change his habits. At least he could keep an eye on the
new family and watch for anything unusual.

If only the young man hadn't fallen on the stairs.

CHAPTER **ELEVEN**

Tuesday morning Will smacked the off button on the alarm before
it woke Sara. He slowly eased into a sitting position on the edge of
the bed. It was an effort to stand, to climb up through the haze of
the predawn gloom that suffused the room. He combed his fingers
through his hair and grimaced at the sour taste in his mouth. The
memory of the woman's maggot infested lips closing over his surfaced, and broke through his mental fog.

He barely reached the bathroom in time. Bringing up bile and
gagging over the toilet bowl. White flashes danced in front of his
eyes. It seemed like he crouched there for hours with his cheek resting against the cold porcelain. Finally, his stomach relaxed.

It wasn't real.

When the nausea passed, he ran some water in the sink and
splashed his face. What a horrible nightmare. It had seemed so real.

But, that's not possible.

He flipped on the light and paused to study his bare arms and
chest. Scratches crisscrossed his upper body. It must have been an-

other vision. He moaned and sank to the toilet, emptying more acid into the bowl. His head threatened to split in half.

Why is this happening now? What does it mean?

Insanity?

Not for the first time in a few days that thought crept around the corners of his mind.

Old Harper, the Vietnam vet who had lived next door when Will was a kid, had been insane. Harper would stand in the back yard dressed in fatigues and shout orders to an imaginary squad to shoot down the invading aliens.

Other kids in the neighborhood thought it was funny, but Will had always worried how he would know if he were insane. His mother had told him not to agonize about it. "When you're crazy, you don't know and you don't care."

Now, he wasn't so sure. Maybe when you go over the edge, you do realize, and have to live through the terror of losing your mind a piece at a time until you're completely bat-shit crazy?

Will slid to the floor, resting his back against the old claw foot tub, closed his eyes, and tried to breathe slowly to calm his pounding heart. No problem other than a few scrapes. Maybe they were self inflicted scratches during the dream?

Sure. You did this to yourself and didn't wake up.

Needing to think and relax, he struggled to his feet and stumbled back to the bedroom. Careful not to disturb Sara, he slipped on his running clothes in the dark.

Hoping his habitual two-mile run would restore some sense of reality, Will stepped into the brisk morning air. His exposed skin tingled. The air stabbed his lungs as he drew a deep breath. The sun peeked over the horizon, casting an orange glow on the world around him. The porch railing felt cold and rough as he braced himself and stretched his calves. After a few deep knee bends and a couple of lunges, his muscles felt limber.

He yawned and thought about his comfortable bed, but the nightmare, *if that's what it had been*, soured the idea of sleep. Before reconsidering, he started down the driveway. The gravel crunched under his feet, creating a rhythmic pattern, and his muscles loosened as he reached the end of the lane.

He ran west along Old Creek Road, increasing his speed until reaching the zone. This was his favorite part, losing himself in the exertion.

The stress drained away. The dream faded in the daylight and now felt distant and thin. Typically, he used this time to mentally prepare for the day, and reflexes and routine clicked into place. Project details started to overlap and bury any lingering memories from the previous night.

The country road climbed a steep grade for half a mile until it intersected with Route 322. At the edge of the highway, he paused to enjoy the view of the Susquehanna River that slowly flowed toward Harrisburg. The haze burned off as the sun heated the air. Will felt small next to the great expanse of sky. The railroad bridges spanning the river to the south seemed miniscule at this distance. Sufficiently awed, he turned around and started home, thoughts of the previous night's nightmare nearly forgotten.

As he reached his driveway, a silhouette backlit by the sun approached from the opposite direction. The tall man with a slight paunch around his middle moved with brisk strides.

"Hello, I'm Harry Weaver. I live on the next farm," the man said as he drew closer.

Will shook Harry's extended hand and the old man's strength surprised him.

"I wanted to say hello and welcome you to the neighborhood."

Will introduced himself as they walked toward the front porch.

The two men paused in the driveway, and Harry stared at the house with a touch of longing.

"She's a fine old place," Harry said.

Will tried to see the attraction. "She needs a lot of work."

Harry chuckled, put his hands in the straps of his bib overhauls and gave the house a real once over. "All old houses do. That's part of their charm."

Old and charm, two words that don't go together in my book.

Will wished he had held out for a nice townhouse somewhere in the Harrisburg suburbs. When he turned to face Harry, the old man still stared fondly at the house. "Yeah, there's a little rot there on the south wall. You could use a few new boards to replace the siding at the bottom."

"I guess I better get right on that. Do you know any good carpenters?"

Harry chuckled and scratched the stubble on his chin like he was contemplating something. "That's not a big job. I could help you with that."

Me? I don't know the first thing about carpentry.

Not able to control his laughter, warmth rose on Will's cheeks when the older man scowled at him. The guy was older than dirt, his face worn like leather from years of sun and wind exposure. Will didn't want someone else dying on the property. But, Harry did have a strong grip.

"I'm sorry. It's just that I'm not a carpenter. I'm into computers. Programming and software design. When it comes to this sort of thing, I'm all thumbs."

Harry studied him for a moment like he was making a decision. "Maybe, but it couldn't hurt to take a shot at it. You'd save a lot of money doing your own repairs. I'd be glad to teach you."

"I would hate to impose."

"Not a problem. It would be my pleasure."

Harry's pleasant smile disarmed Will. He reminded Will of his grandfather. The house did need work. "I couldn't work on it until this Saturday, because of my schedule at the office," Will said.

Harry nodded. "Saturday's fine. We can get the supplies at the lumberyard in Templeton." Harry walked over to the wall and pushed on the bottom board with his boot. Small pieces of wood crumbled.

Will frowned. It was all rotted. "Not to be indelicate, but what do you charge for this kind of work?"

"My going rate is dinner and a bottle of ice cold Yuengling Black & Tan after the job's done."

"That doesn't sound like a fair trade for you." Will poked at the bottom board with his foot and watched another hunk crumble off.

"Well, I'm sort of the unofficial caretaker of this place, and I kinda miss working on her."

Will saw loneliness in Harry's eyes. Will didn't know the first thing about fixing walls. He didn't know the first thing about fixing anything, but the old man had a point. Sara wanted to remodel the place, and he should try to do some of the work himself, or it would cost a small fortune. Besides, worse case if they started the job and couldn't handle it, he would just hire a professional.

Although the whole thing was probably a bad idea, he found himself extending his hand. "You're hired."

He wasn't sure if the old man was pleased or relieved. He was definitely not sure he had made the right decision. One thing was certain, no matter how much Sara loved this place; buying such an antiquated house had been a bad idea.

CHAPTER TWELVE

Two mornings later after long hours at the office, Will squinted at the alarm clock on the nightstand. Red numbers flashed eleven a.m. After his initial adrenalin rush, he realized that it was July Fourth — a vacation day.

He sighed and rolled over to reach for Sara, but found her side of the bed empty. Disappointed, he rubbed his eyes and tried to wake from another night of restless sleep.

Insomnia had never been a problem, but now his nights were plagued with nightmares or long stretches of silent staring at the ornate plaster ceiling in their bedroom, listening to the creaks and groans of the old house and trying to ignore his pounding heart. Exhausted, he considered sleeping for several more hours, but rejected the idea, eager to spend time with his family. Abandoning the soft mattress and warm covers, he plodded to the door and slipped on his old black terrycloth robe. In the bathroom across the hall his pale reflection greeted him in the mirror.

You need to get out in the sun.

Creaking door hinges interrupted this thought. He followed the sound to the bedroom next door. The small space served as his office and a guestroom. The attic door on the far wall stood ajar. Will approached to close it and heard giggling.

At first he thought he had imagined it, but then light feet fluttered across the attic floor, and Ellie whispered, "Okay, over here. See if you can find me."

Images of the open holes in the attic floor where chimneys had once extended flashed through Will's mind. The ceilings in the rooms below had been refinished with thin lattice strips and plaster, but the openings were still in the attic floorboards. Ellie could easily break through one of them and plunge nine feet to the floor below. He raced the stairs two at a time, his heart pounding.

"Ellie," he yelled. Panic raised his voice an octave as he envisioned her fall.

At the top he spotted her, about to step in one of the openings. His heart leapt to his mouth as his hand stretched out to grab her, realizing he was too late. "No."

Her foot rested in the unfinished opening. Plaster cracked and lattice strips snapped. Then her foot disappeared almost to the knee, and Will raced to her, his fingers grabbing her arms too tight and dragging her away from the gaping hole. She blankly stared into his face. "Daddy, what?"

He tried to control his voice. "What are you doing up here?"

In his arms, Ellie glanced around the room as if she was seeing it for the first time. "Celeste and I were playing a game."

The noonday sun had heated the attic to an unbearable temperature. The scent of seasoned wood and dust permeated the air. A wave of wooziness washed over him, and he lowered Ellie to her feet. "Let's get out of here."

She grasped his hand and together they retreated to the room below where they found Sara. Will slammed the door, making sure the old cast iron latch caught.

"What was all the yelling about?" Sara asked.

"I heard Ellie up in the attic and was terrified she would fall through one of those holes, and she would have if I hadn't found her when I did."

Sara examined Ellie. "Will, calm down — she appears fine."

"Are you Okay?" she asked Ellie.

Ellie nodded, burst into tears and buried her head in Sara's stomach. Sara shot Will a see everything is fine glance. "You won't do it again, will you?"

Still clinging to her mother, Ellie shook her head.

Will swallowed and licked his lips. He felt unsteady and wondered why Sara remained so calm about this didn't she understand the implications of what could have happened? But, Ellie appeared fine. He felt foolish.

I'm so tired. Maybe I'm overreacting?

"Come down stairs, I'll fix you some breakfast," Sara said.

Will sighed. Ellie was fine. He glanced at his computer and caught Sara rolling her eyes.

"In a second, I need to check my e-mail."

He sank into his desk chair and powered up the PC.

Sara left the room shaking her head. "Can't you go one day without turning that thing on? I'm sure it wouldn't kill you."

Will nodded, but the girls had already disappeared down the hall, and the list of messages distracted him. He opened one from K. Andersen and began to read. It was a note to tell him she was working, and would have code for him to review tomorrow. She added that he should have a great holiday and enjoy the fireworks.

She's a real go-getter.

He smiled, deleted the file, and double-checked to make sure Sara was not watching over his shoulder. She had left the room, but for a minute he sensed someone behind him. It was probably guilt because he still hadn't told Sara about Kerrie.

There's nothing going on. We're just co-workers.

There was no reason for him to feel guilty, but he realized Sara wouldn't like that Kerrie worked so closely with him. If he told Sara that Kerrie had recommended him for the job it would create tension, and there was no time for that.

Why create a problem where there is none?

Powering down the computer, Will headed back to his room to

get dressed. Ten minutes later he approached the stairs, but detoured when he heard the squeaky door again. Returning to his office, he felt the world fall away as he stared at the open attic door. "Sara, Ellie?"

No answer. He raced to the top of the steps, only to find the attic as he had left it. Relieved, but slightly nauseous from a second adrenalin rush on an empty stomach, he returned to the office below, slammed the door and double-checked that the latch caught. Satisfied it was tightly secured he went downstairs.

In the kitchen Sara chopped potatoes in small cubes, and Ellie sat at the table dunking chocolate chip cookies in milk.

"Did I hear you calling?" Sara asked.

"Yeah, the attic door was open again," Will said and turned to Ellie, "You know not to go up there alone?"

"Yes daddy. I won't, but Celeste likes to."

"I want you to promise me," Will said.

He was sure she didn't grasp the enormity of his paranoia for her. He couldn't drop his guard for a moment. Since becoming a father, he had always felt overzealous about his responsibility for her safety, but lately, his anxiety had increased proportionately with his headaches and exhaustion.

"I promise," Ellie said and climbed down from the bar stool, picking up her Barbie and Ken, and dashing out the back door.

Pouring himself a glass of orange juice and watching Ellie do cartwheels in the back yard he said, "I don't understand. I'm sure I closed that door."

Sara poured the potatoes into a pot of water. "It's an old house. The door frame is probably a little warped from the house settling, that's all."

He smiled and felt silly. It was just an old door that didn't close tight, but then he thought about Ellie's friend Celeste. "She's spending too much time playing with this Celeste."

Sara dropped a half peeled potato in the bowl and stepped closer wrapping her arms around his waist. "She's just an imaginary friend. All kids have them. No big deal."

"Isn't she a little old?"

"Would you rather her out chasing boys?"

He didn't allow his mind to move in that direction. Instead he thought about the scratches on his arms and chest. This morning they were only faint marks, but how had he gotten them? He had been dreaming about Celeste? This was insane. Lately his imagination worked overtime. He had seen the old photo in Ellie's room and just subconsciously incorporated the woman's image into his dream. "I guess, but maybe she should spend more time with other real kids."

Sara squeezed harder, and then rubbed his shoulders. "You're so tense, you need to relax. If you're not careful you'll end up with ulcers."

"Yeah, I guess you're right. I'll take a break from worrying. I better get started on the barbecue."

He gave her a peck on the cheek and turned for the backdoor, but paused when he spotted old keys on a peg by the basement door. "Hey, one of these probably locks the attic."

Will removed the keys from the peg and studied them. A red letter A was painted on one.

Sara rolled her eyes. "Would you just relax?"

He shrugged, returned all but the attic key to the peg. "I'll feel better if I know it's locked. What can I say, I'm just..."

"Paranoid," Sara finished for him.

"I was going to say careful."

Will gave her another kiss on the cheek and hurried up to his office. He slid the key into the slot and heard a resounding click when it turned. Satisfied the door was securely locked, he was convinced that should end it.

CHAPTER **THIRTEEN**

Ellie pointed to the sky over City Island as the fireworks bloomed like giant multi-colored, phosphorus flowers. "Oh Daddy, they're beautiful."

Will sat on a blanket next to Sara and watched Ellie's expression. He was more enthused by her delight than by the actual fireworks display, although the city had obviously spent a small fortune on the exhibition that generated spectacular reflections in the river.

The still air and clear sky created an optimal evening for the celestial display. Thousands of other people had also gathered along the river at Front Street to watch the Fourth of July celebration.

Sara leaned into Will resting her head on his shoulder as he draped his arm around her. "This is more like it."

He watched Ellie watching the fireworks and nodded. "I know. Things will settle down at work soon. I promise."

Sara took his hand in hers. "I don't mean to complain. I just miss you."

He enjoyed her touch. "It's okay. Who could blame you? I'm just so charming."

Sara chuckled and gazed out over the river. He loved the sound of her laugh, rarely heard recently.

The grand finale ended with six huge explosions all erupting simultaneously and the throng of spectators cheering wildly. The evening possessed a surreal, almost ethereal quality that lingered with Will as he maneuvered the car north out of the city toward their home. Glancing in the rearview mirror he noticed that Ellie was already asleep. "I guess we wore her out."

Sara peeked at the backseat and grinned.

"By the way, I met a neighbor," Will said.

Sara studied him. "When? You're never home."

He ignored the jab. "On my morning run two days ago."

Sarah grabbed a handful of popcorn they had purchased from a strolling vendor and offered him the bag: "Who?"

He grabbed a handful of the greasy stuff and wished for a napkin. "The farmer next door. His name's Harry. He offered to help me fix the siding on the front of the house."

Sara turned in her seat to face him. "You're going to fix the siding on the house."

Will shrugged crunching on a mouthful of popcorn before he

spoke. "I know it sounds crazy, but Harry said it wouldn't be that hard."

"How much is the guy going to charge us for this?"

Will swallowed. "Just a home cooked meal and a bottle of beer."

"He should have held out for a whole case," Sara said as she leaned back in her seat and laughed.

Will couldn't get angry. His lack of carpentry skills was legendary in the Shepherd household. In fact he wondered why he had agreed to try in the first place. He didn't have the spare time, and they could afford to hire someone. He couldn't explain it, even to himself; there was just something about the old man's eyes.

He needed to work on our house.

The car's lights reflected off the house as Will turned into the driveway. The large trees in the front yard swayed in a light breeze, and shadows danced across the front of the old building. The entire structure was cloaked in darkness, except Will's office window.

"That's odd, I don't remember leaving the light on," he said climbing out of the car.

"You must have this morning," Sara said.

He shook his head as he walked around the back of the car to the passenger side, and gently lifted the sleeping child from the back seat. "I guess."

"Careful you don't hurt yourself."

Will carried Ellie toward the house trying not to jostle her. He made a mental note that he must be spending too much time behind a desk if it was becoming a struggle to carry the eight-year-old. "She's getting too big for this."

Sara teased that she was going to have to trade him in on a younger model. Will ignored the jab and focused on the long climb to the top of the stairs. He was relieved to place Ellie on her bed. He gave her a peck on the forehead, and she stirred slightly, a wide smile on her face. "You little faker, you."

Ellie giggled and pulled the blanket up over her face. "Good night Daddy."

"Good night Sweetie."

He left Sara to help Ellie get dressed for bed and went to his office.

When he opened the door, chills ran down his spine. He wasn't sure if he had left the light on, but there was no doubt that he had locked the attic door, which now stood wide open. He stared in disbelief and was startled by Sara behind him in the hall. "The attic door is open again."

Sara entered the room. "It's an old door. It probably doesn't close tight."

He examined it moving it back and forth on the hinges. "I locked it."

She touched him on the shoulder. "Will, you're starting to act flaky. I think you need some sleep."

He didn't see any humor in this. Someone had opened the door and they might still be up in the attic. He had to be sure, so he entered the stairway, reached out and flipped the light switch on the wall. The forty-watt bulbs couldn't illuminate the large open space above him. The plaster walls on either side of the stairs started to press inward. Will's stomach felt hollow, and a cold chill crept across his skin.

Sara shadowed him as he climbed the stairs. He could almost feel her against his back. "Why would anyone be in the attic?" she whispered.

He had no idea, but that didn't settle his nerves as he neared the open room above. His muscles tense, he prepared for attack. Halfway to the top he realized that he was unarmed. This thought came too late because the creature sprang.

Their nerves stretched to the breaking point, Sara and Will both screamed. Mr. Whiskers raced down the steps past them into the bedroom below. Will wasn't sure if they or the cat had been more startled. They embraced each other laughing hysterically.

They staggered to the top of the staircase in each other's arms. Will turned in a slow circle, scanning the space. Again the room smelled like antique stores and farmer's markets that Sara had drug him to on many excursions in search of treasures.

The large open space provided no place for an intruder to hide. Will walked to the center of the room where he could see the other wings of the attic. "I guess it is all clear."

He glanced at the small stack of boxes. They were old cardboard grocery cartons, a few antique suitcases, and a couple small wooden crates. All stuff they had brought from Horsham. Nothing seemed disturbed.

Sara prodded one of the cardboard boxes. "Are you sure you don't want to check in the suitcases?"

"Very funny."

She started back down the stairs. "Oh Honey, lighten up. That was like one of those old Halloween funhouses we used to go to when we were dating."

He followed her to the bottom of the stairs. "Yeah, fun like that can give a guy my age a coronary."

She wrapped her arm around his. "Come on old man, I'll tuck you into bed."

They started to leave the room, but Will paused to look back at the attic door. "I still don't see how that door opened. I'm sure I locked it."

"Will, let it go."

"You don't think Ellie went back up there."

Sara groaned and tugged his arm. "No. Not after you told her not to. Besides I think you kept the key."

Will reached into his front pocket and removed it. "Huh, I guess I forgot to put it back," he said staring at old key.

"You probably thought it was locked. That's all."

Will walked over to the doorway, but paused to listen to the thump, thump, thump of something bouncing down the attic stairs. A red rubber ball the size of a small apple bounced against the wall at the bottom of the steps and rolled over to his feet. "What the?"

Picking up the ball, Will turned to Sara. "Where did this come from?"

Sara glanced at it and raised her eyebrows in mock interest. "It was probably in one of the boxes up there. Mr. Whiskers must have been playing with it."

"I don't know…" Will turned the ball over in his hand examining it. He didn't remember seeing it on the floor.

Sara grabbed his arm and started pulling him from the room. "It's only a ball. Would you put it down and come to bed."

Will set the ball on his desk and swung the attic door shut, slamming it tight. He locked it, and tried it several times to make sure it was secure. Sara watched, her hands on her hips, mild amusement danced on her face. "Come on, you're tired. Let's get some sleep."

Will followed her from the room, but glanced back at the old door one last time to make sure it was still sealed. He was afraid to look.

CHAPTER FOURTEEN

The red ball bounced down the wooded trail, and five year-old Will ran to keep up. Twigs and leaves smacked his face and arms as he dashed through the thick forest after the trophy. In the fading light he had to squint to keep his prize in sight.

Up ahead in the darkness he heard voices. Forgetting his goal, Will slowed and approached silently. The acrid stench of a great campfire drifted in the breeze, and through the brush he spotted the fire's glow.

The darkness deepened; his parents would be worried. He had only wanted to catch the ball, now he was lost and alone in the woods at night. He bit his lower lip to stop the trembling. He wanted to cry out for help.

Big boys don't cry.

Crouching close to the earth, he crawled ahead on hands and knees. Pine scent mixed with the burning wood, earthy and primitive. He pulled aside a branch for a better view and gasped. A huge village, hundreds of low, long, curved roof buildings lay silhouetted in the darkness.

At the edge of the clearing, a group of people gathered around a fire dressed in buckskin and fur clothing. Beads and feathers adorned their clothes. Will tried to hide real good and hoped they didn't see him in the brush.

A tall man with long black hair addressed the throng. "The Great

Spirit has not been kind to the people this season."

One of the wizened old men shook his head. "We have always survived in the past."

An ancient looking woman with long white braided hair rose to her feet and leaned on a wooden staff. "It was the others, the pale ones we encountered at the bay. They were a bad omen. We have never seen men of that color walk the earth."

Many in the group bobbed their heads in agreement and turned to listen to the old woman as she continued. "It was no surprise that all the crops have failed when we returned here for the frozen time. Those strange others were a portent."

The tall dark-haired man shook his head. "No, Small Sparrow. Those others brought powerful weapons and new tools and are willing to trade for fur. They are not a bad omen. We can use these things to make our lives better. The crops did not fail because they came. If I lead a party to the north to those grounds, I will be able to bring back more game and feed the village. The people will not go hungry."

The first old man interrupted. "That land to the north is dark. The people have avoided it since the beginning of time; even the others do not hunt or dwell there."

The tall man grunted and rose to his feet. "I fear no shadows. The hunting grounds here around the "Great Rock" are desolate. Game may be more plentiful there because no one hunts. If you do not allow my party to journey to the north we will all starve." He lowered his head in a sign of respect.

The elder man nodded and raised his hands. "Gray Wolf is a brave warrior, but the shadow lands are dangerous. The council must decide."

A group of six elders entered a large wooden longhouse. Others disappeared into scattered lodges, leaving only the tall man named Gray Wolf and another younger man.

Will lay real quiet, like Davey Crockett on TV. Will's daddy, loved to watch that old show. Davey always knew how to deal with Injuns. These Injuns talked funny, but Will understood them. Cold and scared, he wanted to find his way back to the car, back to

Mommy and Daddy.

The younger man picked up a branch and tossed it into the fire. "Will they allow us to go?"

"They have no choice, little brother."

The younger man squatted by the fire, warming his hands. "We have heard tales of that place our whole life. I can't believe we will actually journey there."

Gray Wolf chuckled quietly and punched the younger man's shoulder. "Are you scared of tales told to children, Running Turtle?"

An owl screeched in the distance, and the two waited in the moonlit silence.

Running Turtle tossed another small log onto the fire. "I have always followed you without fear."

"I know, and this time will be no different. I'm confident."

Running Turtle nodded and eased back on his haunches also staring into the flames. "Small Sparrow will not concede. She has seen visions."

"The other five elders will overrule her. They haven't the desire to watch children starve." Gray Wolf leaned forward. "They have no choice and neither do we."

"What about Little Flower?"

Gray Wolf remained silent for a few moments. "She's my mate, she goes where I go."

Running Turtle responded with a silent nod.

Will thought about trying to squirm back farther into the darkness and escape up the trail, but he wasn't sure where to go. He was lost and scared. Why had he followed the ball? His head pounded and his eyes burned from the campfire. He was about to attempt to slip away when the old woman named Small Sparrow appeared in the long house doorway.

She limped over to the two young warriors. Her frail body bent and supported by the long wooden staff.

Gray Wolf rose. "Have they decided?"

The old woman nodded and touched his arm. "They have agreed. There is no choice."

Gray Wolf smiled at the other man. "I told you they would, little brother."

The old woman shook her head slowly and touched Gray Wolf's cheek. "You should not go, my son."

"It will be all right, Great Mother," Gray Wolf answered, "I will return with much game for the people to eat. We will not fail."

The old woman sighed and poked the fire with her staff. "In that forest evil dwells, it is in the land, it is rooted there. If you go, you will not return."

Gray Wolf bowed his head in respect, but would not relent. "I am a warrior, my brother and I have fought many battles with others and are not afraid of any that may attack us."

Her voice became low and her words fierce. "It is not other men you must fear. No man should dwell on that land. It houses an evil that has no form. It has dwelt there since the beginning of time."

Gray Wolf's hands closed into fists. "I fear the starvation of our people more than I fear the shadow world."

Small Sparrow shook her head.

Running Turtle rose and took her hand. "Mother, We will return before the ice is thick on the river."

She embraced the two young men. "My brave warriors, my foolish boys. Go now, rest, you will need your strength for this journey."

The two men started toward the longhouse. "What about you Mother?" Gray Wolf asked.

The old woman stared into the flames and was silent for a moment. "I'll be along."

Gray Wolf and Running Turtle disappeared into the lodge. Small Sparrow hobbled toward Will's hiding spot. He was sure she could see him in the darkness. As she closed the distance, her eyes were shut. When she reached a few feet from him she opened them. He screamed. They were solid white.

"Remember boy, remember well, no man should dwell on that land. It houses an evil that has no form. The veil is thin and the dead slither back across into the land of the living."

CHAPTER **FIFTEEN**

Friday morning the alarm tore through Will's brain like a buzz saw. He almost decided to skip work and take a four-day weekend, but he couldn't afford another day of lost productivity.

Most of the morning he attempted to concentrate on an Excel document, entering data, but then losing his place. The previous night's dream distracted him. It had felt real and familiar, more like a memory than a dream.

After a few hours of this mental battle, he surrendered and fired up his web browser. He always succumbed to the digital world's call far easier than that of the physical.

A Google search on 'Native Americans of Pennsylvania' painted the screen with an extensive list of hits. Will started to follow links, and time melted as he read accounts of the first inhabitants of the Susquehanna Valley.

An article about the Susquehannocks by Sam Gersh was particularly interesting. They were a powerful tribe that lived along the Susquehanna River prior to 1675.

Will was struck by their lifestyle. They planted crops in the spring and then journeyed south to the Chesapeake Bay in the summer, returning north in the fall to harvest their crops. They lived in towns of up to two thousand people and sent out satellite villages to hunt game to help support the main towns in the winter.

Will stared at the screen and frowned. This was exactly like his dream. He had no memory of studying this in school and wondered how his subconscious could have constructed this scenario. He clicked print, and the laser printer hummed to life spewing what he thought was significant data, although he was not sure why.

A knock on the door distracted him. Frank peeked his head inside. "Have a minute?"

Will looked up from the screen, automatically closing the browser. "Sure."

"I have the data model changes," Frank said as he strolled into the office. He handed the pages to Will. Will studied them while Frank idly glanced around the office.

The words and numbers swam on the page, and Will eased himself back into his chair. He prayed he wouldn't have another vision of Frank bursting into flames.

"Have a seat," Will suggested.

"No thanks. I'm good."

Frank walked over to the printer and picked up one of the pages and scanned it. "Susquehannocks?"

Feeling foolish, Will didn't want to get into this with Frank. "Yeah, that's something I researched for Ellie."

Frank dropped the paper back on the stack. "Wow, give the kid a break, it's summer."

Will lifted his gaze from the data model to Frank. The bright sunlight hurt his eyes, and he winced. "We have to give her a head start. It's a competitive world out there."

Frank dropped into the chair opposite Will's desk. He removed his glasses and used his front right shirttail to diligently clean the thick lenses. He rubbed the cloth around and then held the frames up in the light for inspection. "I hope you're kidding, or that child's therapy bills are going to cost you a fortune."

Will smiled. He enjoyed pulling Frank's chain, and it was particularly easy.

Frank must've suffered terrible ridicule as a kid.

"Don't worry. It's just something Ellie saw on the Discovery channel," Will lied. "You know anything about them?"

Frank shrugged and scrunched up his face. "No, history's not my bag."

"Mine neither."

"By the way, you look like shit."

Will ran his fingers through his hair. "Thanks, I'm just tired, not sleeping well."

Frank checked his watch. "Hey, it's almost noon. What you need is grub and a big shot of caffeine."

His head throbbed, and Will thought caffeine was probably the last thing he needed, but he did want to get out of the office. Maybe some fresh air would clear out the cobwebs in his brain, so he agreed to lunch.

"Come on, we'll grab Kerrie on the way to the car," Frank said.

The three usually ate together, taking turns picking different restaurants.

Will and Frank were surprised to find Kerrie's cube empty. In the cube across the aisle, Steve Andrews hunched over his keyboard. Head bobbing up and down like one of those bobble head dolls in time to the music that played in his earbuds. Will tapped lightly on the edge of Steve's cube frame. Engrossed in his work and the music, he obviously didn't hear Will and Frank behind him. Will tapped louder. "Excuse me."

Steve spun around in his chair, the headphone cable yanking his iPod across the desk. Removing the ear buds he stared. "What?"

"Sorry to interrupt. Have you seen Kerrie?"

"Yeah, I saw her head to the parking lot with C.L. I think they were going to do lunch".

C.L. Morris was the C.E.O., "C.L." as he preferred to be addressed, was in his forties. He was tall with a thin athletic build and his brown hair was always immaculately trimmed. He dressed in Dockers and Polo shirts, casual attire for the president of a corporation. He was a likable guy, and Will supposed women found him attractive. Will felt heat rise in his cheeks. He wanted to wipe the smirk off Steve's face.

What a total jerk.

Steve righted his radio and drew the outline of a well-endowed woman in the air. "Have you seen C.L.' s wife? She's one hot babe. I don't know why he would want to slum it with Kerrie."

Again with the smirk, and Will fought down an inappropriate response and instead said thanks. He turned to Frank and said, "Come on, I'm hungry. Let's head out."

In truth, his appetite had vanished. He was more curious about what Kerrie was up to with C.L., and that question only left him inappropriately jealous.

CHAPTER **SIXTEEN**

Harry scraped most of his Friday evening supper of liver and onions into the trash bin under the counter and dipped his plate in the sudsy water. His appetite non-existent, he stared out his kitchen window at the old Courtland House as he wiped the dish. The sunset's orange and purple afterglow exaggerated the silhouette of the mammoth structure that towered over the surrounding foliage.

He had appeased his conscience, but didn't enjoy the quiet. Once again he had stuck his nose in where it didn't belong. He had thought Martin's death had freed him of the whole thing, but now he was sucked back in. There was no escape. He was convinced he would never be free.

Of course sticking his nose where it didn't belong had started all his problems seventy-three years earlier.

He remembered it like it was yesterday the morning sun's heat on his face and the cool breeze that rustled the leaves.

His hands were blood red, and he balanced precariously in the thin upper branches of the tree. The breeze rocked the bough, and he struggled to maintain his perch while stretching out and clutching another handful of cherries and snapping them off the branch. Popping the handful into his mouth, he chewed around the seeds, enjoying the sweet juice.

"I hope you are getting some in the bucket. Mom won't let us have supper till we each fill a pail." His older brother Alvin sat on the top of a rickety old stepladder plopping handfuls of fruit into his container.

"Let Harry alone, he's only eight. He can fill half a bucket, because he's a half-pint." Nevin, their oldest brother was always standing up for Harry. Alvin scowled at Nevin, and while his back was turned, Harry stuck out his tongue.

Nevin grinned at Harry and dropped another handful of cherries into his own bucket.

"You always take his side," Alvin complained.

Nevin shook his head and inched up into a higher branch.

"Well, he is the baby," Nevin said, and Alvin smirked at Harry.

"Hey, I'm only two years younger than you." Harry almost lost his balance as he threw a cherry, pelting Alvin in the head.

"Don't make me come hurt you." Alvin rose off the ladder, starting to scramble up into the branches after the younger boy.

"Stop it you two. You're going to spill them." Nevin who was twelve, commanded his two younger brothers with authority.

Alvin laughed, but stopped halfway to Harry. "You're not worth it Small Fry, besides I want a cherry pie."

Champion, Harry's beagle, sniffed around the tall grass at the base of the tree. Harry kept an eye on him, watching the dog follow trails through the grass, his tail wagging. Their pop had bought Champion as a hunting dog, but Harry had claimed him.

"Champ's on the scent." Harry scurried down the tree, and Alvin scrambled after him.

Nevin called after them. "Hey, where are you going?"

Ignoring Nevin, the two younger brothers followed Champ through the line fence and into the alfalfa field on the old Courtland property.

"Think he's gonna catch a rabbit?" Harry tried to keep up with Alvin as they ran across the field. "Yeah," Alvin said.

The boys were in the center of the field when Harry heard the car's engine. He stopped and turned to scan Old Creek Road. The red Packard kicked up dust on the dirt road as it raced into the driveway and halted in front of the old house.

Alvin turned to Harry. "We better head home."

Champion must have heard the car and found the newcomers more interesting than his prey. The hound started barking and sprinted toward the man, woman, and child that were climbing out of the vehicle.

"Oh no." Harry wanted to flee, but he couldn't abandon Champ.

Mrs. Freedman raised her hands in the air and tried to distance herself from the small dog that was leaping up and leaving paw prints on her silky pink dress. Her large hat skewed, and her huge brown eyes bulged as she danced in a circle trying to dodge Champ's leaps. With her prominent nose, she resembled an ostrich. "Howard help, get this beast away from me."

Harry wanted to laugh, Champ was only playing; he was just excited to meet these new people. Mrs. Freedman was also excited, actually frazzled. A small red-headed boy clung to her skirt, using her as a shield from the dog.

Senator Freedman rounded the car waving his arms. "Get away from her you mutt."

Reaching Champ first, Harry grabbed his collar and pulled him away from the frightened woman and child. Alvin caught up and tried to help calm Champ down by petting his head while Harry clutched the collar.

"Sorry, ma'am," Harry said.

"You should keep that hound on a leash. If I see it running wild on our property again, I'll shoot it," senator Freedman said as he glared at the two brothers.

"Yes sir," they answered in unison.

"Come along, Jonathan." Mrs. Freedman grabbed her son's arm and propelled him toward the old house. Jonathan glanced over his shoulder at the beagle, his earlier terror apparently forgotten.

"Now get that beast out of here, before I call the authorities."

Senator Freedman turned and followed his wife and child into the house. Harry winced when the front door slammed. He was sure the fancy etched glass panes were going to shatter.

Alvin picked up Champ, who thought he wanted to play and tried to squirm out of the boy's arms. Side by side they started back across the field. Alvin carrying Champ, and Harry trying to keep a hold of the collar so the beagle couldn't get free. Halfway home, Nevin met them with some twine they tied around the collar and used as a leash.

"Boy, he is mean," Harry said, glancing back over his shoulder at the old house.

"Yeah, we better keep Champ away from there. Right boy?" Nevin tugged on the twine as Champ tried to veer off, following a scent that caught his attention.

Nevin tied the rope to one of the fence posts, and Harry and Alvin climbed back into the Cherry tree.

Alvin picked up his bucket. "He shouldn't go over there anyway."

Harry looked down at his almost empty bucket, his face still warm from the senator's threats. "Why? Champ wouldn't hurt anything."

Alvin snatched a handful of cherries from an overhead branch and tossed them in his bucket. "No, but the ghosts might get him."

Turning in the tree, Harry stared at the old house across the field. It was kind of creepy, but he had never thought of it as haunted. "That's not true."

Alvin sat on top of the ladder his arms crossed. "Yes it is. Tell him the *story Nevin."*

Nevin frowned, glanced from Alvin to Harry and shook his head. "Keep picking or we'll never get done."

"Tell him the story."

Now Harry was curious, he wanted to know what the other two boys were talking about. He climbed down out of the tree. "Come on Nevin. Tell me please?"

Nevin sighed, dropped to the ground and sat on the grass, leaning against the trunk of the tree. Alvin scurried down the ladder, and he and Harry sat crossed legged in the shade in front of Nevin. Champ tried to lick Harry's face.

"I'll tell you, but then we have to pick extra fast."

"Okay." Both younger brothers agreed.

Nevin glanced over his shoulder at the house, when he started his voice was barely a whisper. "That old house was built back before the Civil War. They say a man named Kiefer Courtland built it for the woman he loved. When the war broke out, he became a captain in the army."

"On which side?" Harry asked.

Alvin smacked Harry in the back of the head. "On the North's stupid, now be quiet, let him tell the story."

Harry picked up a stone to throw, but Nevin continued, and he forgot to toss it.

"During the war Captain Courtland went mad from all the blood and stuff. When he came home he was out of his mind. One night he thought his wife was a southern soldier and shot her dead. When he realized what he had done, he shot himself.

Now they say their ghosts haunt the old house, and if you go up to the front door at midnight, you'll see them standing there looking out."

Harry dropped the stone; Alvin was grinning from ear to ear. "Have you ever seen them?" Harry asked.

Nevin shook his head and smiled as he climbed to his feet. "Naw, Pop would tan our hides if he caught us out after midnight."

Alvin folded his arms across his chest. "Then how do you know it's true?"

Nevin shrugged and started climbing the tree. "Seen their tombstones up on the hill behind the house. They were both buried on the same day, and Robert Tanner said that sometimes at night you can see lights in the house when the senator and his family are back in Harrisburg at their main house. Now come on and fill your buckets."

"Wow, I'd like to see a ghost." Harry said.

Alvin picked up his bucket and started back up the stepladder. "You'd be too scared."

Harry climbed up after him. "I would not. I'll go tonight."

Nevin grinned at Harry and shook his head. "Didn't you hear me? I said Pop would skin us alive if he caught us out of the house at midnight. You better just forget about it."

The boys finished their chores and ate supper, but Harry didn't forget about it. It was all he could think about. The idea of seeing a real ghost was just too tantalizing, and later as he lay in the dark in the bedroom he shared with Alvin, he decided he was going to do it.

"Hey, You awake?" Harry whispered.

"What?" Alvin stirred in his bed like he was trying to get comfortable.

"I'm going to go see the ghost. Want to come?"

Alvin sat up, his hair spiked out in all directions. "You heard Nevin, if Pop catches us..."

Harry slid out of bed and started pulling up his trousers. "Pop's sound asleep. If we're quiet he'll never know."

As Harry drew on his clothes, he was relieved when Alvin eased out of bed. They finished dressing silently in the dark. Harry went over to the window and slid it open. He climbed through and inched his way across the slick slate porch roof, careful not to make a sound. Harry was not real scared of ghosts, but he did fear his father's temper.

At the edge of the roof he stretched to reach the rose trellis attached to the end of the porch. He dangled his feet out over the darkness, carefully trying to get his footing on the unseen lattice below. One slip and it would be all over. His years of tree climbing experience were tested as he negotiated the thorny grid work. The thorns scratched his arms and legs, but it was all part of the adventure. He wiped the sweat from his brow as he watched Alvin scale the framework. Alvin was halfway down when he let out a soft curse. He must have grabbed a thorn and he almost lost his balance. Harry tried to reach up and give him some support. Alvin regained his balance and soon was there beside him on the ground, nursing his one *hand.*

"You hurt?" Harry whispered.

"No, just a scratch. You know what Pop says, a job is never done till you've donated a little blood."

Harry remembered his pop's saying, but wasn't sure what it meant.

He shivered in the cool night air. Thick clouds blanketed out the full moon's light. The barnyard was lost in long shadows, and Harry tried not to think about what could be hiding in the darkness. Alvin grabbed his arm as they crossed the driveway. "Try not to rustle the stones too much."

Harry didn't think their father would hear their footsteps in the driveway, but he didn't want to take a chance on it. He held his breath as they eased across the gravel, relieved when they reached the grass on the other side.

The two boys crossed the alfalfa field and slipped through the line fence. They crept toward the stand of lilac bushes near the old house. After reaching the cover, Harry pulled out the old pocket watch his grandfather had given him. "It say's five 'til midnight."

Alvin glanced at the old house then back to Harry. "I don't think this is a good idea."

The old house sat dark and silent. Harry could tell Alvin was scared, but they had already risked their father's wrath. He had to see the ghost; no turning back now. "I'm going."

Harry stepped from the bushes and inched toward the front porch. Sweat beaded on his forehead, and his heart pounded. He had never felt so alive. Slowly he crept up the front steps, forgetting his scratches from the roses and Alvin who still hid in the bushes. His desire to see a ghost propelled him forward.

His face was almost pressed against the glass when the clouds parted and the moon's light illuminated the front of the house. Fierce emerald eyes stared back at Harry through the glass. At first he didn't recognize the gaunt face, the black disheveled hair, or the fiery eyes.

"Ahh." Harry stumbled backward off the porch as the front door opened. He dodged as a hand grabbed for him.

As fast as his feet would carry him, Harry ran for the line fence. Alvin had already escaped.

The senator followed Harry to the edge of the porch. "You kids come back here again and I'll shoot you."

Harry ran all the way home, and was still running from that house seventy-five years later. He had run from it almost his entire life, but he had learned something the acts of men could be far scarier than ghosts.

Harry sighed and placed the dish in the cupboard. In the morning he would help Will Shepherd with the repairs. After all, Harry was getting too old to keep running.

CHAPTER SEVENTEEN

Will braced himself as the 1964 International pickup truck rattled across the railroad tracks and kicked up dust. Harry brought the vehicle to a practiced stop in front of the renovated freight station that housed Long's Hardware and Lumber Co. Glancing around at the deserted parking lot, Will thought the place looked abandoned for a Saturday morning.

He followed Harry into the building, and a small bell mounted on the door jingled, adding to the old time ambiance. The room was filled from the cracked cement floor to the rough-hewn wooden rafters with a variety of hardware and carpenter tools. Small paths, hardly wide enough to be called aisles, wound through the assortment. The odor of lawn chemicals and fertilizers lingered in the air. Will surveyed the dimly lit room, wondering how the elderly clerk behind the glass counter could possibly locate anything.

Harry approached the thin, redheaded man and they shook hands. Harry said something that Will didn't understand, and then the clerk answered in the same strange language. Will raised his eyebrows in question.

"Pennsylvania Dutch, I guess you don't speak it," Harry said.

"I'll get the wood loaded first," the clerk said and disappeared through a door behind the counter. Will studied a rack filled with flower and vegetable seeds. He slowly turned it reading the names on the small packets.

"Do a lot of people speak Pennsylvania Dutch around here?" Will asked.

"Not as many as years ago," Harry said, "I learned to speak that before I learned English. Mom and Pop spoke it all the time. Now I only get to use it when I run into another old-timer like Red. I guess the younger generation never picked it up."

"That's too bad," Will said, but he was looking past Harry, distracted by a glass showcase along the back wall of the store. Inside an assortment of shotguns and rifles were displayed. Will approached and stared at the weapons. The light reflected off the blue steel of the barrels, and Will's eyes fixed on a Remington 870 Wingmaster shotgun. He couldn't express it with words, but the gun was the most beautiful thing he had ever seen.

Will hadn't grown up around guns. His father, a vocal pacifist, would never have brought a gun into their home. "We will not indulge in the tools of destruction," his father would've said.

Harry joined Will. "Are you a hunter?"

"No. Why?"

"The look in your eyes. I just thought."

"I've never owned a gun, have you?" Will asked.

"Oh sure, I have a few."

Will turned to Harry. "I know this is a strange request. If I buy one of these will you teach me how to shoot?"

Harry laughed and smacked Will on the back. "We'll make a country boy out of you yet."

Red returned and Will asked him to add a shotgun and some shells to the list of supplies. Red said something to Harry in Dutch, the men laughed and Will wondered if it was at his expense.

CHAPTER EIGHTEEN

The noon sun blazed in the cloudless sky as Harry's truck rumbled up the drive. The trip to the lumberyard had consumed most of Saturday morning. Will climbed from the truck and stretched his stiff muscles. The heat felt luxurious, and he stifled a yawn as he approached the tailgate, his enthusiasm for the project rapidly waning. As they removed the lumber and stacked it on the grass, Ellie wandered into the front yard and sat on a large rock to watch.

Harry's tool collection intimidated Will the electric drill and air powered nail gun were serious looking, but the circular saw with its smiling teeth unnerved him the most. Will had never used this type of equipment, and found the thought sobering that one slip could be a life-altering event.

He had spent many hours watching his grandfather work in his woodshop in the basement of his old house in Germantown; although Will had never learned to use the tools himself. His grandfather, Paps as he had called him, had passed away, before Will was old enough to handle the equipment. Now glancing over Harry's collection, it stirred memories of that cool basement on hot summer afternoons; that same dark, damp basement where Will had gone the evening of Pap's wake to retrieve a jar of tomato sauce for his Mom.

Doesn't Harry remind me of Paps?

Will had felt something that evening; he was almost sure — a hand on his shoulder.

Ridiculous, focus on the work or you could lose a finger.

Sure or not, he had never gone down into that basement again in all the years that he visited his Nana.

Satisfied that his tools were in working order, his power cords plugged in, and his saw horses properly positioned, Harry retrieved two crowbars from his large wooden toolbox. Handing one to Will, he walked over to the wall. The crowbar felt cool and heavy in Will's hands. Following Harry's lead he joined him at the wall and they began to pry off the rotted boards at the bottom. It was hard, dirty work, and Will felt blisters forming on his palms before they completed the first hour.

They removed the boards and revealed the wooden skeleton underneath. The lattice strips that were nailed one after another on the frame and then coated with horsehair plaster to form the interior wall fascinated Will.

He was marveling at the craftsmanship when the circular saw's whirling growl jarred him and caused his stomach to flip flop. An image of Ellie, flashed through his mind. Both men spun around simultaneously. Will almost collapsed, his legs turned to rubber when he saw blood spurting out of Ellie's severed wrist. Her eyes wide, she stood over her dismembered hand that twitched on the ground next to the circular saw at her feet.

Oh Lord, no.

Will stumbled backward leaning against the house for support. He couldn't speak all the air had leaked out of his lungs. "Oh…"

He gasped at the gruesome sight, blinked and then it was gone. Ellie stood there, unharmed, staring wide-eyed at the circular beast on the ground.

Will regained some composure. "Get away from that."

She looked up at him surprised by his harsh tone. "I didn't touch it."

Will started toward her. "That's very dangerous, it's not a toy."

Ellie backed away wide eyed. "It wasn't me daddy, it was…"

Will held up his hand for her to stop. "Don't even…"

Even as relief washed through him, angered followed at the thought of what could've happened. He was in no mood for make-believe characters. "Go in to your mother. It's too dangerous out here."

Ellie fled to the house without another word, her shoulders set and her back stiff in defiance. Will hated the way he had lost his temper with her, if only he wasn't so tired. He also felt embarrassed.

He and Harry went silently back to work. It felt like hours before Will's hands stopped trembling.

As the sun climbed higher in the sky they continued to labor. They worked at a steady pace, as the day wore on. Harry taught Will how to fit the new planks into place. By the time Sara called them for dinner, they were finishing the first coat of primer.

CHAPTER **NINETEEN**

After gorging on Sara's delicious meal of roast beef, mashed potatoes, corn, and gravy, the two men adjourned to the front porch. Will handed Harry a cold bottle of Yuengling Black & Tan, and the men settled into wicker rocking chairs.

Will's muscles ached and the blisters on his palms burned. He took a long sip from his ice tea, the cubes in the glass clinking, and he noticed Harry's questioning glance.

"I don't touch the stuff anymore," Will said smiling weakly.

"Oh, I didn't mean to offend you."

Will sighed and gazed out into the shadows in the front lawn. "Don't worry, you didn't."

He could sense Harry growing uncomfortable, and tried to explain to put the other man at ease. "I just don't handle it well."

That was an understatement, because alcohol and Will were like a can of gasoline and a match. He thought about the numerous blackouts and that last time at the Keg House. Will had avoided alcohol ever since, not sure what he would see if he drank again, but lately it didn't seem to matter; the boy on the bike, the vision of Ellie earlier in the day, the strange Indian dreams. Maybe alcohol wasn't the problem?

Maybe I'm just losing my mind.

Will watched small birds land on the edge of the old cement birdbath and changed the subject. "The last owners liked birds?"

"Yep, Martin sure did."

"You miss him." It was a statement, not a question.

Harry nodded, his gaze never left the birdbath. "Yeah, I do." He paused and shook his head slowly, his gaze fixed on some distant point beyond the birdbath. "This old place was built in the eighteen hundreds and required a lot of maintenance even back in '49. Martin was not very handy with a hammer or a saw, but he tried."

Will grinned, and Harry took a swallow of beer.

"Don't tell me you helped him fix up the place."

"Yup. One day, not long after Martin and June moved here, I was out plowing the field over there next to the line fence. Martin was struggling to reattach a shutter and almost fell off his stepladder. I helped him put it back and the rest as they say is history. That's how I became the unofficial caretaker of this place."

Harry grew quiet again, and Will wondered what memory he was reliving. "They were good people, and they had a good life, except for children. They both wanted them, but it never happened. I know it ate at Martin. You know when you love someone, you want to give them the world."

Will understood. That was the reason he was living in this damn house.

"Overall I think things were good for them until June became ill cancer. It took her quick."

Will didn't like thinking about losing Sara, even if it was only in response to another couple's story. Harry also seemed somber.

Harry shrugged and took another swallow of his beer. "Would you listen to me, I'm going on like an old fool."

"That's okay. Your friends sound like nice people."

Raising his bottle in mock salute, Harry nodded. "That they were. That they were."

Harry picked at the paper label on his bottle and grinned when he realized Will was watching. "I think it's good Ellie is living here. It livens up the place. June's niece and nephew used to come up from Philly in the summers when they were kids until…" Harry paused like he'd caught himself, "well anyway it always livened up the place."

Ellie loved the house almost as much as Sara did. Although Will wasn't sure that her presence did much for the house's dismal atmosphere.

The conversation drifted to world events: Harry was an avid news junkie, and Will sat silently listening to Harry's take on the state of affairs. Exhaustion started to take its toll, and Will drifted into longer stretches of silence, but he was disappointed when Harry said he had better be getting home. "I want to thank you for all your help today. I wouldn't have known where to begin."

This was also an understatement; Will knew less than zero about carpentry.

"It was my pleasure," Harry said as he rose from his chair. He glanced longingly around the porch, his hand lightly caressing the porch railing. "There are still a lot of repairs. I'm familiar with them and I would be happy to help you."

Will saw the need in Harry's eyes. Unlike the old man, he was overwhelmed by all the repairs. "I'd like that, but with my schedule this was probably the last free day I'll have for a while."

The older man remained silent for a moment, like he was considering something. "Since you're busy, I could do some of the repairs for you."

Now it was Will's turn to hesitate. He looked at the surrounding porch and realized he was not up to the task himself. "That would be great. If everything waited for me it would never get completed, but we would have to pay you. I insist."

Harry smiled, but shook his head. "I don't need money, but if Sara is willing to cook another fine meal every so often, I'd say we could call it even."

Before Will could consider he heard himself say, "Okay, but I feel like I'm taking advantage."

Extending his hand, Harry said, "Good, then it's settled. Now it's getting late, so I'll head home, but I'll start on some of the repairs this week."

He shook Harry's hand and again was surprised by the old man's strength. "Goodnight Harry, and thanks."

Will watched the older man walk to his truck, wave, climb in and head for home. He couldn't have turned Harry down; somewhere inside he knew they were somehow connected by mutual need. An owl screeched in the trees to the west and for a moment Will thought he smelled a campfire.

He found Sara in the dark parlor on the couch watching an old black and white Jimmy Stewart movie that he didn't recognize. The grandfather clock in the hall chimed eleven. "You and Harry must have had a good time."

Will stretched trying to loosen his sore back. "He's very nice, but lonely."

"I got that too," Sara said.

"He practically begged me to let him work on the house, and he doesn't want to be paid. He just wants to have dinner with us occasionally."

Sara looked into his eyes and smiled, she was beautiful in the television's soft glow. "I guess that's fine."

Will ran his hand through his hair and yawned. "Where's Ellie?"

"Asleep."

He glanced toward the stairs in the foyer. "I didn't get to tuck her in. Since we moved here she's always so busy with her imaginary friends. She's lost in her own little world."

"She's just developing her imagination. Don't worry, she won't forget bedtime stories with dad."

Will tried to cover the hurt in his voice. "I hope not."

He surveyed the shadows and dark recesses of the parlor and shivered, the room was cold. "I'm beat. I'm going to take a shower and go to bed."

He headed for the foyer.

"I'll be up after the movie," Sara called.

Will paused in Ellie's room to check on her. She was sound asleep, her face that of an angel. He covered her with the blanket and smiled.

Mr. Whiskers passed Will in the hall and hopped on the table next to the banister and curled into a tight ball. Will wished he could relax and enjoy his sleep as easily as the animal.

The bathroom light flickered several times before it lit and cast its ethereal illumination over the small room. Will drew the curtain open on the claw foot bathtub and started the tap.

'A nice hot shower is the ticket,' he thought, as he peeled off his T-shirt.

Steam inundated the small room. Running a hand over the stubble on his chin, Will decided to shave. He rubbed a circle clear on the mirror. An old man with bulging eyes in sunken sockets, gray wisps of disheveled hair, and a black, swollen tongue protruding through cracked lips stared back.

"Get out while you can," the face in the mirror shouted.

Will flinched, lost his balance, and sat down hard on the toilet.

Too spent to rise, he bent forward, placing his head in his hands. Nervous electricity coursed through his stomach. After a few minutes of deep breathing he stood up, afraid to look into the mirror. When he did, only his reflection greeted him.

Despite the steam, the room felt frigid, and he started to shiver. He stared at his unchanging reflection as the steam condensed on the mirror obliterating it. Had he imagined the whole thing, like the image of Ellie with the saw earlier in the day?

"I'm just tired," He said to convince himself. Not that he believed his own propaganda. Something was very wrong.

He slid off his jeans and boxers and stepped into the tub and screamed when the icy stream of water hit him. Stumbling to escape, he slipped on the wet floor and went down. Sharp pain jarred his skull. He was disoriented and confused; how could cold water create steam? He slowly struggled to his feet, gingerly touching the knot on his head where he had struck the toilet seat.

Exhausted, but too grungy to give up, he slipped on his black terrycloth robe and stumbled toward the basement. The water heater must've shut off. Sara had gone to bed. His head throbbed as he walked through the dark house to the kitchen. He paused before the basement door.

There is nothing down there to fear. It's just an old basement.

Like Pap's old basement.

Until now he hadn't made the connection.

He screwed up his courage, opened the door, and flipped the light switch. Ozone floated on the air as the bulbs crackled to life casting minimal light. Will didn't consider himself a coward, but the dark hidden places in this house were a curtain worn too thin that he could see through to some shadowy realm.

He slowly started down the steps, cringing as each board groaned under his weight. He felt like the child back in Pap's basement, the desire to turn and flee to the safety above almost overwhelmed him. He held the railings to steady his trembling hands.

At the foot of the steps he paused and listened for movement. From its dirt floor to the rough-cut fieldstone foundation, this room gave the word unfinished a whole new meaning. A musky odor permeated the area. Several bare bulbs hung at intervals throughout the corridors and only made the slightest effort at banishing the darkness. Six chambers that felt like catacombs divided the basement. Will was glad that the gas furnace sat in the corner of the first chamber. He couldn't explain the irrationality, but he hated this basement.

Out of the corner of his eyes all the shadows crawled with life. Not spiders or rats. They would have been preferable to Will's imagined creatures that dwelled there, waiting to drag him into the darkness. The hair on the back of his neck tingled, and he felt someone watching over his shoulder again. He spun around and tried to catch a glimpse of the unseen specter, but found only empty air.

He had almost reached his breaking point, his body trembled, his head throbbed, and his stomach clenched.

No hot shower is worth this.

Through sheer determination Will forced his legs forward toward the old furnace in the corner. The closer he approached, the worse he felt. The temperature dropped, and he saw his breath. Only inches away from the antique behemoth, Will forced himself to reach out and touch the water tank. He jerked his hand away in surprise. The heat from the metal tank almost blistered his fingers.

So how could the water in the shower be so cold?

CHAPTER TWENTY

Saturday's labor with Harry had taxed his muscles more than his usual physical activity, and after the strangeness with the shower, Will tossed and turned and struggled to get comfortable all night. He spent Sunday in a mental fog. The day slipped past him, and much too soon the weekend drew to an end. Restless and unwilling to give up and go to bed, Will stepped into the back yard and flinched when his bare feet touched the wet grass.

He had the *Sunday Night Blues.*

He liked his job, and still he mourned the end of the weekend. Staring into the brilliant sky and studying the stars, he felt like he was standing on the edge of forever one false move and he would plummet into the dark oblivion. His insignificance overwhelmed him. Reality stretched thin.

A gentle breeze caressed the leaves of the trees, and the scent of campfires drifted on the cool air. Will studied the surrounding forest, seeking the smoke's source. The world spun away, and he steadied himself against the porch, his back pressing a column. He closed his eyes, waiting for the vertigo to pass, but when he opened them the ground rushed forward.

Time lost all meaning, and Will struggled to his hands and knees, unsure how long he had blacked out. He was kneeling in front of a longhouse. A palisade constructed of timbers ringed the perimeter of the encampment. Smoke from fires and torches choked the air.

Several women dressed in buckskins squatted near the fence. As Will watched, afraid to trust his own eyes, they arranged the body of a man into a sitting position in a hole. Then they started to cover the dead man with arched pieces of bark. When Will glanced around he saw many other small mounds of bark.

Another odor skimmed along underneath the smoke the stench of decay and feces. Will threw up, but the women paid no attention; they remained intent on their task. He tried to gain his feet, but swayed, his balance unsteady. This was all wrong he didn't belong here.

"You have to listen, brother."

Gray Wolf stumbled out of the longhouse followed by his brother Running Turtle. They continued past Will apparently unaware of his presence. They were the same tribesmen Will remembered from before, only this time Will was not a lost six year old, this time he felt like his adult self. Although he recognized the men, this was a different settlement, and Will didn't know how he knew, but he realized this was his backyard as it would have appeared in the fifteen hundreds.

"We can still make it home," Running Turtle said.

Gray Wolf turned on his brother and ripped back the skins he wore over his shoulders. "Look, The rash, just like the others. I already have it."

A red rash oozed yellow pus on Gray Wolf's hands. A thin film of sweat coated the warrior's body that glistened in the moonlight. He stared vacantly through red-rimmed eyes.

Running Turtle persisted. "Little Flower and I do not have the rash. We could take you and the others back to Small Sparrow. She'll know how to treat this sickness."

Gray Wolf shook his head. "No, this is something she has never seen. It is the land. She was right — the dead slither back across from the spirit world and make us sick. We were fools to come here, and now it is too late."

"You can't just give up." Running Turtle attempted to grab his brother's shoulders, but his sibling dodged him and swayed like a frail rag doll.

Gray Wolf sank to his knees and held his head in his hands. "We are all cursed."

"You need a medicine man." Will rose to his feet, but the others ignored him when he approached. He tried to grab Running Turtle's arm to get his attention and his hand went right through the other man's limb. It was like reaching into a tub of ice water. Will recoiled, stumbling backward and sat down hard on the ground. Apparently unaware of Will, Running Turtle didn't flinch.

A woman ran from the longhouse. "Gray Wolf"

Gray Wolf raised his head at the sound of her voice. "Little Flower, stay back. I have the rash."

She fell to her knees in front of Gray Wolf. "No."

Running Turtle seized her and dragged her away. "He has it. You can't touch him."

She struggled to escape Running Turtle's grasp. "Let me go."

A sound from outside the parameter shattered the night. It sent chills like ocean waves over Will's flesh. He had never heard such a fierce cry. It was the screech of a barn owl combined with the scraping of nails on a chalkboard and the ripping of steel, all amplified to the intensity of a train wreck. Inhuman and unearthly, it demanded submission.

Everyone in the compound froze. Something large and fast circled the camp in the forest outside the fortifications.

The two women dropped their bark and fled the fence, leaving the burial incomplete. Whatever approached sounded unearthly and evil. The women escaped into the longhouse as two men rushed out, causing a moment of confusion. Running Turtle herded Little Flower toward the entrance. "You have to go inside."

She clutched at his shoulders. "No. I will stay and fight alongside you."

He shoved her hard, and she careened backward into the darkened doorway.

Gray Wolf grabbed a stone hatchet and struggled to his feet while the other three men lit torches mounted around the perimeter fence, perhaps trying to scare the creature back into the forest or maybe to improve their vision.

Another cry pierced the night air. This time it originated on the opposite side of the village. Whatever prowled the camp circled faster, and every few moments the ear shattering, nerve-jarring explosion occurred from a different location around the encampment.

As he scanned the darkness, Will crabbed backward against the side of the longhouse. He did not want his back exposed to the night. He trembled as he huddled there, trying to see in every direction at once. This couldn't be real. It must be a hallucination or more likely a dream. He wasn't in the middle of an Indian hunting village in the fifteen hundreds; he was lying in bed next to Sara having an incredibly realistic dream. There simply was no other explanation. But he couldn't dismiss the sights, sounds, and smells that overwhelmed his senses.

"Keep her inside." Gray Wolf yelled at Running Turtle. "It is the dead. They have come over from the spirit world to take revenge because we disturbed their peace."

Will heard this, but didn't believe. He continued to scan the darkness, but could see nothing. Only the piercing screams announced the presence in the woods. It drew closer to the outer walls with each rotation.

A tall haggard man with long black braids turned on Gray Wolf.

"It's you they want. You led us here. It's your blood they cry out for." The tall warrior raised his flintlock toward Gray Wolf. The moon danced in the man's bright blue eyes revealing his hysteria. His lips curled back in a sneer.

"No, Long Fang." Running Turtle dashed toward the delirious man with the rifle, who turned and fired. The flintlock hammer's crack and the black powder's explosion reverberated off the compound walls.

Will clutched his ears, trying to ease the pounding in his skull. The noise, the heat, and the acrid smells of sweat and blood that now mingled with the decay and feces overwhelmed his senses. The lead ball's impact hurtled Running Turtle backward through the air, and he collapsed in a bloody heap by the longhouse doorway.

Even sick, Gray Wolf was still a skilled warrior, and his stone hatchet sank into the tall warrior's chest before he could reload. The technology the white men had brought from Europe and traded for furs was obviously not that much superior to the weapons of these savage warriors.

Will watched as everything slowed down into a brutal ballet. The other warrior with the necklace of animal's teeth around his neck raised his bow and fired. Obviously Gray Wolf had chosen the best hunters for this expedition, and the arrow found its mark in Gray Wolf's left side. The arrow penetrated to the feathered end, the stone tip protruding from his back.

Will pushed away from the longhouse and stumbled to Gray Wolf's side, but it was too late, he could hear the gurgling in the man's chest. Little Flower burst from the shelter's doorway and uttered a cry that rivaled the banshee outside the stockade. The knife flashed in her hand as she lunged for the warrior with the bow.

Her ferocity amazed Will. She tackled the larger man and they rolled against the outer wall dislodging a torch. Flames sprang across the dry grass and leaped up the side of the longhouse. The blaze greedily lapped up all the dry timbers and danced across the encampment.

On any given day, the larger man should have outmatched Little Flower. Perhaps the fever had stolen his strength, because she struck home repeatedly with the blade. The blood soaked archer grabbed a rock and smashed the side of her skull. When he pulled it away, blood matted her hair. He struck a second time and bone gave way to unyielding stone with a dull crunch. The two were locked into a grotesque death pose   intertwined like hellish lovers.

The flames licked the side of the building, and Will scrambled trying to find something to smother the fire, realizing the futility as he heard the laughter from outside the stockade walls. In the confusion Will stumbled, falling once more as he lost his way in the suffocating smoke.

CHAPTER **TWENTY-ONE**

Monday started bad and grew worse as the day progressed. Sara shook Will awake when he slept through his morning alarm.

"Get up, you're late."

She tugged and released the shade, inundating the room with sunlight. Apparently wide awake and in grand spirits, she did not appear to suffer from the residual effects of another night of horrible sleep.

Will despised the lilt of humor in her voice. He shielded his eyes, which itched and burned, with his pillow. Every muscle screamed.

"Arrgh."

Sara snatched the pillow. "I've done my part. Don't come crying to me if you're late."

He squinted at her, trying to focus. "Holy shit. Give me a break."

Sara crawled on top of him, straddling his waist. "Rough night? Maybe you need some encouragement to wake up."

She tickled his ribs in a surprise attack that sent a jolt of pain through his sore muscles.

"Hey."

She giggled, he did not.

His mind wandered in fog and his head thumped. "Stop it."

Sara froze. He could see the hurt in her eyes. She slid off him and backed away.

"Sorry." She muttered and turned toward the door.

"Wait." Ashamed of his outburst, Will threw back the covers to pursue her.

She paused to stare at his feet. "What happened?"

Will followed her gaze to the foot of the bed. The sheets were soiled with black earth, and his bare feet were stained with soot. Will remembered the fire, the massacre, the dream or vision and swallowed the acid that rose in his throat. For a moment the vertigo returned, and he steadied himself on the edge of the bed. "I don't know."

"It looks like you were stomping around in a campfire. Honestly Will, how did you make such a mess?"

He looked into her eyes and wanted to explain, but how could he when he didn't understand himself? He hadn't left the room he was almost sure, yet the evidence at the foot of the bed suggested otherwise. "I think I might sleep walk."

Will stood and gave Sara room as she started stripping the bed. She frowned and shook her head. "You've never done that before."

"Maybe I'm just trying to adjust to a new place."

She smiled. "I guess I'll have to start strapping you in at night."

Will nodded as he fought for control. Something was very wrong and growing worse, something connected to this place.

Although Sara made light of the situation, it disturbed him. The rest of day became the kind of day that caused him to wonder why he had ever gone into the tech field in the first place. No monumental problems, just the usual setbacks, but his lack of focus intensified even the minor situations. He couldn't ban the images of the previous night's dream from his mind. The sights, sounds, and smells clung to him through the day. The experience seemed too intense to be a dream, and there was the charred dirt on the sheets in his bed that morning that he couldn't explain.

He must have walked in his sleep while he was experiencing a very lucid dream — that seemed logical.

By the end of the day he surrendered and returned home dispirited and exhausted.

Will groaned when he saw Harry's truck in his driveway. He wanted a nice stiff drink and a quiet evening. He knew he would do without the drink, he always did, but apparently he could kiss the quiet goodbye as well. He liked Harry, but he was too exhausted for company.

Ellie met him at the door. Her emerald eyes alive with excitement, she threw her arms around him. "Daddy, Daddy, Mr. Weaver brought a tire. He says I can use it as a swing."

Will hugged her.

"He says we can hang it on the big tree in the back yard."

Will grinned and surrendered because he didn't want to crush her enthusiasm. He missed her smile; he missed a lot lately and knew it would only grow worse according to his work schedule over the next few weeks. Ellie grabbed his hand and led him to the kitchen like he was a returning conquering hero.

CHAPTER TWENTY-TWO

Harry pulled the wooden ladder from his truck bed and motioned to Will to grab the old tire. He was stuffed and realized how much he missed eating meals prepared by someone who could actually cook. He had survived on his own throw-together meals since Martha passed, and Sara's fare was a welcome change, although he would not fit through the door if he ate Sara's cooking all the time.

He positioned the ladder under a tall maple in the back yard, and turned to Will. "This should do fine."

Will dropped the tire and studied the thick branch just above them. "Do you think it's strong enough?"

Harry smiled, climbed the ladder and leaned hard putting all his weight on the limb. "Hell, this could hold you and me."

Will nodded and ran a hand through his hair. The young man looked dead on his feet. Harry had never worked for a corporation:

he spent all his days on the farm, but it appeared that Will's career was taking a tremendous toll on him.

"We're going to need a rope," Harry said as he climbed off the stepladder.

Will shrugged and glanced at the shed. "I think I remember seeing some in the shed the other day."

Will sighed and started for the old structure. Harry could tell the young man wasn't into this project, and he probably should've waited till Will was at work to hang the swing.

Too late now.

Harry followed Will toward the old tool shed.

Suddenly Will turned and paused. "Do you smell a campfire?"

Harry froze in his tracks. He thought about it for a moment, sniffed the air and felt silly like an old bloodhound. The air was arid, but sweet. "Nah, it's been kinda dry with the drought and all. A fire could be dangerous."

Will stared at Harry for a moment like he had just been hit in the stomach — his eyes wide, his mouth open slightly. "I forgot about the drought."

Harry kicked at the dry grass. "Yeah, worst in years. There's a ban on open fires right now. If a small fire got out of hand it could burn the whole mountain."

"I guess you're right. I must have imagined it."

Will turned and entered the shed, slump shouldered. He looked defeated. When Harry entered, he paused for a moment to let his eyes adjust to the dim lighting. This was his first time in the shed since the estate was sold. He remembered the assortment of garden tools, lawnmowers, and other clutter Martin and June had piled from floor to ceiling. Only a small stack of items remained in one corner. It struck him how the objects amassed over a lifetime were unceremoniously scattered to the wind after a person abandoned this mortal coil.

Harry shivered when he recognized the rope Will pulled out of a box filled with old life jackets.

"Think this'll do?"

Will held out the rope for Harry to inspect. Harry realized it wasn't the same piece, only another section of the towrope from the old motorboat that the Martin and June had owned in happier times, but it still disturbed him. After a moment he nodded, it would do the trick.

Besides, ropes don't kill people, people kill people.

They returned to the tree in silence, Harry lost in nightmarish memories, and Will appeared almost asleep on his feet. They quickly suspended the tire at the appropriate height for Ellie and retreated to the back porch to watch her try out the swing.

Sara brought them tall glasses of ice tea. Harry noted it was a pattern that the women who tended to fall in love with this house were all elegant. Fine featured and stylish. Harry felt almost embarrassed when he looked into Sara's sparkling emerald eyes; she had that same presence that June had possessed.

There was something else about those eyes, something memorable. Harry had noticed it when he first met Sara on Saturday and he felt it again. He wasn't sure why she seemed so familiar; he glanced down at the drink, not wanting to hold her gaze too long.

He sipped the drink. The cool liquid offered a reprieve from the day's heat, even at dusk, sweat coated Harry's skin. "It's good to see a child playing in this yard."

Will looked like he was going to slide off the chair into a puddle on the porch. Harry took a long swallow of tea. He figured he'd better not outwear his welcome. "We can go out to the shooting range one night after you get home from work and I can give you a few pointers on that shotgun of yours. If you want to."

Exhaling slowly Will studied his glass. "Sure, if I have the time."

"Oh, no rush. When you're ready the offer stands."

Will smiled, leaned forward and sat his glass on the porch next to the railing. "Not so high, Ellie."

The sun disappeared over the horizon in a brilliant display of oranges and purples, and as the last fleeting beams vanished, a fruit bat fluttered through the twilight.

When Will spoke again, there was a slight hesitation. "Do you think Native Americans ever lived on this property?"

Harry was struck with déjà vu, although it really wasn't because he remembered when Martin asked the exact question one night a few years ago. He stared at Will's vacant eyes and was chilled by the fear that lingered there. This young man who reminded him of Martin with a wife who reminded him of June was starting to resemble Martin more and more. Right down to the same questions.

Harry answered exactly the same. "Might have, I've found a few arrowheads in my fields over the years. Why do you ask?"

"Just curious," Will replied, but Harry was sure there was more to the question. He thought it had something to do with the vacant stare in both men's eyes. Perhaps there was a bigger secret here than the one Harry kept.

CHAPTER TWENTY-THREE

Tuesday afternoon Sara watched Ellie in the back yard and listened to Gretchen on the phone. Ellie flew through the air with reckless abandon, swinging the tire to the utmost zenith of its arc. Sara tapped her fingers on the Formica and tried to concentrate on Gretchen's voice.

"I'm sorry I haven't visited, but my show at Renaldy's has been overwhelming. I've already sold several of my paintings."

Sara winced and turned from the window. "I should be there. I've never missed one of your openings. I feel terrible."

"Chill. It's okay, you're still settling into the new place, but I'll expect the royal treatment when I visit your new estate."

Sara chuckled and stared out the window. "Nothing but the best for you."

"Hah. So fill me in. How's the mansion?"

Tap, tap, tap, Sara's fingers machine-gunned against the counter. She was barely aware of the motion. She held her breath as she watched Ellie. She exhaled and smiled.

"It's wonderful, but it's not a mansion, just a nice country house." Sara glanced around the kitchen, visualizing future renovations.

With some work it would be a spectacular kitchen.

"Is it old and spooky?"

Gretchen's question jarred Sara out of her daydream. "You're starting to sound like Will."

Gretchen laughed, but Sara thought it sounded forced. She could always read her friend's voice. "Well it is a Gothic Victorian, right? It probably looks like that house in the Addams Family, no — I know, the one in the Munsters."

Sara picked up the dishcloth and wiped the counter, trying to use up some of her nervous energy. "Yes, but it's not like that… I can't explain… it's like coming home. I feel like I belong here."

Gretchen's voice almost sounded sincere as she continued. "It sounds wonderful. I can't wait to see the place."

Sara folded the cloth and placed it in the sink. "When will you come?"

Gretchen paused for a moment, it sounded like she was shuffling papers. There was a soft curse, and an electronic beep. Sara smiled and tried not to laugh. Gretchen hated the computer that Will had talked her into getting to keep track of her business records.

"I'll never get the hang of this thing… My show ends tomorrow, so how's this weekend?"

Sara was thrilled; she couldn't wait to see her friend. "Great. I'll stock up on Häagan Dazs."

Laughter floated through the receiver. "Then count me in for sure. I guess you're getting excited about your own show?"

Sara thought about her latest collection 'Exiled From the Garden, the figures of Adam and Eve.' They were already in the back room of Versalis gallery. This was her best work to date, and it would be her largest show.

"Saturday, August 3rd, right?"

Sara realized she was tapping again. "Yeah."

"I'll mark it on my calendar."

Sara felt another twinge of guilt. "Thanks, but don't make a big deal out of it."

"Getting a show at Versalis is a big deal. It's the hottest gallery in center city, you lucky dog."

Sara grinned. It felt wonderful to have her work validated. "Will thinks it's all hype."

Sara missed the laughter she heard on the other end of the line. Had they only lived here a little over a week? It felt like years since she had gossiped with Gretchen. Ellie was picking up speed in the tire.

"Then I want some of that hype for my work. You always get the breaks in the hottest galleries first. Not that it's a contest, but it's not hype honey, it's talent."

Sara was embarrassed, wanting to change the subject, she said, "I'm expecting the delivery of a large block of translucent alabaster."

Gretchen's whistle almost deafened Sara. "Big Bucks. I guess we know who is rolling in the dough."

Sara started toward the door to warn Ellie to slow down. "Just taking a big gamble."

"I'd ask what your latest idea is, but I know you'll never tell, so on a safer note, how does Will like his job?"

Sara paused, she didn't know. "You know Will. He spends every waking hour there, but says nothing about it when he comes home. I'm sure he loves it."

A short pause on the other end of the line, then, "Why does that not sound convincing?"

Sara caught herself tapping her fingers on the counter again. It felt warm in the kitchen, and Ellie was swinging much too high.

Gretchen didn't wait for an answer. "Is everything okay with Will?"

"I don't know… I think so."

"I've been worried, I keep getting flashes of him in trouble." Sara heard the concern in Gretchen's voice, but smiled. Gretchen was famous for her faulty premonitions. This did not dissuade Gretchen from the notion that she was psychic.

Careful not to hurt her friend's feelings, Sara stifled a laugh. "Your premonitions are never right. In tenth grade you said you were going to marry Bobbie Turley."

"Sara, this is different, besides, I didn't say *when* I was going to marry him."

Opening the door, Sara called, "Ellie, not so high."

Gretchen persisted. "I saw him, and he was hurt."

Ellie dragged her feet and slowed down, and Sara closed the door. Distracted Sara asked, "Bobby?"

"No, Will, I'm serious about this."

Gretchen had too much time on her hands, but then again, she probably just missed them. She had spent most of her free time at Will and Sara's when they lived in Horsham. Now alone, she was just letting her imagination run wild.

Sara understood how an overactive imagination could conjure all sorts of drama. She was experiencing a little of that herself. She never could keep a secret from Gretchen and the need to unload overwhelmed her. "I'm a little worried about him too," she confessed. "It has nothing to do with premonitions. I think he's started drinking."

Gretchen sounded confused. "Alcohol?"

"Yeah."

Gretchen sighed, and Sara could picture her rolling her eyes. "I've never seen him with a drink in all the years you've been together. I always thought it was some sort of religious thing."

Sara paced back in forth in front of the sink, glancing outside to keep an eye on Ellie who was still swinging too wildly for her comfort. "No, even before he starting attending church with me, he didn't drink. He said he didn't like the stuff. A few days ago, I found five empty beer bottles lined up on the kitchen counter."

"You guys don't keep beer in the house. Where did they come from?"

Sara explained how Harry had helped with the repairs, and Will purchased the beer because he knew the older man liked it.

"Maybe the old guy drank them."

Sara wished that was a possibility, but she knew better. "No, he only drank one before he left. There were still five full bottles when I went up to bed. Will was all alone down here."

Gretchen was quiet for a moment then said, "Did you ask him about them?"

"No, I felt silly. What would I say? Hey did you drink five beers the other night? It sounds ridiculous. I mean even if he did, it's not like he broke any laws."

Tap, tap, tap, Sara caught herself again.

"Maybe he just poured them down the drain," Gretchen said, obviously trying to see the glass half full.

Sara bit her lower lip. "I don't think so, I'm not sure why, but it seemed like he left the bottles there to taunt me."

"That doesn't sound like Will. I've had a few flashes that he was in trouble, but I don't think the guy would deliberately tease you. He adores you."

Sara fought back tears. "He's acting strange since we moved. He's tense, paranoid, and even walked in his sleep once. I think he's trying to hide something."

Sara felt foolish; everything in their lives was perfect. Their careers were great — they were all healthy, why was she looking for problems? Gretchen must have thought the same thing. "It's probably just the transition, he needs to assimilate into his new environment."

Sara laughed, sniffed, and rubbed away the tears with her palms. "He's not Borg. I worry that the stress of his new job might be too much."

Gretchen chuckled "I know, honey. I'll never understand why, but he loves the Techie crap. He thrives on it — you said it yourself."

Sara grabbed a paper towel off the roll and blew her nose. "I know, but he's different. What if he's an alcoholic and never told me?"

"Sara, get a grip. I think you would have noticed in all the years you've known him, if he had a problem with alcohol. You shouldn't be so rough on him. He's a good guy. If I met a guy half as good, I'd marry him in a minute."

Sara leaned against the counter. Ellie was gaining height in the back yard again. "There's always Rupert."

"Yeah, I'm sure Vance would love that," Gretchen shot back. They laughed at the thought.

Vance and Rupert were life partners who owned 'Picture This', a small gallery in New Hope that prominently displayed Sara and Gretchen's work. Rupert was the first gallery owner to give Sara a chance, and over the years both women's work became a fixture at the trendy shop.

"I love Rupert, but he's no Will," Gretchen said.

Sara sighed. She felt better. Talking to Gretchen always lifted her spirits. They had been friends since they were five. Sara thought of her as a sister. After the accident when Sara moved in with her aunt and uncle in Northeast Philadelphia, it was Gretchen, the little girl next door, who made her laugh and forget her pain. Over the years, Gretchen was always there with some crazy scheme that would lift Sara's spirits. "You're right. You're right about the whole thing. Even if Will did drink the whole six-pack, it's not the end of the world, right? I can't wait for you to come. I miss you."

Sara thought she heard Gretchen's voice crack. "I miss you too. Don't worry, when I get there I will cleanse Will's aura, we'll have him right as rain in no time."

Sara remembered how Will always teased Gretchen about her mother earth philosophy. "He'd love that."

Ellie's wild swinging distracted Sara. The two friends exchanged farewells. Gretchen promised to arrive early on Friday.

Sara opened the door. "Ellie be careful or I'll make you spend the afternoon in your room."

"Awe, mom, I'm not going that fast."

Sara realized she was starting to sound like Will. It was only a swing, a few feet off the ground. Why was she acting so over protective?

"Have fun, but be careful. I'll be in the studio if you need me."

The day melted away when Sara was in her studio. She lost all sense of time as she journeyed through her imagination.

The afternoon heat radiated through the studio's glass ceiling. A warm cross breeze from a couple of open windows washed over Sara as she studied the large, orange stone that sat in front of her like an ancient obelisk. Four feet tall and three feet wide by three feet deep — it was magnificent. Sara knew this would be her greatest piece.

Three strong men had to work together to move it from the delivery truck to her studio. Working with dollies and a hand truck, the men maneuvered it through the large outside double doors. Watching them revived memories of moving day, and Sara expected the large stone to topple over and crush one of the worker's legs. In her mind she heard the crunch of bones as the stone landed. The screams of this man would not end as abruptly as Tony's had.

She watched in horrid fascination, almost disappointed when the stone was in place without incident. Not typically a morbid individual, Sara had no idea where this thought had originated. It made her skin crawl.

She slowly walked around the stone. Usually, she would have to live with a rock for a while before she saw the form trapped inside. This was a time of discovery that she didn't like to rush, sometimes it required weeks or even months for the hidden shape to reveal itself. She liked to relax and enjoy the journey. This time seemed different, the shapes were almost screaming for her to release them as she stared trancelike, her fingers twitching to begin. Sara had no idea how long she stood there until Ellie's screams jarred her out of her stupor.

CHAPTER TWENTY-FOUR

Will sprinted up the stairs and into Ellie's room. The fear subsided when he saw her, but his stomach sank after he spotted the cast on her left arm. She looked so small.

Sara repositioned pillows, helping Ellie get comfortable among all the stuffed animals on her bed. Will rushed over and gently wrapped his arms around his daughter. "Are you okay, Sweetie?"

Ellie tried to smile. "Yes, Daddy."

Sara brushed past Will and moved a couple of stuffed bears to a chair by the bed. "She was so brave at the hospital."

Ellie nodded and her smile almost broke his heart.

"The doctor said it's a hairline fracture."

"What else did he say?"

"If you wanted a full report you should've showed up at the hospital."

Will lowered his eyes to his daughter's cast.

Sara busied herself arranging Ellie's dolls and toys that lay scattered across the floor. She avoided eye contact as Will hovered over Ellie's bed and examined her cast.

He was relieved when Sara went downstairs to fix dinner.

Ellie appeared exhausted, but she wanted to tell him all about her emergency-room visit. She said the doctors and nurses were very nice.

Her resilience was amazing. "I'm so sorry you fell."

Ellie's face contorted as if she were concentrating on something important. The grownup look seemed out of place. "I didn't fall, she cut the rope."

Will was confused. "She?"

Ellie glanced at the corner. Will followed her gaze and had the uneasy sensation of being watched. The corner remained empty, but he shivered in the frigid air. When he turned back to her, he saw the fear in Ellie's eyes. She stared wide-eyed at him as if she was afraid to let her stare wander back to the corner. "Nothing, Daddy."

"What do you mean? She cut the rope?" Will strained to maintain an even voice.

"I can't tell. It's a secret. She made me promise."

Will wanted to push. He wanted to know what had happened, but Ellie looked like she was going to burst into tears. He held his tongue, distracted by noise in the hall. Sara entered the room carrying a tray with a bowl of chicken soup, a sandwich, some animal crackers, and a glass of milk. Was Ellie afraid to speak in front of Sara?

She placed the tray on the nightstand. "Here you are."

Will glowered. He could feel the heat radiating off his cheeks. He wanted to lash out at Sara, but held his temper. He didn't want to further upset Ellie. He couldn't understand how Sara could have done such a thing. The woman he loved wasn't capable of such betrayal and deceit. Or was she?

He hugged Ellie and quickly fled the room before he lost his temper. He needed answers. He had to see for himself. He took the stairs two at a time, racing to the backyard.

When he returned to the kitchen he tossed the rope on the table. "She didn't fall. The rope was cut."

Sara turned from the stove where she prepared two bowls of soup, and stared at the length of cord on the table. "What do you mean?"

"I mean — it didn't break. Someone cut it."

Sara cocked an eyebrow and shook her head.

"Someone deliberately cut this. Someone tried to hurt our daughter. You aren't even concerned?"

Sara dropped the ladle into the pot and turned on him like a mother lion. "How can you say that?"

Either Sara was psychotic or ready for an Oscar because she truly appeared confused. This only increased Will's rage. "She said someone cut the rope, then told her to keep it a secret."

"She was alone in the back yard."

Sara's sarcasm soaked laughter scared Will. He might have pushed her over the edge.

"That's ridiculous. You think someone climbed the tree and cut the rope while she was swinging. You think I did it?"

Will looked down at his hands. "No…"

"You think I'm capable of hurting her? She's my daughter for God's sake."

Will saw the shock and hurt and immediately regretted his words. What was going on? Nothing made sense. He sighed. It sounded foolish when she said it out loud. Of course he didn't think she would do anything to hurt Ellie.

Sara sank into a chair and studied the rope. "Ellie actually said I did this?"

"Well…" Will thought for a moment. All the rage drained away with his uncertainty. It left a cold empty spot in his chest. Ellie hadn't said that Sara cut the rope. "Ellie said, 'She cut the rope,' Who was she talking about?"

Sara tossed the rope across the table at Will. "Maybe one of her imaginary friends."

He grabbed it. "Maybe, but it's not frayed, and it wasn't cut with an imaginary knife. Somebody sliced through this."

"Listen to yourself. Who would want to hurt Ellie? I reached the back yard right after she screamed, and I found her alone. There was no one there."

Will ran a hand through his hair. "I can't explain it, but something's going on here. Don't you feel it?"

Sara crossed her arms. "I don't feel anything. What I felt today was alone. I tried to call you on your cell phone, and your office phone. I couldn't reach you. Where were you? Lately you spend all your time at the office. You're up and out in the morning and don't come home until late at night. I needed you and you weren't here."

Will shrugged; he couldn't face her, because he didn't want to fight this battle right now. "I turned off my cell, I was in a meeting. I'm sorry, you know my schedule is going to be crazy for a while."

Sara rose from her chair and dumped a bowl of soup back into the pot. "The only thing wrong with this place is that you're never here."

His anger flared again like hot coals fanned by a breeze. "Ellie is upstairs with a busted arm, and this rope was cut."

Sara shook her head, moisture gathered in the corners of her eyes, and her cheeks grew crimson. "I'm sorry you're stressed, but you're talking crazy. Are you listening to yourself? I think you're just looking for someone else to blame because you know you're never here for us anymore."

Will turned and stormed out the back door, he needed some air.

CHAPTER TWENTY-FIVE

What made Will a great programmer was his ability to compartmentalize problems. Reduce large, almost insurmountable challenges into smaller, more defined tasks and then deal with them in an orderly, precise fashion. He also applied this technique to his life, some days more effectively than others.

The next morning when he woke, he went to work and tried to concentrate on his responsibilities. By lunchtime he had almost convinced himself that nothing out of the ordinary had happened. Things felt normal when Kerrie, Frank, and he returned from one of their typical Wednesday lunches at the Golden Dragon. As they entered the lobby, Will held the door for the other two, stifled a yawn and listened to Frank whine. "She sounded great when I talked to her online, then I show up for the date, and woof."

Kerrie scowled at Frank. "That's a little harsh, and what do you mean, 'talked to her online'?"

"It's a dating service I joined. Haven't you been listening? It cost me a grand. I chat with babes on the web and set up dates."

"You don't see any pictures first?" Will asked as he followed them into the lobby.

"No, but I will from now on."

Will stifled a smile. What would prospective dates think if they saw a picture of Frank?

"So you liked her when you talked to her, but were turned off by her body?" Kerrie said.

"What can I say? There's got to be a spark. Am I right?" Frank turned to Will for confirmation.

"There's got to be a spark." Will agreed.

Kerrie rolled her eyes, then shot Will a knowing glance. Frank continued his tale about the disastrous date, and Will politely tried to listen. He also tried to divert his eyes from Kerrie's form-fitting skirt as he followed her across the lobby.

Betty, the receptionist, a sophisticated woman in her mid-fifties, glanced up from behind the counter. She was always helpful and pleasant.

"Kerrie, I have some paperwork for you-all from human resources." Will loved her southern accent.

Kerrie shrugged and approached the counter. "Sure, what is it?"

Betty retrieved a file from the corner of her desk and handed it to

Kerrie, who flipped through it and groaned. "Another glitch with my SSN. I've had nothing but trouble since I changed my address. Will, I have to take care of this, but I'll stop by your office with the mid week status reports when I'm finished." She touched his arm, sending a shiver through his body. He prayed Betty and Frank hadn't noticed a change in his expression.

He nodded in what he hoped was a nonchalant gesture and quickly followed Frank into the office area. He felt confused, and worse, he felt exposed. Perhaps he compartmentalized his life too much.

Will reached his office, collapsed into his desk chair and stared out the window. In the moment of idleness, thoughts of Ellie crashed through his defensive mental barriers. How could he sit here and do his job when his daughter was at home with a broken arm? Was her injury tied to his dreams and strange blackouts? Was this like the time in college, and if so were worse things still to come?

Sweat formed on his brow, and he coughed attempting to loosen the tightness in his chest. He gulped air and rubbed his forehead. The moment quickly passed when his phone buzzed. Will swallowed and answered the call from Rob in Marketing home life would have to wait till the end of the day.

Later, totally absorbed scanning the completed code for a Java object, he almost didn't notice Kerrie enter his office. Her rap on the half-open door startled him and he jumped.

"I'm sorry, I didn't mean to surprise you."

The slight curve of her lips betrayed amusement.

He felt foolish for overreacting. "No problem. I guess I lose track of the world when I'm dissecting code. I'm reviewing some of Jim's work."

"Oh, can I take a look at that?"

Kerrie rounded the desk and studied the code on the monitor. He was immediately aware of her hand on his shoulder and the press of her right breast against his back as she leaned forward to get a better view. "Jim does nice work."

Will agreed, only now she distracted him from the cryptic symbols on the screen. In his mind he stood up, taking her in his arms. Their lips locked and they tumbled backward into his chair. Her words jarred him out of this fantasy.

"My monitor burned out again. It's the third one that's gone bad. I need to finish some coding, and we don't have a spare system."

"Use my desktop," Will suggested, "I can work on my laptop."

Kerrie continued to lean in close, and he drank in her sweet scent, lilac and a touch of cinnamon. "That'd be great. You sure you don't mind?" she asked.

Will pulled another chair over to his desk. "Not at all, I'll work here."

He opened his laptop, and they settled in, only the click of the keys echoed in the silence. Will fumbled through his report and tried to ignore her presence.

Impossible.

Acutely aware of her every movement only inches away, after half an hour, he needed a break and rose to stretch.

Kerrie also paused and rummaged in her handbag.

Why do women carry all that crap?

Kerrie extended her hand, offering gum. "Would you like a piece?"

"Sure," Will responded absentmindedly.

The mischievous smile vanished as she followed his gaze into her handbag. The levity of her suggestive joke rang flat as he stared at the handgun. She grabbed the purse and zipped it shut.

"You can't bring that on company property."

Kerrie grabbed his hand. "Please don't make a big deal out of this."

"You could get fired, maybe even arrested."

She dropped the purse on the floor and rose. "Come on Will. Don't you ever break the rules?"

The undercurrent in the question threatened to pull him in and drown him. "I don't know…"

"I need this for protection."

The necessity in her eyes touched him.

I'm in so much trouble with her.

He could feel his resolve crumbling. "What do you need protection from?"

"I work a lot of late nights, and sometimes I show up before the sun rises. I don't know who is lurking outside the building."

"You didn't carry that thing in Philadelphia."

Kerrie crossed her arms. Holding herself, she appeared fragile. "I didn't start till after my contract with Automated Technologies expired."

Her eyes glazed over as she spoke, and her voice quivered. "I was out on the town with some friends. We'd gone clubbing on South Street. It was late, and I was tired. My judgment was more than a little impaired. My friends wanted to hit another club, but I decided to call it a night. I left on my own, a very bad idea. I almost reached my car when the guy jumped me... He had a knife... I never saw him coming. I tried to fight, but he was too big. He forced me to the ground, I was no match for him..." Kerrie paused, staring into space, reliving the nightmare.

Will was speechless.

"Some other people came along and scared the guy away," Kerrie continued in a whisper, "If those strangers hadn't stumbled on the scene, things might have turned out worse."

She paused and her body trembled slightly. Before he could react she was in his arms, quietly sobbing. "I need it, Will. I can never let anything like that happen again."

He tried to comfort her. To tell her it would be okay, but his words sounded hollow. He struggled to express something that didn't ring false or sound cliché. The knock on the door interrupted him as C.L. stepped into the office. "Sorry, didn't mean to interrupt."

The usually smooth businessman paused and his eyes grew wide, but he quickly recovered. "Will, when you get a chance, we need to discuss some last minute changes marketing has requested."

C.L. fled the office, and Will sighed.

"I hope I haven't created trouble," Kerrie said.

He slowly released her and pulled away. "Don't worry. I won't say anything, but please be careful with that thing."

She smiled through wet eyes and gave him a tight squeeze.

"Thanks, you're a good friend."

They slowly broke their embrace, and he stared out the window, not able to look her in the eyes. He didn't feel like a friend. "I'd better go see what C.L. wanted."

Kerrie nodded and sat down at the computer as Will escaped from his office. He felt a thousand years old, and a dull sensation swept over his forehead as he pursued C.L. down the hall. He knocked on C. L.'s partially opened office door, wishing the other man wasn't so accessible to his employees.

"Enter," C. L.'s voice boomed from behind the door.

"You wanted to see me?" Will said as he entered the office. He closed the door and eased into the chair across from C. L.

"Yes, there are a few last minute requests from Marketing."

Will accepted the spreadsheet from C. L. and glanced down the list. He thought several of the proposals weren't bad. He had learned long ago not to outright refuse the suggestions of others. He would give at least a little of what they ask for, and try to push the rest back to the next code release. Will knew from experience that the site would go through constant life cycles of enhancements and updates to stay current. "Some of this looks doable and a few of these things are very good."

C.L.'s face brightened.

"I'll try to get as much of this in the first release as possible, but I may have to hold off on a few of the larger pieces until next release," Will said as he waited for C. L.'s pleased expression to disappear.

To Will's surprise it didn't. "I knew you'd do your best to appease them," C. L. said, "You're doing a fine job, and I'm very pleased with your work."

Will waited for the 'but' and observed the change in C. L.'s appearance. Slight downturns formed at the corners of his mouth and a pained expression settled into his normally jovial eyes. "Will, is everything okay between you and Kerrie? Earlier when I walked in on you two ..."

Will didn't let him finish the thought. "Everything's fine. Kerrie was just upset about something, and I tried to comfort her. There's no problem."

Will hoped he didn't sound too defensive, and he tried to relax. C. L. shifted in his chair; apparently he didn't handle confrontation well. "To be honest, I've been a little worried about you even before today. You look exhausted. I know you have been putting major effort into this project, but I don't want you to destroy your health, and as for the other thing, well, I just wouldn't want anything to happen that would compromise your ability to continue doing your job. I'm counting on the both of you," C. L. paused.

Will gave his best 'everything is fine' smile. "There's no problem. We're old friends, and I'm just a little tired, but I promise I'll catch up on my rest as soon as the first release is completed."

C. L. shoulders sagged a little and he leaned back in his chair. Will hoped this would be the end of the discussion.

"I'm not trying to butt into your personal life, but I've already lost your predecessor to a similar situation."

Will's ears perked up. "He had to resign because of illness?"

C.L. shifted in his chair. "No. Not exactly, it was an affair. He never admitted it, but I believe his wife found out. It was a nasty situation, and he had to leave the company to save his marriage. I can't afford to lose you, not at this juncture."

Will stood up. "I appreciate that, but there's no affair. My marriage is strong. I'd better get back to my office and see about assigning this extra work to the team."

"Thanks, I appreciate all your fine effort." C. L.'s smile was broad, and Will almost felt touched, but in some way, on some level, it was still a salesman's smile.

He's the real deal.

Will left the office and wondered if he had fooled C. L. any more than he had fooled himself. He walked back to his office, the spreadsheet forgotten in his right hand. All he could think about was holding Kerrie in his arms, that tight embrace, her scent. He was in over his head, and as he opened his office door, he definitely felt like he was entering the shark tank again.

The question is: who is the shark?

CHAPTER **TWENTY-SIX**

By Friday afternoon an exhausted Will reluctantly ducked out of the office early for Gretchen's arrival. Kerrie had spent much of her time the last two days using his desktop computer, and he found it impossible to concentrate on his work. Her perfume, the soft curve of her upturned lips, the sparkle in her eyes — all unwanted distractions. To fortify his resolve he fled to his family.

Alone on the front porch, he watched the sun descend in a fiery spectacle that seemed more appropriate for an autumn evening than the twelfth of July. He watched the fading light with a sense of dread, like it was the last fleeting brightness in a brittle world that was quickly slipping out of his reach.

The silence and his contemplation were shattered by the hum of the small car's engine and the crunch of gravel when Gretchen navigated her Bug up the drive. She was barely out of the car, and Ellie dashed out the front door, across the dry grass and into the petite woman's arms. Sara followed, and together she and Will crossed the driveway to greet Gretchen.

"Oh, you poor little sprite. I'll have to do a special drawing on your cast. " Gretchen lowered Ellie and turned to hug Sara.

Will couldn't hear the exchange, but both women grinned.

"Give me a hug, big guy," Gretchen said and almost tackled him.

Gretchen gave the house a once over. "Wow, would you look at this place."

"Our house has a name," Ellie announced, "It's Shadow's Forge."

"Really?" Gretchen said raising her eyebrows.

"Where did you hear that?" Will asked.

"Celeste told me."

Will felt a chill.

Gretchen winked at him. "A property with a name, you guys certainly have moved up in the world."

"Let me help you with your bags."

Will approached the car, but Gretchen shooed him away. She reached into the back seat and removed a beat-up backpack. "I travel light."

The four of them approached the house, Ellie chattered excitedly, and to Will it felt like old times. But as they entered the foyer the mood changed. Gretchen winced and stroked her left temple.

Will touched her arm. "Something wrong?"

Gretchen grinned, but her eyes betrayed discomfort. "It's just a slight headache, probably from the long drive."

Sara seemed oblivious to her friend's uneasiness and started up the steps. "I'll show you the upstairs first. The guestroom's up there, and you can settle in."

"I'll pour some ice tea for after your tour," Will volunteered.

CHAPTER TWENTY-SEVEN

At the top of the stairs, Gretchen nodded her approval after Sara pointed out the round stained glass window. She would have enjoyed studying the beautiful piece if only the pressure in her head would have eased.

The pain had started when she entered the front door, exactly when she had crossed the threshold.

Hopefully it isn't the beginning of a migraine or something worse.

She drew a deep mouthful of air and surveyed the landing. The drab house screamed for a makeover, and she tried to hide her disapproval.

Not wanting to hurt Sara's feelings, Gretchen approached the family cat stretched out on the antique side table next to the banister. She stroked him a few times, and he extended even more, if that was possible. "Hey, it's Mr. Whiskers. How're you baby?"

He twisted on his back in that elastic way that only cats can. Gretchen laughed, but flinched at the sharp jab in her head.

Sara gave Mr. Whiskers a scratch behind his ears. "This is his favorite perch. He lays up here like the master of all he surveys."

Gretchen fought vertigo as she scanned the foyer floor below. "That's quite a drop."

Sara stared trancelike at the room. "Isn't it spectacular?"

Ellie tugged at Gretchen's sleeve. "This way first, Aunt Gretchen. I want to show you my room."

She followed the little girl without commenting, glad for the interruption.

Ellie's room overflowed with frills and stuffed animals, and she proudly pointed out all her treasures. Gretchen recognized Ellie's possessions, but ooed and ahhed to please the little sprite.

Icy chills danced across Gretchen's bare arms. The place was frigid.

Gretchen loved Ellie, and the two of them had had fantastic tea parties back in Horsham. Their relationship was playful, and Ellie didn't so much as wrinkle her nose when Gretchen brewed herbal teas for their healing properties. Ellie was excited and explained that she had planned an early evening tea party with several of her new friends, so Gretchen could meet them.

Gretchen tried to be polite, but struggled against a wave of nausea. "That sounds like fun, but we might have to wait till tomorrow. I'm a little jetlagged."

She steadied herself against the canopy post.

"Okay." The disappointment was thick in Ellie's voice.

It tore Gretchen up inside to disappoint the child, and she fought hard to maintain her composure. This had hit her so suddenly. She had felt great on the drive from Philly, now she wanted to collapse into bed. Maybe a nice cup of herbal tea was the answer.

Thankfully Sara interceded. "Aunt Gretchen will play with you tomorrow. Let's show her the rest of the house, and let her relax a little."

Ellie nodded and seemed to recover quickly. "I'm going to draw you a picture of Celeste."

Gretchen smiled and glanced at Sara with one raised eyebrow. "Celeste?"

"She's her imaginary friend." Sara said as she led the way down the hall.

Gretchen followed, leaving Ellie in her room. Passing the banister she fought another wave of vertigo. Sara pointed to the first doorway on the left. "Bathroom, and this is your room right across the hall."

Sara entered a small space furnished with a computer desk and a bed. "This is the guest room and also serves as Will's office."

Sara closed a door that stood ajar. "Don't mind this. It's just the attic door. It doesn't stay closed."

"See what you get for buying an old place." Gretchen had meant it to be funny, but Sara didn't laugh. Instead she seemed to tense up. Gretchen lowered her pack to the bed and turned slowly in a circle admiring the room. She wanted to say something encouraging, undoing the last remark, but couldn't find the words to compliment the old, dingy room. She shivered and undid her pack in search of her sweatshirt.

Sara studied the room with the same vacant stare from the foyer. "I know it needs work, but think of the possibilities."

Gretchen pulled on the sweatshirt. "It'll be fabulous when you finish redecorating. I've always said if the sculpting doesn't work out, you could make a fortune as an interior decorator."

Sara chuckled and touched Gretchen's arm. "That's sweet of you to say."

Huh? Since when had Sara become so polite and formal?

Before she could respond, Sara was out the door and down the hall. Gretchen followed, but paused in front of a large cabinet in the corridor. The new piece of furniture's presence shocked her.

Sara hates guns.

"What's this?"

Sara returned to her side and stroked the hardwood cabinet almost lovingly. "Will's purchased a few guns."

"A few." Gretchen studied the shotgun, two rifles, and a couple of pistols with a sinking feeling. "What's he trying to do   arm his own militia?"

"The neighbor got him started. Everyone in the country owns guns."

Something's wrong.

It wasn't just the guns. Sara seemed distant, and Will appeared exhausted. Gretchen rubbed her temples; maybe she was coming down with something and projecting her bad vibes on her friends, but Sara being fine with Will owning guns just didn't fit. "Sara, is everything all right?"

Sara looked down at her hands, averting her eyes from Gretchen's. "I don't know. Will has been acting odd since we moved. He spends almost every waking hour at the office."

Gretchen shrugged and wished her head didn't feel like it was going to explode. "You knew his new job would be more demanding."

A small tear trailed down Sara's cheek. "Yeah, but he's so distant. I think there's someone else."

"What?" Sara's statement caught Gretchen off guard.

"I'm just not sure."

"Not Will, he's crazy about you. He always has been."

Sara jammed her hands into her jean pockets and shrugged. Gretchen felt weak and overwhelmed. Sara had always been serious, but never this somber.

"At night when he's asleep, I hear him talking. I can't make out much, but I think he's talking to another woman."

This sounded paranoid, and Gretchen tried to lighten the mood. "You can hardly blame a guy for what happens in his subconscious."

Sara's expression didn't change as she stared at the guns, her eyes distant and vacant. Gretchen shivered, she wasn't sure about Will, but something was definitely off with Sara. "What about the drinking?"

Sara slowly shook her head, her voice a whisper. "I haven't seen any other signs. I couldn't stand to lose him. If he left me, I don't know what I would do."

Her gaze still fixed on the weapons, Sara delivered this last line in a hollow tone and with such expressionless eyes that Gretchen wanted to shake her. "I don't like guns. I thought you hated them. I can't believe he would bring them into the house with Ellie. Don't you have a problem with this?" Gretchen waved at the cabinet, her cheeks felt hot. She wanted to jar Sara out of her funk.

Still focused on the cabinet, Sara smiled and shook her head. "He says they're safe. He keeps the cabinet locked, and the little trigger guards lock into place."

"It's just, so not like him." Gretchen said this more for her own benefit than for Sara's.

CHAPTER TWENTY-EIGHT

Will tried to balance the four glasses of ice tea on the tray wile flipping the dining room light switch with his elbow. The brown liquid sloshed over the rims of the glasses pooling on the silver tray.

Shit.

With most of the bulbs burned out, the chandelier failed to satisfactorily illuminate the room.

I guess we will be dining by candlelight tonight.

He lowered the tray to the table and glanced around the ill-lit room. The shadows made his skin crawl. He would have to ask Harry if he knew a good electrician.

Ellie's laughter echoed in the foyer as the girls approached. For a moment it raised Will's spirits. There hadn't been a lot of laughter since the move. Maybe Gretchen's visit would change things.

Sara seemed pleased with herself as she entered. "And this is the formal dining room."

Gretchen glanced around, her attention seemed drawn to the chandelier for a moment, she frowned, and then noticed Will staring at her. "Nice high ceilings. Nine foot tall?"

"Actually ten," Will said and handed Gretchen a glass of ice tea. She grinned and took a small sip. "This house is great. You guys must be thrilled."

Will detected some insincerity, but smiled and handed Ellie a glass. Ellie gulped hers, swallowing half the liquid before she came up for air. "Thanks Daddy, I'm going to finish my drawing for Aunt Gretchen.

She started toward the foyer.

"Careful on the stairs with that glass." Will caught Sara's sharp glance and realized what he had said.

Sara continued with the tour, obviously not wanting to explain the incident on the stairs to Gretchen.

"Now, I want to show you my favorite space in the entire house."

Sara opened both French doors and led the way into her studio. Will and Gretchen followed. He had not entered the studio since Sara had adorned the doors with white curtains. He smiled. Sara had covered her latest work in progress with a large tarp. He assumed that Gretchen knew better than to ask to see one of Sara's sculptures before its completion. Gretchen walked around the room admiring the space, but avoided commenting on the covered statue.

The sun had set and the harsh white glare of the spotlights positioned around the studio hurt Will's eyes.

"It's wonderful to work in the natural daylight," Sara said.

"It must be fabulous to have a view of the surrounding property to inspire you while you work," Gretchen said.

Will didn't comprehend the aesthetic advantages of the room and thought that Gretchen was trying a little too hard to seem impressed.

He shivered, the studio felt icy. He decided to head back to the dining room, but a movement under the tarp distracted him. He caught it out of the corner of his eye, just a glimpse of motion. Studying the large shape carefully, he dismissed it as a trick of the light. It was probably a shadow cast by one of them as they walked about the room. He squelched the desire to lift the edge of the tarp and peek underneath.

Sara almost danced about the room, practically giddy. "I have so many ideas for pieces. This place inspires me so much."

Gretchen politely nodded, but seemed tense. Will wondered if she was also uncomfortable, or if he was just projecting his own discomfort.

Sara grabbed Gretchen by the arm. "It's getting late and you must be starved."

"I could eat," Gretchen agreed.

"Good and don't worry, it's eggplant Parmesan, so no animals were harmed to produce the meal." They all laughed as Sara led them from the studio, but the humor felt forced to Will.

Gretchen paused in the dining room and turn to face him. "What's with all the guns, expecting an invasion?"

He shrugged and felt his cheeks grow warm. "A neighbor is teaching me to shoot. You know how it is, when in Rome…"

This was not true   something had compelled him to purchase that first shotgun at the hardware store, but he couldn't explain his new obsession to Gretchen, even if he wanted to. He didn't understand the warm sensation when he held one of the heavy weapons in his hands, or the powerful energy that radiated from the object, the notion that pulling the trigger could change the course of someone's life, not just the victim, but the wielder as well.

"We'll talk more about this later," Gretchen said over her shoulder as she followed Sara into the kitchen.

Gretchen on a crusade, just what I need.

CHAPTER **TWENTY-NINE**

While Sara and Gretchen finished preparing the meal, Will returned to the dining room with his hands full of utensils. He ignored the shadows in the room. They crawled with unseen inhabitants that would vanish if he spun to catch the motion he detected in the corner of his eyes, and approached the table to place the silverware. A wave of coldness splashed across his flesh. The room's temperature plummeted. His breath crystallized, and goose flesh rose on his arms. He steadied himself on the edge of the table.

Slowly a female formed in the dimness. One minute she wasn't there and the next she emerged from a roiling mist. Her details solidified like a developing photograph. He drew in his breath and held it because he recognized her — *Celeste.*

Will moaned.

She hovered in the entranceway between the parlor and the dining room. Her large blue eyes peered out from sunken cavities. Hollow defeat floated in the cold murky orbs, her expression broke Will's heart. Sadness washed through him so strong it overwhelmed his fear. Tinged green, her pale flesh glowed with a green luminescence. Dark cracked lips pulled back in a cruel sneer, and long tangles of filthy blonde hair cascaded over her shoulders. The white silk nightgown once intended for seduction, now a rotted rag, exposed an emaciated carcass; only a withered husk remained.

She clutched a long silver knife in her left hand. Dark liquid covered the blade.

A powerful force radiated from Celeste's translucent body, a hate so strong it sent a shockwave across the room. At the same time, she emitted an attraction that Will struggled to resist. Like the sensation of glancing over the railing on the balcony of a tall building and feeling pulled to lean out further to get a better view.

He felt drawn toward her. It required all his strength to stay rooted.

If she touches me, I'll die.

He couldn't explain this flash of knowledge, but he believed it. This glorious and horrific apparition held only death. A large chasm opened in the center of the ceiling replacing the chandelier. Light emanated from inside, and dark clouds swirled in the thunderous sky. The glowing turbulent circle in the ceiling sucked the air from the room.

"You're dead. Go into the light," Gretchen shouted.

Will was so entranced by the vision that he hadn't noticed Gretchen enter the room until she spoke. His heart pounded. Forgotten silverware crashed to the floor when his hands involuntarily opened. Gretchen's presence interjected a new terrifying reality into this experience. She also saw Celeste.

"That's it — you're free. Go into the light," Gretchen repeated.

Celeste stared longingly at the chasm, then back at Will and Gretchen. She shook her head slowly and pointed at the floor. Was this some admission that she belonged in hell? Celeste's thin lips pulled into a tight line and her eyes grew dark and menacing. She radiated hate like the wisps of vapor from a block of dry ice. A vile bitter taste flooded Will's mouth. He wanted to run, he wanted to scream, but he remained frozen in place. She was too wretched to face and too compelling to ignore.

Please don't come any closer.

The stench of decay carried the hint of death from across the room, and the thought of her lips touching his paralyzed him. Will squeezed his eyes closed. Her touch was only millimeters away, her maggot infested kiss closing in from across the room, Will could almost feel it. The anticipation sent a shudder through his body.

CHAPTER THIRTY

"What's going on in here?" Sara's voice shattered the vision.

Celeste, the hole in the ceiling, and the bright light all vanished, leaving Will with a sense of dread and a longing he couldn't explain. Even though the thought of her touch terrified him, for a second, he had anticipated it so strongly that when it didn't occur, he felt a sense of loss.

"You saw that?" Will asked Gretchen, his heart pounded and he felt like he had just run a marathon.

"Saw what?" Sara persisted.

Will paused and inhaled deeply, trying to fill his lungs. Blackness slid into the edges of his vision. He fought to stay conscious. "The woman in the doorway."

Gretchen examined the archway between the parlor and dining room, like she expected to find some secret to the illusion. Gretchen had remained calm. She gazed at Will with shining eyes. "That was incredible."

Will pointed to the arch. "She just vanished. She was right there."

Sara started to speak. "What are… "

"That explains it," Gretchen said cutting off Sara's question. "The manifestation we saw…"

Will rubbed the bridge of his nose. "Manifestation?"

Sara glared at him, and he suddenly felt foolish.

"Yes – the apparition. I was wondering why I felt so bad after I arrived," Gretchen continued.

Sara stared at Will almost ignoring Gretchen completely and repeated, "What?"

Doubt lingered there below the surface of her voice. Will shrugged and stared at the archway. "We saw something."

"It was dark in here. How could either of you see anything?"

"I'm not sure what we saw. I'm sure there's some logical explanation." Will shivered and thought about the other visions, dreams, or whatever they were. The Native Americans, the boy on the bike, all these things were unexplainable. He struggled for logic to hang onto, but found none. How could he, a man who believed in things he could see and touch, a man who had struggled with his faith in God for years before believing, how could he explain all these unexplainable events?

Gretchen continued to examine the floor in the archway. "It was a trapped spirit, you could tell she wanted to go into the light, but couldn't."

Sara bent and picked up the scattered silverware. She laid it on the table in front of Will. "You're exhausted. You don't get enough rest. You're probably hallucinating."

"It wasn't a hallucination, we both saw her." Gretchen said.

"Saw who?" Ellie asked as she entered the dining room.

Silence. The three adults didn't move.

Will prayed Gretchen wouldn't say anything that would disturb Ellie.

"Nothing Sweetie, Aunt Gretchen and Daddy were talking about someone back in Philadelphia," Sara said.

Ellie smiled and appeared to accept the statement at face value. Will sighed, relieved that she did not pursue the issue, and Gretchen remained silent.

"I wanted to show Aunt Gretchen my picture of Celeste."

Ellie held out a crude pencil drawing.

Gretchen studied the drawing. Her pupils dilated and she cast a quick glance at Will, raising one eyebrow in question. She must have realized the apparition was a deteriorated incarnation of Celeste. Will slowly shook his head to silence her. He didn't want to talk about this in front of Ellie. Thankfully, Gretchen seemed to understand. They would discuss this later, after Ellie went to bed.

CHAPTER **THIRTY-ONE**

Will still felt rattled hours later when he tucked Ellie into bed. He'd found it impossible to concentrate on her bedtime story, repeating the same lines several times. This amused her, but frustrated him. Before he left the room, he asked her if he could have the photograph of Celeste to show Aunt Gretchen. Ellie said she'd lost the photo, which was why she had drawn a picture. Will was disturbed by this, but tried to hide his displeasure.

Disappointed and troubled, he returned to the parlor to find Sara and Gretchen seated in silence at opposite ends of the couch. He remembered happier times back in Horsham when Gretchen's laughter had permeated the air. He picked up the cup of black coffee that Sara had left on the coffee table for him, and eased into an old armchair, careful not to spill the hot liquid. He guessed that Sara and Gretchen were drinking their usual French Vanilla.

He rubbed his right temple. "What a night."

Gretchen rested her drink on the coffee table spilling some of the creamy liquid onto the table. "We have to talk about what we saw."

Will glanced toward the dining room, his pulse quickening at the thought. "It happened so fast."

"Will, you're exhausted. You should get some sleep." Sara's eyes were bright, and her tone warned that he should drop the subject.

Gretchen leaned forward touching Sara's arm. "This is important. We need to talk. It was a trapped spirit."

"Come on Gretchen. You're not going to start with that supernatural crap." Sara folded her arms and glared at her friend.

Her open hostility shocked Will.

"It's not crap. Tell her what you saw," Gretchen said.

They both stared at him, and he felt foolish, like he was under cross-examination.

"I saw a woman." He proceeded to describe what he had witnessed. "I think it was Celeste."

Gretchen nodded. "It all makes sense. I haven't felt right since I've arrived. There is something wrong with this place, and I think you might be…"

"Stop it." The severity in Sara's tone silenced Gretchen, who looked to Will for help.

He tried. "Let's just calm down. I'm sure there's some explanation."

Gretchen pushed on, "Sara, this woman was dead. We could see right through her. It was a classic apparition. I spoke to her, and she shook her head before she vanished. She actually responded to me."

"What's your point?" Sara asked.

"I think you need to get someone in here who can do a séance and contact this spirit, find out why she's trapped here."

Sara rolled her eyes.

"I'm serious. I feel the negative vibes here. Maybe the three of you should come back to Philly with me until we can get someone in here to check it out."

Sara slammed her mug down on the coffee table. "Look, I know you're unhappy we moved. I know you're probably lonely, but we live here now, and there's nothing wrong with this place."

Will could see Sara's anger building; he could hear her rage as she continued.

"This psychic shit used to add color, give you some character, but it's not funny anymore. Grow up and start acting like an adult. Maybe if you weren't so flaky you'd have a man."

"Sara." Will reached out to try to calm her, and she turned on him, her eyes filled with tears.

"And you. I don't know why you want to spend every waking moment at the office, but there's nothing wrong with this place. You're just looking for an excuse to stay away."

Will wanted to argue, but he knew she was right. He involuntarily thought about Kerrie. The guilt silenced him because the house was only part of the reason. He watched silently as Sara verbally attacked Gretchen again.

"I'm not going to sit here and listen to the two of you create some kind of paranoid fantasy. I love this house. It's the first place that's ever truly felt like home. I spend every day here, all the time, and I never see anything strange. I'm the one with the imagination, not Will. I'm sorry you're jealous of my life. I guess I've always known you were. I just didn't know how far you'd go to try to ruin it."

Sara stormed out of the room, up the stairs, and slammed the bedroom door.

"Oh, Sara, no," Gretchen said, but it was too late.

"I'm sorry. I know she didn't mean what she said. She loves you like a sister," Will said. He felt bad for Gretchen. She'd done nothing to warrant Sara's hysterical outburst. He licked his lips and wished the black coffee in his hand were something stronger.

"It's this place," Gretchen said as tears ran down her cheeks.

"Are you okay?" he asked and felt helpless again thinking about a drink.

"Yeah, I'm fine. I'm just a little surprised. Sara's never let me have it like that before."

"I'm sure she didn't mean it."

"No, I think she did. Maybe she's right, and I'm jealous, but mostly I miss you guys. Either way, I was hit with bad vibes as soon as I got out of the car, and I think something is going on here."

Will glanced at the dining room and tried to reason through the dull ache in his forehead. "You really think we saw a ghost?"

Gretchen didn't hesitate or flinch. "Yes."

Will considered. Until now he had experienced all his visions or whatever they were alone. He wasn't comforted that Gretchen had shared this sighting. After all, she qualified as the flakiest person he knew. "Have you ever seen anything like this before?" Will sipped from his drink waiting for her response.

"No, but I've read all about this sort of thing, and have talked to others who've encountered spirits. What about you?"

The question hung in the air between them. Will set his empty cup on the table and rubbed his hands together trying to generate some warmth. The room was brisk again. He didn't want to explain, wasn't even sure he could. "You know I don't drink. I haven't had one in fourteen years…"

CHAPTER **THIRTY-TWO**

Will drank his last drink fourteen years earlier on a cold Saturday night in October at a party at Millberton University.

"You're smashed," Gina Zimmerman said and leaned in and kissed him hard on the lips.

When her soft lips pulled away, he responded. "Oh yeah."

She smelled like springtime, flowers and grass. Her lips were sweet. The music blared, and Will's head swam.

She waggled her plastic cup back and forth. "I need a refill."

"I'll get it." He upended his cup, sucking down the last of his suds. He grasped hers, rose from the ratty sofa and started to stagger away. She snatched his belt and yanked him back on top of her.

"Hey, wait. I need more lovin'." They both giggled.

She kissed him again, her tongue probing his mouth. Her body soft and inviting under him, he almost forgot the drinks. She combed her fingers through his hair. He nuzzled her neck, and her long blonde hair tickled his nose. He chuckled again.

"Hurry back." She winked and raised one eyebrow. He shivered. "I will."

She broke into a spasm of uncontrolled laughter. "You Will, me Gina."

He gripped the back of the sofa to steady himself as he struggled to his feet, impaired by his laughter that summoned a wave of light-headedness. The room swayed as he tried to navigate between bodies in the dim light. The Keghouse, the most notorious frat house on campus, brimmed at maximum capacity. He apologized as he bumped into others, spilling their drinks. Some were trying to slow dance in the crowded living room.

"Oops, sorry."

He stumbled into the kitchen. His roommate Brian DeLaurino was drawing a draft. Foam overflowed the edge of the cup, and Brian raised it. "Some blowout."

Will grinned and raised his empty cup in salute. "I aced my Cobol test."

They high-fived, and Will staggered.

Brian grabbed his arm to steady him. "Better slow down, partner."

Will laughed and held his cups out for Brian to fill them. "I'm just getting started. Did you see who I'm with?"

Brian splashed beer into both cups until the foam overflowed. "Man, Gina, she's hot."

Will grinned, took a sip of his drink and held it out to be topped off. "You think you can make yourself scarce later?"

Brian howled and sprayed a blast of beer at Will. "Acing a test and bagging Gina in the same day, you're a god."

Will's response died on his tongue as a slash of pain exploded in his right temple. The room spun, and everything faded for a moment. Will dropped the drinks, doubled over, and grabbed his head. His skull pounded, and his stomach lurched. He staggered backward against the kitchen table, the top pressing into his back.

He opened his eyes and blinked against the overhead light that was now too bright. "Hey kid, what're you doing here?"

A small blonde haired boy stood in front of the keg, between Will and Brian. Dressed for trick or treat, he wore a blue and white silk clown costume. His face was painted white with a red nose, and drawn on big red lips, and a blue star that covered his left eye.

Will laughed in spite of the pain in his forehead. "That's quite a getup."

Apparently confused, Brian cocked his head. "Huh?"

The boy's gaze never left Will as he reached into his paper sack and pulled out a shiny red apple. Will's stomach tightened, and his fogged brain tried to comprehend.

Trick or treat and apples – not a good idea – nobody really let their kids accept them?

He tried to warn the kid, his voice sound high and whiny. "No, you don't want to do that..."

Before Will could finish, the boy raised the apple to his mouth. His bizarre red lips parted as he chomped into the polished fruit. The crunch reverberated off the walls, and the child's eyes went wide. He lowered the fruit, and blood spurted from his mouth, racing down the white painted chin. Will's legs buckled, and he grabbed the table for support.

Brian stepped toward Will. "Will, what's wrong?"

In blinding speed the clown turned and slashed at Brian with the apple. Will spotted the glint of the razor blade and lunged toward them, trying to knock the boy away. In a blur he piled into Brian, missing the child. They both crashed to the hard linoleum tile. Chills scurried across Will's sweat soaked body as he stared at the long slash on Brian's right arm.

Screams distracted him, and he turned to see the small clown howling, and blood flecks from his mouth splattering the white tile floor.

Gina burst through the kitchen door. "Hey what's taking so..."

Double images of Gina and the clown danced in Will's blurred vision. Their mutual screams merged into a dull roar. The wave started at the base of Will's skull and slowly washed over his mind, until he lost himself in the quiet soothing grayness.

CHAPTER THIRTY-THREE

Will finished his story and gulped a swallow of coffee, but wished for an ice-cold beer. "I didn't wake up till the next morning. Brian had to get sixteen stitches and the most bizarre thing was neither he nor Gina had seen the boy in the clown outfit."

Gretchen nodded, leaning forward. "You think he was a ghost?"

"I didn't at the time. I thought it was a drunken hallucination. I swore off alcohol and haven't had a drink in fourteen years, but lately, I'm not so sure."

He explained everything, the boy on the bike, the apparitions, and the dreams since they had moved into the house. He left nothing out, trying to recall as many details as he could. When he finished, Gretchen sat there staring at him, her eyes wide, her mouth ajar. "Have you told Sara this?"

Will shrugged and felt foolish. "How could I? The thing in college was just a drunken delusion. It happened before I met her. This other stuff, to be quite honest, all sounds crazy. You saw how she reacted. She thinks I'm nuts or making it all up."

Gretchen stared at the bottom of her empty coffee cup. "Will, it's not nuts. I'll bet if you checked out the history of that intersection you'd find out that a boy was hit by a car and died there. That's probably true for the frat house as well."

Will slumped back into the chair. "But, why would I see these things and not Sara? She's the one with the great imagination."

Gretchen lowered her cup to the table. "Imagination has nothing to do with it. What you saw tonight was real. Some people are just more sensitive."

Will pondered this and decided that exhaustion and insanity made a lot more sense than some sort of supernatural specters. Maybe he had a brain tumor. "Why one time almost fifteen years ago and then nothing until now?"

Gretchen shrugged and pursed her lips. He expected her to rev up for a long debate. She obviously wasn't going to let go of the ghost concept without a fight. "There are spirits around us all the time. Most people don't notice. Then there are others who have keener senses, like some people can hear or smell better than others. Maybe that night at the frat house the alcohol lowered your inhibitions, so you were more open to the world, and maybe now in this place the spirits are stronger or the veil is thinner."

Small Sparrow's words returned to him, 'The veil is thin and the dead slither back across into the land of the living.' He hugged himself to stop the shivers.

"What you need to do is try to figure out why these spirits are revealing themselves to you. There are three types of ghosts: The first is a spirit who has unfinished business, it is trapped in purgatory here on earth. The second is a messenger from God who brings good news or some kind of aid, and the third is an evil spirit straight out of hell. The third type is deceitful and dangerous. You need to figure out which one we saw and what it wants," Gretchen said. Although she spoke with authority, he fought hard not to laugh. He couldn't believe this absurd conversation.

"Okay, I'll admit I saw something, but Sara is here all the time and she never sees anything."

Gretchen nodded and paused for a moment. She seemed to struggle, trying to figure out how to say something diplomatically. "Just because she doesn't see it that doesn't prove it's not there. She might not want to see. She said it herself; this is the first place that feels like home. I'm scared. I really think you should all come back to Philly with me until we can get a medium in here."

"Sara will never go for that, besides we have every penny tied up in this place, and I'm in charge of a million-dollar project. I can't just run off."

"Will, this is serious. Ellie sees this Celeste as an imaginary friend; maybe she has the same senses you do. What if this Celeste tries to hurt her?"

Will thought about Celeste holding the knife.

Gretchen continued, "Ellie's already hurt, if you stay I'm afraid thing will get worse. Someone may end up dead."

CHAPTER THIRTY-FOUR

Upstairs, Gretchen stalled in the guestroom doorway, not ready to say good night, and Will gave her a quick peck on the cheek. "Things will be better in the morning," he said.

She returned his grin and wished she believed him. Before he could escape she gave him a quick hug. He disappeared through his bedroom door, and she felt queasy. The hallway's shadows seemed alive with unseen entities, and she fled into the guest room.

Behind the door, she flipped the porcelain wall switch, and the overhead light lit. Satisfied that nothing sinister stalked her, she continued farther into the room. Her heart pounded and her head ached. She felt ridiculous — Will and Sara were right down the hall. That fact provided no comfort when she considered the evil that dwelled in the house. She could feel its presence, and it made her skin crawl.

An icy draft from the partially open attic door caressed her skin, and she shivered again. She slowly crept toward the doorway and peered up into the darkness.

"Great, the attic. I won't get any sleep tonight," she announced to the room and slammed the door.

The overhead light went out, plunging the room into darkness. Gretchen yelped. Instinctively, she wanted to dash across the floor to the light switch, but the darkness disoriented her, and she bumped her hip into the desk chair. Clutching the post at the foot of the bed for support, she gasped when she saw the naked couple there.

As her eyes adjusted to the dim moonlight, she could see them plainly. The man continued to rise up and down on top of the woman, silently thrusting into her, apparently unaware of Gretchen's presence. The scene played like an old silent film — some sort of imprinted memory on the place. Their monochromatic flesh remained translucent like Celeste earlier in the dining room. Gretchen could see through them.

She turned for the door, but froze when a similarly colorless man in a Civil War uniform burst through, blocking her escape. His face wore an expression of pure rage.

Gretchen trembled and backed away from the unhinged intruder.

The naked man, now distracted, tried to gain his footing as he scrambled from the bed. With his long mutton chop whiskers and tussled hair, he resembled a deranged barbershop quartet singer, but any hysterical laughter died in Gretchen's throat. The dark haired woman clutched the quilt in an attempt to cover her naked body. Her not-so-modest lover rushed the soldier, who had drawn a long black six-shooter from a holster on his belt.

The nude man tried to reach him before he squeezed the trigger. Flames erupted from the end of the barrel. Gretchen smelled burnt gunpowder and flinched as she felt the vibrations of the silent pistol's report.

The first bullet hit muttonchops in the center of his chest; a dark splotch grew there. The force of the projectile propelled him backward across the room. The second bullet caught the man in the shoulder.

The naked woman leapt from the bed. Gretchen winced at the slap of cold when the woman dashed through her and grabbed the latch to open the attic door.

Crazed, the wide-eyed soldier pursued, stepping over the naked dead man without a glance. The dark-haired woman fell to her knees, pleading for her life as he raised the gun. A hole silently appeared in the center of her forehead, and black liquid splattered the door and wall behind her. Gretchen fought the urge to vomit, swallowing a mouthful of bile. The woman crumpled to the floor in a limp heap.

The soldier turned to face Gretchen, and she knew she was going to die. Unlike in the dining room her voice failed her. His pleading gaze met hers and revealed a damned soul begging for forgiveness. He raised the pistol and inserted it into his mouth. Gretchen felt her sanity slipping away with each heartbeat.

"No, don't do it," she tried to scream, but the words caught in her throat.

As tears ran down his cheeks, the soldier squeezed the trigger. Gretchen watched in horrid fascination, as the ghostly bullet shattered the back of his skull, and black, white, and gray matter surged through the air like a grotesque fountain.

Gretchen's screams died in her throat as she gulped air. Her heart pounded, and her head threatened to explode. She vomited in the corner, unable to escape the vision … or the room.

CHAPTER **THIRTY-FIVE**

The next morning, dark clouds promised to end the drought and unleash a deluge on the parched earth. The sky matched Will's mood as he stepped onto his porch, stretched, and tried to psych himself for his morning run.

The first large rain drops exploded in the dust, giving Will the final excuse to skip his morning regimen. He slowly turned to re-enter the house, but paused when his cell phone rang.

"Will, is that you?"

Gretchen's voice jarred him fully awake, and he realized her car was gone. "Gretchen where are you?"

"I couldn't take it. I had to get out. I'm at a hotel here in Templeton."

Will frowned. "I know it was a little crazy last night, but…"

"You don't know the half of it."

Gretchen told him about the murder-suicide scene in the bedroom going into very graphic detail.

"Come back. Sara will wake soon, and you can tell her what you saw."

"Sorry. I don't think so. Besides I don't think Sara would believe me anyway."

Will ran a hand through his hair. "Look, I'm sorry things got all messed up this weekend. Maybe if you come back, you can help me talk some sense into Sara."

"It'll take more to convince her. I have an idea. In the meantime, you have to find a way to get her and Ellie out of that place before it's too late. It's dangerous there."

Will thought about their conversation as he showered and dressed for work. He found Sara and Ellie in the kitchen.

Ellie ate cold cereal. The absence of the aroma of frying eggs and bacon, their usual Saturday morning fare, was a bad omen.

Sara slouched in her chair staring at an untouched cream cheese slathered bagel on the table in front of her.

She frowned when she saw Will's attire. "Not today."

"I'm sorry. Only two weeks until the release."

She slid the plate with the bagel across the table. "You can't wait to get out of here."

Will didn't want to have this discussion in front of Ellie. He sensed the tense undercurrent threatening to explode. Sara's gaze burned into him, and he fought hard to restrain his own temper.

"Where's Aunt Gretchen, Daddy?"

"She had to leave, honey."

He knew Ellie sensed the tension. "Why didn't she say goodbye?"

Will stared at the shabby kitchen cupboards as if the answer to his daughter's question was hidden behind their faded doors. "She wanted to, but she had to leave in a hurry."

Will turned to Sara for help, but she simply rose from the table.

"I'm not hungry. You can have my bagel," she said and left the kitchen.

Kneeling beside his daughter, he tried to find the proper explanation in his muddled mind. He glanced at his watch. "Aunt Gretchen had to leave because something real important happened, and she had to go home to take care of it."

Ellie nodded and seemed satisfied with the explanation. He stood up, kissed her on the forehead, told her he loved her, and headed for the door.

"Have fun at work," Ellie called.

Will smiled as he left the kitchen, amused by the view of life through the eyes of a child. Unfortunately the pressure and deadlines had killed the thrill of learning something new, or solving a problem, leaving only the bitter residue of disillusionment in its wake.

Will heard Sara's air compressor humming inside her studio when he approached. He rapped lightly on the French door and waited for her to answer. The humming ended, and Sara cracked the door, glaring at him. "What?"

He swallowed and braced himself. "We need to talk about what happened last night."

Sara narrowed her eyes and glanced toward the kitchen, lowering her voice. "We already did… last night."

Will shook his head. "There's more. Gretchen saw something horrible in my office. She saw a Civil War soldier murder a man and woman, and then kill himself."

Sara raised a hand. "Stop, I don't want to hear anymore of this craziness."

Will stepped closer, and Sara narrowed the opening. "I think you and Ellie should come down to the office with me. You could spend the day shopping in Harrisburg, and then we can figure something out tonight."

Her sharp laughter cut him. "You think this place is dangerous, but you need to get a day's work in before you can deal with it. Just where do you think we would go and for how long?"

He felt the heat rise on his cheeks. "I'm worried about you here."

"There's nothing wrong with this place. Please, Will, you're acting insane. For years you've busted on Gretchen's Mother Earth beliefs, now all of a sudden you're willing to embrace them? Go to work." The door slammed shut, rattling the glass panes.

Will glanced at the parlor entranceway, remembered the apparition from the night before, and shivered. Now in the daylight the whole thing felt like a bad dream. The air compressor behind the studio doors resumed humming. Maybe Sara was right. Maybe he was losing his mind.

On the drive to the office, he replayed in his head all the strange events that had occurred over the last few weeks. With the exception of Gretchen, he remained the only witness to anything unusual. Unfortunately, Gretchen lacked credibility. It disturbed him how Sara remained enchanted by the house, spent all her time there, and never noticed anything out of the ordinary. As he pulled into the office parking lot, he wondered how he could possibly persuade her to leave. She had possessed an abnormal love for the house from day one.

The gleaming chrome and polished glass interior of the office complex was a welcome change from the dark, shabby interior of his house. Glad to escape the gloom, Will entered this otherworldly cathedral to high-tech. He was pleasantly surprised when he entered his office to find Kerrie seated at his desk, working on his computer. It was good to see her friendly face.

She stopped typing. "I hope you don't mind. My monitor's still on the fritz."

He nodded as he sank into a chair next to his desk. "No problem."

He felt Kerrie study him as he opened his laptop, hit the power switch, and watched the screen spring to life. "Is something wrong?"

The concern in her voice moved him and he glanced up from the screen to meet her large brown eyes. He felt them scour his face as she slid her chair next to him and placed her hand on his. He tried to act casual as his heart pounded. Her soft touch, intimate and exciting, sent a thrill through his body.

Struggling not to move his hand, he said, "I had a rough one last night."

Kerrie leaned in closer. "What happened?"

Will didn't know where to begin. It all sounded crazy. Sitting in his nice polished office, he felt distanced from the events, but still could not explain them objectively. He didn't want to appear foolish in front of Kerrie.

"Nothing that interesting," he said and forced a smile.

She gently patted his hand. "If you need to talk, I'm here for you."

The awkward pause lingered, and then she released his hand and slid back behind her computer. He tried to focus on his reports, but the phantom specter kept resurfacing in his mind, interrupting his progress. They worked for hours in silence. Neither one speaking, both okay with the quiet, until later in the afternoon when the phone's shrill ring interrupted them.

Kerrie raised the receiver to her ear and answered, "Will Shepherd's office."

She frowned and handed him the receiver. "It's Sara."

He rose and grabbed the phone, and a wave of panic rippled through him. How would he explain a woman answering his phone? Any thoughts of explanation vanished when he heard Sara's flat emotionless voice. "It's Gretchen…"

CHAPTER **THIRTY-SIX**

Large drops of rain exploded against the windshield, and Gretchen strained to keep her focus as the bug's wipers failed to clear her view. The weather had chased most of the citizens indoors on this quiet Saturday morning. She had hated to leave in the middle of the night without saying goodbye, but it had been too much. Now she was a woman on a mission   she needed to demonstrate the house's danger to Will and Sara. The sooner she made her point, the sooner they would be safe.

She drove along Templeton's deserted, rain-soaked streets, and again cursed her luck for the way the weekend had turned out. At least her headache had cleared. Only a dull queasiness that reminded her of a hangover remained. She ignored the ill feeling and followed the desk clerk's directions from the hotel until she located the building. She parked the VW by the curb, flipped the latch on her seat belt and climbed out from the bug's dry shelter into the cold summer shower.

Gretchen felt like a child as she sprinted up the steps into the old stone building's lobby. Inside, the institutional smells of strong floor cleaner, dust, and something that she associated with her elementary school days, assaulted her senses, further enforcing her memories of childhood, and emboldening her to save her best friend. She studied the small, deserted office, not sure if anyone was in the building. She suspected that someone had accidentally left the front door unlocked.

"Hello, is anyone here?"

Receiving no answer, Gretchen turned to leave and was surprised when a voice replied from the open doorway behind the counter. "Just a moment please. I'll be right there."

A frail woman, with dirty blonde hair pulled back in a bun, appeared in the doorway and greeted Gretchen with a thin smile. Her fair skin indicated that she spent a great deal of time indoors locked away from the sun.

"I'm sorry. I was in the back setting type for this week's edition and I didn't hear the bell," she said as she motioned to the little bell at the top of the doorframe.

"No, I'm the one who's sorry to disturb you. My name is Gretchen Himmel, and I'm doing some research on a property just outside of town."

The women accepted Gretchen's extended hand in her own bony one and shook it limply.

"Your newspaper has been in existence a long time, right?"

"Yes, it's been published for about 150 years. It's one of the oldest papers in the region. I'm Lillian by the way."

"Nice to meet you Lillian. You're born in March right?"

Lillian studied Gretchen through her coke bottle glasses with a perplexed stare.

"I get feelings about these things," Gretchen said.

"Oh."

"I'm sorry. I'm rambling. I came here because I thought your paper might have done some stories on this property I'm interested in. It's located at 1410 Old Creek Road. Is there some way you could look up the name of this property in your old newspapers?"

Lillian leaned against the counter, pursed her lips, and stared up at the ceiling for a moment, apparently waiting for inspiration from some heavenly region. "Well, the best way to learn about the history of a property would be to go down to the Dauphin County Courthouse and do a title search for the deed. You could probably find a list of every owner of the land. To find an old story we really should have a date to go on."

Gretchen sighed. She had not anticipated this complication.

Lillian shrugged.

Gretchen tapped the counter, trying to think. "I thought I could tell you the address of the property, and you could do some kind of data base search."

Lillian laughed. Then bowed her head in apparent embarrassment. "I'm sorry. I don't mean to be rude, but this is a small paper. I'm the only full-time employee besides the owner and his wife. I only started using a computer to lay out the paper about two years ago. I'm afraid there's no database of all the articles we have printed over the years."

"Oh, now I'm starting to realize what a ridiculous idea this is. I'm sorry to have disturbed you."

Gretchen turned to leave the office and had her hand on the knob when Lillian interrupted her.

"This is really weird. You said the address is 1410 Old Creek Road. That's a property located out there near the river? A big old Victorian House?"

Gretchen brightened. "Yeah, that's the place."

"About a year ago someone was in here asking about that same property."

Gretchen's heart nearly jumped out of her chest. "Who?"

"The previous owner — Martin Darkas. You know him?"

Gretchen shook her head. "No. My friends Will and Sara must've bought the place from him."

"Will and Sara Shepherd?" Lillian asked.

"Yeah, that's them. Do you know them?"

Lillian looked a little embarrassed. "Not well. They've attended my church a few times. It's a small town so everyone sort of knows everyone."

Gretchen thought it was odd that Will and Sara had only attended the new church a few times because they were very active in their church back in Horsham. Then again they had both been acting weird yesterday. Will with all the guns, and Sara with her insane jealousy and short temper.

"Thanks to Martin I think I can help you. If you'll just follow me please."

Gretchen followed her through another small office furnished with a few metal desks, computers, and clutter. Gretchen wondered how anyone could function in this room. Every surface was stacked high with file folders and sheets of lose-leaf paper.

They entered a much larger room that overflowed with junk. The dim bulbs suspended about thirty feet in the air on the open rafters did little to exterminate the darkness. Gretchen fought claustrophobia as she picked her way along the narrow path between the piles of stacked antiques. It was like someone had started in the back of this room and layered one old item on top of another. Even in the dim light Gretchen spotted an old 1940s love seat, a 1950s jukebox, World War II helmets, an Indian motorcycle, and a precarious tower of cardboard boxes that disappeared into the rafters. Gretchen estimated it would probably take a few years to catalog all this stuff, if someone had the inclination, but where would they start?

"This used to be the pressroom in the old days. Somewhere under all this old junk there is an actual printing press. Now we send the paper down to Lancaster to a larger newspaper company that prints the weekly edition for us. The boss loves to collect antiques, hence the mess."

They had traversed the maze about fifty feet when they arrived at the back wall of the room. Lillian opened another door and flipped a light switch.

When Gretchen entered this room her eyes had to adjust to the dim yellow light that was even fainter than in the previous room. The scent of dry pulp paper as it decayed into dust permeated the air. A large, heavy-looking wooden table occupied the center of the room, and metal cabinets with wide, flat drawers covered the entire twenty feet of the far wall. Someone had painted over the small windows above the filing cabinets. Gretchen guessed to block out the sunlight. She still felt claustrophobic, because newspaper bundles were stacked high against the other walls, and only a small path remained clear around the center table.

"This is our morgue. We have a few copies of every issue of the Chronicle that was ever published."

Gretchen shook her head and studied all the bundles. "How do you possibly keep track of them all?"

"It's not that bad. The drawers are labeled with years so we can check for an issue by the publication date. The ones stacked around the walls are just extras. Mr. Grimes, the owner, doesn't like to throw anything away, so things tend to pile up around here."

Lillian started to search through a stack of file folders she picked up off one of the metal cabinets.

Gretchen wondered why the entire place hadn't burned to the ground years ago. Lillian triumphantly held up one of the manila folders that she had retrieved from the stack. "Here it is."

Gretchen looked at the folder. "What is it?"

"Well, like I said, Mr. Darkas came in about a year ago, asking for any old stories about his property. I told him the same thing I told you. He could start with the title search at the courthouse. That's exactly what he did. A few weeks later he returned with a complete list of the previous owners of his property."

"Did you find anything else out about the history of the property?"

"No. Actually, I never got that far, and then Mr. Darkas died. It wasn't too long after he had dropped off the list. I thought the research might come in handy for a human-interest story so I saved it. Sometimes Mr. Grimes will run a story I've researched if he likes it, but I just kind of forgot about it until you asked."

"You never helped Mr. Darkes look up any of the people?"

Lillian's face darkened. "No. He passed away before I talked to him again."

Gretchen wondered about a connection between Martin Darkas' interest in his property and his death. Maybe he, too, had seen spirits in the house. She thought about the murderous soldier and shivered. "I'm looking for someone who would have owned the house around the Civil War."

Lillian's eyes scanned the list. "This guy here — Kiefer Courtland — he owned the house from 1856 to 1865. We can check if he made the papers. We'll start with the papers in 1865 and work our way backwards."

Gretchen was grateful for the help and slumped onto one of the stools at the table. "I don't want to take you away from your work."

Lillian blushed and glanced down at her feet. "Actually I'm kind of ahead. I love my job, so I come in on the weekends to work on different stories; it's sort of like a hobby for me. Maybe I could write a story about your friend's property. I would check with them before I ran it. I wouldn't want to intrude on their privacy."

Sara would love that.

Not wanting to discourage Lillian, Gretchen said, "That's great, I'd appreciate your help."

Lillian opened a large metal drawer and placed a stack of old yellow newspapers on the table.

"Well then, let's get to work," Lillian said as she pulled out a metal stool and sat down at the table.

Gretchen joined her. The newspaper felt brittle as she picked one up and carefully paged through it.

The two women searched through newspapers for the remainder of the morning. The lack of sleep the night before started to wear Gretchen down. Her fingers were coated with dry ink and her lungs felt tight from breathing in stale paper dust. She began to have serious doubts until Lillian gave a shrill, "Yes!"

"You found him?"

Lillian leaned in over the yellowed print. "Here it is, but you're not going to believe this."

Excited by the discovery, Gretchen jumped from her stool and rushed over to Lillian.

"According to this article, Kiefer Courtland was a captain in the 57th Regiment Infantry, Pennsylvania Volunteers. He mustered out in June of 1865 and returned home from the Civil War to Shadows Forge where he discovered his wife Elizabeth in bed with another man…"

"…and He shot them both dead and then turned the gun on himself," Gretchen finished.

"How did you know that?" Lillian asked, astonished.

"Lucky guess," Gretchen said and gave her a weak smile. "Could I make a copy of these things? I need to show them to my friends."

"Sure, do you think you could mention the article? I think it would make a fascinating piece."

"I'd be glad to put in a good word for you." Gretchen promised trying hard not to sound too enthused, because she knew Sara would veto any story about her haunted house.

Lillian gathered up the newspaper, and Gretchen picked up the list of previous owners. Following Lillian to the front office, she glanced down the page. When she read the second name her stomach tightened   senator Howard Freedman. She stopped cold in her tracks. Lillian paused after a few more steps and turned around. "Gretchen, are you OKAY?"

Gretchen could only whisper. "The owner before Martin Darkas..."

Lillian smiled and nodded. "Oh yes, Senator Freedman. He was a state senator. Have you heard of him?"

Gretchen steadied herself against an old desk because she knew that name too well.

CHAPTER **THIRTY-SEVEN**

Gretchen slid behind the wheel, and water trickled down her forehead into her eyes. She wiped it away with the back of her trembling hand and fumbled with the seatbelt and keys. Struggling to stay calm, she slipped the car into drive and pulled away from the curb. A garbage truck swerved to avoid smashing into her. The angry driver sounded his horn, jarring Gretchen. She blinked and glanced into the review mirror.

Get it together Girl.

She eased her foot off the brake and cautiously started down the road, resisting the urge to floor the accelerator. Armed with the information in the folder on the seat next to her, she knew she could convince Will and Sara that they were in real danger. The sooner she revealed her findings to Sara, the sooner they would all be safe.

She shivered as she guided the car along the winding road out of Templeton. More than the chill from soaked clothes caused her hands to tremble. The research had confirmed her worst fears, and now the first storm in months made visibility almost impossible. The road twisted through a dense pine forest with a steep hill on the left and a sheer cliff on the right that dropped thirty or forty feet to a rocky ravine. Gretchen kept her speed low, because of the many blind curves, but it felt like something was trying to deliberately slow her down and keep her away from Will and Sara.

A wave of adrenalin surged through Gretchen's body when she rounded another curve and almost ran down a woman standing in the center of the road. She jerked the wheel to the right and stood on the brakes, trying to avoid the lady. Time slowed, and her stomach clenched when the tires failed to grab the macadam's slick surface. The car hydroplaned off the road and went airborne. It felt like an eternity before the V.W. plowed into a large oak.

The driver's side airbag exploded, stunning Gretchen. Everything was fuzzy, and her left ankle screamed. The small car had collapsed in on itself.

Gretchen shook her head and remembered the woman in the road. She didn't think she had struck her, thank goodness, but wanted to be sure. The seatbelt was jammed, and as she struggled with the clasp, another cold chill washed over her body. The air had turned frigid like someone had opened a freezer door. Something hissed. Gasoline vapors grew stronger inside the car, and Gretchen's composure slipped away. The seatbelt wouldn't budge.

She frantically clawed at the latch. Her lungs grew tight, and she fought to suck in deep breaths as invisible bands constricted her chest. Hot fumes from burning plastic choked her.

She struggled harder against the restraints. Overcome with panic, she almost didn't notice the woman in front of the car. Celeste. At first she stood there, the vision of despair from the dining room, but then her image shifted and she glowed brilliant like a white-hot flame. Long blonde curls blew free in the wind, and the white silk nightgown, saturated from the storm, was plastered against her body. Fire danced in her eyes as she held out her arms toward Gretchen like a demon lover.

Tears streamed down Gretchen's cheeks. She had failed her friends.

The apparition threw her head back. Celeste's inhuman laughter echoed through the forest. Gretchen, wracked with pain, struggling to break free, shivered at the sound and realized that she had underestimated the true power of the evil in the house, and that her friends were doomed.

Thick, acrid smoke seared Gretchen's eyes, and blurred her vision. She lost sight of Celeste, but still heard her spiteful laughter. Wreckage pinned Gretchen's left foot to the floorboards that were growing steadily hotter, and she winced as she tried to move her left leg. A thousand jagged bone shards snarled and bit inside her trapped ankle as she attempted to free herself from crushed metal encasing her foot.

The heat sparked a memory from childhood, when Gretchen had touched her mother's stove, only this time she couldn't pull away. Acrid smoke spasmed her lungs, and white starbursts appeared in her vision as she wheezed for oxygen.

She yanked harder on the restraints, ripping several of her nails off as she frantically clawed at the latch and threw her body against the straps. I'm not ready to die, not like this.

There was a dull click, and she slammed against the steering wheel before she realized the clasp had let go. Hysterical laughter filled her mind, but her lungs had no oxygen to support an outburst. Unbearable heat and jagged pain in her ankle reminded Gretchen that she was still caught in the wreckage. She had to free her foot.

Her body convulsed in another wave of choking spasms. Long shards of glass sliced her hands as she gripped the door frame in a frantic attempt to pull free of the wreck. The cracking of dry twigs filled her ears, and she realized with horror that the sound was the snapping of her own bones as she tore her left ankle free. Struggling to work the door handle with blood-slicked hands, Gretchen saw Celeste's cruel, gleeful face flash in front of the driver's side window.

There was a popping sound and a large whoosh like the pilot light on Gretchen's apartment's gas stove as the car erupted in a ball of flames around her. The last sound she heard was the hellish symphony of the apparition's laughter as the flames licked and caressed her skin, causing it to sizzle and pop in inescapable searing pain. In the white-hot heat, her world went red, then white, then mercifully black.

CHAPTER THIRTY-EIGHT

Will mindlessly steered the car, his thoughts disjointed. He couldn't get past Gretchen's death. Only two days ago she had visited them, but now it seemed like a lifetime had passed. Sara silently stared out the passenger window. Ellie slept in the back. Mesmerized by the monotonous repetition of highway driving, Will jerked to attention when the car started to drift toward the berm. Sara seemed unaware of his momentary lapse.

"The memorial service was nice," Will said, trying to break the ice.

Sara nodded, but remained focused on the passing countryside. "Um."

She had barely spoken to him in the past two days, and he hated the silence. He had loathed the memorial service, but he was attempting safe conversation. In keeping with Gretchen's wishes, Vance and Rupert had displayed a collection of her work in "Picture This" as a memorial service. An urn containing her ashes had perched on a pedestal in front of a horrible abstract self-portrait. Friends, family, and potential clients loitered and drank champagne like they were attending a subdued gallery opening.

Will wondered how many vultures swooped in for a purchase after the event. It irritated him that Vance and Rupert had the nerve to capitalize on Gretchen's death. The whole thing seemed sordid.

Sara absentmindedly twisted a strand of her hair. It was a nervous habit. "Mrs. Himmel looked so devastated."

His stomach tightened at the thought of losing Ellie. "This is horrible for her," he said.

Sara nodded and dropped her hands to her lap. "She's all alone now. I don't know how she'll get along."

He wanted to comfort her, but had no words, nothing that made sense, or could fix this.

Sara's hand wandered to her hair again. "She invited us to stay with her when my show opens."

"Oh." Will flinched when he realized how he sounded, and Sara glared.

"Don't worry. I know you won't be able to tear yourself away from the office."

He frowned; he was making things worse. "I'm sorry. I want to come, but there may be issues with the site. It's only a week after the release. I'm nervous about leaving so soon after the project goes live."

Sara stiffened, but her stare remained on the passing countryside. "I understand. I guess Gretchen should be honored you could find time on a Monday for this. It must be killing you."

"Sara, please don't…"

She turned on him, her voice rising. "Oh, that's right. I'm supposed to understand, it's your career, it's important."

Sweat formed on his forehead, and he reached for the air conditioner. "I feel guilty thinking about work today, but I have responsibilities."

"You also have a family and friends."

He stared silently out the window as he clenched his jaw and tightened his grip on the steering wheel. He kept his gaze on the distant horizon, not wanting to see the hurt in her eyes. Her voice sounded bad enough.

"You've always been dedicated, but lately it's the only thing you live for."

She had a point, but he had to try to justify his actions. "I don't live…" he paused. "If it seems like I don't want to be at home, it's not you, it's the house. Something's not right with the…"

Sara slammed her hand on the dash. "Not this again? I think you're losing it."

Will inhaled deeply, trying to control his temper and remain calm. "I don't know what Gretchen and I saw in the dining room that night, but it scared both of us, and she was convinced it was a ghost."

With her shoulders hunched forward and head bowed, Sara appeared as exhausted as Will felt. "We've been through this before. I know you think the house is old and creepy, but you're letting your imagination run wild."

"It's not just me. I told you about the ghosts or whatever they were that Gretchen saw after we went to bed."

Sara closed her eyes, and a small tear traced her cheek. "You can be a real insensitive jerk. How can you bring this up today, of all times?"

Will knew she was right, but he couldn't let it drop. "Gretchen thought the house might be dangerous, and that guy died on moving day, and Ellie broke her arm."

Sara folded her arms. "Stop, no more. I loved her like a sister, but Gretchen was always flaky. You used to make fun of her all the time. Now you're going to sit there and tell me you believe in ghosts?"

Ellie whimpered in her sleep, and Will realized how loud their voices had grown. Sara turned away, and stared out the passenger window. Another tear ran down her cheek.

They finished the journey in silence. Sara bolted from the car before it came to a complete stop. She entered the house without a backward glance, slamming the door. Ellie stirred in the back seat, and Will told her he had to go to the office. He watched with uncertainty as his daughter ran to the porch and followed her mother inside. He sat for a moment and struggled with the idea of leaving them alone, before he slammed the Civic into drive and smashed the accelerator to the floor. The small car's tires spit stones and left a trail of dust in the driveway.

Chapter THIRTY-NINE

The countryside sailed by, as Will raced his Civic down Old Creek Road like a test driver going for a new land speed record. He had traveled this same route every day since starting at Compu-Gear. This however, was the first time he noticed a small bar on the right, just south of Templeton. The sign called out to him like a flame to a weary moth, and he slammed on the brakes and turned into the gravel parking lot. For a moment he feared the car would roll, but then it skidded to a stop.

Tiny's Roadside Lounge occupied a gray, cement, one-story building about a hundred feet from the lonely country road. Will eased the Civic farther into the almost empty parking lot and stopped next to a rusted, red Mustang. A faded sign hung over the door. Someone had painted the two small windows on the front of the building shut with black paint.

A familiar ache formed behind Will's eyes, and he clutched the steering wheel and watched the sun disappeared over the horizon, the last twinges of day fading into twilight. After a few tortured minutes, he opened the door and climbed out. He inhaled deeply and steadied himself against the car when the world spun for a moment. Praying he wouldn't black out, he fortified himself with another deep breath and approached the bar.

Inside, he paused to allow his eyes to adjust to the subdued lighting. Only the muffled sound emanating from a small TV mounted on the wall behind the bar disturbed the silence. Two men in jeans and threadbare T-shirts played pool in the far corner of the big room, and a heavyset man sat on a stool behind the bar, his attention fixed on the TV.

Will glanced at the empty booths, a few vacant pinball machines, and a couple of old arcade games. The place emitted that dingy, less-than-profitable ambiance. He concluded that he had beat the evening crowd, and that was just fine with him.

He approached the bar and sat down. In the quiet emptiness he felt exposed and on display. The bartender stirred from his stool and ambled down to Will. The massive man labored for breath from the exertion. He rested his thick arms on the bar and leaned forward to support his bulk. "What are you drinking?"

Will's mouth grew wet with anticipation. The bartender eyed him with impatience.

"Bud Light, I'm trying to watch my weight," Will said, and immediately regretted his attempt at humor because of the bartender's size, but the large man didn't seem to notice. He retrieved a frosted mug from the cooler and placed it under the tap. Will watched with growing anticipation as the amber liquid filled the mug. The bartender set the mug down carelessly, spilling beer on the counter.

Will's hands trembled as he fished his wallet from his pocket and placed a five on the counter. "Keep the change."

The bartender grunted, snatched the bill, and wandered back to his perch. His attention locked onto the small screen as soon as his huge frame settled.

Will glanced around the room. The pool players were engrossed in their game and there would be no other witnesses to his tumble off the wagon. He turned back to the mug on the bar and stared at the drink. Sweat ran down the sides of the glass, and the white foam on top started to settle. The odor of stale popcorn and beer permeated the air. Will remained immobile, his body rigid, his eyes fixed on the prize, while the internal battle raged.

For fourteen years he hadn't touched a drop of alcohol, convinced it would cause more bizarre hallucinations. He knew if he started, one drink would lead to another, and another. He had never been able to stop until he was fall down, pass out drunk, and he realized today would be no exception. Today of all days, the pain hurt too much and the need cried out too great. Besides he was already having hallucinations without alcohol, did it really matter? Somewhere deep inside he feared it did.

How has life become such a mess? What the hell am I doing?

He stared at the drink, unsure of what he wanted anymore. His emotions felt scoured raw. Sara had become a stranger   someone he hardly recognized.

He reached for the mug with a trembling hand and knocked it over. The golden liquid spread across the bar and spilled on the floor.

"I'm sorry," he mumbled, stumbling from the stool.

The bartender hoisted himself from his perch.

Will backed away, turning to flee from the overwhelming temptation, his head pounding, and heart racing. He almost bolted for the door, but a wail distracted him. The sound drifted from behind double doors on the left wall. Will hadn't noticed them before. Shuffling forward, the hair on the back of his neck tingled. With a shaking hand he eased the door open.

Men in tuxedoes and women in long black gowns congregated at the far ended of the long narrow room. Their clothing sharply contrasted with the open beams and rough hardwood floors. Will couldn't see their faces because their backs were to him.

Curious, bur wary, Will approached, and they cleared a path for him to enter their inner circle. Will ignored them, his attention focused on the silver casket with chrome handrails.

A tall, thin man served drinks behind the casket, using it as a bar. Will paused to study him because his features seemed familiar. Will couldn't match a name with the face, but felt like he knew him.

The bartender set a frosty mug of beer on the casket, the foam overflowed and slid down the glass onto the coffin lid. "Have a drink Mr. Shepherd. You spilled your last one."

Will backed away from the casket. "I have to go."

The bartender produced a cloth from air like a magician conjuring a handkerchief and started polishing the coffin lid. "Surely, you can have one drink. Who would ever know? What could it possibly hurt? We're all friends here."

The tall man laughed, his yellow teeth flashed like dull pearls.

Will stepped closer and reached for the drink, his internal battle almost lost. It had required every ounce of strength earlier to resist the tempting liquid. Now at this wake for some stranger his resolve weakened. This was all wrong. How could the bartender know his name? He dismissed all the strangeness because every fiber in his body screamed out for the amber liquid.

Pausing, he lowered his eyes to the casket. "Who's in there?"

The bartender shrugged and winked. "It's not you, lad, so drink up."

Laugher erupted around him, and Will felt foolish. He froze caught between his desire for the drink and his curiosity about the casket. On some level he knew he could not have both. He made his decision and lunged for the box, trying to heft the lid. He knocked the mug off the curved top. It disappeared over the back. Before he raised the lid high enough to see inside, the bartender slammed it down. "That's the second drink you've wasted today. You're starting to piss me off."

"I just wanted..." Will began, but before he could finish, an arm draped over his shoulders, and the scent of lilac flooded the air.

A familiar woman's voice said, "My friend needs a fresh drink."

Will tensed as an icy wave flowed from his shoulders to his groin, slowly seeping down his arms and legs.

The tall man behind the casket adjusted his coat and smiled warmly. "Sorry, ma'am, but of course."

Will turned to face Celeste — not the ravaged apparition from the dining room, but an idealized version of the seductress. This young woman glowed with unnatural radiance. Her formfitting white silk gown, long cascading blonde curls, and seductive pouting lips ignited Will's desire.

"You're not real. This can't be real," Will said.

She pressed her body against his, crushing her breasts into him and touching his lips with her finger. "Shhh. Of course I'm real, don't I feel real?" she asked, slipping her arms around his waist.

Remembering their last encounter in the parlor, Will tried to break her iron grip. She squeezed tighter, and he inhaled her intoxicating perfume. His vision clouded, and he relaxed and forgot his panic. No longer afraid, he wanted to lose himself in her arms. Her lips caressed his. He quivered. Although wrong, it felt very right.

His resistance gone, his body reacted on instinct, and he felt himself growing hard. He wanted to take her there on the floor. Nothing else mattered but having her. Before he could act, the casket lid sprung open with a loud shriek, breaking the spell as the charred cadaver inside sprang into a sitting position like a hellish jack-in-the-box, pointing an accusing finger at Will. The hollow stare of its eyeless sockets combined with the skin around the mouth stretched into a permanent black grin, and the smell of charred flesh, all caused Will to cry out as he broke free of Celeste.

"Run," The corpse screeched in Gretchen's voice. "Save yourself, before it's too late."

The lights died and the coffin burst into flames. The crowd fled the inferno. Will saw them clearly for the first time; their deformed skeletal faces, eyeless sockets, and strange smiling jaws all laughing at his terror — a party of the dead.

Turning to escape, he dashed across the room and slammed

through the double doors into the main bar. In his confusion, he tripped over rubble and went down hard onto the scarred wooden floor. Jagged splinters bit into his palms as he tried to break his fall. Ignoring the pain, he scrambled on his hands and knees in the darkness in search of an exit. Unsure of what pursued him, Will crawled toward the brighter light of the night sky visible through the front door. He climbed to his feet and sprinted toward the opening, praying he wouldn't trip over anything else.

He gasped for air outside in the cool night as he raced across the deserted, weed-choked lot to his car. Falling into the driver's seat, he fumbled for his keys and hit the headlights. The beams swept over the front of the burned out, abandoned building, as Will steered the car out of the lot, barely missing the "No Trespassing" signs. This did little to steady his hands, slow his pulse, or quiet the pounding in his head.

Backward glances in the rearview mirror failed to reassure him the whole drive home, and Will stumbled into the foyer still looking over his shoulder. The midnight chime of the grandfather clock surprised him. He was disoriented and unsure how he had spent six hours in the abandoned building when it had only seemed like minutes.

Maybe it had been another blackout. The fall would explain his aching palms. None of that other stuff could've been real. He had probably imagined the whole thing. That made sense. Of course that meant he was losing his mind. Will stared at the damn smiling cherubs on the newel posts and fought back tears.

Chapter FORTY

The next morning Will studied the front of the burned out shell that had once housed Tiny's Roadside Lounge. It was impossible to mistake the place for a functioning business, but he realized that he hadn't made an error. The previous night Tiny's *had* been open for business, at least in his mind.

Will leaned against the car door and massaged the bridge of his nose. His head still felt fuzzy, and he ran a hand over his stubble feeling like a disheveled mess.

The dark doorway beckoned. Will checked his watch and cursed, he was already a half hour late for work. It didn't matter, he had to look inside. He approached the doorway and felt eyes watching him from the dark recesses of the building. He tried to shake it off; convinced it was only residual effects of the previous night's hallucination, but he still slowed his pace, even in daylight Will felt uneasy about the shadows.

The front door leaned against the inner wall, like someone had ripped it from its hinges. Will wondered if he had really entered the building the previous night, or simply imagined the whole thing in the parking lot. Staring into the darkness he saw that the floor, beams, and bar were charred and the ceiling had collapsed in several places. Fire had destroyed Tiny's. From the weeds in the parking lot and the cobwebs covering the charred inner remains, Will guessed that it had happened years, if not decades earlier.

His footsteps echoed off the walls as he picked his way across the main barroom, careful not to break through any weakened floorboards. As he approached the double doors, he told himself it was ridiculous, he didn't need to do this. But he knew that he would doubt himself if he didn't verify that the casket wasn't there.

When he pushed the left double door open, his hand recoiled from the heat. For a second the door felt hot. That was impossible, but he had felt it.

The shadows were deeper inside, and Will wished he had brought a flashlight. The large room appeared empty, but it was impossible to see into the far corners. His heart raced, and he waited for something to spring out of the darkness. When it did, he yelped. The flapping wings pounding the air startled him, and he reflexively covered his head as he ran for the front door. Outside he saw the pigeons that he had disturbed take to the sky.

He broke into hysterical laughter, and couldn't have explained why. At least it was better than the scream that lingered there under the hysteria. Somehow Will realized if he left that scream escape insanity would consume him.

CHAPTER **FORTY-ONE**

Later in his office, Will dropped into his leather desk chair and closed his eyes, ignoring the flashing message light on his phone. It was probably Frank, or one of the business analysts from marketing with another issue that required his immediate attention, he was just not ready to deal with them. In a rare move, he also turned off his cell phone. When the desk phone's *breep* echoed off his office walls, driving shards of pain through his head, he ignored it. Instead he glanced out the window, squinted at the sunlight and longed for his missed morning run.

He thought of Sara alone in the old house. He should have stayed home and comforted her. She had only said three words to him the previous evening. She was shutting him out, or maybe he was shutting down. Probably breaking down — the kind of mental tailspin where they would place him in a room with men in white coats and pretty colored little pills. The thought wrung another small hysterical chuckle from him.

Leaning back in the chair, he closed his eyes again, trying to quiet the pounding behind them and almost leapt to his feet when Frank burst into the office. "Hey buddy, were you asleep?"

"Huh, no, just deep in thought," Will lied and spun around to face Frank as he flopped into the seat on the other side of the desk.

He was surprised when he glanced at the clock in the bottom right corner of his monitor. He had slept for an hour.

Frank fumbled with a folder in his lap, not lifting his eyes. "I was real sorry to hear about your friend."

Frank's unusual solemn sincerity moved Will. He thanked him and tried to change the subject, not wanting to dwell on Gretchen's death. "You have something for me?"

Frank studied the documents in his hands. "I hate to bother you with this today, but I thought you'd want to know."

Frank slid the stack of documents across the desk. Will picked up the report and studied it. He ran his hand over his jaw again, irritated by the stubble. His whole day felt out of kilter.

"It looks like there's a problem with these sequel queries, they are running too slow and timing out." Will stared at Frank, waiting for a response.

"Yeah, that's how it looks to me too. That's why I brought them to you. I don't want to stir up trouble, and if I'm wrong, I'll apologize, but something's hinky with these queries."

Will frowned. This indicated a major setback. "This will cause pages to fail and throw java exceptions if it takes too long to retrieve the data."

"I know how the tables work, I designed them."

Will tried to remain calm and not let the anger creep into his voice. "Did you talk to Steve? He wrote all these queries."

Frank nodded, meeting Will's stare. "I talked to him the beginning of last week. He said he would look into it. I don't know, sometimes I get the idea that he is screwing this stuff up on purpose."

Will closed his eyes, trying to clear the haze. "Just to make me look bad?"

Frank squirmed, obviously uncomfortable with the conversation. "The guy was next in line for lead, and then you showed up out of nowhere and got the job. He was really pissed when he was passed over."

"You think Steve would sabotage the project to get me fired?"

"I'm not accusing him, it's just awfully suspicious."

He raised his hand for Frank to stop.

Office politics; the last thing I need.

Dropping the report on the desk, he leaned back and ran his tongue over his dry lips. He needed a drink, and Diet Coke wasn't going to cut it. "Thanks for the heads up. I appreciate it."

Frank nodded and started to rise. "I just thought you should be aware. I'm sure you're safe as long as Kerrie has C.L.'s ear."

"What?"

Swallowing hard, Frank looked like he wanted to bolt from the room. "I'm sorry. It's just that Kerrie likes you, and C.L. listens to her. I didn't mean anything else by it."

He wondered why Frank was so uncomfortable with the whole conversation. Then it occurred to him that perhaps the rumor mill was in full gear, spewing sordid tales about him and Kerrie. He glanced down at the report and decided he really didn't want to know, what he really wanted was that drink.

CHAPTER FORTY-TWO

Through crusted eyes, Will read the blinking numbers on alarm clock — six a.m. Smashing the *off* button with his fist before it roused Sara only mildly satisfied him. She murmured and stirred, rolled over on her side and settled back into a soft breathing pattern. He dragged himself to a sitting position on the edge of the bed. Blinking several times, he fought the urge to fall back onto the mattress.

Although he had resisted the temptation to drink. His stomach was sour, and he belched up a mouthful of acid. Swallowing, he tried not to gag. The burning in his throat spurred him to pull on his running clothes and quietly slip down the hall to the bathroom, where he gulped cold water.

He shivered when he stepped into the morning chill. It was mid-July, but he could see his breath. His muscles protested as he leaned against the porch column and stretched his calves.

Today he was running out of habit and discipline. He was not in the mood for it and considered turning back, tempted by the thought of his warm bed. But by the time he turned west toward the river he had gone into his zone.

CHAPTER **FORTY-THREE**

A mile and a half to the west Buford Parnnel eased his green Pontiac Bonneville onto the gravel shoulder. His wife, Mary Scarlet, scanned the river with wide, excited eyes. Buford smiled. His hunch had paid off — the small road had led to a scenic overlook that provided a gorgeous view of the Susquehanna River as it snaked south toward Harrisburg.

The morning mist burned off the river, and Buford could see for miles. He felt humbled next to the open expanse.

"Oh, Buford, it's beautiful."

He couldn't stop smiling as he opened the door and climbed from the vehicle. "I reckoned it would be best early. I'll get some great snapshots to show the grandkids."

Mary rounded the car and joined him. "Retirement's even better than we thought."

He nodded and raised his camera. "I always wanted to visit these parts. Stand over yonder. I want to get a shot of you in front of the river. Those train bridges in the distance are fine."

"You and your trains."

He chuckled and looked through the viewfinder. "I can't help it, they're in my blood."

She walked to the edge of the overlook and struck a pose. "Thirty five years working for the railroad, I'd reckon you'd have had enough of them."

He grinned, shook his head, and then snapped a few more photos. Satisfied, he surveyed the countryside for other interesting subjects. He had parked on the edge of a meadow that bordered a dense forest. To the north, the mountains rose to meet the fluffy white clouds. The rise and fall of the land fascinated him, the rolling hills so unlike the flatness back home in Georgia.

Mary slipped her arm around his waist. "The view takes my breath away."

Buford aimed to head north to a coal-mining village he had read about in a brochure. He was about to suggest returning to the car, but something distracted him. "Would you look at that?"

He set off across the field toward the north fence at a brisk pace, the mining village forgotten. He knelt at the first stone and cleared some of the taller weeds away. He could barely read the writing: years of weather had almost erased the letters.

"Tombstones?" Mary asked.

Buford traced the date with his index finger — 1865. "I'll bet he was a soldier in the War Between the States."

Mary knelt in the grass beside him. He knew she was only mildly interested in history, but she always indulged his passions. "Why are they buried here instead of a church cemetery?"

He shrugged and considered for a moment. "There's another stone, maybe it's a family plot. Let's see if there are others."

CHAPTER FORTY-FOUR

Sara leaned against the kitchen counter and stared into her beautiful backyard. The morning sun illuminated patches of grass where the sunbeams pierced the canopy of leaves. It reminded her of an enchanted grove from the fairy tales her aunt had read her when she was a child.

She had heard Will go out the front door for his morning run and wanted to surprise him with breakfast when he returned. She needed him… and missed him. Maybe the gesture might heal some of the hurt between them.

Ellie's greeting startled her. She had been lost in thought, which happened a lot lately. So inspired by the surroundings, she simply lost track of reality. She vowed to pay more attention to Ellie. "What would you like for breakfast? Cereal or french toast sticks?"

Ellie vaulted into a kitchen-chair. "French toast sticks."

Sara was searching the freezer when Ellie asked, "Do you think it's okay for a soldier to kill?"

Puzzled by the question, Sara turned to face Ellie. "Why do you ask?"

"Because I think the Captain is going to kill someone."

She studied her daughter, not sure where this was going. "The Captain?"

"Yes, he's very angry, and Celeste said he is going to blow his top."

Sara only half listened as she pulled the frozen toast sticks from a box and arranged them in the toaster oven. "Honey, the Captain is imaginary, he can't hurt anyone."

When she turned to face her daughter, the little girl's eyes frightened her. They flashed with an intensity she had never noticed before. "No Momma, he's real, and he's very mad."

Maybe Will was right, maybe it was unhealthy for Ellie to be so immersed in her own little world.

"Why?"

"He just left my room. He said he was going to kill some damn Johnny Reb. What's a Johnny Reb?"

Sara frowned and threw the empty toast box into the trash. "Johny Reb was a slang term for a southern soldier in the Civil War. And I don't like you swearing. Where did you hear that kind of language?"

"From the Captain."

Sara grasped Ellie's small hand. "Sweetie, I want you to listen to me. There is no Captain, you made him up."

Ellie nodded, but her eyes lacked conviction.

CHAPTER FORTY-FIVE

Buford took several pictures of the stones, but couldn't get the details. He wished he had some tissue paper and charcoal to make a rubbing. The fellas back home would be very interested in these. He and several of his buddies were amateur historians fascinated with the War Between the States, and Gettysburg had been the focal point of his entire vacation.

He stood to try another angle, but froze when a man stepped out of the forest dressed in what appeared to be an authentic civil war uniform. The man carried a rifle with a fixed bayonet. Buford chuckled; this would be a real prize to show the boys back home. Bobby Spencer would be green with envy when he saw the photos.

Buford started across the field toward the soldier. "That's quite an outfit."

"You shouldn't have come here, Johnny Reb."

Buford laughed good naturedly and raised his camera. "I just want a couple of shots."

The soldier raised his rifle and charged. The swiftness of the man's attack caught Buford off guard. The impact knocked him back a step and forced the air from his lungs. The pain of the cut only beginning to register when the soldier thrust again, and a sharp jab caught Buford in his left ribs. The blade on the end of the rifle came away wet and dark. The heat spread across his chest, burning and squeezing. His balls tightened and his legs buckled. Suddenly he couldn't breathe. Buford dropped the camera, hearing the casing crack as it hit a large stone at his feet.

He touched his chest, searching for the wound. But his gaze was fixed on the warrior whose skin turned gray and sloughed away from the bones. The face deteriorated into a horrible mask of rotted flesh, earth, and darkened cavities where piece of the skull had been shattered.

Buford collapsed to his knees, clutched his throat, and wheezed. Lights danced in front of his eyes, and the rag clad specter's curses flooded his ears.

Mary realized something was wrong when Buford plummeted to his knees and grabbed his throat. "Buford," she called across the field.

He didn't answer, instead he fell face down into the field.

She steadied herself on the tombstone as she struggled to her feet. Stomach clenching, she stumbled toward him and lost one of her shoes. Her hands trembled, and, her heart pounded. Frantic, she dropped to her knees in the tall grass next to him. She struggled to roll him over on his back and shrieked when she saw his ashen face.

His eyes stared at nothing.

CHAPTER **FORTY-SIX**

By the time Will reached the river, he felt great. Lost in the rhythm of his stride, muscles loose, he decided to continue farther north along the edge of his property.

A shriek jarred him out of his runner's high, and he spotted the woman kneeling in the field.

"No Buford, don't leave me, please?"

She clutched the prone figure of an elderly man whose head rested in her lap.

He called to her as he ran toward her, not wanting to startle her. "Ma'am, can I help?"

She looked up at him through tear soaked eyes. "He collapsed, I don't know what happened." Then she burst into tears.

Will knelt and gently rested the man's head on the ground. He fished his cell phone from his pocket and handed it to the woman, forcing it into her hands. "Dial 911."

Will didn't like the color in the man's face, and he couldn't locate a pulse. There was no physical sign of trauma. Was it a heart attack, a stroke? Beeps sounded as the woman jabbed numbers on the keypad. Will inhaled and positioned himself over the man. He had taken a CPR course in college, but hell that felt like ancient history, and he had never performed it on a living person. Trying to remain calm, he placed the heel of his right hand over the notch where the man's ribs met his breastbone. He locked his hands and elbows and started the steady up and down motion.

The woman frantically explained the situation to the emergency operator on the line.

"We're located along the river, north of Harrisburg. I'm not sure of the address."

Her eyes pleaded.

Will kept pumping, and shouted. "Tell them we're on Northridge pike, just off Old Creek Road."

She repeated the location into the phone, adding. "Please hurry."

CHAPTER **FORTY-SEVEN**

By the time the ambulance arrived, Will's shoulders and arms ached and his chest felt like it was going to explode. One of the paramedics relieved him, and he struggled to his feet and staggered away from the fallen man, certain he was dead. Will couldn't face the woman. Her sobs echoed in his ears, and he felt powerless. A beefy state trooper that Will remembered from moving day tried to calm the hysterical woman. The officer vaguely resembled a younger, version of Muhammad Ali.

Will drifted away from the gathering and surveyed the field. It was his first glimpse of this section of his property. He had a general idea of the entire layout, and planned to explore all twenty acres when he had the time.

The sound of the ambulance door closing startled him from his thoughts. The trooper approached. "Thanks for your assistance, Mr. Shepherd."

"Sure, no problem. Officer Wilson, right?"

The tall man nodded.

Will glanced at the woman. "Do you think she'll be all right?"

"It's always hard."

They both watched her climb into the Pontiac with another officer. "You didn't know the Parnnels?"

Will explained how he had discovered them on his morning run. "I guess they stopped to look at the river."

Officer Wilson gestured to the tombstones along the fence. "They were examining those stones when he had the heart attack."

Will was halfway to the fence before he realized he was moving. "I didn't know anyone was buried here."

The trooper followed, keeping pace with him. "Old family plot, I suppose."

When Will knelt in front of the grave markers, the dates sent a shiver down his spine — July 1865 — both the man and woman had died on the same day, and it coincided with the end of the Civil War. The man could have been a returning soldier.

Will tried to commit the name Kiefer Courtland to memory. He wanted to research him. Rising to his feet he wiped the dirt from his knees. "It's been crazy. Two people have died on our property since we moved in, and now a graveyard in the back twenty. I'm starting to think this place is cursed."

He was half kidding, but there was something in the officer's face Will couldn't read. Some hesitation, as if he wasn't amused. Will wondered what the trooper knew that he didn't.

CHAPTER **FORTY-EIGHT**

That evening when Will returned home from work, he was surprised to find Sara waiting at the front door. She greeted him with a hug. "Are you okay?"

Before he could answer she kissed him long and hard. When she paused to catch her breath, he attempted a smile. "I'm fine."

She hugged him tighter. "The State Police called. An officer Wilson, he wanted to let you know that the woman from Georgia's son is coming to get her. Why didn't you tell me what happened this morning? Officer Wilson said you tried to save a man's life."

Will held her close, enjoying her soft body pressed against his, and the scent of her vanilla shampoo.

"I didn't even hear you come back this morning, or leave for work."

Will touched her cheek and traced her jaw line with his index finger. "You were in the studio hard at work. I didn't want to interrupt. I guess I just needed some time to kind of work out what happened."

She stepped back and took his hand. "I have dinner waiting."

Will resisted when she started for the kitchen. "Wait, I want to show you something."

He retrieved his black leather computer bag from the floor. "I found something remarkable today. There are two people buried up on the hill in the field. Kiefer Courtland and his wife Elizabeth, and they died on the same day in July of 1865."

The corner's of her lips dropped and her eyes narrowed. "What are you talking about?"

"This is the proof that Gretchen was right. I did searches online and discovered that this guy was a Captain in the 57th Regiment Infantry of Pennsylvania Volunteers. He served at Chancellorsville and Gettysburg."

He retrieved the folder with the printouts and handed it to her. Sara opened the folder and examined the pages. "I know you're under a lot of stress, Honey, but I think you need to get a grip."

"I'm fine." Will started and then stopped as he stared at the blank pages in her hands. He grabbed at the folder knocking the contents to the floor. "No, that can't be. I saw them."

He couldn't breathe; it felt as if all the oxygen had leaked out of the room. Will fell to his knees and rummaged through the stack of blank papers. He rifled through the black bag searching for the documents. He had printed them and placed them in the folder earlier at work. The bag had rested on the floor under his desk all afternoon, but Will had spent most of that time at Frank's cube helping him with a database issue. Someone could have taken the papers in his absence, but who would want to, and why?

Sara touched his shoulder, and he jumped. "Come eat. It's all right."

"No, no it's not."

He staggered to his feet and stumbled up the stairs. "I can prove it. I can print them again."

"Will?"

He didn't stop. He had to show her his proof. He fell into his desk chair and fired up the computer without turning on the light in his office. He sat there in the dark room illuminated by screen's faint light as the web browser loaded. He tried to retrace his steps, but when he found the link to the regiment page and clicked it, the message — page cannot be found, displayed on the screen.

A cold draft caressed the back of his neck. He looked up to see the open attic door and a demented laugh rose from somewhere deep inside his chest.

CHAPTER FORTY-NINE

A few hours later, the warm night air rustled the leaves and tall grass as Will climbed from his car and lit the flashlight. He had to know for sure. All through dinner Sara had watched him, tense and wary, as if she expected him to go crazy at any moment. After the meal, he told her he needed to run out for a few things. She nodded, but he could see the coolness in her eyes. They were losing each other, and he didn't know how to hold on to her.

The summer had been the driest in years, but Will felt a storm coming as he crossed the grassy field. The air carried an electrical charge. It crackled with anticipation. He shivered as he played his beam across the area where he had examined the stones that morning. His heart sank when he did not see them.

Was it possible he had imagined the whole thing? More hysterical laughter built in his chest when he spotted the grave markers. In his haste he had walked too far east. Quickly running to them, he fell to his knees and read the inscriptions. They were just as he remembered. It was a small comfort, but at least *they* were real.

Kneeling in the dark, he didn't know whether to laugh or cry. He needed answers. His head throbbed again, and his eyes ached. This was ridiculous; he was swamped at work, he didn't have the time for this. The thought made him laugh to himself. The idea that he would simply put some supernatural phenomenon on hold because he was too busy at work seemed ludicrous. But that was his life;

everything came after the career, including this.

By the time Will returned home, the wind had picked up, and raindrops splattered around him as he hurried to the porch. Inside the dark foyer, he listened to the storm building outside and a sense of foreboding washed over him. He felt a power growing in the house. He couldn't explain it. He squirmed in insanity's clutches. Something grew in the air around him. He climbed the stairs, acutely aware of the old structure's creeks and groans.

Sara was already asleep, so he quietly gathered his clothes, careful not to disturb her. A hot shower might release his tension. Inside the claw foot tub with the shower curtain drawn around him, he let the water's hot stream pound his back. He hated this tub and the way the plastic curtain closed in on all sides, and how it felt if it touched his skin.

Steam filled the air, and the stress drained off his body with the hot water. He closed his eyes and tried to force everything from his mind. It didn't work. His usually ordered thoughts were scattered in a thousand directions. He would have to make time to relocate that information about Kiefer Courtland... prove to Sara that Gretchen had seen something real.

He stepped on the cloth mat in the center of the small room and pulled one of the large, white, heavyweight towels from the rack on the wall. As he dried off, the room's temperature plummeted. He shivered and goosebumps formed on his arms. He could see his breath. He gazed at the steam-fogged mirror where an invisible finger drew letters. It slowly spelled GET OUT.

The room spun, Will clutched the sink and sank to his knees, his head lowered, he squeezed his eyes closed, trying to ward off the vertigo. Bright starbursts of light bloomed behind his eyelids. He feared looking in the mirror, not sure what he would see.

As quickly as it started, the sensation vanished. Will opened his eyes surprised to see three small feathers resting in the sink. He blinked, glanced at the steam-covered mirror and then back down at the sink. The feathers still rested there.

He carefully picked up one of the brown and black sparrow feathers and examined it. The feather turned to dust and slipped through his fingers. Where the other two had rested there was only powder. Was Small Sparrow trying to warn him?

Did she even exist?

CHAPTER FIFTY

Will straightened, rolled his shoulders, and stretched, trying to loosen his lower back. The blisters from the shovel handle on his fingers and palms burned. He examined the four holes he had dug several feet apart scattered across his back yard. Sweat coated his forehead and back.

Nothing. You really didn't expect to find anything did you?

His plan had seemed logical several hours earlier when he had arrived home from work and started digging. If the Native American village had existed in this clearing then he should find some remnants   broken pottery, perhaps a grave, there should be over a hundred of them if his vision had been real. Now as he stood sweating in the fading daylight, he had serious doubts.

He had found no sign of the missing printouts at work that morning and could not relocate the website. It was July 18th and with the release deadline only a week away, Will couldn't afford to lose focus at work, but he had to make this last ditch effort to prove he was not losing his mind.

He stood thinking as long shadows slithered across the lawn and the sun disappeared over the horizon. He scanned the back yard and wondered about the feasibility of his plan. He could dig a thousand holes and never discover anything. He sighed, walked a few feet, and inserted the shovel blade into the dry earth.

"Planting something?"

Will jumped. "Huh?"

It seemed like Harry had materialized behind him. He turned to see him holding a long wooden box.

"Sorry."

Will wiped his hands on his pants. "That's okay. Just didn't hear you coming."

Harry smiled and handed Will the planter. "Thought Sara might like it for the front porch."

Will examined the skillfully crafted dovetail corners on the window box.

Harry nodded toward the holes. "Doing a little planting of your own?"

Will felt heat rise in his cheeks. He had no explanation. It had never occurred to him that he would have to explain his actions with Sara locked away in her studio, and Ellie playing in her room.

"Something like that. Nice work on the planter. Sara will love it."

He handed the box back to Harry. The old man smiled, but his scrutiny made Will uncomfortable. He felt like a small child caught stealing cookies.

He repositioned the shovel. "Remember when I asked you about Native Americans? I had this idea that I might find some evidence of a settlement."

This sounded ridiculous when he said it out loud and he immediately regretted saying it. He wished he could pull the words out of the air and take them all back.

But Harry didn't laugh. Instead he scanned the yard with a thoughtful expression on his face. He sat the box on the ground and asked Will to follow him as he headed for the shed.

Inside, Harry rooted through a pile of old stuff the estate had left behind, pulling from it a large circle constructed out of branches. Strings were strung across the three-foot circle in intersecting patterns. There were beads and feathers wove into the design.

"What is it?"

Harry held it closer to the light for Will to get a better view. "It's a dream catcher. You're not the first person to ask me about Indians living around here. Martin asked me the same thing a few years back. He was obsessed with them."

The familiar chill tickled Will's spine. "Indians?"

"Yeah, he started reading everything he could find on them."

"Do you know why?"

"Nah, but he found an article about a Native American lady out west that was producing these dream catchers. They're based on a legend about an old woman who found a spider's web in her house when she was cleaning. She thought it was so beautiful that she did-n't kill the spider or destroy the web. In gratitude the spider taught her how to make these. They're supposed to catch all the bad dreams, only allowing the good ones in."

Will studied the object, it was old and worn from the elements; the strings were faded and frayed. "Did Martin have bad dreams?"

"Not that he ever said, but I wonder. He bought six of these and I helped him hang them in the gables."

Will didn't like the expression that crossed Harry's face like a shadow. He wasn't sure if it was pity or contempt.

CHAPTER **FIFTY-ONE**

Harry to the rescue again.

Will savored a piece of Sara's tender roast. It was the first sit-down meal they shared as a family in over a week. Sara insisted that Harry stay for dinner when he presented her with the planter. She then threw herself into preparing a pork roast, rice pilaf, salad, and gravy. It was one of Will's favorites. They relaxed around the dining room table enjoying the meal. Sara seemed almost embarrassed by Harry's praise for her cooking.

Will enjoyed the small talk, but caught himself glancing toward the parlor throughout the meal, afraid Celeste's ghost would appear and ruin the evening.

After dinner the adults adjourned to the front porch with tall glasses of ice tea. They lounged in the old wicker rockers, and Will wondered if this is how Harry and Martin had spent many of their evenings.

Harry and Sara compared gardening notes.

"You have to mix in some cow shi… uh, manure." Harry said, "If you want tall healthy plants. They grow taller to get away from the smell."

Sara laughed.

What a wonderful sound.

It felt like ages since he had heard it.

He listened quietly, but his mind was speeding like freight train. He hadn't found proof of the settlement, but he had learned something that might be important. Martin had been obsessed with Native Americans. Maybe Martin had experienced the same nightmares or delusions that Will had. It would certainly explain why he wanted a dream catcher.

Harry rose. "I want to thank you young people for a wonderful evening."

He turned to Will. "You look like you're going to nod off. I better let you folks get some sleep."

Sara pecked Harry on the cheek. "Thank you for the planter. I love it."

"You're going to make an old man blush."

Will slipped his arm around Sara as they watched Harry stepped off the porch and head for the path to his own home.

When they reached their bedroom they fell into each other's arms. It was the first time since Gretchen's death that Will felt like the wall of isolation was cracking a little. Peeling off one another's clothes they took their time, slow and gentle. Touching her sent ripples of excitement through him, and she giggled, almost giddy as he traced her contours with his hands. Naked, he eased her down onto the bed. When she guided him into her, he felt complete. They moved together in cherished familiarity, until they climaxed in unison. Afterwards, they held each other in the moonlight with only a sheet covering them. For the first time in recent memory Will felt relaxed and safe.

CHAPTER **FIFTY-TWO**

The spring of 1948 was a tough time for Harry. The crops grew slowly. Both his brothers moved off the farm, and his father passed away. Harry dreamed of moving away himself, but now with a bride and a mother to support, he felt tied to the farm more than ever.

"Why do you have to go over there?" Martha said.

Harry scrubbed his hands with the thick bar of soap and stared out the kitchen window at the newly plowed field. "Because he asked me to come. The man's all alone."

His young wife stood with her hands on her hips. He glanced at Martha and tried not to smile at what she considered her best withering scowl.

"I don't like it. They say he's crazy," Martha said.

His Ma dumped another small basket of sugar peas on the kitchen table. "She's right, Harry. Your father never thought much of the man."

Harry grabbed a tea towel from the peg on the side of the cabinet and dried his hands. "I know Pop didn't like him, and he was a good judge of character, but the man's all alone over there in that big house since Jonathan moved to Philadelphia."

Martha grabbed the towel from Harry and folded it neatly and returned it to the rack. "They say the kitchen fire that killed his wife drove him over the edge."

Harry finished wiping his hands dry on his bib overalls. "He was never that nice."

Martha harrumphed and folded her arms across her chest. "And you want to go talk to him?"

He gave her a quick hug and a peck on the cheek. "Don't worry. I'll just go see what he wants. I won't be too long. I haven't spoken to the fella in years."

Martha frowned and shook her head. "Now is no time to start."

His Ma continued to snap sugar peas. "That was a horrible day. Lord knows that poor woman had a hard life living with that man. To die that way was just awful."

Martha joined his Ma at the table. "They had a cook and a maid, didn't they? Why was she cooking?"

"They did when he was a senator. She never lifted a finger in the kitchen then, I'm sure, but I think things were pretty hard on them the last few years after he was voted out."

Harry shook his head as he stepped into the midday sun. Living with those two was entertaining. He decided they would still be chattering about the crazy old ex-senator when he returned. Harry dismissed most of the gossip, but he found himself slowing down as he crossed the field. It was true that he hadn't spoken to Mr. Freedman in years, and probably not more than a few words in his whole life.

Harry had always been afraid of the old coot and with good reason, but that was when he was a kid. It was ridiculous for him to still be frightened. He caught himself holding his breath as he crossed the front yard and approached the double doors.

As Harry stared at the frosted glass windows inset in the doors, he was transported back to a night twenty-three years earlier. Sweat beaded on his forehead, and he considered turning and fleeing across the field like he had as a terrified boy.

Summoning his courage he reached out to knock. His hand never hit the wood. The door slowly swung open. He swallowed. The latch must not have caught, allowing the slight breeze to move the door. Harry smiled at his runaway nerves, but it was dark in the foyer and he hesitated. "Hello?"

Even in the warm still midday air he felt a chill. "Hello? Anyone here?"

Nothing. The silence was unbearable. The old man must have forgot he had asked Harry to come. That was fine with Harry. Now he could go home and forget the whole thing. After all, he had stopped by. It wasn't his fault if the old guy was asleep, or maybe worse.

Soft music played in the parlor. It was an old song Harry thought he recognized, but he couldn't remember the title. Not sure why, he stepped into the shadows of the foyer, and closed the door.

"Hello, Senator. Are you there?"

The curtains were drawn in the parlor, and he paused to let his eyes adjust to the darkness. The scent of mildew clung in the air, and Harry's skin felt clammy.

"You took your time getting over here."

Harry jumped. He hadn't noticed the old man sitting in the high-backed wing chair by the window. The man shifted in his seat and lit a small oil lamp on the table next to him. Harry thought it was odd to be inside such a dark room on a bright sunny day.

With a trembling hand the old man set the box of matches gently on the table. "I told you I needed to talk to you. It's important."

The soft light exaggerated the senator's hawk-like nose. His eyes were wide and shiny, thin wisps of white hair puffed out in all directions.

Harry glanced at the old couch, but decided he would stand. "I had to finish my plowing. I told you that at the line fence this morning."

The old man's head bobbed more wildly and he cackled. "Plow and plant, sow and reap, young Master Weaver. You will soon reap what we have sown."

His high voice, brittle with age, cracked like glass, and Harry was not amused by the old man's humor. "I don't know what you're talking about."

The senator leaned forward in his chair. His wide grin revealed large toothless gaps. "Of course you do. Sow and reap. Reap and sow. The harvest is soon upon us."

His impatience growing, Harry turned to leave. "I have chores waiting."

The old man's voice rose to almost a shout. "You know what I'm saying. I saw you that night."

Harry froze.

Pointing his long, shaky index finger at Harry, the senator almost growled. "All those years ago. You knew."

Turning back to the old man, Harry clenched his fists at his side. "I didn't know anything. I didn't see anything."

The large gaping grin sent a chill down Harry's back. "Sure you did. Reap and sow, Harry Weaver, sow and reap."

Harry stepped closer and felt the heat rising on his face. "Listen,

I didn't know anything. I was just a kid, and you're not making any sense, old man."

The gun appeared as if by magic in the senator's trembling right hand. "Stay back."

It was a large revolver, like something out of the old west. Hands up, palms open, Harry backed away. "Why don't I just take that from you before someone gets hurt?"

The old man swung his bobbling head back and forth, his eyes darting about the room. "I just wanted to warn you. She's back, and she wants revenge."

Harry swallowed. "That can't be. She'd be in her…"

"She's coming for me, and she'll get you too."

A spasm twisted Harry's guts, and grew more intense as the old man swung the gun around in a wide arc. Facing the business end of the large revolver was bad enough, but the man wielding the gun was off his hinges.

Harry backed toward the foyer, hoping the old man's finger wouldn't twitch on the trigger. "Remember Harry, I warned you. She's here, and she's coming for you soon."

Harry ran out the front door and across the lawn. He felt like the young child who had fled that house years ago, it was only when he reached his line fence that he slowed down. "Foolish nonsense," he muttered to himself just before he heard a gunshot.

CHAPTER **FIFTY-THREE**

The fuel gauge indicated half a tank, but the Civic chugged a few times and stalled at the stop sign. Will slammed his fist against the steering wheel. "Now what?"

The lights and radio went dead, and nothing happened when he turned the key.

The last edge of the sun disappeared beyond the horizon and the surrounding countryside grew menacing in the last vestiges of light.

The trees seemed twisted and the shadows crawled with unseen creatures. It unnerved him, Will cursed his luck.

Going through the motions only because it seemed like the right thing to do, he found a flashlight in the glove box and pulled the hood release, undid his seatbelt, and climbed from the vehicle. His mechanical ability paled in comparison to his carpentry skills, which meant that, other than driving a car, he had no idea how one worked.

I'm screwed.

He found the latch and lifted the hood. The engine compartment revealed nothing in the dim beam provided by the flashlight. It looked like all the hoses and wires were still connected   at least as far as he could see. Since the lights and radio didn't work he suspected a problem with the battery. That was as far as his mind could travel down the path to a solution. Will understood computers, but he had no idea how to troubleshoot an automotive problem. He was lost.

He fished his cell phone from his pocket and uttered another curse. No signal.

Sara had to live in the frickin' country.

He leaned against the fender and shoved the phone back into his pocket, his frustration growing. He was exhausted and irritable. The normally dependable Civic now seemed like a huge paperweight.

Will read the street signs — Old Creek and Pine roads. The heat drained from his body. It was the same intersection where he had seen the boy "die" on moving day. Maybe it was a coincidence; after all he drove this road every day on his way to work. He was stranded a mile-and-a-half down the road from home, not much of a walk, *but it had to be this spot*. Will scanned the area. No houses in sight. Deeping shadows crept away from the trees, swallowing the remaining daylight. He'd have to hoof it home. Maybe he could get Harry to come help him with the car, or he could call Triple A. Either way, the sooner he was away from this intersection, the better he would feel.

Will shifted the car into neutral and tried to push it onto the berm. There was a slight incline, but he was able to guide it into the grass on the edge of the road.

The other car's engine growled across the valley before he saw the lights. The possibility of avoiding an evening hike was appealing. It wasn't that far, but after twelve hours at the office, he was exhausted and anxious to get away from this intersection. Will slammed his door and hit the automatic lock on the key chain. When he turned to face the approaching car he had to shield his eyes from the bright headlights' glare.

Turning away from their brightness, Will saw the boy on the bicycle. He sucked in air and held his breath. The boy raced toward the intersection straight toward the oncoming headlights from Will's left.

Neither slowed, and Will realized he had to warn them. The seconds seemed to expand into hours. He ran toward the intersection, frantically waving his arms. The boy didn't see him, or ignored him and continued full speed into the intersection. The large vehicle, a mid-seventies station wagon, plowed into the boy. The bike pin wheeled across the road and the boy soared through the air, his arms and legs flailing as if he could fly. The left fender clipped Will, spun him in a circle and hurtled him across the road. He lost sight of the boy as he slammed to the hard road.

The driver didn't slow down, and sparks sprayed from beneath the wagon, as it ran over the bike. Will imagined the vehicle erupting into a giant fireball. He read the license plate as the green Chevy wagon sped away into the darkness.

The oddly contorted child sprawled on the road, just a few feet away, staring into the sky with unseeing eyes. Will climbed to his feet. It hurt to breathe. Pain stabbed through his ribs; his right hip throbbed where the car had clipped him. He stumbled toward the boy's lifeless body. He collapsed to his knees next to the boy, who appeared to be about the same age as Ellie. It was like knives jamming into his kneecaps when they hit the pavement. His anguished cry echoed through the trees when he realized the child was beyond help.

Tears ran down his cheeks as he closed the boy's eyelids. It was too horrible to gaze into those empty orbs. Will's head throbbed. He swallowed, and closed his own eyes for a moment to stop the spinning.

He cringed when he thought about lifting the dead child in his arms, he didn't want the lifeless body against his, but knew he had to move the child out of the intersection. He didn't want to touch the body, but couldn't leave it there for another unsuspecting motorist to hit. Images of bloated deer by the highway flashed in his mind, the ones who were repeatedly hit until they were only bloody pulp splattered across the freeway.

Gently, Will slid his arms under the boy's neck and knees. He winced when he felt the moisture at the base of the skull. The limp body was awkward, and he almost dropped it as he tried to stand. Will struggled to balance the weight and heard another motor approaching.

He knew he had to act fast, they were in the middle of the intersection, and the car approached from the same direction the station wagon had. Will took one step and the boy opened his eyes and screamed. "You have to help me."

The boy's eyes were wide, his pupils large and dark. His breath putrid. Will tried not to gag. Stunned by the sudden movement, he froze, dropping the boy. The body hit the road with a wet slap.

Will only had time to turn and see the approaching headlights. He stumbled backward, lost his balance. Mind shattering pain halted the freefall.

CHAPTER FIFTY-FOUR

When the darkness cleared, Will flinched at the bright light.

A man's voice said, "Just take it easy."

Will swallowed and opened his eyes. "Where am I? What happened?"

"You're en route to St. Vincent's hospital."

Will tried to sit up, but pain stabbed his right side and he collapsed back on the gurney. The young man by his side touched his shoulder. "Hey, relax, don't try to move."

He was in an ambulance. Pressure intensified on his left arm as a blood pressure cuff inflated. The man he assumed was an EMT listened to his chest with a stethoscope. "Any pain, any trouble breathing?"

Will inhaled and a sharp jag stabbed through the right side of his chest. "Yeah, sharp pain."

The EMT jotted something on a clipboard. "We're almost there. I need to take down your personal information."

The EMT ran through a series of questions, Will answered without really thinking — name, birth date, etc., all the information that defined who Will was to the world. Trying not to move or breathe too deeply, he gazed out the back window of the ambulance into the void of blackness and wondered how this had happened. The motion of the ambulance lulled him into a stupor, and he was only vaguely aware when they lifted his stretcher from the ambulance and wheeled him through large glass double doors.

A deep voice said, "Get him to room eleven."

Closing his eyes, he tried to will himself awake from this nightmare, but it didn't work. When the gurney stopped, the EMT from the ambulance ask if Will could slide over onto an examination table. He found he was able to move with only a little stiffness. A nurse with a warm smile and a blonde ponytail raised the examination table so he could sit up slightly. "Let me help you with your shirt."

She opened the buttons and helped Will slip out of it. Another nurse slipped a blood pressure cuff over his left arm. She had dull yellow teeth when she smiled. The blonde started taping electrodes to his chest. "We need to get an EKG, he's had chest pain. Any trouble breathing now?"

Will gasped, but not because of her question. Standing in the doorway to the emergency room was the little boy from the accident. The child's head was cocked at an impossible angle, bent almost 90 degrees and the left side of his body was twisted in an unnatural way, like a cat stretching its spine. Blood pooled in a spreading puddle around the child's feet. His eyes were dilated and completely black, no whites showed. "Help me, pleaded through broken teeth."

The nurses both grabbed Will's shoulders to restrain him as he struggled to escape his bed. "You have to help the boy."

Yellow Teeth followed his stare and turned quickly back. "There's no one there."

Will glanced at her, momentarily distracted. Her discolored teeth almost glowed in the harsh light of the emergency room. When he looked again the boy was gone. Ponytail pulled a curtain blocking the view to the outer room. "Let's give you a little privacy."

Exhausted, Will eased back into the reclining position and tried to convince himself he hadn't seen the boy at all. His breath came easier, and the pain faded on his right side. Ponytail was swabbing the inside of his right elbow. "We need to put in an IV and draw a little blood, there will be a slight prick."

Will looked away when the jab came. It was quick and only burned for a second. He wasn't particularly squeamish about his own blood, but he didn't watch them draw it just the same.

Yellow Teeth wheeled in a machine and plugged it to the monitor behind the examination bed. She studied it for a few minutes, holding up a long coil of paper. "EKG is fine."

Will sighed and closed his eyes, only stirring slightly when Ponytail slipped an oxygen tube over his head and inserted the nasal cannula into his nose. He looked at her, but before he could ask, she responded. "Standard procedure, Mr. Shepherd."

Will nodded, he let go and drifted into a light sleep, until he was disturbed by the glare of another light. The illumination vanished; someone had been shining a small penlight into his eyes. He tried to sit up. "Just take it easy," the woman said.

Will blinked several times, forgetting where he was and glanced around. A dark haired woman in a white lab coat extended her hand. "I'm Doctor Harris. How are you feeling? I understand you had some chest pain?"

Thinking about it for a moment, Will realized the pain was gone. "I feel fine now."

Doctor Harris jotted something down on the chart. Will wondered what was happening, and for a moment he considered his own mortality — the possibility that this might be the night he died.

Smiling, the doctor lowered the chart, but seemed practiced at holding it so that he couldn't get a glimpse. She leaned in and told him to take a deep breath and listened to his chest, then asked him to sit forward. Will eased forward in the bed. It was hard to move, not because of pain, but from the encumbrance of wires and tubes. The stethoscope was cold against his back.

His mouth felt like he had swallowed a large cotton ball. "How did I get here?"

Doctor Harris made a note in a chart. "A state trooper discovered you collapsed along the road and called for an ambulance."

Will tried again to sit up. "What about the boy?"

The Doctor didn't stop him this time. "Boy? No one mentioned a child."

Will's head felt thick. "He was hit by a car. That's why I was in the intersection."

Deciding he wasn't ready to sit up, Will eased back down. The world was still a little fuzzy.

Doctor Harris added a few more lines to the chart. "I want you to relax. You took a blow to the back of your head, and there is quite a nasty bruise. You don't have a concussion, but I'm going to run a few tests. Because of the chest pain I would like to run another EKG and blood test in four hours just to be sure you didn't have a heart attack. I'll also do a chest x-ray. We don't have to admit you, we can handle all this from the ER."

Nodding, Will closed his eyes. "What about the boy?"

Doctor Harris cleared her throat. "I'll ask the officer about the child."

Will decided to just go with it for the moment, even though he didn't have time for any of this. It was a major inconvenience, but the thickness in his mind overwhelmed him, and he drifted in and out of sleep, and vaguely remembered lying on a table and some sort of scan inside a large tube, possibly a MRI. He also remembered Sara, Ellie, and Harry by his bed.

"Will, we're here honey." Sara said, and he felt her hand on his.

He nodded then floated back into darkness. When he woke again, he wanted to dismiss the whole thing as a dream, but he was still in the ER. Bright sunlight streamed in through tall double doors in the outer room. He rubbed his eyes, clearing away particles of crust and felt like he had slept for a long time. Expecting a lot of pain, he was surprised he was only a little stiff. His ribs and hip felt fine. He examined his side and found no bruises.

Will was pondering this when Doctor Harris entered the room. "Good morning, Mr. Shepherd."

"It's Will, and good morning to you. So what's the word, Doc? I feel fine."

Picking up the chart and studying it, the doctor circled to the front of the bed. "Your blood work's fine and the scans all came back normal. No sign of lesions or tumors. No heart problems. I can't find a physical explanation for why you collapsed last night."

Will was not sure if this was good news or bad. "I was hit by a car."

The doctor frowned, checked the chart, and shook her head. "There was no sign of impact."

Confused, Will felt his ribs, there was no pain; modesty stopped him from lifting his hospital gown to check again for bruises. "What about the boy?"

The doctor crossed her arms and pursed her lips. "I asked the officer who found you. There was no child."

Will tried to hide his surprise. "So when they found me I was alone?"

The doctor nodded and shinned her penlight into his eyes. "Yes, you apparently collapsed in the middle of the intersection. Have you experienced any other blackouts or seizures?"

Will's mind raced in a thousand directions and he answered quickly. "No."

"Shortness of breath, chest pains?"

Shaking his head, he looked down at all the electrodes attached to his chest. "No."

She nodded again and made a note on the chart. "You were exhausted. You slept through the night without stirring. Have you been under a lot of stress?"

After a moment's consideration, Will nodded. "I'm in charge of a huge project, so there is plenty of stress. Over the past few weeks, I've been dizzy a few times, and maybe I had a blackout, but I feel fine. Friday is the release date for my project. I have a lot to do. I really need to get back to work."

Adding another comment to the chart, Doctor Harris smiled and shook his hand. "Well, I'm ready to release you. Perhaps you were simply exhausted. As I said, your tests are fine, but I would suggest you get more rest, and if the symptoms recur, you should contact me, I have a practice in Templeton."

Will nodded and smiled, but he was plotting his escape.

The doctor paused at the door. "Officer Wilson is here to speak with you. He's the one that found you last night."

Will felt his smile fading as the tall state trooper entered the room. "Mr. Shepherd, I hope you're feeling better. I wanted to stop by and make sure you're okay."

"You're the one who found me?"

The older man nodded and smiled. "Yeah, it seems we keep meeting under the worst circumstances. I almost ran over you."

Will tried to suppress that image, his head hurt, and he wasn't in the mood to chat. "What about the boy on the blue bike?"

The officer's face darkened, and Will immediately regretted the question. "Boy? What boy?"

Will, knew he had struck a nerve, and hesitated. "The boy that was hit by the car."

The intensity in the officer's eyes scared Will. "Who put you up to this? Is this some kind of sick joke?"

Will sighed, he was still exhausted, and he didn't have the energy for this. "No. The boy who was hit by the car that almost ran me down. It was a green seventies station wagon, one of those with the wooden panels on the side. I even got the license plate number."

The officer suppressed whatever agitated him. Will could see him struggle to regain his composure. "I'm sorry. Long night."

Will wondered if there was more to it than that, but he let it pass.

He recounted the entire incident. Officer Wilson produced a note-book and jotted down the details. When Will finished the story, the state trooper promised to check it out. Will wasn't sure if the other man believed him. He wasn't sure if he believed himself, but he was positive that he saw fear in the officer's eyes.

CHAPTER FIFTY-FIVE

Kerrie paused as she opened his office door Friday evening. "That's the last of it. It's finished."

At the sound of her voice Will glanced up from the screen. Sitting in the darkness, working only from the illumination of his laptop, he enjoyed her figure silhouetted in the doorway. Trying to remain focused; he glanced back at his screen and read his e-mail message one last time before he hit *enter*. "I'm just giving Steve the go-ahead to launch the site."

Kerrie closed the door. "Marketing has signed off. We've done it. We've hit the deadline."

Will yawned and stared out the window. The night sky swirled, stirring large storm clouds that alternately blocked out and revealed the moonlight. He rose and stretched, trying to loosen the kinks in his stiff back and neck. The bruise on the back of his head still ached, but at least the swelling had gone down. "When I came on board, this seemed like an impossible deadline."

Kerrie rounded his desk. "I think congratulations are in order."

She surprised him when she laced her hands behind his neck, drew his face close to hers and kissed him. Her lips were soft and warm, and without thinking he kissed her back. He slid his hands around her waist and pulled her close. He had wanted this for so long, and it exceeded his expectations. He realized it wasn't a dream or hallucination, but the dark office with the storm clouds gathering outside, gave an ethereal quality to the moment.

"How about we go for a drink to celebrate a job well done?" she said when their lips finally parted.

Will didn't answer. He still held her, smelling the faint hint of cinnamon on her breath. He wanted to kiss her again. He moved to, and was interrupted by a knock. They stepped away from each other as Frank burst through the door. "Hey guys, the team has decided to go to Neil's to celebrate."

Will felt exposed, almost naked and was relieved when Frank pretended not to notice how close they were standing. "Sounds great. Give us a minute," Will said.

Frank stared for a little longer than Will liked, then he shrugged and turned for the door. "No problem, we'll all meet over there in fifteen. Steve has even agreed to grace us with his presence."

Frank's nervous laughter did little to reduce the tension. Will and Kerrie nodded, and Frank hurried from the room.

"I guess we have to do the group thing tonight," Kerrie said, her voice thick with disappointment, "a rain-check on the two of us."

He wanted to take her in his arms. He wanted to smell her perfume and taste her lips before the moment passed, but it already had.

CHAPTER FIFTY-SIX

Will bumped Frank's arm, spilling some of his drink. "Sorry."

"No problem-o, boss-man."

Will tried to adjust his chair so he had more room. It was a tight fit with his team packed around two small tables in a back corner of Neil's. He banged his head on a football helmet fastened to the wall and cursed the decorator. What genius had thought it was a great idea to plaster every inch of the walls with trophies, memorabilia, and sports equipment? He knew this was a hot spot for young professionals, but he was uncomfortable in the tight quarters.

Will bit into one of his hot wings and quickly chased it with a swallow of Coke. Frank exploded in a raucous burst of intoxicated laughter at some inane story someone was telling. The alcohol on his breath was almost enough to give Will a buzz. Everyone around him was drinking, and Will struggled to resist joining in. He rationalized that he was already plagued by bizarre visions, so what could one drink hurt? But inside, deep at his core, he knew one drink would lead to another and another, so he abstained. It was almost unbearable.

Will tried to avoid staring at Kerrie. She was radiant, and he found it almost impossible not to devour her with his eyes. For her part, she played it cool, talking and joking with other team members, pretending Will didn't exist, although several times, he caught her furtive glances directed at him.

When he could stand no more, he excused himself, claiming he had to get home to his wife and daughter. He wondered if he threw that in for Kerrie's benefit. Driving home, he tried not to think about what might have happened if Frank hadn't interrupted them. He felt guilty and ashamed. He was sinking fast and he knew it.

The silver moon dodged in and out of the clouds, causing long shadows to appear and vanish on the front lawn when Will turned into the drive. His headlights momentarily illuminated the exterior of the large house, painting it with dramatic starkness that increased its sinister appearance. Will hated his all too-familiar current routine of returning home long after the girls had gone to bed. Studying the outside of the house he cursed under his breath. All the windows were dark *except his office*.

Checking the dash clock, Will cursed — 1AM. Ellie and Sara were certainly asleep.

He climbed from the car, a knot in his stomach, his heart pounding. Dread swept over him like an icy gale. He stifled a maniacal laugh. He blinked and rechecked the office window. He prayed that he had only imagined the illumination, or that it had been reflected moonlight. The window went dark.

For a moment the ground seemed to drop away. Someone or something was stirring upstairs in his office. Fumbling with his key in the darkness, Will could barely control his trembling hands. He pushed the door open cautiously, entered, and paused in the dark foyer, listening for any telltale sounds.

The temperature in the room was bitter cold. Will thought of Tony Legaro. Not wanting to relive moving day in some bizarre hallucination, Will flipped on the foyer light and took the steps to the second floor two at a time.

A quick glance in Ellie's room verified she was sound asleep. Will paused outside his office and glanced at the gun cabinet. He felt ridiculous, a grown man afraid to open a door in his own house.

'I should've had a drink,' he thought as he turned the knob.

Of course the attic door stood open. Dim moonlight streamed in the windows, illuminating the room enough to make that obvious. Will had expected it. However, the man standing in the attic doorway surprised him.

It was the same older man from the bathroom mirror. The man's old-fashioned pinstripe suit exaggerated his thinness. Wild wisps of gray, uncontrollable hair and large bulging eyes underscored by hollow shadows exaggerated his gauntness. Ignoring Will, the man turned and climbed the attic stairs with slow deliberate steps.

Will wasn't going to let some stranger wander around his house. "Hey, wait."

Will reacted without thinking, racing across the room; he flipped on the attic light and pursued the man up the steps. At the top of the stairs Will paused, turned in a circle, and searched the large open space. His heart pounded, and he sucked in deep breaths. There was nothing but floating dust motes and the familiar scent of dried timbers. The man had vanished.

Will stumbled to the center of the room and peered down each of the gabled wings. He was not sure what to do if he found the man there. Not sure what to think if he didn't.

The attic was empty, but Will's heart continued to race. Beads of sweat broke out on his forehead, and the room started to tilt. 'Not again,' Will wanted to scream. He stumbled forward and steadied himself on a rafter as he caught his breath.

The stairs provided the only escape. Will felt reality slipping away. The doctor had found no physical explanation for his blackouts. That left him with two possibilities — he was losing his mind, or the dead were appearing. Neither thought offered much comfort. He gripped the rough wooden beam above him thankful for its reassuring substance.

The vertigo passed, and Will felt steady enough to let go of the beam. He turned to leave, but stopped at the creak of rusty hinges. He turned to see the man kneeling in front of an old trunk. Hidden in the shadows, the man was only momentarily illuminated by the moonlight.

The stranger held an old framed photograph toward Will. "Take a look."

"Who are you? How did you get in here?"

The old man frowned and shook his head, slowly dissolving into mist. The photo fell back into the trunk.

Will closed his eyes and clenched his hands into fists this wasn't real. He opened his eyes. Only the trunk remained. More curious than afraid, Will approached and knelt to examine the old steamer trunk. He did not recognize it and was positive it didn't belong to him or Sara. Old photographs, leather bound scrapbooks, and yellowed documents filled the inside.

A framed color photo on top showed a young man and woman and two small children — a boy and a girl. They posed in front of the fountain in the front yard. Will picked it up to examine it closer and froze, not sure what to make of the scene. The man was a younger version of the guy he had followed upstairs. In the dim light it was difficult to see, but there was a strange mist next to the little girl. It was an odd photo, and Will had no idea what it meant.

He laid it aside and reached for one of the leather bound albums, but stopped when movement in his peripheral vision caught his attention. Through the nearby window he had a clear view of the back yard. The movement was subtle, and if he hadn't been pumped up on adrenalin, he might have missed it.

In the moonlight, Ellie held Celeste's hand as they stepped into the woods at the edge of the yard. Will dropped the photo album and sprang to his feet. "Oh, my God. Ellie, No!"

His warnings failed to reach Ellie as they continued toward the trees. Will's mind raced. He scrambled out of the attic. Sara met him on the landing. "What's wrong?"

He didn't hesitate. There wasn't time. He sprinted down the stairs and toward the kitchen. "It's Ellie."

Dashing through the kitchen and into the backyard, he didn't hear Sara's reply. His lungs burned, and his muscles protested as he raced toward the trees. Panic gripped him. The two were gone now, consumed by the forest's dark shadows. Twigs clawed at his face and arms as he stumbled across the rocky ground, plunging deeper into the undergrowth.

It was maddening. Will increased his pace and tripped over a large rock, pitching headfirst onto the ground. Pain echoed through his left knee and up his thigh. His hands burned where small rocks bit into them when he tried to break his fall, on top of the cuts in his palms from the splinters in the burned out bar, this new abuse brought on a fresh agony of pain.

He crawled forward and struggled to his feet. "Ellie."

No answer. He couldn't see because the overhead canopy obscured even momentary glimpses of moonlight. "Ellie."

Still no answer.

Sweat trickled down Will's forehead and back, and his legs felt like jelly. He stumbled through the darkness with branches slapping his face. This seemed so familiar. Had it happened before when he was a child? Had he been lost like Ellie? Or were his memories and hallucinations starting to merge?

He ran blindly, tripping, stumbling, and crashing through the undergrowth. Ellie was out there with that monster, and he had to save her.

"Will."

At first Will didn't recognize the familiar voice. Bright light blinded and disoriented him. It sounded like his father. Will remembered the light, the strong hands gripping him, but this time it had to be different. He was supposed to be the rescuer.

The man called again from behind the light. "Will?"

"Harry?"

Harry lowered the beam toward the ground. "Will, what are you doing out here?"

Will fought back the tears of frustration and panic. "It's Ellie. She's out here. We have to find her.

The older man grabbed him by the shoulders. "No, Will. Ellie's fine. She's in bed, sound asleep."

Will shook his head, convinced this was another trick of the house. "No. I saw her enter the woods. We have to find her."

Harry squeezed his shoulders tighter. "Everything's fine, come back to the house. Sara's worried. She called me. I've been out here looking for you for over an hour."

Struggling to break free, he almost swung at the old man. "This is some sort of trick."

Will saw it in Harry's eyes again, pity and apprehension. "Come back to the house. You're scaring Sara."

Will shook his head. He couldn't give up on Ellie. Finally, he let Harry lead him back home. He felt like a child. It was too confusing, he knew what he saw, but he had also been sure about a lot of things lately that didn't add up. In truth, Will wasn't sure about anything anymore.

Ellie was indeed sound asleep in her bed. When he could bring himself to leave her, he returned to the landing, and found Sara and Harry whispering by the front door. The older man glanced up at Will and nodded before he left. Will hated the look on Harry's face, like the old man knew something, but wasn't telling.

Sara remained calm as she climbed the stairs. Will wondered what she and Harry had talked about while he had checked on Ellie. "You're bleeding. Let me clean that."

Will followed her into the bathroom and sat on the edge of the tub while she cleaned the gash on his knee and his multiple abrasions. "I was positive I saw her enter the woods."

Sara nodded and soaked a cotton ball with some antiseptic. "What were you doing in the back yard at this hour?"

Will jumped when she dabbed his knee. "Hey, that hurts. I wasn't. I was up in the attic."

Sara shot him a sharp glance. "Not the attic door again?"

"I saw a man in the stairway."

Will explained how he followed the old man up to the attic and found the trunk of photos.

Sara seemed to struggle with frustration. "Like you saw Ellie go into the woods?"

Feeling like an idiot, he started toward his office. "I can prove it. The trunk."

Sara quietly followed him up to the attic. Will supposed she was letting him rant and rave to get it out of his system. He led her over to the north gable, explaining how he had looked out the window and spotted Ellie entering the forest. Not sure why, Will omitted the part about Celeste. He was already worried that Sara was ready to commit him. He stopped when he reached the window where he had spotted Ellie and didn't know what to say. The trunk, scrapbooks, and photographs were gone.

Will turned in a slow circle, doubling checking that he was in the right spot. "How can this be? They were right here."

His heart pounded in his chest like a hummingbird's wings.

"You're exhausted. It's been a rough week, and you've been through a lot. Let's get some sleep. The doctor did say you needed to get more rest."

Sara's suggestion sounded patronizing.

"I'm not crazy, they were here."

Touching him gently on the arm, Sara guided him back toward the stairs. "We can figure this out in the morning."

He nodded, but wasn't convinced.

CHAPTER **FIFTY-SEVEN**

Friday evening's events plagued Will the rest of the weekend. There was something familiar about stumbling through the woods. But he couldn't decide if memories of the red rubber ball and Small Sparrow's solid white eyes were something from his childhood, faded images that were more of an impression than an actual memory, or the residue from one of his recent visions. He tried to separate what seemed real from the recent hallucinations, but he struggled to distinguish between the two. His most vivid images or memories remained a bright light, and the strong hands lifting him from the ground.

Perhaps he had been lost in the woods as a very young child. This thought nagged at him, following him to work Monday morning, taunting and distracting him.

He sat at his desk trying to work out the implications. Kerrie burst into his office interrupting his thoughts. "We're a hit. How does it feel to be the manager of a bona-fide mega-success?"

Will spun his desk chair from the window to face her. "Pretty damn good."

The corners of Kerrie's mouth turned up in that hint of a smile that he found sexy. "That would be more convincing if you didn't look exhausted."

Will glanced at the window, trying to get a glimpse of his reflection. "Do I really look that bad?"

"Worse. Look, if you ever want to talk, you still owe me that rain check on dinner."

Will turned back to her and smiled. "I'm fine. Just not sleeping well."

C.L. appeared in the doorway before she could respond. He draped his arm over her shoulder, and a pang of jealousy stabbed Will. "I wanted to let you know that Marketing and the investors are thrilled with your team's accomplishments."

Kerrie grinned, and Will tried not to stare at C.L.'s arm.

"Keep Thursday night open. As a small token of our appreciation the company's throwing a little party at the Penn Harris Hotel. They're hiring a band, the whole works. Betty can get you directions if you don't know the location."

Will faked enthusiasm. "I'll check with her. Sounds great."

In his head, he tried to think of a way to convince Sara to attend a party on Thursday when he had claimed he would be too busy to join her at her gallery opening on the weekend. Besides, a party was the last thing he wanted. He wanted answers. He wanted to know if he was losing his mind.

Distracted, he hadn't noticed Kerrie and C.L. leave his office until he heard them continue their conversation as they moved down the hall. He had zoned out again, thinking about Friday night.

The shrill *breep* of his phone jarred him from his thoughts. "Hello, Will Shepherd in Development."

"Son, it's me, Dad."

Will leaned back in his chair. "Hey, where were you this weekend?"

His dad cleared his throat, a nervous habit. "Your mother dragged me off to one of those bed and breakfasts up by the lake. Is something wrong? Are Sara and Ellie all right?"

Will smiled, his mother never dragged his dad anywhere. His dad was the one with wanderlust. "Everyone is fine. I just wanted to check in and see how you were."

There was silence on the other end of the line. "You usually don't call six times, just to see how we are."

Concern colored his father's voice. His dad was too smart for subterfuge. Will slouched in his chair. The guilty six-year-old feeling struck him again. He wanted to ask, and had to know, but felt silly at the same time. He felt that way most of the time now — silly and slightly off balance, like he had slipped over some imaginary line into an alternate world he alone could see. But wasn't that the definition of insanity?

"Is there something on your mind, Son?"

He had zoned out for a moment again. "Yeah, sorry. Do you remember when we used to go for Sunday drives when I was a kid?"

The familiar sound of his dad's chuckle comforted Will. "We used to call it *On Adventure*. I sure do. Those were good times."

Will remembered how his dad would wake him on a Sunday morning, all excited about the day ahead. "I was wondering, did we ever drive to Harrisburg?"

"Sure, I guess we might have."

Will felt certain they had. "This will sound strange, but it's kind of important. Did I ever wander off into the woods?"

There was another long pause. Will waited and knew the answer before his dad spoke. He knew and didn't want to know.

His dad cleared his throat again. "I'm surprised you would re-member that. You were just a little guy."

Will listened to his dad's voice travel the distance between his Chicago kitchen and Will's Harrisburg office — the digital signal crisp and clear. "It was a Sunday drive. We traveled along the Susquehanna River. I was shooting a lot of landscapes that summer and I wanted to get some scenic shots at sunset. We parked the car on this hill that had a beautiful view of the river. Your mother sug-gested we eat our dinner there. Remember how she used to pack a picnic?"

Will nodded and smiled. It had been a weekly routine.

"I was absorbed in my photos, and your mother was unpacking the picnic. We only turned our backs for a moment. I swear. You know how kids are. You were gone. Your mother and I were frantic. I spotted a path into the forest, and don't ask me how I knew you had followed that path, I just did. Have you ever just known some-thing?"

Will nodded again and felt foolish when he realized his dad couldn't see him. "Yeah, that's happened to me."

"I followed the path, and your mother ran behind me. She was a mess. I'll tell you one thing. You were fast as a kid. It was getting dark, but luckily we had a flashlight. We caught up to you and you were fine. We were both so relieved." His dad's voice trailed off.

Will swallowed, afraid to ask his next question. "Was there some-one with me?"

His dad didn't seem to even consider the question. "No. You were standing there alone on the path. You didn't seem upset at the time. Of course your mother and I were upset. You did start having night-mares that night, and that went on for a couple of months. Your mother thought we had damaged you for life. She was afraid you would end up in therapy. We felt so guilty."

Will sighed and leaned forward in his chair. "Like you said, it only takes a minute."

He said this because he felt like he had to absolve his father. It wasn't that big a deal. He hadn't been scarred for life. The memory hadn't surfaced in thirty years. Until recently everything had been fine. Will could hardly blame the probable nervous breakdown he was having on being lost in the woods when he was a kid.

His dad's voice interrupted his thoughts. "What brought this up? I didn't think you would even remember that."

Will didn't want to alarm his parents. "It's nothing. I was walking in the woods behind our house on Friday and it all seemed familiar. I guess I remembered that incident when I was a kid. I think maybe we bought that property where I was lost."

His dad's chuckle echoed loud and clear across the phone line. "I'm sure it's not the same place."

This certainty surprised Will. "No. Why not?"

"Your place is north of Harrisburg, right?"

"Yeah."

"The place you wandered off was south of Harrisburg. Down near Chickie's Rock."

Running a hand over his jaw he glanced out the window. "I was so sure. It seemed so familiar."

His dad was moving about his kitchen. Will heard the refrigerator door close. "The woods all look alike. It's not hard to see the similarities. It's probably just a coincidence."

Will wanted to agree, but something was still nagging him. "Chickie's Rock. What's that?"

His dad laughed, and Will thought retirement must be good for him. "You really should get out and learn about your area. It's beautiful country. Chickie's Rock is a large rock outcropping. A big rock."

For a moment everything fled from Will's mind. The world turned upside down. His hand clutched the receiver so tight his fingers ached. His dad's words hung in the air. Was the big rock the same as the people's great rock? Small Sparrow's solid white eyes burned in his memory, and he closed his own, fighting to ignore a roar in his mind that started low and grew in intensity until it sounded like a jet engine. He licked his dry lips and ignored his incredible thirst.

CHAPTER **FIFTY-EIGHT**

Will spent the afternoon staring at his computer screen, and accomplishing nothing. He found it impossible to concentrate after the phone conversation with his dad. He had too many unanswered questions. Despite the distractions, and his lack of progress on any work, he still lingered several hours past quitting time. Finally, he gave up and left, but not wanting to go home, he found himself in Templeton. Everything jumbled in his mind, and he drove aimlessly around the small town, trying to resist his desire for a cold beer. His resolve crumbled, and in desperation, he drove to St. Mark's Lutheran Church.

Streetlights bathed the church in an unearthly florescent glow. The old brick building, stark and desolate, lacked any of the charm Will remembered from the few Sundays he had attended services. He climbed from his car and approached the wooden double doors with conflicted emotions. In Horsham his old church had been a mainstay in his life, but now he felt like a stranger in unfamiliar territory.

His footsteps echoed off the hard tile floor in the dark outer hallway. Through the glass panes in the doors, he spied Pastor Wheeler kneeling before the altar. Careful not to disturb him, Will eased open the doors and slipped inside. In the candle-lit sanctuary, he could barely read the gold letters on the wall above the altar — Jesus is Lord. The usually reassuring words provided no comfort. He was beyond consoling.

The long carpeted aisle seemed to extend as Will quietly approached the praying pastor. He felt like he walked on a long, red treadmill.

Pastor Wheeler's head remained bowed as he spoke. "Will Shepherd. Would you look at what the cat drug in?"

"I need to talk. I think I'm losing my mind."

The pastor didn't turn, but replied. "It's always the same. When things are going good who needs God? But when you hit a bump in the road, then it's time to come calling. A little heart disease or cancer, and then it's 'save me Lord.' Otherwise when it comes to

God fahgettaboudit."

The pastor's harsh words and severe tone shocked Will. "No. It's not like that. I've just been busy with the new job and relocating."

The pastor snorted, his shoulders shook with laughter. "Well, God is too busy now. He's on a coffee break. You have blown it. No more time for you, sorry."

Will grabbed Pastor Wheeler by the shoulders and spun him around. "I need help."

The older man almost lost his balance, but surprised Will with his agility, when he sprang to his feet. "It's too late for you. God has seen your sins and washed his hands of you. The Lord knows about your lust and drunkenness. He has measured you and found you wanting."

Pastor Wheeler delivered this pronouncement with such vehemence that Will fell to his knees. The candles erupted like flame throwers, shooting fire high into the air. Will raised his arms to shield his eyes from the brightness. The pastor's hysterical laughter boomed throughout the sanctuary. Will felt the world start to spin even with his eyes closed. When he opened them Celeste had replaced Pastor Wheeler. Her long silk nightgown rustled in an impossible breeze, and her blue eyes pierced him to his soul. He felt naked before her. "You're pathetic, beyond help."

Will stumbled backward away from her disoriented. "You?"

He reacted too slowly; she moved like a cat, pounced on him and grabbed his arms with an iron grip. "Don't you see? God won't help you. I'm the only one you can turn to now. It's your destiny. We will spend eternity together."

Dark chords from a funeral dirge blared from the organ, and flames continued to erupt from the candles. Will struggled to break free as Celeste crushed against him. Her body blazed, and her lips burned when she kissed him. He resisted, but his world exploded in a bright flash of fire and light when her mouth crushed his.

CHAPTER **FIFTY-NINE**

Will opened his eyes and squinted at the bright sunlight. His tongue felt swollen, his lips dry and cracked. He swallowed, wishing for a drink. Aches and pains bloomed everywhere on his body as he straightened up in the driver's seat and stared at his house trying to remember how he had gotten there. Everything was a blank after the fiery kiss in the church the night before.

That couldn't have been real.

He stumbled toward the house, deciding if he had time for a shower before work. When he entered the foyer Sara launched from the couch in the parlor. "Will, where have you been?"

Her eyes were swollen and blood shot.

"I don't know," he said.

Hurt and betrayal played across her features. "You don't know? I tried calling you on your cell. I waited down here all night. I was terrified. The police wouldn't look for you because you weren't gone long enough. I called all the hospitals."

He tried to hug her and she brushed his arms away. "Sara, I'm sorry. I had another blackout. I went to the church after work and then I blacked out."

He wasn't sure if she believed him. Her body language and facial gestures indicated cynicism. Not that he could blame her. If she came to him with this story he wouldn't believe it either. "What were you doing at church?"

The heat exploded on his face. "I needed to think. To work some stuff out."

Rising above her doubt, she threw her arms around him. "Are you okay?"

She was soft and warm, and when she hugged him and kissed his neck and cheek, he struggled not to think about Celeste in the white silk nightgown. The incredible kiss at the church had left him dazed and longing for more. And guilty. The woman had cast some sort of spell.

"I'm fine now," he whispered.

She squeezed tighter. "I want you to see another doctor. These blackouts aren't normal."

No way, I'm done with doctors.

"I will."

It was a small lie, but it seemed to satisfy her. Will was still convinced this was all connected to the house. Letting it slide, he enjoyed a moment in her arms, not wanting to initiate another argument.

He left for work, exhausted. He drove without paying attention so it came as a complete surprise when he found himself returning to St. Mark's parking lot.

The red brick building stood like a stone citadel, a gateway to the divine. Will timidly approached and tried the door. He was ambivalent when he found it unlocked. Not sure if he wanted to enter the building, after the previous night's events, he stepped into the dark entranceway and closed the door behind him. The building lay quiet in that way that public places are when empty. Will glanced in the glass doors to the sanctuary. No burning candles, no pastor praying at the altar.

"That's a good sign I suppose," Will said out loud and chuckled.

He entered and settled into a pew. He found some comfort sitting there in the quiet. His gaze drifted to the gold letters painted above the altar. Jesus is Lord.

Will bowed his head. "Lord, have mercy. I'm frightened. I think I'm losing my mind."

The silence overwhelmed him. He needed to find his bearings, nothing made sense. Everything was slipping away; his job, his marriage, his sobriety, and his faith. Everything he had worked for, everything he valued. The worst part was that he was a willing participant in his own destruction. If he didn't control his desire for Kerrie and find out why he was seeing these hallucinations, he was going to lose it all.

A door opened on the west side of the sanctuary and startled him. Pastor Wheeler entered. The reverend looked older than Will remembered. He supposed it could be a trick of the light.

Will rose. "I'm sorry, I didn't know anyone was in the building. I needed a quiet place to think."

The pastor smiled, glancing around the sanctuary. "Then you've come to the right place."

"I didn't mean to impose."

Running his hand along the top edge of the pew, the minister seemed distracted. "No, it's fine. I was just finishing some work on this Sunday's sermon. I must have left the front door unlocked. I thought I heard someone enter so I came to check."

Glancing at the back of the sanctuary, images of the night before flashed in Will's head. "You normally keep the doors locked?"

Wheeler's face darkened. "Yes. Unfortunately, the insurance companies require it. I hate the idea of a locked church, but in this day and age I'm afraid they're right."

Wanting an explanation for the night before Will persisted. "The doors were locked last night?"

"Of course. When I arrived this morning I had to unlock them." He paused and studied Will's face for a moment. "Is there something wrong? Would you like to talk?"

Embarrassed, Will checked his watch. "I don't know. It's... I wouldn't know where to begin."

Motioning toward the side door, the pastor started in that direction. "Why don't we go to my office?"

Will followed him to a small office next to the sanctuary where the older man eased himself into a leather chair behind a large oak desk. Will dropped into a straight-backed chair in front. The white plaster walls were lined with bookshelves loaded with thick old leather bound volumes. It was a tight space, but comforting and secure. The window behind the pastor looked out over what, at first glance, appeared to be a tranquil garden. Only upon closer inspection, Will realized it was the church cemetery.

Wheeler picked up a pipe from the desk and filled it from a pouch. He struck a wooden match and puffed on the pipe to light it. The sweet fragrance of cherry tobacco permeated the room.

The pastor leaned back in his chair, smiling apologetically. "Afraid it's the one vice I haven't been able to give up."

Watching the ribbon of smoke waft into the air, Will thought about the events of the last few weeks. "I don't know where to begin. I stopped by last night."

But that couldn't have been real, not if the doors to the church were locked when the building was empty.

But what was reality? Lately it was as elusive as fog; there was nothing to grip.

Wheeler frowned and leaned forward. "I'm sorry I missed you. Why don't you start at the beginning?"

Will considered his options. He didn't know this man very well and he was a little intimidated. The last thing he wanted was the whole town to think he was crazy like his old neighbor lady when he was a child. She claimed Jesus visited her on the back porch. Although the things that were appearing to Will, lived far south of Jesus.

He thought there was some sort of pastor/parishioner confidentiality rule. Still, maybe it was better to keep this whole thing to himself. He thought about Gretchen. Maybe it was safer for all concerned.

Will inhaled deeply, held his breath for a moment and made his decision. "I've been having blackouts. Sara thinks it's pressure from the new job, but I don't think it is."

The reverend nodded. "Have you seen a doctor?"

Will watched the smoke continue to curl from the pipe. It looked like a question mark. "Yeah, I had a little incident along the road and was taken to St. Vincent's. They ran all kinds of tests and found nothing."

"That's good."

Will shrugged, slouching in the chair. He felt defeated. "I guess so, but that only left more questions on why I'm having the blackouts."

Pastor Wheeler puffed on his pipe, not pushing too hard. "How are things between you and Sara?"

Will gazed at his hands. "Not good, pretty bad, there's a growing distance between us. Maybe it's just my long hours at the office."

Embarrassed by his misdirection, Will couldn't look in the other man's eyes. Wheeler fidgeted with the wooden match, and Will watched in fascination as the tobacco glowed in the bell of the pipe.

The smoke continued to dance into the air in a thin, almost transparent ribbon.

"Have you tried to discuss this with her?"

The pipe went out again, and the Pastor sat it on the round metal plate on his desk.

"No. Not really. It's my fault. I've been shutting her out."

Pastor Wheeler folded his pudgy hands on the desk and studied his pipe as if he was considering whether to light it again. "You need to talk to Sara about your feelings. Only through confession and forgiveness is true reconciliation possible. You know it takes a lot of effort to keep a marriage on track. Just as it does to keep your spiritual life healthy."

Will felt trapped. He didn't want to be pressured about his attendance record at services. He wasn't ready to come clean about his attraction to Kerrie, or his increasing struggle with alcohol. He was sure not ready to admit he was seeing things that weren't there, or that he was probably going insane. The only reason Will had visited the church was to prove that he hadn't seen anything the night before.

Will gave his best "I'm okay, you're okay" smile. The one he had perfected to convince others that he was confident and in control. "You're right. I'll talk to her about it."

It was another lie, but it seemed to satisfy the pastor. Not typically a man of deception, Will was amazed and ashamed at how easy it was becoming.

Wheeler smiled, leaned back in his chair and studied Will for a moment with a thoughtful expression. "How have you settled into the house?"

There was something in the other man's eyes, a troubled knowledge. Before Will thought about his answer he blurted out, "I'm not comfortable there."

A flicker of understanding passed over the Wheeler's face. "I can certainly appreciate that. The tragedy of your first day there must certainly color your experience."

"Maybe. But Sara still loves the place. She seems to have gotten completely beyond it."

Wheeler looked uncomfortable. He leaned forward and his whole frame seemed to tense. "I hate to admit it, but I've been obsessing about your house. I'm having a hard time escaping the vivid memories of that afternoon. Nothing in my thirty-nine years of ministry prepared me for that."

Will thought he saw the other man shudder. "Yes, it was terrible."

Wheeler continued. "When I left that day I felt somehow tainted. I was ill for almost a week, not able to eat or sleep. Horrible nightmares tormented me. I can certainly understand how you might be uncomfortable living there."

It was shocking. Here was another person claiming there was something wrong with the house. "So you felt it too?"

The reverend fumbled with his wedding band, turning it slowly on his finger. "Yes, I did, and I have been trying to come to grips with it."

Will's relief was almost palpable. At last someone who thought something was askew, besides he and Gretchen. "What can I do? Sara thinks I'm losing my mind or there's something physically wrong with me. I've been seeing things I can't explain. Some days I do think I am going crazy."

Will started recounting all the strange events, the visions, and the blackouts. Explaining how he was starting to have trouble distinguishing between what was real and imaginary. Relief washed over him as he fully described the events of the past month.

Wheeler listened without interrupting, and when Will finished they sat in silence. Will saw the internal struggle playing out behind the pastor's face. "I believe God has given you the gift of discernment. Some people are blessed with this ability."

Will snorted and ran a hand through his hair. "I wouldn't call it a gift or a blessing. I certainly wouldn't have asked for it. I'd call it dark discernment."

The pastor picked up his pipe, emptying the tobacco into a trashcan under his desk. "God doesn't always give us what we want, but he always blesses us with what we need."

There was no answer for that, and Will remained silent.

Wheeler fumbled with his pipe, turning it over in his hand carefully examining it. When he spoke, he started very quietly, almost cautious that someone would overhear their conversation. "The events of that day were a terrible tragedy. That alone would be enough to ruin your life in that place. I'm sure it's hard to forget the horrible scene, but I felt something from the moment I arrived that day. It was like I had stepped into a dark cloud. Something didn't feel right.

"Many of my colleagues would find the idea of demons quaint, naïve, and outdated. Today all the evils of the world are explained by illness, poverty, and the cruelty of men. Most of my contemporaries would laugh at the notion of Satan and demons. I probably would have too, before that day at your house, but now I'm sure. I truly felt the presence of evil that day.

I believe the only way to defeat this type of evil is through faith, prayer, and calling on the name of Jesus to drive it out."

The silence was oppressive when he finished. Will contemplated their options. Finally, he shifted in his seat. "You mean like some kind of exorcism?"

The older man nodded. "That's exactly what I mean."

Will realized he was gripping the chair handles and eased up. "You will perform one?"

The pastor flinched. Apparently he was not keen on reencountering whatever evil he had felt that day. "Lutherans don't have a specific rite of exorcism, but I could make a few phone calls. I have a friend who is a Catholic priest."

Will almost laughed, the idea was absurd. Six weeks ago he didn't even believe in ghosts and now he was keying in an exorcism on his Droid. Not to mention that Sara would explode. She seemed to have a huge blind spot were the house was concerned. This was the same kind of thing Gretchen had suggested. Yet it might be the chance to make things right. If others felt it too, there was hope that he wasn't going insane. "Thank You. I appreciate any help you can offer."

The older man smiled. "I'll gladly do what I can."

There was comfort in the man's smile. "I should be going, I'm keeping you from your sermon."

The two men rose and shook hands. "Remember, when we are weakest in ourselves that's when we are strongest in God."

Will nodded and turned to leave, then paused. "Does He ever give up on us? God I mean."

The pastor's smile didn't waver. "No, He never does."

CHAPTER SIXTY

By Wednesday the air crackled with electricity. The power Will had sensed at the old tombstone on the hill the other night gathered around him with the weight of a funeral shroud. The bedroom hummed. He half expected something to reach out of the darkness and grab him. He wanted to chalk up the sensation to his exhaustion and dismiss it, but it still unnerved him.

His initial relief that Pastor Wheeler shared his feelings about the house had faded. If he ruled out insanity, then he, Sara, and Ellie were in real danger. He had spent the better part of two days trying to figure out a way to broach the subject with Sara without starting World War III. She hadn't been herself lately either. She was vague, distant, and perfectly at home in this house — especially her studio. Lately every conversation ended in an argument.

It didn't help that he found it impossible to think clearly. He felt like he was mentally wading through mud. Restless and disjointed, sleep left him more exhausted each morning than the night before.

Standing by the bed in the moonlit bedroom, he watched Sara sleep. He loved her so much, and this growing chasm between them tortured him. In sleep her serene face resembled an angel's. He watched her for a while before he slid into bed, careful not to wake her. In the darkness he resolved to find a way to convince her to let the pastor and his priest friend try to help.

Will started to drift off and then heard voices and old, far-away sounding music. The kind that played on a Victrola with skips, pops, and echoes. The alarm clock read four in the morning. He had slept for five hours, it felt like minutes.

Quietly, he slid out of bed and crept to the door where he slipped on his old black terrycloth robe. At first he thought that Sara had left on the TV in the parlor, but then he remembered the silence when he had gone to bed.

Someone was downstairs. He retrieved the gun cabinet key from the nightstand drawer, carefully opened the door, and edged along the hall to the cabinet. He removed his pistol, it felt heavy in his trembling hand. Holding his breath, trying not to make a sound, he inched toward the banister.

The music blared, and it seemed odd that it didn't wake the girls. Will crouched by the table at the banister and tried to get a better view of the parlor. The furnishings in the parlor had changed. Spellbound by the parlor's transformation, Will startled when the figure next to him on the landing sighed. It was the old man from the attic. They were so close they almost touched. The man's thin wisps of white, disheveled hair and sparkling eyes reminded Will of an asylum inmate. The old man raised a bony finger to his lips and whispered, "Watch."

Will tried to speak, but the apparition dissolved into mist. Will almost dropped his pistol. Heated words drew his attention back to the parlor. When Celeste stepped into view by the fireplace, Will couldn't take his eyes off her.

She placed her champagne flute on the mantle. "Howard, I don't understand."

From somewhere in the parlor beyond Will's view, Howard spoke. "I'm sorry, but this has to end."

"I thought you loved me. You said you were going to leave her," Celeste said, her voice cracking.

A tall, dark haired man with a pencil thin mustache stepped into view. Must be Howard. Will recognized him as the casket bartender from Tiny's. Howard placed his hands on Celeste's shoulders. "I want to, but don't you see? The scandal would end my career."

"You could leave office. We could go away together."

"Celeste, no."

Howard grasped her wrists and forced her hands away from his face. "I can't. My wife has all the money. She inherited it from her father. If I left her I would have nothing, and if we continue together and I get caught, my career will end. Don't you see? I have no choice."

Tears welled in Celeste's eyes as she backed away. "You said you loved me. Was that a lie?"

Howard released her wrists and tried to touch her cheeks. "No. It's just too dangerous. My wife is starting to suspect."

She slapped his hand away. "What if I go to the papers?"

Howard laughed. "You wouldn't dare. Your reputation would be ruined. You'd have no future. Who would want you after the scandal?"

"I don't care. If I can't have you, I don't care at all."

Howard reached for her trembling shoulders. "Of course you care. Be reasonable."

"Get your hands off me!" Her words were a lash. He backed away.

His momentary surprise faded replaced by anger. He approached with clenched fists. She ran into the foyer. Will slid back against the wall, not sure if these apparitions could see him, or if he was watching some rerun of the past play out like an old movie. Celeste fled up the stairs with Howard in pursuit. They passed Will on the landing without a glance.

Howard caught her and seized her shoulders spinning her around. "You can't tell anyone about us."

She started to laugh, a weaker version of the loud hysterical laughter that Will recognized. Howard smacked her hard, leaving a red mark on her cheek. "I will not be made a fool."

She continued to laugh. Hysteria danced in her eyes. The man raised his hand to strike again, and Will raised his gun. He realized this was futile what was he going to do — shoot a dead man?

The second blow cracked, and a bloody tooth flew across the floor.

The strike knocked Celeste to her knees. Howard raised his hand again, but before he could strike, she clutched a large silver letter opener from the table by the banister. She lunged. The sharp blade sliced through his silk smoking jacket and came away covered in dark liquid.

Howard froze, staring at the slash across his waist. "You bitch. You're insane."

Celeste bolted for the stairs, but Howard grabbed a fist full of her hair. Will winced at the snap like dry twigs in her neck as her head jerked backward. The letter opener clattered to the floor. Apparently surprised by the sound, Howard released his grip. Celeste staggered toward the staircase. She stumbled in a circle. Terror filled her eyes and blood dripped from her mouth. Howard reached for her, but his fingers fell away from her nightgown's smooth fabric, failing to gain a grip. Reminiscent of Tony's fatal descent, she stumbled down the stairs, a scene in slow motion. Her arms flailed like a wounded bird's.

Her head smashed into the hardwood floor and sounded like a watermelon dropped from the back of a pickup truck. Will sprang toward the steps. "No. What have you done?"

Halfway down the stairs Will froze. A small boy peered through the glass panes by the front door. There was something familiar about the child who turned and fled into the night. Will grabbed the railing to steady himself. His gaze only left Celeste for a second, but when it returned she had vanished.

Howard stood in the foyer, holding her limp form in his arms. Will's heart sank when he saw her blood matted curls. He wasn't sure how Howard had beaten him to the foot of the stairs, or picked up her body.

Howard's sad eyes drilled into him. "I never meant to do it. I loved her. You saw it wasn't my fault. I lost my temper. Oh God, what have I done?"

The two forms dissolved into the foyer's darkness.

CHAPTER **SIXTY-ONE**

Will's concerns about Sara's attendance at the Thursday evening release party were groundless. She readily agreed to go, and with Ellie tucked away at the babysitters, she seemed eager to enjoy the evening. The setting sun cast final sparkles on the Susquehanna River as Will steered the Civic through heavy traffic on the Wade Bridge. Sara glowed in the setting sun's light, her perfume, a combination of citrus and vanilla, floated in the air. Will wanted to enjoy her and his success, but he felt out of sync. Haunted by the previous night's vision of Celeste's death, he couldn't generate any sincere enthusiasm for the evening's festivities.

Sara finished applying the final touches to her makeup and raised the sun visor with mirror into the up position. "So what happened to you last night? I woke up and you were gone."

Trying to act nonchalant, Will kept his eyes on the traffic. "I had a bad dream. I couldn't sleep, so I went downstairs. I must have fallen asleep on the couch." He wondered if that's all it had been. In the morning he had woke on the couch with no sign of a struggle, everything in the parlor returned to normal.

Sara fidgeted with his collar and looked at him critically, as if it were the first time in weeks that she was really seeing him. "You've got dark circles under your eyes. You haven't been sleeping well. Promise you'll see someone."

Will still hadn't found the opportunity to approach Sara about the Reverend Wheeler's offer. He smiled. He would fight that battle in the morning. He didn't want to upset her tonight in front of all his co-workers. He parked the car in the large lot in front of the elegant one-story Penn Harris, and Sara whistled.

"Very nice."

"My company spares no expense."

They both laughed, and the mood lightened. Sara stepped out of the car and stole his breath. She wore her dark blue dress, hair up, and just the right touch of makeup. His hand found hers as they entered the hotel, and as Will remembered how much he loved her, the tensions of the previous weeks dissolved.

His joke about expense proved true. A large crowd of people ate, drank, and danced in the Windsor ballroom. Uniformed waiters carried trays of assorted hors d'oeuvres, a band played, and a crowd gathered at the open bar.

Will and Sara helped themselves to some appetizers, and Will realized he was famished. He especially enjoyed the fried triangles of flaky dough filled with cream cheese and crab that Sara told him were crab puffs. He scanned the room, searching for the waiter with that tray.

Frank approached wearing a hideous, light blue leisure suit that he probably had purchased from some vintage seventies shop. "Hey boss man, what a blast."

Will agreed and introduced Frank to Sara.

Frank extended his hand. "Nice to finally meet you. I've heard a lot about you."

Sara grasped his hand and shot Will a grin. "No wonder my ears burn some days."

"It's all good," Frank said and laughed. "He hardly ever refers to you as 'the little ball and chain.'"

Sara raised her hand in a mock conspiratorial whisper. "Looks like he'll sleep on the couch tonight."

Frank guffawed, and slapped Will on the back. "You're so busted man."

Will rolled his eyes.

Frank was still attempting to be charming when Kerrie made quite the entrance in her tight black cocktail dress, her bare shoulders accentuating her long neck. Frank uttered something he thought was clever and Sara chuckled politely, but Will missed it. His attention fixed on Kerrie. As if on cue, her eyes found his. Will was lost for a moment, everything in the room vanished except her eyes.

Kerrie approached, a mischievous smile playing on her lips. The band should have played the theme from 'Jaws'. She nodded to Will and Frank and turned to Sara. "Sara, isn't it? How good to see you again."

If Sara was surprised, she hid it well. "Kerrie, right?"

"Yes, we met at an Automated Technologies Christmas Party a few years ago when I was a contractor."

Sara smiled, raised an eyebrow and glanced at Will. "Yes, I remember the party."

Will felt trapped. Suddenly the ballroom seemed small. His unease intensified by Frank's grin. "I didn't know you two worked together before?"

If half the company's upper management hadn't been in the room, Will probably would have strangled Frank. Kerrie touched Will's arm. "Yes, that's why I recommended him for this job. I was so impressed when I worked under him before. He was the first man I thought of for the position."

Sara spoke too quickly, and Will didn't like the dawning realization he saw in her eyes. "You recommended Will for his new job?"

Kerrie continued apparently oblivious to Sara's shock. "Yes, didn't he tell you?"

Sara stared into Will's eyes, and he felt her struggle to maintain control. "Yes, I'm sure he did. It must have slipped my mind."

Will glanced at the open bar. "Yeah, I'm positive I did."

Kerrie went on. "I mean he is just so impressive."

Sara grasped his hand and smiled. "Yes, that's my Will." Outwardly she seemed calm and composed, but her performance failed to fool Will.

He wanted to end the conversation before it intensified. "I wonder if we should find our seats for dinner?"

"I think it's going to be a while," Frank said, "They're still serving appetizers."

Kerrie seemed to be enjoying the conversation too much. "So how do you like the house?"

Sara's hand almost crushed Will's fingers, but he hid his discomfort. Her voice cracked a little when she responded. "The house?"

"Yes, when Will told me you wanted an old Victorian, I knew that place would be perfect."

Sara's composure slipped. "You picked out our house?"

Kerrie smiled. "I thought it would be wonderful for your family."

Sara dropped all pretense of politeness. "If you will excuse me, I think I need a drink." Without waiting for a reply, she left for the bar.

"That's a great idea," Frank said and trailed after her.

Will lingered in the blast zone wondering why he hadn't seen this coming. He had never expected Kerrie to deliberately taunt Sara. Then again, he hadn't told Kerrie that he had failed to mention her or her aid to Sara.

Kerrie executed her well-practiced pout. "I'm sorry. I hope I didn't cause any trouble."

Will was not convinced. Her eyes sparkled too much, and the corners of her mouth flirted with a grin. He shrugged it off. "It's just a misunderstanding, everything is fine."

He wished that were true.

Kerrie followed his gaze toward Sara. "I better say hello to C.L., talk to you later."

Will thought about a stiff drink, the smooth burn. "Sure."

Spending the rest of the evening at the party proved excruciating for Will, anticipating Sara's building fury, and the unavoidable confrontation. Sara played the proud, supportive wife; she had too much class to cause a 'Jerry Springer' moment, but Will noted she had more than her usual amount of wine with dinner. They only stayed until the first opportunity to slip away unnoticed.

Sara had arranged for Ellie to stay overnight at the babysitter's, a young woman from church who sort of reminded Will of Gretchen, so they returned home alone in silence. Will followed Sara into the house and up to the bedroom, waiting for the outburst. When he could stand the silence no longer, he provoked her. "Say something."

She turned on him, her face red, her cheeks wet. "I don't know where to begin. Why didn't you tell me she recommended you for the job?"

"Would that have made a difference?"

Sara sank to the bench at her vanity. "Obviously you thought it did, because you conveniently forgot to mention it, and the fact that the two of you have been working together for months. That just slipped your mind?"

"I remembered how you reacted the first time you met her."

"When I told you she had a thing for you."

Funny, that seemed like a long time ago. At the time Will had dismissed it, back in Philadelphia Kerrie had just seemed like some kid. He hadn't thought of her as anything special until Sara had pointed out her apparent crush on him. Even then he had only felt flattered, but now something felt different.

How could he respond when he knew she was right? He undid his tie and hung it on the rack in the closet, stalling for time. "I'm sorry. I thought you would be jealous."

Sara removed her earrings, slamming them into a drawer. "When another woman finds you a job and picks out our house, maybe I should be jealous."

"It's not like that."

Sara rose from her vanity and approached him, her voice low and steady. "She picked out our home, and you didn't even mention she was here."

Will wanted to fix this. He had to make her understand. "She only gave me the name of the realtor. It wasn't like we drove around together looking at houses."

Sara stood only inches from him, hands on her hips. "No, you were too busy at the office working."

"What are you talking about? I was at the office working."

Sara clenched her fists. "You think I'm a complete idiot. All this extra time at the office, and when I question it, you invent some story about blackouts and visions."

"I didn't invent that. Gretchen saw the same thing. Last night I saw Celeste's murder on the stairs."

Sara seemed momentarily confused. "Who?"

"The ghost from the dining room, her name is Celeste."

Sara laughed and threw up her hands. "You mean Ellie's imaginary friend? You're losing it."

"She's not imaginary. I think she was murdered here. I think we all are in danger, and we need to get out."

"Stop it, no more crazy talk. No more blackouts. No more flashbacks to childhood, no more ghosts in the dining room or attic doors that won't stay shut."

"But that all happened."

Sara turned her back to him and slipped out of her dress. "Are you sure? Maybe it's just your conscience."

Even angry she was beautiful. He closed his eyes, trying to control his own anger. "Sara there is nothing going on between me and Kerrie. There never has been."

She sat on the edge of the bed and removed her stockings. "You mean you haven't got into her pants yet? What's the hold up? She looks willing."

Will slumped next to her on the edge of the bed. "I wouldn't."

She ignored him and pulled on a pair of old sweatpants. "What are you planning? To trade me in on a younger model?"

"No."

Showing him her back again, she dropped her bra, and ducked into one of his old T-shirts she liked to sleep in. "That's a lie."

Will tried to touch her shoulder. "I'll never leave you."

She recoiled from his touch. "Everybody leaves. My parents, My Aunt, Gretchen   why should you be any different?"

He tried to hug her. "I am."

She shoved him away. "Don't touch me. I know you've been keeping secrets."

"No, it's this house. Something is going on here."

She turned her back to him. Rejecting any attempt to reconnect. "It's not the house. The only thing strange here is you. You've changed since we moved. You're secretive, you started collecting guns, and creating these paranoid fantasies. I found the beer bottles. I know you're drinking."

"Beer bottles? I don't drink. You know that. I haven't had a drink in all the years we've been together."

She pulled back the covers and sank into bed. "You expect me to believe that?"

"It's the truth."

She waved him off and rolled over on her side facing the far wall. "Why don't you go tell your little friend 'the truth?' I'm not interested."

Blinded by rage, he stormed from the room. She had blown everything out of proportion. He had no idea where he was going. He just knew he needed to go.

CHAPTER SIXTY-TWO

The slam echoed in Will's ears as he stormed downstairs. The front door offered escape from the madness, but he glanced over his shoulders at the upper landing. A chill ran down his spine. The carved cherubs on the banister glared at him in the moonlight, accusing him of desertion. He was angry, but he couldn't abandon Sara to the house. He had to find a way to convince her that something was wrong.

Temporarily defeated, he wandered into the parlor and flopped onto the couch. Slouching there in the darkness, he grew acutely aware of the house's noises and the shadows that seemed to crawl with unseen beings. He considered sleeping in his office, but the thought of the attic door and Gretchen's tale of the Captain changed his mind.

Alone in the dark, Sara's words tormented him. *"It's not the house. The only thing strange here is you. You've changed since we moved."*

He wanted to refute that, but lingering doubts had silenced him. The possibility that this was all in his mind still terrified him the most.

His anger dulled, and he was almost asleep, fading into the dark abyss, when the music startled him. It was faint, and seemed to echo down a long corridor from some distant place in the past. He didn't remember the title, but recognized the tune. It conjured a feeling of nostalgia.

On some level it, was apparent that this was a dream, but it felt real in every sense. The cold hardwood floor beneath his bare feet, the scent of the kerosene lamps on the mantle, even the music with its hisses and pops created the perfect illusion of reality.

Celeste entered from the dining room. Thoughts of the kiss at the church warmed him. He rose to greet her. She glided across the parlor with poise and grace. She slipped her arms over his shoulders and whispered in his ear. "Hello, Lover."

Running his hands up and down her back, he felt the smooth silk beneath his fingers. She pressed tighter against him, and he gazed into her sparkling blue eyes. They started to sway to the rhythm of the music. It was a slow tune, the haunting melody an auditory fragment from another time.

Will closed his eyes and felt her body move against his. The song continued for what felt like forever. Her fragrance — lilac — overwhelmed and intoxicated him. Springtime, new life, and the promise of new beginnings. She guided him toward a table by the fireplace.

A bottle and two glasses rested on a silver tray. She circled behind him and rested her hands on his shoulders. Her hot breath tickled his left ear. "Go ahead. Pour us a drink, we need to celebrate."

Frozen with indecision, Will told himself it was only a dream. Sara thought he was drinking anyway, so what did it matter? The thought of Sara startled him. In his dream he belonged to Celeste. Her soft lips and warm skin beckoned. In the end, he reasoned it didn't matter   who could hold anything against you that you did in a dream?

His trembling hand lifted the bottle for examination. White Horse blended Scotch whiskey. It was hardly his drink of choice. He was a beer man. Maybe that's why he removed the cap and splashed generous amounts of the amber liquid into each glass. Turning, he handed her the glass. She clinked it against his. "To us. Together forever, just as it was always meant to be."

"To us." Will echoed, and raised the glass to his lips. The whiskey's scent overwhelmed him. He closed his eyes and threw back his head emptying the glass in two swallows. The liquid burned all the way down, but he relished the sensation. "Smooth."

Celeste handed him her empty glass. "Fix us another."

Will turned back to the bottle. The warmth spread from his stomach.

I'm home boys. Pull up a stool because the good times are here again.

He refilled the glasses and turned to find Celeste reclining on the couch. "Don't be too long with that drink."

Laughter bubbled up from inside his chest and he felt giddy. Crossing the room, he knelt next to her, careful not to spill any of the precious liquid. Celeste took her glass, sipped a little of the Scotch, leaned in and kissed him on the lips, letting the liquid pour into his mouth.

He kissed her again and she pulled back with a giggle. "Finish your drink."

Will knocked back the second drink, and the room started to sway. It had been too long since he had experienced the euphoria. Dropping the glass, he pulled her off the couch and on top of him on the floor. Her warm breath, her sweet scent, he was reeling, and the room swam. He fought unconsciousness. 'Not yet,' he thought, 'I deserve a celebration.'

Like the music earlier, he heard her voice from far away down the tunnel. She was behind him again. She whispered in his ear. He was astounded when he opened his eyes and found himself standing in front of his gun cabinet with no memory of climbing the stairs.

That's okay, Dreams are like that.

Celeste pressed against him, and he tried to turn and take her in his arms, but her grip tightened on his shoulders. Her strength surprised him. Pain radiated from his shoulders, and he couldn't turn around.

"Not yet," she whispered, "You have to do one more thing so we can be together forever."

He had the key in his right hand, but no memory of retrieving it. The dream thing again. He unlocked the door and picked up the .44 Magnum.

"I have to buy it," he had explained to Harry with a wry smile, "It's Dirty Harry's Gun."

It felt heavy in his hand. Best not to think about it, he told himself. Transfixed, he gazed into the cabinet. Tears streamed down his cheeks because he knew what he had to do. There was no other way, so he turned toward the master bedroom door.

CHAPTER SIXTY-THREE

Every muscle hurt when Will opened his eyes Friday morning. Not quite with it, he came awake at once when he read the alarm clock. He had overslept again. His head pounded, and his sour stomach clenched — the familiar symptoms of a hangover.

Hello my old friend.

He would've laughed, except his blood ran cold because of the .44 Magnum next to the alarm clock. His head thumped harder and his pulse raced as he rolled over to the other side of the bed. Sara was gone.

Will struggled to his feet and called to her. Only the house's silence greeted him.

His last memory was storming out of the bedroom the night before. He grabbed the Magnum and stumbled toward the door. Holding the cold steel drove it all home. The memories flooded over him Celeste, the alcohol, and the gun. *Where was Sara?*

The pain intensified, and his head felt like it was going to explode. His stomach lurched, and he swallowed bitter acid that threatened to flood his mouth. If the night before with Celeste was only a dream, then how had the Magnum ended up on the nightstand? His stomach clenched tighter.

Will staggered into the hall and returned the gun to the cabinet. No signs of foul play. He called to Sara, and again only the silent house answered. The last thing he clearly remembered was standing in front of the gun cabinet the night before, and Celeste whispering in his ear. Then everything disintegrated. The accusing scream echoed in his mind — 'What have you done?'

He flung open the office door and expected a scene of carnage. Nothing was disturbed. Even the attic door was closed. Uncontrollable, hysterical laughter exploded from deep inside his chest. Now it surprised him when the door was closed. How odd that the normal now seemed strange.

Back in the hall he shouted for Sara.

If it was only a dream, how did the gun get in your room, and where is Sara, and what about Ellie?

His heart leapt into his mouth along with the sour contents of his stomach. He charged into the bathroom and collapsed in front of the toilet. Stomach acid spewed, burning his throat and nose. After his stomach had jettisoned the foul liquid, he pulled himself up to the sink. Gulping handfuls of cold water, he tried to rinse away the bitterness. He gripped the sink until he regained his balance and composure. As soon as he was steady, he fled the bathroom, dashing to Ellie's bedroom. The undisturbed room reminded him she had spent the night at the babysitters.

Back on the landing, he called for Sara. He took the staircase two steps at a time. His heart raced. Afraid to look in the parlor, he began to repeat the mantra that it had only been a dream. Doubts lingered — the gun on his nightstand.

The parlor was intact, and he was thankful there was no sign of a whiskey bottle. Yet his heart still pounded. He didn't need to see the bottle, his hangover was proof enough, and he swallowed bile again.

Back in the foyer, the image flashed in his mind like a stabbing blade. He had fired three shots — the empty casings discharged across the bedroom floor; the bullets tore into her flesh, her face exploded. The sheets saturated with pooling blood, the coppery scent had overwhelmed him as he hauled her corpse from the bed. He remembered the long trail of blood that stretched out like a ribbon as he dragged her body down the stairs, through the foyer, and into the basement. The smell of earth as he dug a grave in the soft dirt basement floor lingered in his senses.

He saw the blood trail, and his knees buckled. He steadied himself on the parlor doorframe, paralyzed with grief. What had he done?

Pounding startled him. Someone knocked on the front door. He drew a deep breath, filled his lungs, and tried to compose himself.

The pounding repeated. His legs felt like lead as he approached the doors. He could see Harry through one of the side windows. The old man clutched a cardboard box.

Will cracked the door. "Hey, morning."

Harry nodded and held up the box. "I got the circulator pump for your furnace."

Will didn't move aside. He held the door open only a few inches. "The what?"

"Sara told me about your trouble with the hot water. I checked it out. You need a new circulator pump. The old one was going bad, and the overflow would kick off and spray your hot water across the basement floor…"

Will started to ease the door shut. "I'm sorry it's not a good time right now. I need to get ready for work."

Something in Harry's stare alarmed Will. It was like the old man saw something. "Sure, that's fine. I can come back later and fix it. Can I set it inside the foyer? The box is heavy to carry back and forth."

Harry started coming through the door, and Will had no choice, but to open it and step aside. He clenched his fists as he watched Harry set the box by the staircase. He was ready to spring if the old man noticed the blood on the floor. Harry sat the box down and turned to face Will, apparently oblivious to the swath of blood leading back the hallway. "I'll come back when you leave for work."

Harry paused, cocked his head, and studied Will for a moment. "Are you okay? You look like something the cat drug in."

Will glanced at the floor, unable to meet Harry's eyes. The blood was gone. "I'm fine, just a late night."

Harry patted Will on the shoulder. "I'll let you get ready for work. I hope you feel better."

Will held the door open for Harry, but continued to scan the foyer floor and the stairs. There was no sign of the blood trail.

"Thanks," he said, as Harry retreated down the front porch steps.

Will slammed the door a little harder than he intended to, but Harry didn't seem to notice. He watched as the old man walked over to his truck, climbed in and drove away. When he was sure

Harry was gone, he started toward the hall, but dull thumping interrupted him. It took a moment for the sound to register. It was Sara's air compressor motor in the studio.

He felt a wave of relief as he rushed through the dining room and pounded on the locked French doors. "Sara."

"Go away, I'm working."

Even hostile, they were the sweetest words he had ever heard. He inhaled deeply and leaned against the doorjamb. The jackhammer in his chest eased. "I need to talk to you."

The compressor stopped. "Not now. I'm still angry."

"Sara, I'm sorry."

The compressor started again, and Sara's pneumatic chisel pounded out a rapid rhythm cutting into rock. Will sank into a hard Windsor chair and trembled. With his head in his hands he wept, sure of it now. He was losing his mind.

CHAPTER SIXTY-FOUR

An hour later, Betty greeted Will with her usual smile as he entered the office building. "Looks like you had a late night."

He forced a grin and wondered if he looked as bad as he felt. "You don't know the half of it."

She laughed, a sound that lifted Will's spirits a little, and gestured over her shoulder with her thumb. "You weren't alone. Half the staff called off today. I guess that'll teach C.L. to throw a party on a Thursday night."

"Yeah, I guess you're right."

Hopefully it would be a quiet day since half the staff was missing.

On the way to his office, Will noticed most of the cubes were empty. However, his e-mail was still filled when he checked. Whether he was ready for it or not, the day promised to be busy. He started to read the first message, but something on his screen distracted him. His FTP program was open, but he was sure he hadn't touched it the previous day. It appeared that someone else had used his machine.

"You made it in."

Kerrie startled him. Her amusement was evident as she stood in his doorway. The corners of her mouth turned up in that mischievous way that drove him wild. Any lingering irritation he held against her for the previous night evaporated. He hated that she had this power over him. Just looking at her made his body react.

He eased back from the computer. "You too."

"I didn't stay that late, but I think you and Sara must have left before I did. I looked for you to say goodnight."

"We called it an early night because of Sara's Philadelphia trip today."

Kerrie stepped into his office and pulled the door shut. "I want to apologize again about last night. I didn't mean to cause any trouble. I hope Sara wasn't too upset. I'd hate to think I ruined your evening."

Unsure why he felt the need to continue the deception he said, "No, everything was fine. Sara just forgot that you had told me about the job and the realtor, I'm sure I mentioned it to her."

"So you're not going to Sara's gallery opening tonight?"

Something in the way she asked the question disturbed him. Her words implied a whole world of meaning and suggested endless possibilities.

"No. I think it's better if I stay in town. Just in case there are any problems with the site."

Kerrie turned from the window and moved toward a chair. "There are other people who can cover for you. I would. I'm sure anyone on the team would, and you could always remote in if there is a major crisis."

Of course she was right. But Will felt compelled to stay. Something called to him, a feeling he couldn't explain, maybe a premonition. "Thanks, but I'm a little possessive of the project right now, since it's still so new."

Kerrie ignored the chair and started toward the desk. "Well I think it's horrible that you have to miss the show. I guess you'll spend the night with Ellie."

Will appreciated the way she moved like a cat circling in on its quarry. Her steps were slow and deliberate, her shoulders back, her chest out. "No, she is with Sara."

"So, you'll be home all alone?"

Starting to feel like prey, Will smiled and crossed his arms. "I'll be fine; I have spent an evening alone before."

Her smile broadened and she leaned in over his desk. "You know that's crazy. Why don't you come to my place for dinner? I'm not the greatest cook, but I make a pretty mean spaghetti and meatballs, and men have been known to fall in love with me for my garlic bread."

Struggling not to follow the lines of her neck down into the plunging neckline of her blouse, Will turned toward the window again. "I wouldn't want to interrupt your plans."

Kerrie shrugged and even managed to make that gesture sexy. "No plans. I was going to spend a quiet evening at home. We both have to eat, so you might as well come over. It's no trouble, really. Besides, you still owe me that rain check on dinner."

Will's resistance slipped, it was only dinner, and what would he do if he didn't accept? He would spend the evening alone in that creepy old house seeing ghosts around every corner. He thought about Sara for a brief moment, and grew angry. If she intended to convict him anyway, he might as well do the crime. "Sure, what time should I arrive?"

Kerrie straightened and turned for the door. "Make it seven that will give me time to prepare the meal, and we'll both be hungry by then. See you later."

She left the office, and Will smiled as he watched her go. His heart was racing again, only this time it wasn't terror. He decided he liked anticipation a whole lot better.

CHAPTER **SIXTY-FIVE**

Will gripped the steering wheel and stared at the Charter Arms apartments. The bushes that bordered the two-story brick building were neatly manicured and the wood trim around the doors and window sported fresh paint. The complex was located in a neighborhood of small single homes near the Colonial Park Mall, only ten minutes from the office. He glanced at the dash clock again. It was quarter till seven. He didn't want to arrive too early and felt nervous, almost nauseous, like his first date when he was a kid. Not wanting to arrive empty-handed, he picked up a bottle of wine and arrived at seven sharp.

An anxious twinge danced in his stomach. What the hell was he doing? As bad ideas went this was right up there — he would call Kerrie on his cell phone and beg off. He would say he felt ill. After all, this was exactly what had Sara accused him of — sneaking around behind her back.

He grew angry again.

If I'm going to do the time, I might as well do the crime.

A ridiculous excuse to justify his actions, but he didn't care. Logic and reason were buried under exhaustion and the emotional turmoil of the last few weeks. The thought that this all might be a dream alleviated some of his reservations. With dead boys vanishing, colleagues bursting into flames, and burned out bars open for business, the definition of reality began to blur. If he was going crazy, he might as well enjoy life while he still could.

Will retrieved a packet of mints from his drink holder and popped one into his mouth. The setting sun cast everything in a surreal orange glow adding to the evening's unreality.

At the door, he checked for the correct number. He drew a deep breath and rang the bell. Kerrie answered the door dressed in a tight blue skirt and low-cut white cotton blouse. He forced himself to focus on her face.

She gave him a peck on the cheek. "I hope you're hungry."

He felt flushed. "Starved."

She took hold of his hand and moved back into the apartment.

"No trouble finding the place?"

"No, your directions were perfect."

Closing the door behind him, she released his hand and he immediately missed her touch. She gestured around the room. "This is it. Home sweet home."

"It looks like a nice neighborhood."

Ouch, did I really just say that?

He felt awkward and couldn't smother his nervousness.

She smiled and seemed not to notice. "It's nice, and it's close to work."

Nothing semi-intelligent to say came to mind. "It must be nice to have such a short commute."

"You bet. I'm not a morning person. I always have way more fun in the dark."

She winked, and he tried not to grin like a self-conscious teenager. Anticipation hung in the air. Tonight just might be the culmination of all the suggestive flirting over the last few months. He tried not to let his thoughts wander too far ahead. He tried not to think at all and let his body drift into auto pilot.

Turning toward the kitchen, she waved at the couch. "It will be a few minutes until dinner's ready, make yourself at home. I'll open the wine."

He hesitated, and hoped his apprehension wasn't too obvious. "I'm good, thanks."

She gave him another warm smile and bit her bottom lip. It was a nervous habit he thought was adorable. "When you're ready for a drink, just say the word."

She entered the kitchen, and he watched her through the opening above the counter that separated it from the living room. He enjoyed the way she moved as she checked on the dinner. The aroma of simmering sauce filled the apartment. His stomach growled. Tonight his appetites were ravenous.

Not wanting to stare, he turned his attention to the living room. It was sparsely decorated with a couch and two thick-cushioned chairs. An entertainment center covered most of the west wall. Hundreds of books lined the shelves, many of them programming manuals, but he smiled when he noticed a large section of paperback romance novels.

A twenty-seven-inch TV occupied the center of the large unit. Photos in metal frames were propped against books on different shelves, giving the entertainment center an uncharacteristically untidy appearance compared to the rest of the room. Two end tables with lamps completed the eclectic décor. It resembled a college student's dorm room, filled with pieces that didn't match, because the young person wasn't yet established — they hadn't matured into the person they would ultimately become. He pushed that thought away; he didn't like to think of Kerrie as immature.

Kerrie poured the sauce over the dish of pasta. "I think it's ready."

He joined her in the kitchen. She had two places set at an old metal kitchen table that resembled his and Sara's first kitchen set in Philadelphia. A slight pang of guilt tweaked him. Shoving it aside he sat down at the table. "This looks delicious. I'm starved."

Kerrie approached the table with two glasses and his bottle of Elmo Pio Moscato white wine. "How did you know it's my favorite?"

He smiled, but said nothing as she filled the glasses and joined him at the table. "Let's dig in before it gets cold."

The flavor of fried garlic, green peppers, and oregano melded perfectly in the tomato and meat sauce, and again his hunger surprised him.

"I hope it's okay," Kerrie said, "I rarely get the chance to cook for company."

"It's great. I don't think I've ever tasted better."

Smiling, she picked up her glass. "I wanted tonight to be special, a private celebration of our accomplishments."

Will picked up his glass to be polite, and she raised hers a little higher and continued. "A toast to us."

She paused, and he stared at his glass.

She took a sip, and he smiled and said, "Here, here."

Returning his glass to the table untouched, he thought she seemed agitated, but it faded quickly. He bit into his slice of garlic bread, and it melted in his mouth. "You said you have an uncle who lives near Harrisburg. Do you get to see him often?"

Her face darkened. "No, he passed away."

Will watched something hard pass in her expression. He didn't like the anger that flashed in her eyes for a second. He felt awkward. "I'm sorry."

She shrugged and her face softened, the darkness disappearing. "He was old, and these things happen."

He agreed, wishing he had not brought up the uncle. "It must be hard living so far away from the rest of your family. Do you ever think about moving back to Philadelphia?"

Kerrie shrugged again and took a sip of her wine. "I guess it depends on what happens here. I mean, it's not that simple to move back. I like the job, and I would hate to have to start all over again."

"Starting over is never easy, and it's not always clear if things will be better." His words felt like more than he had intended to say. What the hell was he playing at? He didn't want to start over. Coming here tonight was not about that. He wasn't sure why he had come. In honesty he knew, he just wasn't ready to admit that to himself. This path led to danger.

Kerrie nodded and searched his face. He felt naked under her scrutiny. He held up his slice of garlic bread. "This meal is wonderful, and you're right, men could fall in love with you for this."

Her face brightened and she laughed. Will could listen to that sound forever. It was hard to think of anything else when they were together. The way she moved, the way she tilted her head, the way she reached over and touched his arm when she spoke. "You've always made me smile, that's what I love about you," she said.

He felt a rush. She took another sip of wine, and he tried to ignore his glass. She touched his arm again and continued. "Do you remember how hard that project was in Philadelphia? That was my first big project, and I thought I would never get through it, but you always had something to say that made me feel better."

He hadn't realized he had done that. "You were pretty upbeat yourself as I recall."

Her hand squeezed a little tighter on his arm. "No, really, you made the difference. You helped me get through it. You believed in me and encouraged me. That meant a lot."

Her touch sent another thrill through his body. He didn't want her to let go. He was letdown when she did.

Kerrie finished her glass of wine and reached for the bottle. "You haven't touched yours."

He shook his head. "I'm not supposed to drink."

"And do you always do what you're supposed to?"

He glanced around the small kitchen. "I guess not."

She raised her glass again. "To not doing what you're supposed to."

Will chuckled, but still couldn't bring himself to lift the glass. His hand moved closer, but stopped. He told himself this wasn't a dream, and picked up his fork instead and ate another bite of pasta. They made small talk about the office, a subject that seemed like safe ground, and Will ignored the glass of alcohol in front of him. Kerrie only picked at her food, but the wine bottle was almost empty when she rose with a full glass in hand. "Why don't we relax in the living room?"

He popped another mint into his mouth and followed, leaving his full glass behind on the kitchen table. She proceeded to the couch, but he paused by the entertainment center. "You have a lot of books. I didn't know you were such an avid reader."

"It helps me pass the time, and I think books make a place feel homey."

He had always thought the same thing. "You're into romances; I would have pegged you for action-adventure."

Smiling, she took another sip of wine. One eyebrow rose slightly as she patted the couch next to her. "I guess I'm just a romantic at heart."

Ignoring the invitation, he realized that he neared the point of an unretractable action, if he proceeded, it would alter him and his life forever. The internal melee raged between the desire of what he wanted right now, and the sense of who he was. If he accepted Kerrie's offered pleasures, he would pay with a large piece of his soul. But, he wanted her. No thought, just an unsatisfied hunger that threatened to consume him. Instead of joining Kerrie, he turned to the pictures on the shelves. "Are these photos of your family?"

"Most of them, yes. You know, grandparents, uncles, aunts, and a lot of my brother and me. When I was a kid, I had this old black and white camera, and I loved to take pictures."

He listened, but was distracted. He lifted one of the photos from the shelf, and the world dropped away, his body felt almost weightless. He held it out for her to see and tried to steady his trembling hand. "Is this one of you and your brother?"

"Yes, he's my twin, that's when we were kids."

It was the same photo he had found in the trunk when he had followed the man into the attic. The room started to spin, and Will fought for control. "What were you doing in front of my house, and who were these people?"

Kerrie stared at the carpet, avoiding his eyes. "That's my Aunt June and Uncle Martin. It was their house."

Will backed against the wall for support. "What?"

She pleaded with her eyes — her vulnerability laid bare — no flirtatious seduction, just naked urgency. "Please don't be angry."

He struggled to make sense of this, but nothing was clear. "I don't understand. Why didn't you tell me I was buying your uncle's house?"

She rose from the couch and crossed the room with her half full glass in hand. "I didn't know how you would feel about that."

His vertigo lessened. "How I would *feel?*"

"My brother and I would visit in the summer. I loved it there. We would run through the woods and swim in the river. It is the place that contains my most cherished memories, and I wanted you to have it."

Will stepped away from the wall and glanced at other photos, noticing that there were many taken in the front and back yard at his house. "I just don't understand."

Kerrie moved closer, almost touching him. "I remembered when you said that Sara always wanted to own an old Victorian house. You told me that one night while we were working on the project in Philly. So when you accepted the position and moved here, I knew Sara would love my Uncle's house. My parents were trying to sell the place after he died. I didn't know how you and Sara would feel if you knew it was my family's property. That's why I told you about the Realtor, and let her show you the house. I just didn't want anyone to feel uncomfortable."

He stared at her pouting lips and her doe eyes and his defenses melted. "You remembered something I said in passing back in Philadelphia?"

Kerrie sat the wine glass on the shelf and stepped closer. "I remember everything you said in Philadelphia."

She ran her fingers through his hair, pressed her body against him and kissed him hard on the lips. Her lips were soft. He dropped the photograph, drew her closer and kissed her back. His world spun out of control, but he didn't care. The only thing that mattered was the here and now, nothing else, not strange visions or vanishing children, or delusions or reality. Her breath was sweet and fruity, her breasts pressed warm and tantalizing against him. He closed his eyes, lost in the moment, and surrendered to his desires. He wanted her, no matter the cost, but suddenly he felt the .44 Magnum in his hand and his finger tightening on the trigger, the unretractable action. The explosion roared in his head as a vision of Sara's face disintegrated.

Will jerked away. "I can't do this."

Kerrie ran her hand over his crotch, her fingers gently caressing him. His erection grew harder at her touch. "It feels like you can."

"No. Stop, *I mean I won't do this.*"

"Will?"

He backed away. "I'm sorry."

Her face a mask of confusion, she scanned his, seeking confirmation. "What do you mean? I know you want me, and I want you. We're perfect together, a perfect match."

She stepped closer, reaching for him, trying to kiss him again. He pushed away harder than he intended to, and she stumbled backwards, landing in a heap on the floor.

The look of surprise and rejection in her eyes crushed him. Will stepped forward reaching for her. "I'm sorry…"

"Will, don't make me beg."

He froze. "No. Sara… and Ellie, I don't know what I've been thinking. I never meant to hurt you. But I won't hurt them."

Kerrie crawled to her knees. "No one needs to know. It will be our secret."

He couldn't stand the pleading in her voice, and he realized if he didn't escape now his defenses would crumble. As much as he loved his wife and daughter, his attraction to this young woman threatened to consume him. "I can't."

She reached for him, tears welling in her eyes. "After everything I've done for you, the house, the job, and all I've gone through to be with you. Now you come here leading me on. What kind of sick joke was this?"

Will stared at the floor. "It was never like that. I was flattered and I guess I…"

He wanted to take this evening back. He wanted to take the last three months back. He didn't understand why it had reached this point, or how he had allowed himself to go this far. "I never meant to hurt you."

Fury flashed in her eyes as she climbed to her feet. "Hurt me? You never really thought about me at all, did you? This was all about how *I* made *you* feel. You were flattered. What did you do? Laugh to yourself every night as you drove home to your wife and daughter? You enjoyed letting me make a fool of myself."

Trying to find a way to salvage the situation, Will struggled for the right words. "It wasn't like that. I swear. If I wasn't married… When I'm with you…"

Kerrie stood defiant with quivering shoulders. She fought back sobs. "Even now, it's still all about *you*. Now you can walk out of here a righteous man, self-congratulatory because you can do the right thing in the face of temptation. You're still using me to make yourself feel better."

"I didn't mean to do this, I'm sorry."

She picked up the wine glass and hurled it at his head. It shattered on the doorframe, fragments exploding across the rug. "Sorry. Get out, you bastard. I hate you, I hate you."

Will fled her apartment for the safety of his car. He sat there in the parking lot for a long time and stared at her window. His heart pounded and his hands trembled. He tried to convince himself that he had not come there to use her. It was no use, she was right.

The lights went out in her living room.

I hope she's okay.

He regretted everything, including the problems that might result at work. He had been a fool. He sat there castigating himself for his stupidity, when another thought stopped him. He was afraid to go home alone.

CHAPTER SIXTY-SIX

The old Victorian loomed in the mist waiting for his return. The moss-covered ground was slippery, and a thick canopy of leaves blocked most of the moonlight. Will's stomach clenched as he crossed the driveway. He forced his leaden legs forward. Cold sweat trickled down his back. Every instinct screamed not to enter the house. If he left now, he could join Sara and Ellie in the city. Maybe patch things up with Sara. And what? Never come back. It had been his idea to move here, following his own desires, now the situation had grown beyond his control. He tried to shake the jitters as he opened the front door. Inside the dimly lit foyer, he paused to stare at the intricately carved angels on the banister. Rapture filled their faces, mocking his fear. A bout of nervous laughter bubbled forth; he couldn't contain it, the sound echoed in the still house, and surprised him into silence.

Standing there in the darkness, paralyzed, afraid to move forward, Will wished he had never seen this place. His actions earlier in the evening were going to have repercussions possibly damaging his marriage and career. He stood on the brink of eternity. One wrong move and he would fall into the eternal void.

Footsteps in the upstairs hall distracted him. The hair on the back of his neck tingled, and his stomach tightened. He should have gone to Sara and Ellie in Philadelphia. Sara's anger would have been preferable to enduring the night alone in this hell hole.

He paused and listened, but heard no other sounds. Doubt clouded his mind. He had probably imagined the footsteps and fought the urge to go room-to-room turning on lights to make sure that he was alone. This impulse was further evidence that he was losing his mind. He climbed the stairs, intent on crawling into bed and pulling the covers over his head, like a small child, until morning.

He listened intently, and the footsteps did not repeat. He sighed. The darkness transformed the most mundane noises into something sinister. Still tense from his encounter with Kerrie, his imagination was in overdrive, and it was best not to give any energy to delusions. This seemed reasonable; however, the events of the past few weeks cast uncertainty on everything.

The phone rang in the foyer and shattered the silence. Will yelped. He felt foolish and prayed it was Sara. He longed to hear her voice. He scrambled for the receiver and forgot about the footsteps.

Through the earpiece he heard a timid woman's voice. "Hello, Mr. Shepherd, my name is Lillian... work at the Chronicle. I'm sorry it's so late, but... I don't know if you remem... church when you moved."

They had a bad connection; the woman's words kept cutting out. Will searched his memory, trying to match a face with the name. "I'm sorry, the connection's bad, there's too much static. I can't understand you."

The woman continued, but static drowned out many of her words. "It's urgent... I have some... I need to share..."

"Did you say you're from the paper?"

"Yes... Chronicle... Your friend Gretc... a few weeks... I discov... your house... need to see this."

It had something to do with Gretchen. This woman had some information, and Will needed anything to explain the last few weeks. "We should meet," he said.

There was a long pause on the other end of the line, and he

thought he had lost the connection. About to hang up, Lillian's voice returned. "I would pref... is important... at the paper..."

Will glanced at his watch, and it was almost midnight. Unsure what the caller had just said, he took a chance. "I can stop by the paper tomorrow. How about nine?"

The line went dead. Although static had distorted most of the conversation, this seemed to be the break he sought. Gretchen must have discovered something about the house, something that got her killed. Excited and terrified, Will undressed and slipped into bed. As he lay awake in the darkness, he tried not to listen for sounds, and prayed for the morning's speedy arrival.

CHAPTER SIXTY-SEVEN

It felt like he had just drifted off to sleep when he opened his eyes. The white bedroom curtains billowed in the moonlight. All the windows were open. *What the hell?* Disoriented, he searched for his alarm clock. It read four AM. He had slept for five hours. Sleepy and confused, he stumbled from bed to close the windows that he was sure had been shut when he went to sleep.

Will turned from the last one, and felt like someone blasted him with icy water from a fire hose. He gasped. Kerrie's Uncle Martin knelt next to the bed, holding his wife June's hand. Will recognized them from Kerrie's photos. Although June looked sick and fragile. The scent of disinfectant, bile and urine clung in the air.

The couple ignored him. June was still, her eyes closed, her face pulled into a permanent mask of discomfort. Martin held a syringe in his left hand. "I know the pain is too much, please forgive me? I love you."

With trembling hands, Martin carefully injected June. She stirred momentarily and then exhaled a shallow breath. Her face relaxed. Martin buried his in his hands.

Will couldn't decide if he was dreaming or hallucinating. The couple faded, leaving only the foul smells that reminded Will of disease and death. He swallowed, trying not to vomit; the overwhelming stench permeated the air. He crept toward the bed and examined it, but found no trace of June. It didn't matter; it was too much. He wouldn't spend another night alone in this house. His heart pounded as he went to the bureau and grabbed a clean pair of jeans and a T-shirt. He pulled them on in the darkness and fumbled for his shoes. Footsteps echoed in the hall, and a moan drifted from the bed. Will scrambled to his feet, ready to bolt for the door, but froze when he saw an older version of Martin reclining in the bed and Celeste standing in the doorway. She was beautiful, and seductive, but because of the hardness in her face, Will suspected she had not come for amorous reasons. She casually leaned against the door-frame, folding her arms under her breasts.

"Martin, I'm sorry, but I think we are through with you," she said.

Will watched with fascination, unable to move, as a rope snaked through the open doorway and across the bedroom floor. Celeste's sinister glare fixed on Martin, who inched toward the edge of the bed away from the door. The rope slithered up the bedpost and inched closer to him. It sprang with incredible speed, a piece of the same old towrope that Harry had used on Ellie's swing, Will felt sick to his stomach as he made the connection.

Martin struggled as the one end of the rope coiled around his neck and formed a noose. The other end rose into the air like a cobra following the melody from an unseen flute. It weaved effortlessly through the ornate openings in the center-ceiling beam and jerked taut to lift Martin into a standing position on the bed.

A corner chair slid to the center of the room at the foot of the bed as Martin pulled frantically at the tightening noose. He struggled to keep his balance as he was towed toward the chair. The rope kept circling the beam, slithering around it, with a life of its own, reeling in Martin toward the foot of the bed. He stumbled awkwardly onto the chair and gasped for air. Desperate fingers clawed at the noose.

Celeste studied him, like a predator sizing up prey.

Martin spoke, his voice barely audible. "You can't have me."

Celeste's cruel laughter echoed off the bedroom walls. "I had you a long time ago. The day you murdered your wife you became mine."

Tears rolled down Martin's cheeks.

Will had been so shocked by the scene he hadn't moved, now he lunged toward Martin. He reached out to grab the old man around the waist to support his weight, but passed through him and the chair. It was like running through a spring-fed mountain waterfall. The frigid temperature stole his breath. He staggered around to face Martin, who continued, unaffected by Will's efforts. "She was in pain. The cancer. She asked me — begged me."

"You little worm," Celeste said.

The chair toppled, plunging Martin into a freefall. Will heard something snap in Martin's neck like the dry crack of breaking twigs. Martin's lifeless body dangled in the center of the master bedroom, and Will groaned as urine ran down Martin's leg and pooled on the hard wood floor.

Will wheeled around to face Celeste, but only caught a glimpse of her image as she dissolved into the darkness, her manic laughter echoing through the house.

Will didn't want to, but he had to turn around and look at Martin, just to prove the man didn't exist, that this was all some lucid dream. He groaned again when he saw Martin's limp body still hanging from the rafter. A gunshot's crack interrupted his thoughts, the sound faint and far away like an echo from the past. It had originated downstairs, probably the parlor. Someone had fired a gun. Will fished his keys out of his front pocket with trembling hands. He'd be damned, if he was going to face an intruder unarmed. He grabbed his twelve gauge Wingmaster Remington shotgun. With the spray of buckshot, he had a better chance of hitting a target. He worked the pump to chamber a shell, gaining some courage from the sound, he inched toward the staircase.

CHAPTER **SIXTY-EIGHT**

Halfway to the stairs another cold chill washed over Will. A man dressed in a tattered union soldier's uniform blocked his path on the landing. The haggard soul shook with rage; his face gaunt and his eyes black holes. Will leveled his shotgun at him.

The man laughed. "You can't kill a dead man, son."

Will raised the shotgun, his finger lightly touching the trigger. "You know you're dead?"

The man's face twisted with torment, and he reached up and pulled away the left half of his skull. It cracked and popped like old straw. "We're all dead. Me, you, everyone, we're bound to this forsaken ground. You just don't understand it yet."

The soldier shambled forward like a zombie, and Will squeezed the trigger. The shotgun blast erupted, and the apparition dissolved into mist.

Will's heartbeat thumped in his ears, as he pumped another shell into the chamber. He tried to steady the shotgun as he moved down the stairs. He told himself he hadn't just murdered a man, there was nothing there. His muscle tense, his mind on edge, the adrenalin coursing through his body, he yelled out when he heard the thump in the parlor. Only inches from the front door, he considered fleeing, but a low, gurgling sound from the parlor called to him, and God forgive him, he couldn't help himself; he had to see the source of that sound. He started toward the parlor doorway, the shotgun raised high in trembling hands. He walked through a curtain of frigid air, his breath misting before his eyes.

He promised himself he would only take one quick glance and then run like hell for the front door. He licked his lips and swallowed hard, trying to slow his pounding heart. Shadows enveloped the room and at first it appeared empty. Then he spotted the body slumped to one side in a high backed wing chair. A revolver lay on the floor under the man's left hand.

Will tried not to notice the dark stain on the back of the chair and the pieces of spongy material splattered there. It was Howard, much older than Will remembered him from the vision were he'd killed

Celeste, but it was the same man.

It was obvious the man was dead, so when Howard sat forward and shouted at Will with the moonlight shining through the back of his mouth where the rest of his skull should have been, Will crashed backward over the coffee table. "She's beautiful, but deadly. She'll get you too. She already has."

Will crabbed away from Howard, the Remington clutched in his right hand. When Howard awkwardly tried to rise, Will fumbled the gun up, aimed in Howard's direction and fired. The buckshot tore through the old man, the chair, and Window behind him. The spectral corpse slammed back into the chair and slumped there.

Will gulped air as he struggled to his feet. He stumbled for the foyer, and almost tripped when Tony Legaro's severed body blocked his path to the front door. Will couldn't look away from the top half of the young man's torso that crawled toward him with entrails trailing out behind. Will inched backward toward the dining room. Tony's eyes were wide. The horror reflected there hinting that the young man was in his own secret hell.

"It's your fault," Tony rasped, reaching bloody hands out to grab Will.

Will fled farther into the dining room, not turning his back on Tony and keeping the shotgun pointed at the corpse that he knew couldn't possibly exist. "Stay back. Please? I don't want to shoot you."

Tony crept after him, leaving a swath of blood in his path. "You've already killed me."

Will's back bumped against the studio doors. He kept the shotgun aimed at Tony, his finger on the trigger. A loud crash thundered inside Sara's studio. The noise surprised Will and he lurched away from the French doors. Reflexively, he squeezed the trigger. Because his aim went wide, the blast destroyed the glass front and most of Sara's favorite china in her china cabinet.

Will regained his footing, hoping to escape through the kitchen, but froze when he saw a woman engulfed in flames blocking the doorway. Cornered by Tony and the flaming woman whose shrieks bespoke hellish torment, Will backed toward the studio doors, dreading whatever fresh horror surely waited inside.

With the shotgun raised he spun and fled into the studio, seeking escape. The dim moonlight cast the room in cold blue and white starkness. The broken bodies of hundreds of small dead birds littered the floor among thousands of shards of glass. The studio's ceiling was all jagged edges, as if all those small sparrows had crashed against the panes, demolishing them and shredding themselves.

In the middle of the studio, the canvas tarp fell away to reveal Sara's current sculpture. The translucent orange alabaster statue mesmerized Will. A multitude of grotesque depictions ascended around the man-sized pillar. Each scene a brutal act, starting at the bottom with a ball of fire that fell to earth and crashed into the base of a mountain that looked remarkably like Will's property. From the smoking ash a flaming man-shaped figure rose and shook its fists at the heavens.

The next scene was the slaughter of the Gray Wolf's village.

An apparent trick of the light the figures seemed alive. The blood flowed, and the flames sprang to life. Each three-dimensional scene repeated like an endless movie loop. The warriors butchered each other in the brutal massacre Will remembered from his vision. The orange stone pulsed like living flesh, sensuous and horrific.

Will didn't recognize most of the events that encircled the column. But some of the scenes were familiar. Here the Civil War Captain shooting his wife and her lover in bed, there Celeste falling down the stairs. Near the top, Martin Darkas hung from a rafter in the master bedroom.

It was too much. Will needed to escape. He couldn't breathe. The final unfinished scene at the top sent a wave of weakness through his body, his legs threatening to collapse. It depicted Sara and Ellie lying motionless on the foyer floor. The hand of an unfinished figure held a smoking gun over them.

Anger burned away Will's fear. "You can't have them," he screamed to the house and all its spectral inhabitants. He squeezed the trigger again, and the buckshot tore through the statue like it was living flesh. The blast shredded the demon rock, and sent pieces splintering in all directions. The stone's blood splattered the floor and walls like some hellish abstract painting.

A cold fist clenched Will's ankle, and he screamed. Distracted by Sara's living sculpture he had forgotten the horrible apparition that pursued him. Tony's bloody teeth bit down hard on his right calf, tearing away a chunk of flesh and muscle. Hot pain exploded in Will's calf, and he tried to jam the shotgun butt into the creature's head, but it passed harmlessly through. Will tore himself free and stumbled away from Tony, who now resembled an animal more than a human. Will pumped the shotgun, praying he had another shell, leveled it, and fired. He did not wait to see if the blast destroyed the phantom. He turned and sprinted out the side door into the night, his heart pounding, his lungs on fire, pain searing his right leg.

CHAPTER SIXTY-NINE

Lillian Arnold arrived at the Chronicle at eight thirty Saturday morning. She wanted to meet with Will Shepherd, give him the information she had gathered and be done with the whole business. The previous evening's phone conversation still disturbed her. Mr. Shepherd couldn't seem to hear her, although she could hear him just fine. It was probably the old phone lines, still there were too many strange events tied to that house for her liking.

Even in the familiar surroundings of the newspaper office, she felt unnerved. The paper's office had been her home away from home for the past ten years, but today the place felt different, somehow desperate. Lillian was fifty, single, and had no real future; even the future of the small town weekly paper was in question. For the first time, it occurred to her how depressing her work and life truly were.

She sat at her desk and tried to shake the feeling before Mr. Shepherd arrived. She reached for the file to go over it one more time, but it wasn't on her desk where she thought she had placed it last night. She must have left it in the morgue. "Lillian, every day you become more forgetful. I hope you're not getting Alzheimer's."

She chuckled at her humor. If talking to oneself was a symptom of the disease then she had been infected since childhood. She flipped the light switch in the pressroom. There was a loud "pop" and the windowless room remained dark. "Great, a blown fuse. Just what I need."

She felt her way through the maze of junk in the darkness. The fuse box was in the basement. She hoped the lights still worked in the morgue. When she opened the door and flipped the switch, she was relieved that the dim yellow bulb sputtered to life. The file rested at the far end of the table where she must have left it on Friday afternoon when she finished her research. "Lillian you'd forget your head if it wasn't attached."

Halfway to the folder she heard a loud whoosh in the pressroom and the steel door slammed shut, but not before she caught a strong whiff of smoke.

The building was on fire. She ran to the door, touching it with her left hand and recoiled from the heat that left her palm stinging.

Smoke snaked under the door. Lillian tried to remain calm.

How could a raging fire have started in seconds?

She dropped to her knees. Her lungs ached and she coughed uncontrollably. The hiss of flames and crackling and popping of years of antiques being consumed echoed in the outer room.

She steadied herself against the large wooden table. Her vision blurred, and she started to choke. The smoke crowded out the oxygen, and the heat grew unbearable. Her body was slick with a film of perspiration and soot. In the back of her oxygen-starved brain she remembered that smoke rose. She needed to be near the floor.

Lillian glanced at the file, she realized the fire had something to do with the secrets she'd uncovered. It was too important. She couldn't fail. She needed to deliver that folder.

Her eyes stung, and tears ran down her cheeks as the room grew dimmer and the soft buzz in her head grew louder.

The fresh air was near the floor, and it would possibly give her another breath or two of life. The voice in her mind protested and whispered, "Not down, Lillian. Up. The painted-over windows."

She berated herself as she tried to feel her way to the outer wall. Why hadn't she thought of the windows before? They were small, but maybe she could squeeze through, if she could just open one. A coughing jag wracked her thin body as she searched for the darkened panes.

CHAPTER SEVENTY

Will parked by the curb and watched firemen swarm around the old brick building down the street. Flames danced across its roof, and huge black smoke clouds billowed into the morning sky. Fire trucks obscured a clear view of the scene at ground level, so he climbed out of his car, and started up the sidewalk on foot.

His leg still throbbed where Tony had bitten him, but when he had checked there had been no wound, not even a red mark. Still, the ache was real, or perhaps a phantom pain like one that amputees feel in their lost limb. He tried to convince himself that the apparitions at the house couldn't hurt him, but he thought about Martin and reconsidered. It overwhelmed his fevered mind, leaving him to wonder where the delusions ended and reality began.

A police officer called to him. "Sir, you can't get any closer. It's too dangerous."

Will stopped, the man's words drawing him out of his own thoughts. "What building is on fire?"

"*The Chronicle.*"

His heart skipped a beat. "I'm supposed to meet someone there. Was there anyone inside?"

The officer's poker face revealed nothing. "Yeah, one employee, but I can't release any information at this time. Are you a reporter or something? Did you work there?"

Will shook his head. "No."

Motioning for Will to move up the sidewalk toward his car, the officer guided him away from the building. "The best thing you can do is stay back."

Will took a few steps, then turned to watch the firemen direct their powerful streams of water at the burning building. The fire ebbed and flowed in battle with the firemen like a huge beast determined to consume everything in its grasp.

It was a fire just like the fire that killed Gretchen. The thought assaulted him as he licked his dry lips and tried to steady his shaky hands. Lightheaded, he couldn't bear to watch anymore so he turned to walk back to his car. He stopped short when he heard his name. "Mr. Shepherd, please wait?"

A small thin woman approached. Her hair tousled, and her clothes covered with dirt and soot. Will felt a wave of relief. "Lillian?"

She nodded and steadied herself on a porch railing. Reaching for her arm, Will tried to assist her. "Are you okay? Do you need medical attention?"

Lillian shook her head, tears running down her smudged cheeks. "I'm fine. I need to talk to you before anything else happens."

Will noticed the thick folder she clutched. "About what's in that file?"

She looked down at the manila folder in her hand like she was discovering it for the first time. She extended it to Will who took it and helped her over to the porch steps of the old house behind them. She coughed several times.

"Please, Lillian, sit down."

Will sat on the top step next to her. The stench of smoke was strong, and he wondered if it originated from the burning building or the woman sitting next to him. "That's the history of your house."

He studied the outside of the folder. "You look like you need a doctor. Let's get you some help, then we can talk."

"No!" The small woman's shriek unnerved him. "I need to talk to you *now*. I don't think I'll get a second chance."

He thought about Gretchen and decided that perhaps she was right. "You know what's going on at my house."

A fit of coughing overcame her, and she struggled to regain her composure. "It's all in the file. I'll try to explain."

He feared she would collapse, so he started scanning the street for that police officer or an EMT, but her words distracted him. "My story starts about a year ago, when the previous owner of your house visited me at the paper."

"Martin Darkas?" Will's gaze settled on her as she nodded.

She proceeded to explain the same story she had told Gretchen. It intrigued Will that Martin had also been curious about more than Native Americans. He thought about the towrope around the old man's neck and shuddered. The idea that the entities in the house could really hurt him and his family didn't seem so farfetched anymore.

"Mr. Darkas was interested in anything I could find in the paper's archives about his home or its previous owners. We usually don't offer that kind of service, we're a small paper, but I knew him from when he'd worked at the bank, so I offered to help him on my own time." Lillian stared at her hands and sighed. "I'm afraid I didn't get too far before he died. It was a terrible thing."

Will's stomach tightened as he thought about Martin's death. Apparently Lillian had heard about the suicide. A dark shadow crossed over her face. "I had the list of names he gave me, but I forgot about the research after he died. When your friend stopped in a few weeks ago, I dug out the list of names and we started searching the records again. We found a couple of things that day, but I guess she didn't get to tell you."

A chill danced down Will's spine at the thought of that day. "No."

Lillian nodded. "I didn't think so. After her death, I didn't stop. I'm not sure why, but it felt important to continue. The more I learned, the more I grew convinced. It's all in the folder. I'll just give you the highlights. The first owner Joseph Sullivan, an Irish Immigrant had been issued a land grant in 1815. He named the grounds 'Shadow's Forge' because he learned that the local Native Americans called that area 'The place where shadows are formed.'"

Will's heart pounded because it was just like what Small Sparrow had said in his hallucination or vision. It couldn't have come from his subconscious because there was no way he could have known that on his own.

Lillian continued, "He built a two-story log structure and opened it as an inn. It was a popular stopover between Harrisburg, Halifax, and Templeton."

"You found that in your paper's archives? An article about the Inn?"

Lillian swallowed and shook her head. "No not exactly. It turns out that Mr. Sullivan was infamous in these parts, that all happened before the Chronicle was published. I found that at the State library, in archived copies of *The Union* — a weekly paper that was published in Harrisburg at the time of the trial."

Will stared at Lillian. "The trial?"

"Yes, I'm sorry, I guess I'm a little dazed. It turns out that in 1819 Joseph Sullivan married Mary O'Rourke, one of his tavern girls. They apparently had a good marriage until 1820, when in a fit of jealous rage, Joseph bludgeoned Mary to death with a flaming log from the tavern fireplace."

Will's skin crawled as he remembered one of the lower scenes on Sara's sculpture — the crazed eyes of the man as he brandished the burning log.

"It made the *Union* newspaper because the trial was held at the county court house in Harrisburg. Joseph was found guilty and hanged for murder."

Will thought about the gun beside his nightstand. "I guess that was the end of the Inn?"

"No. Joseph left the Inn to his brother James. He and his wife lived there until the original house burned in 1855. They both died in the fire."

"Not exactly a lucky place for the first owners." Will inhaled deeply trying to ease the growing tightness in his chest.

Shaking her head, Lillian was wracked with another fit of coughing. When she regained control, she spoke so low Will could barely understand her. "Not a lucky place for any of the owners. It goes on and on. Your friend was most interested in the Civil War era. When I showed her the list of owners, she homed right in on Kiefer Courtland. He owned the house from 1856 to 1865, bought

'Shadow's Forge' as a wedding gift for his wife and had the current Victorian house built on the site. I think they used the original tavern foundation for part of the new construction. It took us most of the morning, but we found him in early editions of *The Chronicle*. He was the son of a wealthy businessman who owned Courtland Mills, and he was also a captain in the 57th Regiment Infantry, Pennsylvania Volunteers."

Will Leaned against the porch rail and tried to control his trembling hands by gripping the folder tighter. He now had the evidence to back up his research. Sara would have to listen. "I know he's buried on the property. Let me guess — he returned from the Civil War discovered his wife in bed with her lover, shot them both and then turned the gun on himself."

Lillian stared hard at him for a few minutes. "How did you know that?"

It was odd that he was surprising her. "Something Gretchen saw at the house."

Nodding knowingly, Lillian hugged her arms. Her fragile appearance alarmed Will. "When she saw this she was excited, but she never did explain why."

Will imagined Gretchen thrilled with evidence that would prove to him and Sara that they were in danger and the she wasn't crazy. He fought back tears because he felt the same way. She had been right — they were in danger.

Lillian whispered, "There's more. Gretchen was even more agitated by the fact that Howard Freedman had owned the property."

The world fell out from under Will. Howard Freedman, *Freedman* — Sara's maiden name. The connection clicked into place like a cell door slamming. Howard the bartender was actually never a bartender at all. He had been an esteemed State senator. His familiar features now made sense because it was a family resemblance to Sara.

The frail woman touched his arm. "You didn't know?"

Trying to escape his daze, Will shook his head. The folder in his hands grew heavier. "No, we had no idea any relative of Sara's ever owned the house."

They sat and stared at the folder for a moment, both lost in their own thought.

"May I keep this?" Will finally asked.

Lillian looked at the folder with a hint of regret and then glanced over her shoulder at the burning building. "I was going to write a story about your place, you know, a human interest piece. But after today, I don't think I want any more to do with your property. If you don't mind me saying so, I think you should get out of there as soon as you can."

Will looked past her at the burning building. "You think the fire at the paper had something to do with my house?"

She gaped at him. "Yes, that's exactly what I think. I know it sounds crazy, but a demon dwells on that land, and it didn't want me to tell you."

"A demon?" Will didn't find the idea as absurd as he would have a few weeks ago.

"Yes. It's a demon Mr. Shepherd. It fell to earth during the Great Rebellion, and has been linked to the location where it crashed. Maybe the beauty of the place kept it there, more likely, the dimensional veil caused by the demon's fall enables it to draw spirits back from the other side. Either way, it has remained and it feeds on the suffering and pain of anyone who lives there, until it sucks them dry. Then it either kills them or drives them to kill themselves and others."

Will sat in stunned silence. He remembered the first scene on Sara's statue, the burning man falling from the sky. It seemed to be the explanation he was seeking, but it was still hard to grasp. He thought about Ellie, Sara, and his .44 Magnum and shuddered. He looked down at the thick folder, assessing the weight.

"Thank you…" He realized he didn't remember the woman's name. "Louise, Luann, Lillian."

He turned to her, but she was gone. He glanced up and down the sidewalk and scanned the opposite side of the street, but came up empty. In front of the burning building some firemen loaded a gurney with a body bag into an ambulance. The folder in his hands felt icy, and goosebumps rose on his flesh as his cell phone buzzed.

CHAPTER SEVENTY-ONE

Will shivered as he entered the air-conditioned lobby. His mind still reeled and, momentarily forgetting that it was Saturday, he was confused by Betty's absence at the reception desk. Frank's phone call had propelled his addled brain from one nightmare into another. He couldn't remember the drive from Templeton to the office. Some of this he attributed to shock and the rest to exhaustion.

He hurried to the Development department and spotted several team members congregated at Steve Andrew's cube. Frank rolled his eyes when he saw Will. Steve glanced at Will and was obviously surprised to see him there. Steve cleared his throat, not at all his usual cocky self. "We have a problem."

Not letting on that Frank had called him, Will nodded. "What's up?"

When he answered there was no victory in his voice, only quiet disbelief. "The site's gone."

Will studied Steve. The words made no sense. "What do you mean, gone?"

Steve slid back from his desk, shrugging. "Gone, vanished, everything. I'm not talking about a little data, or a few pages. The whole damn thing's gone. All the JSP pages, the Java classes, even directory structures, the web app servers   it's all gone."

Frank had explained the same thing on the phone, but Will thought he was exaggerating, as he was prone to do. Will wasn't amused by what he thought had to be a bad joke. He had more pressing matters at home, and what Steve was saying was impossible. There were too many safeguards and backups built into their development cycles.

"It's even the databases," Frank added.

Steve nodded. It was the first time Will had ever seen him without a shred of arrogance. "It's like someone hit it with an EMP. The drives are wiped clean."

Will leaned over Steve's shoulder to get a better view of the blank screen. "Did you implement the disaster recovery plan?"

Obvious insulted by the question, Steve frowned, looked away and swore under his breath. "Of course we did, but the backups are blank and our mirror site is also wiped clean."

His words struck Will like a sledgehammer. "You're telling me we have no back-ups of anything. The site's completely gone?"

Both men nodded, and Will's legs went weak. He sank into a chair. "How did this happen?"

What they were telling him was impossible. There was no way for this to occur, but it had. Just like the specters the night before and the meeting with Lillian earlier in the day. Will prayed that this was some hellish nightmare and that he would wake up from and his life would be back to normal. Back to the way it had been before he moved to Shadow's Forge, before he had worked with Kerrie. "Kerrie... she programmed the batch files to back up data."

He was drowning, trying to grab onto something to stop himself from sinking deeper. Kerrie had been in charge of the disaster recovery process. If what Frank and Steve were saying was true then somebody had deliberately sabotaged the system, but that was impossible. The system was too big, and there were built in redundancies and safeguards. Even if it had been possible who would have done such a thing, a competitor, maybe?

Then it hit him. Will knew the one person who would have had a reason. "Where's Kerrie?"

Frank shrugged and searched the faces of the others in the cube. "No one's seen her since yesterday afternoon and she's not answering her cell."

Will rose. "I have to find her."

He left the cube, walking fast for the exit, fighting to swallow the acid that rose in the back of his throat. Frank trotted after him trying to keep up as he headed for the lobby. "Just tell me you didn't sleep with her?"

"No, but you were right, she's trouble."

"What are we going to do?" Will heard the concern in Frank's voice.

He was touched by Frank's loyalty. "Nothing rash. I have to find her and talk to her. I can't believe she destroyed the entire project."

Frank grabbed Will's shoulder, causing him to pause. "There's something I should've told you about your predecessor. He had to resign."

Will nodded, impatient to leave. "I know. He had an affair."

"Yeah, but what you may not know, is that it was with Kerrie, and it was kinda weird the way the guy's wife got an anonymous call. I think Kerrie might've engineered the whole thing."

Will stared at Frank, fully realizing the meaning of his words. Kerrie might have slept with the guy just so she could force him out to get Will the job. Frank fidgeted, staring down at his hands. "I just thought you should know. I think she might be dangerous."

The pieces started falling into place. "Thanks."

Frank glanced back at the office. "What should I do?"

Will realized Frank was waiting for instructions. "Stay here and see if you can recover any of the data from the database, and if you're a praying man, start praying because if we don't recover this site we're all out of a job."

He had almost reached his car when C.L.'s Mercedes screeched into the lot and skidded to a stop, blocking his retreat. A rumpled C.L. sprang from the car. He towered over Will, his eyes flashing like a rabid beast's. "Is it true? Is it all gone?"

There was no way to ease the blow. "Yeah, it looks like it."

C.L.'s shoulders slumped, and Will thought he was going to collapse. "How?"

Will didn't have time to explain, he needed to find Kerrie. "We're not sure. I have Steve and Frank researching it."

Crimson rose in C.L.'s cheeks. "When were you going to let me in on this? I had to hear it from Steve."

Will almost laughed. Steve had made his move. In all likelihood he would end up with Will's job. Will was too exhausted to care. "I just found out myself."

C.L.'s fists opened and closed. "Shouldn't you be inside trying to save my company?"

Will saw the man was near his breaking point, but he didn't have time for any of this. "I need to find Kerrie. She's in charge of disaster recovery." Will doubted she could do anything to save the project, but he needed to know what part she had played in everything.

The muscles in C.L.'s jaw tightened. "You couldn't listen. I told you to stay away from her. Now because you couldn't keep it in your pants, my company is destroyed."

Will tried to protest, but C.L. lashed out, striking him on the jaw. Will staggered, crashing to the ground. Loose gravel dug into his left elbow as it slammed the macadam. The large man was on him like a flash, grabbing him by the collar and punching him repeatedly. White lights flashed in his narrowing vision by the time the security guards pulled C.L. off him.

C.L. struggled free. "Let me go. He's the one you should be grabbing. He's the one that destroyed the company."

He turned to Will. "You're fired. I don't ever want to see you again." Not waiting for an answer, he tossed his keys to one of the security guards and walked toward the building. "Park it."

Will tasted blood from his split lip and his left eye had started to swell. He struggled to his feet. One of the men, Smitty, a young guy right out of high school, glanced in C.L.'s direction then extended his hand. "Sorry about that, Mr. Shepherd."

"That's okay Smitty." Will tried to smile, but winced.

"You'd better get some ice on that."

"I think you're right." Will made his way to his car, fumbled for his keys, and collapsed into the driver's seat. He had to find Kerrie, he had to have answers fast.

CHAPTER SEVENTY-TWO

The Charter Arms apartments seemed different. Will noticed the subtle changes from the previous night as soon as he parked the Civic. The late afternoon light revealed broken glass in the parking lot, and tall weeds growing by the side of the buildings. The faded and chipped door and window trim needed paint. Something else seemed different. He couldn't explain it. Maybe it was the lack of anticipation he had felt the night before. Now he only felt desperate dread.

Was it only yesterday? It felt much longer as he sat in his car, trying to ignore the throbbing in his elbow and swollen cheek. He wasn't prepared for another confrontation with Kerrie. What was the point?

Curiosity compelled him, the same inquisitiveness that had urged him to look in the parlor the previous night, when he should have fled through the front door. He couldn't fight it. In all his experience he had never seen a system destroyed so completely. The engineer in him had to know how she had accomplished it.

Aching and exhausted, he climbed from the car and went to her door. He pushed the bell. No answer. He rapped loudly, his knuckles ached as they collided with the solid door. Still no response from inside the quiet apartment. She wasn't going to elude him that easily. He walked to the patio and pressed his face against the glass sliding door, wincing when his bruised flesh contacted the cool glass.

Shielding his eyes from the sun's glare, the empty room surprised him. Kerrie's furniture, books, and pictures were gone. Will stepped back, double-checking the apartment number-143. It was the same apartment.

"No one lives there anymore, young fella."

Will spun around to find an old black woman leaning on her cane. She studied him with quiet speculation. She eyed his face, and he reflexively touched his cheek. "If you think I look bad, you should see the other guy."

She continued to silently stare at him. Will surmised she was deciding how much of a threat he was with his greasy hair, five-o-clock shadow, and scuffed up clothes. "He hurt bad?"

Will shook his head. "Not a scratch on him."

The old woman cackled, and Will attempted another smile, but winced from the sharp stabs of pain that radiated from his wounds.

"You should put a nice thick steak on that," she said as she inspected his bruises over her spectacles.

He ran a hand through his hair and glanced back at the empty apartment. "Yes, ma'am. Do you know where the young woman went who lived here?"

Silent for a moment, the woman stared at Will like she was deciding if she was going to release any information. "Wasn't a young woman. As I recall it was a family. Nice young couple with two small children."

The panic grew in Will's stomach, and his pulse quickened. "No, I'm sure a young woman lived here. I had dinner with her at this apartment last night."

Chuckling and shaking her head the old woman stared at him over her spectacles. "You must have been hit harder than you think. This apartment has been empty for almost three months."

Will glanced at the door, double-checking the apartment number again. "I'm positive this is the place."

"Young man, I live right there. I know who my neighbors are." She thrust a scrawny finger at the next apartment door.

Backing away he mumbled, "Sorry — my mistake."

He hurried to his car. The throbbing in his cheek had moved up along the side of his face. Everything felt wrong. A cold knot tightened in his stomach. Time was running out, he could feel it. Whatever festered in his house continued to grow stronger. The electricity danced in the air like that night on the hill in front of the Captain's tombstone. He felt the storm coming. If he didn't find a way to prevent it, it would destroy his family.

CHAPTER SEVENTY-THREE

Trooper Franklin Wilson tried to silence the unrest that churned in his mind since Wednesday morning. Will Shepherd's perfect account of the hit-and-run bordered on the fantastic. Franklin knew, because he had tried to wipe those images from his mind for the past sixteen years.

It happened his first year on the force, while on a routine patrol; he had discovered Ricky Andersen, the boy's broken body sprawled across the intersection at Old Creek Road and Pine. The child's pale, lifeless face and wide, staring eyes still haunted Franklin's sleep. No witnesses came forward to the hit-and-run, and Franklin failed to discover evidence to lead to a suspect. The guilt of not catching the killer haunted him as much as the horror of the boy's body.

Franklin couldn't explain Will's account. How could he have come up with all these details? Of course this Shepherd fellow could be a crackpot. Ricky had been visiting his aunt and uncle for the summer. The boy had stayed in the house Shepherd now owned. Maybe Shepherd had discovered an old newspaper article left in the house and was just playing some sort of sick twisted game with him, but Franklin didn't think so.

Franklin ran a background check on Shepherd. The guy checked out, no record. He seemed like a standup guy, and he had worked like hell to try to save the old guy with the heart attack. Still, how could Shepherd have come up with a plate number for a hit and run that happened all those years ago — the short answer was that he couldn't.

Sure that it was a waste of time, Franklin gave in at the end of the day on Friday and ran the plate. He was shocked to find it was still registered to a 1970 Chevy station wagon owned by a Charles Peifer. Jotting down Mr. Peifer's address, Franklin struggled with following up. He had no probable cause. He had nothing but a hunch.

It certainly didn't stand the litmus test of the law, but in his experience, Franklin had found that sometimes following a hunch was all he had. Sometimes it could save your life. Like the time he stopped an erratic driver on interstate 78 and instinctively knew before he approached that the man had a gun drawn. He had literally dodged that bullet, drawing his own service revolver and bringing the suspect down as the perp fired. The bullet had caught Franklin in the shoulder, but narrowly missed his heart and lungs. Sometimes you just had to follow the hunch, so Saturday afternoon, Franklin guided his cruiser up the long dirt lane to Charles Peifer's farm.

The place had survived way beyond its glory days. Weeds choked the overgrown alfalfa fields, and hundreds of broken branches and rotting bee-infested apples littered the ground beneath the twisted, unkempt skeletons of apple trees that lined the lane. At the end of the lane, the barn and outbuildings caved in under their own weight, their unpainted planks rotting off large sagging beams. Years of neglect testified that prosperity had fled, leaving a faint reminder of what must have once been a productive property. Franklin climbed out of his cruiser and drew a deep breath of the dry summer air.

A rusted Gremlin sat in front of the two-story farmhouse that fared only slightly better than the barn. Franklin scanned the overgrown fields and visible areas around the outbuildings for the station wagon. He felt foolish for being disappointed when he didn't find it.

He swallowed and approached the front door, carefully testing the wooden planks on the front porch before he stepped on them. Finding no button for a bell, he rapped on the door and waited in the shade of the sagging front porch roof. After a few minutes, he rapped again and heard stirring behind the door. It sounded like a heavy piece of furniture dragging across a hard wood floor.

The door cracked open, and a young man peeked out. "Yeah, sorry, we don't use the front door much."

Franklin nodded and tried to sound official. "I'm here to speak to Charles Peifer."

The door opened a little wider, the man's face grew pale. "That's me."

For a moment the kid's age confused Franklin. This kid was barely out of high school if he was lucky. Franklin checked his notes. "I have a birth date of nineteen thirty-four?"

The young guy sighed, obviously relieved. "Oh, you want my pop."

Opening the door the rest of the way with a hard shove, the young man turned calling over his shoulder. "He's back here. Watch your step."

Franklin stepped into the dim hallway and climbed over a stack of newspapers and magazines. He tried not to gag on the smell of sour milk that seemed to permeate the air under an overflowing cat litter box odor. In the dark and narrow, hallway, Franklin felt like he was walking into an ambush.

The young man opened a door on the right. "He's in here. I think he's awake."

Franklin glanced to his left and saw a dingy kitchen, its tables and counters covered with dirty dishes, empty jelly jars, and overflowing ashtrays. His senses alert, he followed the young man into a dark, crowded bedroom. Thick curtains drawn over the windows blocked out the sunlight, and clothes littered every surface. Against the far wall an old man reclined in bed, an oxygen mask strapped to his face. Young Charles grabbed a string on a bulb in the center of the ceiling yanking it to life. "Pop, there's a Statey here to talk to you."

The older Charles pulled the oxygen mask off and hacked into a Kleenex. A thin streak of red spittle ran down his chin. "Son-of-a-bitch, I always knew you'd show up."

Franklin stepped past the younger man. "Mr. Peifer, I'd like to talk to you…"

Before he could finish, old Charles broke into a coughing fit and dropped his Kleenex to the floor. It landed on a pile of other darkened, discarded tissues. He clutched a handful of new ones from the box and covered his mouth. They came away containing more blood. "So, the little bastard finally sent you. I've waited all these years for you to show up."

The man broke into another coughing fit, then grabbed his mask and took a hit of oxygen. The younger Charles turned and walked toward the door, apparently unconcerned. Franklin grabbed his arm. "Shouldn't we do something for him."

Charles Jr. stared back vacantly. "Why? He's dying."

CHAPTER SEVENTY-FOUR

A faint drizzle splattered the windshield as Will drove his Civic up the drive and parked in front of the old farmhouse. Pale light emanated from one window on the bottom floor. Will stared at the glow, debating his next move. He was trying to make sense of everything.

After Kerrie's empty apartment, he had spent the afternoon and early evening in a small cyber café in Harrisburg, reading through old *Chronicle* articles that Lillian had given him and surfing the Internet to verify other suspicions. He had sipped coffee and wished for something stronger as pieces fell into place.

He sat in the dark in front of Harry's old farmhouse thinking about Sara's sculpture. She sure had carved a masterpiece this time. That scared him more than anything. If the evil spirit in that house could influence her to carve that statue, then could it force one of them to harm the others? The mantra that it was not safe for them to return home kept playing in his head.

He checked the dash clock and was surprised to find it was two-thirty in the morning — late to call Gertrude's, but he couldn't exactly afford manners. He had to talk to Sara. He punched in the number on his cell phone. The phone rang several times, and then he heard the familiar voice. "Hello?"

He tried to hide the fear in his voice. "Hi. Gertrude, it's me, Will"

It took a moment for her to respond. "Will…"

He hated to impose, even though Gertrude was like a mother to Sara. "I'm sorry to wake you. I really need to talk to Sara. Is she back from the gallery opening?"

"Yes she is. Is something wrong?"

Will fought to keep his voice even. "No, I'm fine."

"Just a minute."

He heard movement through the receiver and a faint knock. More rustling, and Sara's voice came on the line. "Hello."

His heart pounded and his hand trembled. "Sara I need to talk to you."

"Will, what time is it?"

Trying not to lose his nerve, he pushed on. "It's late. I'm sorry to wake you."

"What's going on?" He could hear the concern in her voice. He tried to calm down. He had to convince her. "I'm fine. Look, I want you to stay with Gertrude for a few more days."

There was a long pause on the other end of the phone as she digested this request. "What?"

The words came out too fast. He knew it sounded crazy, but he had to persuade her. "I need you to stay there for a few days, until I work something out."

This time the pause was shorter. When she spoke, he could feel her anger through the phone. "It's about her, isn't it? What's going on up there?"

"No. This has nothing to do with Kerrie..." that wasn't exactly true, but he couldn't explain it all over the phone, and she wouldn't believe him anyway.

The question came quick like a knife stab. "Have you been drinking?"

His anger flared. How could she doubt him? "Sara, I'm stone sober. I swear. I love you. I don't have time to explain this all right now, and even if I did you would think it's crazy. You have to trust me. I will explain everything later. I just need you to stay away for a few more days."

Sara remained silent. The pause grew longer this time, like she was struggling with the decision. "If that's what you want."

He could tell she didn't believe him. It hurt to be so disconnected from her. "I'll call in a few days, when I have things worked out."

"Sure." Her last words were flat and distant, and then the line went dead.

CHAPTER SEVENTY-FIVE

Pounding on the front door roused Harry from a deep sleep, leaving him momentarily disoriented as his eyes focused on the TV screen. An infomercial had replaced the John Wayne movie he had been watching when he drifted off.

More pounding goaded Harry out of his chair. His muscle ached and joints creaked as he shambled to the front door. He cracked the door enough to see Will standing on the porch. He had a swollen eye and a split lip, and he swayed on his feet like he was ready to collapse. Harry swung the door open. "You look like you were hit by a truck."

Will nodded and reflexively touched his cheek. "I'm sorry it's late. I need to talk to you."

"No problem. I was still up," Harry lied, "Come on in."

Will stepped into the living room, and in the TV's glow his appearance seemed worse. He was almost green. Harry inspected the bruise. He thought the guy might actually collapse. "Come back to the kitchen, I'll get us something to drink."

Will followed and sank into a chair, tossing a thick manila folder on the kitchen table. Harry pulled two bottles from the fridge. "You like cream soda?"

Will nodded.

Opening them with a bottle opener he kept on the refrigerator, Harry handed Will one and joined him at the table. The two men sat facing each other. "I hate to tell you this, but you look like hell."

Will started to smile, but grimaced instead. Sipping from the bottle, he shrugged. "I know, it's been a rough day."

Harry waited, not sure where this conversation was going. He didn't like the look in Will's eyes, it reminded him of Martin. He saw an intensity that bordered on obsession in them. Harry felt a chill. He studied the folder on the table between them. "What's that?"

Will stared at the folder for a while, and Harry thought he was zoning out. "I'll get to that in a minute. I need to talk to you about my house."

A stronger chill ran down Harry's spine. His Ma had always said that only trouble came to the door in the middle of the night. She was right, and he regretted answering it. Will shifted uneasily in his chair. "You never told me how your friend Martin died."

Harry stared at his hands and shrugged. "No point to that."

Will's voice was slow and steady. "You think he did it himself."

"I know he did." Harry tasted venom in his words. "After all, seeing is believing."

In his mind he was back there. It had been the evening after Martin had returned home from the hospital. He had gone to check on him. When Martin hadn't answered the door again, Harry opened it with a sickening feeling in the pit of his stomach. He had called out, but heard no answer.

He had made his way to the kitchen hoping Martin was fixing supper and hadn't heard the door. In the hall he had paused to inspect the gun cabinet. Martin, an avid collector, had a fine assortment of rifles and pistols. Harry remembered feeing relieved that they were all in their place.

After an unsuccessful search of the downstairs, he had headed for the second floor. His feet felt like lead as he climbed the stairs. Harry hated those pretentious angels on the banisters that seemed to mock him with their grins. He had tried to ignore them as he passed. The dark hallway had felt narrow, and he recalled the unidentifiable low buzz coming from the master bedroom. He had paused outside the door and took a deep breath before he opened it.

His hand had tightened on the knob as he stared at Martin's lifeless body suspended from the ornate beam in the center of the room. His neck had been oddly bent in a noose tied from an old towrope. His body had been bloated like an overstuffed, fleshy piñata waiting to explode. Outside snow had covered the lawn, but in the master bedroom the temperature had to have been well over one hundred degrees. A sickly-sweet spoiled meat stench had permeated the room.

The unidentifiable noise had been the hum of millions of flies that swarmed around Martin's body like a ghastly cloud. They had crawled across his black, protruding tongue and over his open glazed eyes. Overwhelmed by the sight and smell, Harry had retreated to the bathroom and lost his supper before he called the ambulance. He didn't remember the flies when the paramedics arrived and he often wondered if he had imagined them.

"Martin was alone and depressed." Will's words called Harry

back to his kitchen, reviving him from the memory.

"Because of his wife June, because of how she died." Will wasn't asking. It was a statement.

Harry felt the heat rise on his face. "Watch what you say, or I may have to knock you on your ass."

He didn't like the course of this conversation. It wasn't like he hadn't thought of it himself, but it wasn't right for someone else to question. Will raised his hands. "Okay, I'm just saying you think he was depressed over his wife's death."

Harry appreciated that Will was trying to be diplomatic. "Martin never did get over it."

It was true. Harry gazed at his untouched bottle of cream soda, tormented by guilt. He had done nothing to help. For years he had sat on Martin's porch and drank beer and acted like everything was fine. Maybe it was guilt that made him hope for some other explanation, something that would absolve him of failing his friend. He guessed that living with that last terrible image was penance for his failure to save him. Maybe that was a fair trade, or maybe he owed just a little more.

Will turned his bottle around, studying the printing on the glass. "He didn't do it, he was murdered," Will said.

Harry wasn't expecting this. "What? How could you know that?"

Will slammed his bottle down on the table. "Because it happened again last night, and I saw the whole damn thing."

Harry's mouth felt dry, and he licked his lips. It was disconcerting to stare into Will's exhausted and tormented eyes. "You're not making any sense."

The younger man slumped back in his chair, his shoulders sagging. "I know."

Will started at the beginning. Harry listened silently as he described the events from moving day till the present. It was all fantastic: the strange feelings, the weird apparitions, and nightmares. It was obvious that Will was losing his mind. Harry wanted to dismiss the story, but when Will started describing Celeste a cold chill washed over his flesh. A beautiful blonde woman? Was it possible?

"She's the key to the whole thing." Will finished.

Harry shifted uneasily in his chair. "That's quite a tale."

Will slid the folder toward him. "There's more. Take a look in there."

Reaching out for the folder like it was a snake, Harry opened it and started scanning the articles. The news clippings went back into the eighteen hundreds chronicles of murder and suicide repeatedly occurring at Shadow's Forge.

Will spoke in a low voice. "Everyone who ever lived there died tragically. You knew the last two owners committed suicide and you didn't tell me."

Harry reached for his bottle, took a long pull and wiped his lips on his sleeve. "Of course I didn't tell you. Who'd want to know that the previous owner died horribly in the master bedroom of their new house? You think you had bad feelings about the place before."

He stared at his hands because he couldn't face Will. It felt like he had committed another betrayal. "I never saw anything out of the ordinary over there, nothing like what you're describing anyway. No ghosts or nothing. I thought Martin was depressed, that's all…"

When he looked up he realized that Will was looking at him with more pity and concern than anger. Harry swallowed the last of his cream soda. He got up, threw the bottle in the trash, and went to the refrigerator to grab another. He really wanted a cold beer, but he glanced at Will and decided against it. "As for the senator, well, he was a mean old son-of-a-bitch."

Harry slid back into his chair. His eyes fixed on the papers scattered across his kitchen table. Will nodded at the pages. "What you say about Martin and the senator may be true, but this has been going on for a lot longer than them. What scares me the most is that I can't find an account of Celeste's death. I think the senator killed her, and I have a feeling you know something. I can see it in your face. Harry I need your help. I have this feeling that if you don't tell me what you know, Sara, Ellie, and I are going to die. Just like the others."

CHAPTER SEVENTY-SIX

The first time mortality surprises someone is always traumatic. For Harry, death slithered into his life on a dark overcast evening in the summer of 1929. It was a devastating blow to the long-legged 8 year old. He didn't expect it, no one ever does.

The baseball was hard and smooth in his hand, and he heaved it high into the air, watching it hang in space for what seemed like an eternity before it bounced several times and came to rest at the far end of the yard. Champ, his small beagle, raced after it like his tail was on fire. Harry laughed as the dog seized the ball in his mouth, turned almost skidding on the dew coated grass, and raced back to deliver it. It was part of their daily routine. Next to fishing, playing catch with Champ was Harry's favorite thing in the whole world.

The sun disappeared over the horizon, and the moon rose into obscurity in the thick bank of clouds. Harry shivered, chilled by the evening breeze. His pop chuckled from his spectator's seat on the front porch steps. He stood up and stretched. "It's getting late, better get to bed."

Harry begged for just a little longer, not ready for the fun to end. His pop nodded and said, "Not too late."

Champ jumped up and down, apparently proud of his feat. Harry grinned, patted the dog, and retrieved the saliva soaked ball, wiping it on his pants leg. He gave it another strong toss and watched with delight as Champ tore after it. In his exuberance he hefted it a little harder than usual. The ball arched across the moonless sky, bouncing several times before it stopped in the field across the road. The sound of the screen door slamming distracted Harry. He watched his pop disappear into the living room and thought about a nice piece of his mother's cherry pie before bed.

At first he was oblivious to the engine's whine as it raced up Old Creek Road. The bright headlights drew his attention first. Harry screamed a futile warning, but was too late. Champ was so intent on returning the ball, he charged out into the road, probably never noticing the large car before it crushed him beneath its left front tire. There was no hesitation. The senator's car, the one his pop called the *'Gangster car'* never slowed down.

An icy fist clutched his heart in a vice-like grip as he ran to the road and fell to his knees. The moon materialized from behind the clouds, and its pale light illuminated his beloved dog's motionless form. Harry gently cradled his pet in his arms and started toward the house, tears streaming down his cheeks, blood soaking through the front of his shirt.

His mom and pop were sympathetic and tried to calm him down, but he was inconsolable. When he finally climbed into bed he couldn't sleep. He tossed and turned, missing Champ, who had slept at the foot of his bed for the previous two years. Ashamed to admit it to his older brother Alvin who shared his room, he silently cried himself to sleep in the dark.

The next morning, after the milking was completed, his older brothers helped him dig a grave for Champ. The burial was short and to the point, not much of a service. Harry stuck a small cross he had fashioned out of two branches bound together at the head of the grave. It didn't make him feel better. He just stood there and tried not to cry. His brothers were somber. They returned the shovels to the shed and went about their other chores in silence. Harry couldn't understand how everything had turned so bad in only a few seconds. He stood staring at the grave almost waiting for his beloved pet to spring forth. Lost in his own thoughts he didn't hear his pop approach. "Come on, we're going to pay a visit to the senator."

They silently walked across the field, climbed through the line fence, and approached the old house. A slight breeze rustled the alfalfa, and the scent of lilacs wafted across the lawn, the beautiful day only marred by Harry's sorrow. His muscles tensed at the sight of the red Packard parked in the driveway.

His pop knocked on the door, and they waited. His father was an unassuming man he worked hard for his living. He feared God, loved his country, and believed in right and wrong. He told Harry that the senator owed him an apology. It was odd to see his pop angry with another adult.

After a long pause his pop knocked again. Harry doubted the senator would answer. It startled him when the door swung open, and the senator stood there in a silk smoking jacket. It was 8:30 a.m.; apparently he wasn't up for the day. "What can I do for you?"

Harry's pop crossed his arms over his chest. "I believe you owe my boy an apology. Last night you hit his dog and never stopped to see if he was okay."

The senator glanced at Harry and back to his father. "Your boy should learn to take better care of his pets. His dog shouldn't have been running down the road in the middle of the night. Now if you'll excuse me, I have many pressing matters. Good day."

Before his pop could say a word, the senator slammed the door. For a moment Harry expected his father to kick it open and grab the senator by the collar and force him to apologize, but the moment passed. "Come on Son, he's not worth the trouble."

Harry followed him back to their barn in silence.

By mid-afternoon, Harry completed all of his chores. He grabbed his favorite bamboo pole and headed for the river, following the path that cut through the woods behind the old Courtland house. He and his brothers used it all the time, sticking to the trail that carefully skirted the back lawn.

Harry never liked the place and still had nightmares about the time his brothers had dared him to walk up to the front door at midnight. Following the shaded path, he was on the west side of the house when he glanced through the undergrowth and noticed that the Packard was gone. This was not uncommon because the senator, his wife, and son lived somewhere in Harrisburg. Harry only remembered the wife and son spending one night in the place and never coming back. Alvin said it was because the place was haunted. The senator seemed to only come there on the weekends by himself.

On any other day Harry would have continued to the river, but he wasn't really in the mood to fish, so instead he stepped from the path. The light that seemed to dance across the glass panes in the solarium hypnotized him. He stood there quietly for a long time watching the way the clouds created patterns on the glass surface. The anger welled up in his chest. The idea that the man thought he was above the law infuriated him. It was a strange thought for an eight-year-old, and he had no idea where it came from. Without thinking he dropped his fishing pole and picked up a rock. It was like the glass roof cried out for justice.

The rock felt right clenched in his fist, rough and heavy. He threw it, and a chill ran up his spine when the first pane shattered. Picking up another stone and hurling it like a fastball the thrill repeated at the sound of the glass raining down on the stone floor inside. Again and again, he picked up rocks from the edge of the forest and threw them at the glass. He went berserk. It resembled some legendary battle rage. Tears ran down his cheeks as he hurled one rock after another. By the time he collapsed in the grass, he had smashed at least fifty glass panels.

He lay motionless in the lawn, staring at his path of destruction, but found no satisfaction in his accomplishment. His anger spent, he only felt shame. The sound of the approaching car spurred him into action. He sprang to his feet and dove for the underbrush at the edge of the yard.

From the cover of thick brush, he watched, as the senator pulled into the driveway in his red 'Gangster Car.' His heart pounded, and he prayed the senator hadn't seen him. Afraid to move, he crouched at the edge of the forest trying to remain still. He could see the driveway, but didn't think the senator could see the arboretum from the front yard.

Harry held his breath as the senator climbed from the driver's side and went to open the passenger door for the beautiful blonde. She gracefully stepped down off the running board, and the senator took her in his arms. He planted a kiss on her like Harry had never seen before. Harry was shocked, not just by the kiss, but because the beautiful blonde was not the senator's wife. He had met Mrs. Freedman the one time she had accompanied her husband, and that was definitely not her.

Arm and arm they went in the front door, and Harry slipped farther into the woods, trying to move silently down the path to avoid getting caught. He returned home before he realized he had forgotten his fishing pole in the senator's back yard. Staring out the kitchen window at the old house next door, a chill scurried across his sweaty flesh.

At dinner Harry couldn't eat. He sat looking at the steaming vegetable soup his mother ladled into his bowl. His stomach twisted in knots, and he asked to be excused without touching the meal. His family probably thought he was upset over Champ's death. That was true, but he also worried about the senator appearing at his front door. His pop would tan his hide, and as scary as that was, it may not be the worst, maybe the police would come and take him away.

He sprawled on his stomach on his bed, fretted, and waited all evening for the knock that didn't come. By the time Alvin drifted off to sleep, he couldn't stand it any longer. Quietly he slipped out the window and down the rose trellis. Moving through the shadows, he prayed that the senator hadn't found his pole.

The hair on the back of his neck tingled. Every sinister sound caused Harry to wish for a light as he followed the path through the woods behind the old house. Moonlight lit the way, but the shadows seemed to shift menacingly, and he constantly glanced over his shoulders to see if someone followed him. The crushing darkness crowded closer on the path, and he tried not to break into a run. It was difficult to find the exact spot where he had stepped into the yard earlier that day because everything looked different in the dark. When he thought he had the right location he moved out into the yard. Crawling on his hands and knees, he felt around in the damp grass. It was no use; there was no sign of the pole. Even in the faint moonlight he should have found it if it was there. The only explanation was that the senator had already discovered it.

Shouts from the house caused him to gasp and freeze. For a moment he thought they were directed toward him, but the voices faded deeper into the house. The senator was arguing with someone. Harry wanted to follow his first instinct to retreat, return home, and wait for the punishment that would come, but curiosity compelled him. Maybe the senator had just discovered the arboretum that could explain the anger.

He couldn't leave without knowing, so he quickly sprinted

around the side of the house to the front lawn. Staying low, he crept along the shrubs in front of the house. Harry swallowed several times, remembering the last time he had peered in the windows by the door. Slowly he inched across the porch, his forehead dripping with sweat. Lights were on in the foyer and parlor, and he prayed no one would glance out a window as he passed. At the door he peered in one of the side glass panes.

Loud, angry voices drew his attention to the landing above the foyer.. The senator had the blonde by her shoulders spinning her around. "You can't tell anyone about us."

The woman laughed. The senator smacked her hard, leaving a red mark on her cheek. "I will not be made a fool."

She continued to laugh, and the senator raised his hand to strike again. The second blow cracked so loudly Harry could hear it from the outside. The blond moaned and fell to her knees. Harry thought she was hurt bad. Howard raised his hand again, but before he could strike, she clutched some sort of large silver knife off the table by the banister. She slashed through his silk smoking jacket. The blade dripped blood. The senator froze, staring at the slash across his waist. "You bitch. You're insane."

The beautiful blonde bolted for the stairs, but the senator grabbed a fist full of her hair. Harry cringed when he saw her head jerked backward. The long silver knife clattered to the floor. The senator released his grip. The blonde staggered toward the staircase and stumbled. She tried to catch herself on the banister. Harry saw the terror in her eyes before she tumbled down the stairs. She seemed to be moving in slow motion. Her arms flailing like a wounded bird.

The impact of her head hitting the hardwood floor sounded like the snap of a dry branch. She lay in a heap at the foot of the stairs. The sound echoed in Harry's ears. He froze, sure the woman was dead, but then she turned her head and opened her eyes to stare right into his.

CHAPTER **SEVENTY-SEVEN**

This was all too much, and Harry was too old to deal with it. He was tempted to tell Will to get out, go home, and take all his questions and insanity with him. That's what he longed to do.

He wanted to throw Will out and probably would have if he hadn't looked into his eyes. They were Martin's eyes — exhausted, sorrowful, with something extra, defiance ... and hope. Harry inhaled deeply, rubbed his own eyes and started in a low conspiratorial tone. "I have lived in this house my whole life and have known the last two owners of your house. You know most of Martin's story, there's nothing more I can tell you about him. The previous owner was senator Howard Freedman. I can't say I liked the guy, I don't think most people did. I also had the dubious honor of finding him on a spring morning in 1948. He was in the parlor with the back of his head blown off, just like you saw last night. It was quite a story at the time. It made all the papers, although the town's folk missed out on most of the tale. For the whole story you have to go back to an overcast evening in 1929. What I'm going to tell you now, I've never told another living soul."

Harry started telling Will about Champ and before long he lost himself in the story. When he reached the end where the blonde woman fell down the stairs, and he had fled into the night, he took a long pull from his bottle of cream soda. Will sat forward in his chair. "So it did happen, just like I saw it."

Nodding, Harry set his bottle on the table. "Yup."

Will was quiet for a moment. "You never told anyone?"

Harry shrugged, feeling embarrassed by this revelation of another betrayal. "I didn't think she was dead. She turned her head and looked right at me. I was more terrified that she had seen me, and that the senator would know that it was me that had destroyed his arboretum. I ran home and waited for a knock on the door that never came."

Will started to gather the clippings and shove them back into the folder. "So who was she? All I know about her was that her name was Celeste."

Harry handed him a few articles that had strayed to his side of the table. "You may know more than me. It never made the papers, but I remember hearing my parents talk about rumors that one of the senator's secretaries had mysteriously left Harrisburg because she was pregnant. This talk started just after that Saturday night. I guess that's also why I thought she wasn't dead. I'm sure that rumor ended the senator's career; of course I didn't know too much. I was just a kid. What I do believe is that when he pulled that trigger in 1948, it was because of that woman in 1929."

Will steadied himself by holding on to the edge of the tabletop. "You ever thought about the sins of the father being passed down to the son?"

Harry thought about his own son, Scott, living out in Ohio. "How do you mean?"

Evening out the contents by tapping the edge of the folder on the table, Will examined it and then set the folder down on the table in front of him. "When Lillian gave me this folder the thing that hit me the most was the name senator Howard Freedman. I knew the last name; it is Sara's maiden name."

It was late and he was tired, but Harry felt a sudden rush. "Sara's related to the senator?"

Nodding in confirmation, Will tapped the folder. "Yeah, that's in here too. I had to be sure, so I spent the afternoon and evening researching on the Internet. It turns out that Sara's the senator's granddaughter."

Harry whistled. The two men sat in the kitchen light's soft yellow glow thinking about the implications. "You didn't know this before?"

Will shook his head. "No. Sara's parents died in an auto accident when she was only five. The senator and his wife were already dead, so Sara moved in with her mother's sister in Philadelphia. I guess they never really talked about her grandfather, probably because he was such a scandalous figure. At least they never mentioned him to me."

Harry rubbed his jaw. "This is all too much. You think you have some sort of gift that lets you see dead people and you think this

Celeste is out to get you, Ellie, and Sara?"

Harry was probably not as subtle as he should have been with someone with an unstable mind, but he was tired. His comments obviously agitated Will, who picked up the folder and tapped it with his finger. "I showed you the articles. I know it sounds crazy, but I think Celeste is trying to kill us because the senator murdered her."

Will looked like he would pass out at any moment, but Harry had had enough. He didn't have the patience for this. "I told you this Celeste was the pregnant secretary who skipped town. She was still very much alive when I left that night. Besides, you said this stuff has been going on for a couple hundred years, and maybe even longer if your Indian visions are correct, so how could Celeste be the one causing all this? And another thing, I don't want to upset you, but isn't it possible you just imagined these things at the house after you started reading all these old articles?"

Will's face reddened. Harry wondered if he had pushed him too far. Harry waited, not wanting to make things worse. Will took a long swallow of his drink. "I'm not sure, but this is what I think. Lillian said she thought there was a demon attached to this property all along. I think she's right. Hell, she may have even had inside information if that was really her today. The point is; I think whatever evil is there, it is using Celeste as its main form because the senator buried her body in the basement."

Harry had to interrupt because this was too much. "What makes you think he buried her in the basement?"

Holding up his hands, Will leaned back in his chair. "It's just a feeling I get when I go down there. Also, when she appeared in the dining room, and Gretchen told her to go into the light, she shook her head and pointed down."

There was no point in arguing with Will, he was obviously beyond reason, but not ready to let the discussion end. "Okay, here's the other thing. I might have imagined all this. I've been convinced of that sometimes in the past few weeks, but I certainly didn't read the account of your blonde falling down the stairs that night when you were a kid."

Harry wasn't sure he bought into the whole ghost thing. It sounded like the kid stuff his older brothers used to scare him when they were young boys, but he did get a chill when he thought about Will's description of the senator and the blonde. He sighed and crossed his arms. "I guess you have some sort of plan?"

CHAPTER SEVENTY-EIGHT

Will ran his hand through his hair   the nervous habit did nothing to calm him. He sighed and glanced down at the shotgun he gripped so tight that his right hand was cramping, and then up at Harry who stood next to him on the porch. "You don't have to do this. I'll understand if you don't want to."

Harry nodded, and for a minute Will thought the old man was going to change his mind. He wouldn't have blamed him if he did. After all, this was possibly dangerous. Harry hefted his shovels. "I guess I always knew there would be some sort of reckoning for the whole senator business."

Will didn't like Harry's tone. He sounded so hopeless, yet Will was grateful for his help and company. Harry gestured toward the gun. "Is that really necessary?"

Feeling the cold steel comforted Will. "It seemed to slow them down earlier. I don't want to go in without it."

The old man looked unconvinced, but Will didn't care. He understood that this was a fight for survival. With a trembling hand he tried the door — it opened easily. He stepped inside and worked the light switch. "Watch your step."

He pointed at the lower half of Tony's severed body by the door and the large pool of blood that surrounded it and was starting to congeal. Harry glanced at the floor and then back at Will as he stepped in the pool. Will stifled a giggle as he watched Harry track blood across the floor, obviously not seeing it, and for the umpteenth time Will questioned his own sanity.

Glancing into the parlor, he saw the good old son-of-a-bitch the senator sitting there with the back half of his head decorating the back rest. Will decided didn't feel like playing tour guide to the house of the damned, so he didn't mention the corpse to Harry. He didn't want him to have any more doubts about helping. Instead, he headed straight back the hall to the kitchen. When he opened the basement door he felt the cold radiate out from the doorway. It was like opening a freezer on a hot day. He reached in and flicked the light switch. The narrow stairway looked old and rickety in the overhead bulb's dim yellow glow. It grew colder with each step down the stairs.

"Chilly down here," Will said.

Harry looked around the dingy chamber. "Yup, these old cellars usually stay pretty cool."

Obviously Harry didn't feel the same drop in temperature that he did. "I thought we would try here in the larger chamber first."

Leaning his shovels against the wall, Harry nodded. "This dirt floor shouldn't be too hard to dig up."

Will gestured toward the pickax in Harry's other hand. "Let me try with that?"

"Sure, be my guest."

Harry handed it to him, and its weight surprised him. This was going to be hard work. He raised it over his head, bringing it down into the earth with a wide swing. The point bit into the ground, and chunks of earth exploded into the air.

They worked in quiet determination. Will lost track of time. He only knew that they had been at it for hours. Sweat ran down between his aching shoulder blades despite the chill in the air. His arms and legs felt like jelly, and he developed large blisters on his palms. Several times he stopped because his vision blurred, and he thought he was going to pass out.

Harry worked the shovel with slow ease, apparently pacing himself. The elderly man's stamina was amazing. Will imagined all those years of labor on the farm had conditioned him. Will on the other hand was getting the workout of his life. He stopped, stretched his back and surveyed the excavation. They had marked out a grid on the floor and dug two-foot wide by two-foot deep holes two feet apart. Will had estimated that if the senator had buried the body, they would intersect some part of it. Now after hours of backbreaking work with no results, he was quickly losing hope.

"She's not here," Harry said as he wiped the sweat from the back of his neck with a red handkerchief. "Like I said, I was never convinced she died that night."

Will stumbled to the steps and collapsed, dropping his shovel at his side. "She has to be. I can feel it. Can't you feel the chill? Even now the hair on the back of my neck is standing up. Maybe the body is deeper? I don't know. I was sure it was this room, not down the other passages. I feel it stronger in here."

He could see the doubt and exhaustion in Harry's eyes. He felt everything slipping away and knew it was just about over. His body screamed in protest at the abuse. Harry leaned his shovel against the wall. "We could get some sleep and try again later."

Will almost nodded, actually Harry had suggested the same thing the previous night, and Will had rejected it. He couldn't explain, but the intensity was growing and he was sure time was running out. "I have to keep at it Harry. I know she's here and she's the key."

CHAPTER **SEVENTY-NINE**

Sara opened her eyes to the blinding glare of sunlight streaming through unfamiliar curtains. She was disoriented for a moment, until she remembered they were in Gretchen's old bedroom. Outside, she heard the familiar sounds of her childhood in the Northeast neighborhood — a car door slam, a barking dog. Traffic from the main thoroughfare a few blocks away softly echoed. She could smell Gretchen's favorite perfume and, for a brief moment, she expected to turn toward the door and see her. But the moment passed, and Sara remembered she was gone. It was a shock — so final and real. She decided that staying here with Gertrude while she attended the opening had been a mistake. It was just too painful.

She rolled over on her side and gazed at her sleeping child's angelic face. Ellie looked so peaceful, and Sara wished she could regain that childhood innocence. It had been ripped away from her at such an early age. She glanced out the window and tried to force away the darkness in her soul. It was too beautiful a day for such thoughts. Her eyes wandered past Ellie to the nightstand beside the bed, and she was surprised to see one of Gertrude's prized porcelain figures from down in the living room.

Agitated, she slid out of bed and started to dress. She struggled to remain calm as she slipped on her clothing. She had told Ellie numerous times not to play with the expensive collectables that Gertrude displayed in the living room, and still she had disobeyed her. Sometimes it felt like she was talking to a wall. Ellie stirred and sat up in bed. Sara didn't want to start the day with an argument, she was still irritated with Will and didn't want to take out that frustration on Ellie. She glanced at her daughter's cast and sighed.

Ellie rubbed her eyes, apparently not ready to face the day. "Hey. Look Mom, it's Aunt Gretchen."

Sara followed her daughter's stare. "What?"

Ellie was examining the small porcelain miniature. "This little girl. She's the one that looks like Aunt Gretchen."

Sara studied the figurine closer and realized it was the one that Ellie had always said she thought looked like Gretchen. "Yes, about that," Sara said trying to remain calm, "I told you never to play with those figurines. They are very expensive."

Ellie's emerald eyes grew wide. "I know, Mom, and I never ever play with them."

It was the wall again. Obviously she didn't understand. "I guess I wasn't clear enough. I meant you should never touch them, or pick them up, and especially not carry them around the house."

Ellie's face darkened. "Oh, I would never do that."

Frustrated, Sara's tone grew sharp. "Then how did it get there?"

Tears started to form in the corners of Ellie's eyes. "Aunt Gretchen put it there last night."

Sara eased down on the bed next to Ellie and put her arm around her shoulders. Outside the sky was darkening to match Sara's growing despair. "Honey, you understand that Aunt Gretchen is dead. She can't come back anymore."

It was heartbreaking. Sara hadn't thought much about how Ellie was reacting to Gretchen's death. She had been so lost in her own grief that she had neglected her daughter's emotional pain. Ellie sniffed back the tears. "I know Mom, but last night she came back and put that doll on the table and talked to me."

Sara fought back her own tears and tried to stop her hands from trembling. "I love your imagination, but it's not nice to make up stories like that. If Aunt Gertrude hears this she'll be very upset. She misses her daughter very much."

Ellie slowly looked at the figurine, then back at Sara. She furrowed her brows and pursed her lips like she was trying to remember something important. "But Mom, it's not a story. Aunt Gretchen really did come back last night. She told me not to be scared, but she said we have to go home right away. She said Mr. Weaver and Dad were in danger."

A pang of guilt stabbed at Sara. She wondered if Ellie had overheard her conversation with Will the previous night. "Look, we're going to stay here and visit with Aunt Gertrude for a few more days."

Cutting her off, Ellie's voice grew shrill. "No Mom — we have to go now."

The room grew darker as gathering storm clouds passed in front of the sun. Ellie was inconsolable. Her tiny body trembled as she burst into tears. Sara tried to comfort her, but froze as the Mac in the corner on Gretchen's desk powered up. She gasped and felt a chill dance across her skin as she read a Word document that sprang up on the screen. The same three words typed down the page repeatedly — WILL HARRY DEATH.

CHAPTER **EIGHTY**

Raindrops splattered against the windshield as Harry inserted his key into the ignition and fired up the truck's engine. The parched earth greedily soaked up the raindrops as they exploded on the dusty soil. Harry felt as parched as the drought scorched earth. He sat staring at the old house. Every muscle in his body was stretched tight and his joints stiff and sore. He slammed his palm on the steering wheel. "It's all bullshit."

All that labor had been a waste. They had come up empty, and now he wasn't even sure the crazy old senator had actually murdered that woman. Sprawled at the foot of the stairs, she had turned her head and looked right at him. He knew she wasn't dead, at least not when he had hightailed it out of there. He'd only agreed to the whole basement thing because Will had been so adamant about it. Then again, the insane usually were. In a warped way it made sense. Will was all messed up over losing his job, and his friend's death. The pressure had been too much, and he'd just snapped. Still, Harry hated to leave him alone. He was afraid of what Will might do. He'd tried to convince him to come back to his house, take a break, and get some rest, but Will insisted that Sara and Ellie were going to die if he didn't stop Celeste. Harry considered calling someone, but he didn't have Sara's number. Finally, when he could barely keep his eyes open he informed Will he needed sleep. Will refused to stop, but told him to go home.

Harry shook his head and repeated that it was all bullshit. He was about to slip the truck into gear when he paused with his hand on the well-worn gearshift knob. He stared at the house where they had replaced the siding boards. The new paint was darker than the old, and something bothered him about the mismatch. Suddenly it struck him, and he knew they had been searching in the wrong place. He stumbled out of the truck and hurried back to the house.

In all the years Harry had visited, this was the first time he really felt the wrongness of the place. It was like a moldy smell of some black fungus that grew under the floorboards and inside the walls hung in the air. The place was contaminated with something he couldn't put into words. He only knew he didn't want to stay any longer than he had to. He felt like that terrified eight-year-old who had raced away into the night.

Harry hurried to the kitchen and tried the basement door. It was locked. He couldn't budge it. Pounding on the door, he screamed for Will to open it. There was rustling on the steps, and after what sounded like a struggle the door swung open. Will was dead on his feet, swaying dangerously. "I thought you were going to get some sleep?"

Harry brushed past him and started down the stairs. This time he felt the cold that Will had described earlier. He wasn't sure why, maybe he was looking for it or maybe it was growing stronger. "I figured it out. I know where he hid the body."

Will followed him back into the basement. "How? Where?"

Harry grabbed the pickax in the center of the room. He hefted it in his hands, feeling the weight. The room felt much colder than before, and he could see his breath when he exhaled. He stepped carefully around the holes, picking his way to the furnace. There it was, what they had failed to notice, but had been there all along like a neon sign. Once he saw it, he couldn't not see it. It was like one of those crazy picture books with the Magic Eye patterns.

Raising the pickax over his shoulder, Harry gave a mighty swing. The edge of the blade bit into the fieldstone wall splintering off shards of rock. "She's behind the wall. Look at how the stones are different in this section."

Will stood hypnotized, staring at the wall. "I think you're right."

Harry raised the pickax to swing again, but before he could, a scream shattered the silence. He could see his own terror reflected in Will's face. "That was Ellie."

"It couldn't be. You said they were staying in Philadelphia."

A second scream pierced the air. "Daddy, help."

Will hesitated, looking at the wall and back up the steps. "It could be a trick."

"You'd better go check," Harry said.

Will nodded, grabbed the shotgun, and headed for the stairs. "No matter what you hear, don't stop digging till you find her."

Harry took another swing. He was going to end this one way or another.

CHAPTER **EIGHTY-ONE**

Will gripped the shotgun tighter as he raced into the kitchen and stumbled through the hall toward the front of the house.

It can't be Ellie — she's in Philadelphia with Sara.

It had to be another of Celeste's tricks. When he saw someone in the dim light of the parlor, he raised the shotgun, aiming it at their head. His finger tensed on the trigger before Sara's scream shocked him to a halt.

He realized what he had almost done, and vertigo and nausea washed over him. Everything was distorted. He almost dropped the gun as he embraced Sara. Through tears he kissed her face. "Sara, I almost…"

"Daddy, help."

Ellie's cry cut him off, and he released Sara, who stood frozen with terror at the scene in the foyer. Following her gaze, his stomach tightened and he grabbed the doorframe for support. Kerrie stood in the center of the foyer, restraining Ellie. Will could barely breathe. He recognized the gun that she pressed tight against Ellie's right temple as the one from her handbag. Tears streamed down Kerrie's cheeks, and she struggled to speak through sobbing shudders. "I had to come. You forced me to."

He looked into Kerrie's deep blue eyes and was lost. She was so vulnerable with her trembling lips and her tearful eyes that everything else in the world seemed insignificant. He imagined holding her close and tasting her lips. He wanted to take her in his arms. Together they could forget the rest of the world existed. He glanced down at the shotgun and turned toward Sara.

He could feel his arms raising the gun. It was like he was watching through someone else's eyes. His head pounded, and heart raced. He swallowed and licked his lips. He sighted down the barrel on Sara's forehead. His finger tensed against the trigger, just like Harry had taught him, his cheeks wet because he couldn't stop the tears. Sara swayed slightly like she was going to collapse and raised her arms in defense. "Will, no. Please?"

The hesitation lasted forever. He was back on the edge of eternity. Standing at the precipice of his life, and his legs were starting to buckle. Sara didn't move. He could see the shock, but he could also see something else in her eyes. It was the look she gave him when she was scared and needed comfort. It was the vulnerability and trust that he would always be there for her.

Ellie's sobs receded to some distant place. The whole room seemed to be fading into darkness. Will heard Kerrie's voice from somewhere down the tunnel. "Just do it. You know you want to."

It was another blackout. He felt himself slipping away. In the distance haunting Victrola music played. He fought the darkness and crawled upward toward the sound of Ellie's cries. It was painstaking effort to escape the surrounding shadows. A million voices moaned in torment and terror. There was no hope, no escape, and no peace. Cold hands reached out of the void, grabbing and clutching him, trying to drag him under forever. He pushed them away. The more he concentrated on Sara and Ellie, the stronger he grew.

The shotgun's blast jarred him back against the doorframe, and the pain in his back sharpened his focus. A large radius of plaster on the parlor wall only inches to the right of Sara had disintegrated. Sara covered her face with her trembling hands. "Oh my God Will. You almost killed me."

The hurt and disappointment on her face drove a sharp knife into his heart. He relaxed his grip on the shotgun, letting it clatter to the floor. He shook his head, trying to clear the cobwebs. Inside he was conflicted   horrified by what he had almost done and thrilled that he had somehow fought off the blackout. Turning slowly, he closed the distance between himself and Kerrie. "Put down the gun. Let her go. We can talk about this."

Kerrie pushed the gun tighter against Ellie's head. "Stay back. Don't come any closer."

Raising his hands, he backed into the parlor next to Sara, who pleaded to him in a whisper. "Do something. Don't let her hurt Ellie."

He nodded and kept his hands raised. Kerrie started toward them, forcing Ellie along. He winced each time the gun barrel seemed to tighten against her head. Kerrie's sobs were horrible. She sounded like a wounded animal. "I love you. And after all I've done for you — the job, the house. All I went through to be with you.... You'll never know."

Will stared into her blue, vacant eyes.

The lights are on, but nobody's home.

He tried to think of a way to get her to lower her guard. "I never meant to mislead you. You knew I was married."

Kerrie violently shook her head. "You were supposed to take care of that. We are meant to be together."

The room started to swim out of focus and his heart raced faster. He was trying to calculate if he could lunge forward and overpower her. He couldn't risk it. He would never cross the several feet in time. How could he go on if something happened to Ellie?

"Daddy, please."

He tried to inch closer, but Kerrie's grip tightened, and Ellie whimpered. He had to keep her talking. "Wait. Let her go and we can work this out."

Kerrie backed away shaking her head. "No. You're lying. You were supposed to choose me."

He glanced at Sara. "I couldn't. I love Sara."

Staring blankly at some point behind Will, Kerrie spoke flatly. "It was a promise."

This confused him. He had never promised her anything. Something seemed wrong. She seemed wrong. She continued in a flat tone. "I came back for you. I was so cold and alone. It was dark, so dark. I couldn't breathe. It was tight, and I could feel the worms crawling over my flesh. You can feel them eating you and you can't move... I couldn't leave, not without Ricky, not without my twin. He's trapped here, reliving his death over and over. I couldn't go without him. That's when Celeste found me again. I knew her from my visits here as a child. She promised that if I helped her I wouldn't be alone anymore…" She trailed off, lost in some bleak memory.

He had to try while she was distracted in this delusional memory. It was his weakness that had brought his family to this place, and it was time for his atonement. He didn't care what happened to him, but he had to save Sara and Ellie. Then he noticed it again her blue eyes. Not brown, but blue like Celeste's. And he knew. Suddenly it all fit. The crazy nightmare he had been living through all made sense. "You're already dead. You died in the attack on South Street."

How had he missed the shifting of her eyes, the lighter hair? "You came back from the dead to lure me here to bring Sara and Ellie."

Terror flashed in Kerrie's face. "You don't understand. Celeste promised I could live again if I helped her get revenge. She said Ricky would be released. I only came back for you and to save him. Celeste's the one who wants revenge."

Sara grabbed Will's arm. "What are you talking about? Coming back from the dead? Who would want revenge on me and Ellie?"

There was no time to explain. "It's about your Grandfather."

He could see Sara's confusion, but he had to concentrate, waiting for the right moment to make a move. Kerrie started to speak. Sara's pain seemed to amuse her, and she started laughing. "It's simple. Your grandfather — Howard Freedman — owned this house and he murdered his secretary Celeste and buried her in the basement. Now she wants revenge on you and your daughter, since you're his last two living descendants. She almost got you with your parents, but this is better."

Sara tightened her grip on Will's arm. "She killed my parents?"

Will wanted her to let go so he could try to save Ellie, but he didn't want tip off Kerrie, who seemed caught up in her explanation. "Yeah, and that effort weakened her. She had to wait and gain strength. This is much better. She wanted to humiliate you first like she was humiliated. This time the husband would choose the lover over the wife and child, killing them both so he could be with her. Will's already started digging in the basement."

Kerrie spoke with a sinister confidence despite the fear in her eyes. Will guessed there was more involved than what she was telling. He decided to try to shake her up. "You failed Kerrie. Celeste loses again. What happens if you fail?"

Apparently failure was not an option, or the results were too horrendous to consider. Kerrie started to tremble. The kerosene lamps on the mantle burst into flames and an inferno erupted from the fireplace. Will knew he had to make his move, but the motion in his peripheral vision distracted him. Martin, who was standing on the second floor landing, launched Mr. Whiskers from the cat's favorite perch on the table by the balcony railing. The cat soared through the air, crashing down on Kerrie's head like a furry missile.

Mr. Whiskers frantically clawed at everything he came in contact with, trying desperately to break his fall. Whatever his intentions, the results were similar to an attack. Kerrie screamed as his claws slashed her scalp, trying to get a grip. In the confusion she released Ellie to fight off the ferocious feline. Free from her clutches Ellie dove across the floor to Sara.

The gun discharged, and a wild bullet shattered the round stained glass window at the top of the stairs, raining colorful glass down over the room.

Kerrie flung Mr. Whiskers against the wall with a sickening crunch, and let out a fierce scream. She spun around, quickly bringing the gun to bear. Will made his move as the revolver spit fire and the percussion echoed off the hardwood walls with a deafening roar.

In his weakest moment, Will knew he had to believe, to trust, and to have faith. Searing red pain exploded in his chest and left shoulder as the slugs tore through his flesh, nerves, and bones. The force of the impact spun him in the air before he landed flat on his back on the parlor floor. The acrid smell of gunpowder mingled with the coppery scent of his blood, and for a moment he also thought he smelled lilac. He chuckled through gritted teeth.

Sara screamed, and Ellie cowered behind her. Kerrie went ballistic; wailing like a banshee when she saw the bullets she had obviously intended for Sara had struck Will. Knowing he would never reach Kerrie in time, Will had hurled himself in front of his family, knocking Sara out of the way and taking the wounds himself.

His vision swam. He could only see out of the one eye, the other was swollen shut. Kerrie froze in shock. She pointed the gun at Sara and Ellie, but kept staring at Will. "You keep choosing her over me. That's not the way it's supposed to be."

Will blinked through the haze of pain. His chest and shoulder were on fire, and he could feel his life spilling out of the torn holes onto the parlor floor. His left hand was numb and his entire left side felt like he had been struck with a sledgehammer.

"Stay away from him, He's mine, *MINE*," Kerrie screamed as Sara crawled toward him. He could barely see her through the pain. Sara was more beautiful than ever. He didn't want to die, but for her he would've died a thousand times. "I love you," he whispered, hoping his eyes conveyed the strength of emotion his voice could not.

Sara fought back tears. "I love you too."

"I'm sorry for every…" He started. The pain caused him to gasp.

"Shhh, don't talk. I forgive you for anything, just don't leave…" Sara didn't get to finish. The red haze washed over his senses. First his extremities, and then his entire body grew cold and numb, and then he felt no more.

CHAPTER **EIGHTY-TWO**

Harry swung again, and more stone splintered away. Soon he had a small opening in the wall at eye level. He dropped the pickax and stepped closer for a better inspection. Harry wished for a flashlight because it was almost impossible to see anything in the darkness. Leaning closer to leverage a better view, he detected the motion too late. The old fieldstone foundation buckled out toward him, and the wall crumbled knocking him to the floor.

In the door-sized opening stood a beautiful woman with the long blonde hair and brilliant blue eyes, her mouth drawn back in a terrible sneer as she reached for him. Her luminous nightgown was blinding; he couldn't look away. His heart pounded faster when he saw the bamboo-fishing pole in her left hand — a cruel reminder of his years of silence. Her scream echoed in his ears. "You!"

As he struggled to sit up and free his pinned legs, she launched out of the opening like a cougar, colliding with him and knocking him flat on his back. Severe pain erupted in his left leg below the knee.

A shotgun blast sounded upstairs, and for a moment Celeste seemed distracted, as if she had gone away somewhere inside her head, but then she was back. Her face only inches from his, he stared into her deep blue eyes, gritting his teeth against the fire in his left leg. Her lips were almost touching his, and when she exhaled he smelled rotten eggs. "You're the one that left me here to die."

"No. Not me — the senator."

Celeste shifted her weight, bearing down on his left leg, and daggers of pain shot up it and into his hip. "But you saw, you knew."

The pain exploded in his brain and white spots danced before his eyes. She leaned in closer, straddling his chest, pressing his back against the stone-littered earth. "The senator buried me alive in the wall. He bound and gagged me. I woke in time to see the last stone slide into place."

Harry struggled to get free. Each time he moved his left leg the fire shot through his raw nerves and he screamed. Celeste was reliving her imprisonment. The deranged sparkle in her eyes seemed to dance as she spoke. "I worked free of the ropes. I knew you saw me at the foot of the stairs. I knew you would bring help. For days I clawed at the wall. I was too weak to break it down. Look at my fingers."

She raised her hands revealing bloody fingertips worn down to the bone, the nails snapped off leaving only gory craters. "You left me there to die."

Overwhelmed by her suffering, he moaned. His silence had condemned her to a horrid death. She slid down and grabbed his left leg below the knee and squeezed. He howled as his world exploded in a haze of red. Celeste bent forward, her lips again almost touching his. "Now, old man, I'll have my revenge."

She kissed him hard on the lips, and he felt the bands of tightness constricting his chest. He couldn't breathe, his lungs burned. She was sucking the life out of him. He tried to fend her off, but the night's exertion had left him too weak. His heart pounded, and panic fluttered in his guts. The spoiled egg smell grew stronger. She was suffocating him, and he was defenseless. He was slipping away when he heard more gunshots.

CHAPTER EIGHTY-THREE

A shotgun blast echoed from the house, and Pastor Wheeler's body went cold. He was too late. His indecision had paralyzed him too long. He ran from his Cadillac to the front porch, charging up the stairs in his haste.

He had hoped to talk to Will and Sara after the morning service, but they had not attended. He had wanted to schedule an appointment for his friend Father Joe to visit. The priest needed to gather information to take back to his superiors to decide if an exorcism was truly necessary. Father Joe told him the Catholic Church always approached possession with skepticism. Pastor Wheeler had no doubts, so in spite of his reservations he had returned to speak with the Shepherds at their home.

Out of breath, he recoiled when he grabbed the front doorknob and it seared his hand. The hot knob almost glowed. He could hear the screams inside and slammed against one of the doors with his shoulder, but it didn't budge. Pounding on the door, he called for Will or Sara to open it, but no one answered. Desperate, he grabbed a rocking chair and hurled it against the parlor window, but it bounced off harmlessly. Inside he could see flames spreading up the wall behind the fireplace. Something was banning him from the house. Something a mortal man couldn't defeat.

All his faith, education, and perception of the world intersected at that point. He knew the Shepherds were in that house and they needed help. He stumbled from the porch trying to catch his breath, and fell to his knees in the gravel driveway. Ignoring the sharp stones biting into his kneecaps and the pounding rain, he took his only recourse. "Lord, hear my prayer."

He praised God and thanked him for all his precious gifts and asked in Jesus' name that the Lord would send his angels to watch over his humble servants and protect them in their hour of need. He was so intent on his prayers that he ignored the pain as his fingernails dug into his palms. He didn't quit when the State Police cruiser pulled to a stop behind his Cadillac. Only when the trooper touched his shoulders did he fully acknowledge his presence.

"What's going on?" the trooper asked.

The pastor stared up into the face of the tall black man. Water running into his eyes blurred his vision, and for a moment he wasn't sure the officer was real. "It's the Shepherds. Someone's in there with a gun, and they're in trouble."

Before the trooper could respond, another shot rang out in the house. "Stay back. I need to call this in."

The officer bolted for his car, and Wheeler heard him say something in his mic about shots fired and requesting backup. Wheeler watched as the trooper drew his own service revolver and dashed for the front door.

CHAPTER EIGHTY-FOUR

Franklin Wilson realized something was wrong as soon as he parked the cruiser. A man knelt in the driveway in the pouring rain, apparently praying. Franklin had stopped by to follow up with Will Shepherd. He didn't understand how he had done it, but Will had given him the lead to solve the case that had haunted him his whole career. The previous night was the first time in the past sixteen years that Franklin hadn't awoke in a sweat from dreaming about the horrible accident scene.

It didn't matter that Charles Peifer wouldn't live to see trial. Doctors said the cancer would kill him long before the state could. At least the truth would come out, and Ricky Andersen would finally have justice. Franklin wanted to thank Will, and try to understand how he had done it.

The man in the driveway said the Shepherds were inside and someone had a gun. It made no sense why he was kneeling in the mud and gravel praying, but Franklin didn't have time to consider it. Another shot sounded in the house and he could see flames in the living room.

When he tried the door handles they were hot. He didn't see any flames through the glass panels next to the door, but he saw a woman pointing a gun at the Shepherds. It looked like Will had been shot. Franklin decided he couldn't wait for backup, so he hit the doors with everything he had. The wood splintered and he crashed through, trying not to lose his balance. He dropped into a kneeling crouch. Bringing the gun up, he yelled for the lady to drop hers.

She left him no choice. She spun around and brought her gun to bear on him. In sixteen years he had only once before fired at a suspect, but the hours of training at the shooting range kicked reflexes into gear. He squeezed off three clean shots, and the suspect went down.

There was no time to think or mourn the loss of life. The flames in the parlor threatened to engulf the entire place. Franklin started toward the Shepherds, covering his head with his arms to fend off the heat. The explosion lifted him off his feet and propelled him back out the opening where the front doors had been. He landed hard on his back and couldn't get his breath; the impact had knocked the wind out of him.

CHAPTER EIGHTY-FIVE

Three more shots thundered in the old house, and Pastor Wheeler concentrated harder on his prayers. He again became so caught up in prayer that he didn't hesitate when the explosion rocked the house, sending shards of glass across the front lawn. Even when he felt sting of the glass, the burn of the gashes, and his blood was flowing into the mud, he did not relent, because he was positive that the Lord would send his angels to drive back the demons.

CHAPTER EIGHTY-SIX

The pain vanished. Will stumbled forward, disoriented. Ellie and Sara's sobs filled his ears, and he turned to tell them he was fine, but his words failed. They knelt cradling his head in their arms. He stared at his own body lying on the floor.

Kerrie's wails eclipsed their sobs. It was the sound of a wounded beast that resonated inside his head. The woman who was Kerrie, Celeste, and something else stood in the center of the foyer. He could see her clearly now, not the living flesh she had donned like a mask, but the compilation of black energy and fire. She was not a single entity, but some unholy union of trapped spirits and a dark human form.

She approached, and the gun in her hand now seemed tiny and insignificant. "You are mine forever. This isn't the way I preferred it. You were supposed to give in to temptation. You were supposed to break in despair. But this will have to do. First, I'll kill your family slowly and painfully, then I'll take you."

The front doors burst open. Will smiled when he saw Officer Wilson crouch in the doorway with his revolver drawn. Kerrie wheeled in surprise. Wilson leveled his gun at her. "Police, drop it."

The Kerrie creature raised her own pistol, but never got off a shot. Officer Wilson fired three times, the bullets struck true, propelling her backward against the north wall. Kerrie's body lay motionless, but the dark beast still stood in the center of the foyer, it was as if Kerrie had been knocked away, leaving a human shaped hole where she had stood. It was the beast from the first scene of Sara's sculpture, its body twisting and mutating and taking on different shapes; it shifted into a hulking black creature with tuffs of fur growing over its shoulders, and large pointed horns protruding from its head. Then it shifted to a large bat-like shape with wings growing from its back for a moment, and then again to a female human shaped form as black as onyx. It howled in fury at the loss of its flesh shell, and the flames in the parlor danced higher.

Ignoring Officer Wilson, the empty female-shaped void approached Will and though the silhouette was that of a woman, Will swore he heard it stumping on cloven hooves, its long clawed fingers twitching. Will laughed. He could sense he had already won. His family's love encased him, he wasn't falling into the void today, and there was something else. A beam of light more dazzling than the sun burst through the round stain glass window frame at the top of the stairs. A circular light bathed Will and his family. He could feel the warmth, the peace, and the purity, because his entire being vibrated with the harmonics of perfection.

The beast lunged at him with its outstretched black claws, but was repelled at the edge of the circle of light. Howling with pain it crashed to the floor and writhed in agony.

"No. He's mine," the beast screamed.

Seven white pillars of fire appeared around the perimeter of the circle, each blinding with their own radiance. Will couldn't make out any details; they were like pillars of pure energy. They raised appendages that he could only describe as arms, in unison, and torrents of energy erupted in a lightning bolt that engulfed the beast on the floor.

CHAPTER EIGHTY-SEVEN

While Officer Wilson bashed down the front door, Harry struggled for breath. He heard the commotion upstairs and more gunshots. Celeste's grip loosened like she was losing strength. He tried to ignore the pain and breathe through his nose. He fought to break the seal of her lips.

After a loud scream from upstairs, Celeste started to change. Harry tried to close his eyes to block out the transformation. The years of rot and decay suddenly caught up with her. The light in her eyes went dim and then they slowly dissolved into empty sockets. Her hair grew dull, matted, and dirt encrusted. Her smooth skin dried, cracked, and crumbled. He gagged, spitting out a mouthful of bitter dust. She stopped struggling, and he rolled her rag-enshrouded corpse off his.

Choking, he tried to climb to his knees, but the pain in his left leg caused him to collapse. He struggled to breathe. The smell of spoiled eggs grew stronger, and panic washed over his sweat-encased body when he recognized the smell, there was a gas leak in the basement.

He had to warn Will, they had to get out of the house. He tried to stand, but the pain was too intense. He couldn't put any weight on his left leg. Tears of frustration ran down his cheeks as he tried to call out a warning, but it was no use, he was doomed. He crawled toward the stairs, gritting his teeth against the pain each time he bumped the shattered leg.

What seemed like hours must only have been minutes, and Harry couldn't believe he had made it to the top of the stairs when he struggled the reach the doorknob and open the basement door. There was a moment of sickening realization at what he had done when he heard the whoosh of the gas rushing past him into the rest of the house. He felt certain he had killed them all, but then he felt the hands beneath his armpits lifting him to his feet and propelling him out the back kitchen door and onto the lawn. Martin's voice shouted in his ear. "Get going, you old geezer."

CHAPTER **EIGHTY-EIGHT**

The beast shuddered and screamed one final time as it exploded into a fireball that consumed the foyer. Flames splashed across the walls and up the banister, engulfing the cherubs. Will, Sara, and Ellie were protected from the blast in the center of the cocoon of light.

Will looked at his family, feeling only love and peace. He felt no concern about their physical safety. In his new form that seemed inconsequential. He knew they were safe. One of the figures on the edge of the circle turned toward him and transformed into Lillian. Will understood that this was for his perception, and that the white column of energy was its true form. "You and your family have to leave the building now."

Will smiled and gestured toward the light. "But I'm already…"

Lillian shook her head. "It's not your time."

Before he could respond, blinding red pain consumed Will. He blinked his good eye several times and saw Sara. He felt rough hands lifting him. Officer Wilson and a badly cut Pastor Wheeler slipped his arms over their shoulders and dragged him from the burning building. He heard Ellie crying in the foreground, and off in the distance, the sound of Native American drums, beating out a celebratory dance as he drifted back into darkness.

CHAPTER **EIGHTY-NINE**

Will watched Ellie run to the birdbath, the only thing left standing. The rest of the house was a pile of charred and twisted wreckage. Sara squeezed his hand. "Be careful, don't go near the rubble."

Ellie nodded and picked up a stick to stir the stagnant water.

Not taking his eyes off his daughter, Will spoke to Harry. "I'm sorry it took us so long to come back and visit. I can't believe it's been almost a year."

Harry leaned on his cane, also watching the child. "I know you young folks have been busy down there in Horsham. How's the new job?"

Will shrugged and smiled. "Not too bad. I keep it down to 40 hours a week, so we have a lot more family time."

Somewhere in the distance birds chirped, and a slight breeze rustled Will's hair. Sara wrapped her arms around his waist and squeezed. "This guy's around so much now, I never get any work done."

Harry chuckled and poked the gravel in the driveway with his cane. "I guess things worked out at Compu-Gear?"

Will noticed a small feather and bent to pick it up. "Actually we parted quite amicably after I agreed not to press assault and battery charges. Although no one can explain how the entire system was wiped away. I could tell them, but they'd never believe me."

Laughing, Will winced at the pain.

"Shoulder still give you trouble?" Harry asked.

Will nodded, turning the feather slowly in his fingers. "Yeah, sometimes. How's the leg."

Harry shifted self-consciously. "Oh, I get by. The doc say's I'll walk with this cane for the rest of my life. That's all right, it adds character."

Will released the feather and watched it swirl to the ground. "You know, I never did get to thank you for everything you did. You saved our lives. I'm really glad you made it out of the basement."

The old man stared intently at Ellie who was now practicing cartwheels, and Will could tell he was struggling to hold back his emotions. "I don't know how I did it. The doctors say I shouldn't have been able to walk on that leg."

Sara again clasped Will's hand. "A lot of bizarre stuff happened that day."

More in control of his emotions, Harry nodded. "I guess they never did figure out who that young woman was?"

Sara shook her head and gave Will a sideways glance. They had been over this a million times in their counseling sessions. "The authorities think she was some escaped mental patient that somehow had passed herself off as Kerrie for years. They never got a positive ID, in fact they couldn't find a body," Sara said.

Will listened and held his tongue. It was too nice a day to ruin with another pointless argument. He knew the truth, but Sara would never accept it. "It's all a jumble in my mind now," Sara said, "I felt like I woke from a nightmare when it was over."

Shaking his head slowly, apparently lost in his own thoughts, Harry walked over to the large tree stump, and slowly sat down. "It's quite a tale."

Will and Sara both nodded, and the three of them watched Ellie do another tumble in the tall grass. They stood there in silence for a while, each lost in their own thoughts. Ellie approached slowly, and Will could see there was something bothering her. "Dad. They're all gone."

He asked already knowing the answer. "Who Sweetie?"

"Celeste and the Captain. All my friends."

Sara hugged her and told her it was fine. She looked at Will and said, "our little girl's growing up."

Will glanced around the yard, feeling the breeze and the warm sun and knew it was true. Ellie may not have needed imaginary friends anymore, but that's not what she meant, and Will understood. The darkness was gone, even with the large charred skeletal frame of the old house, the specters where no longer there. It was the main reason Will had wanted to come back. He had to be sure.

Harry poked at the dirt with his cane. "I heard you had an offer on the place."

Will's gaze drifted back to the old man. "I guess you don't miss much in a small town."

Still hugging Ellie, Sara shot Will a sour glance. "We have a great offer on the place from a developer who wants to build luxury condos, but I can't convince this guy to sell."

Will laughed and sank down in the grass next to Harry. "We'll probably sell in the end. It's too much money to turn down. What about you? Are you still thinking about selling and moving to Florida?"

The wind shifted, carrying the scent of lilac. "Nah, I started out here, and I guess I'll end up here. Who knows — if they build those condos they may need a caretaker." Harry smiled at Will and winked a sparkling blue eye.